HE WAS *HERS*

Diana was relieved to linger in the shadows and observe the spectacle. The place resembled a zoo, but the animals were the most important in TV's kingdom: at least a dozen famous actors and actresses, several top producers and directors, and a clutch of influential journalists.

Luke was the perfect guest of honor—he looked magnificent and smiled with a brilliance that eclipsed all the other carefully calculated smiles.

What did it matter that all the women who flocked around him were super-glamorous, stunningly dressed, and permanently tanned? Diana reveled in the knowledge that he was *her* creation. She had discovered him, nurtured him, and put him where he was.

And after all the smoke and Giorgio perfume had cleared, Luke would be going home with her. . . .

PROTÉGÉ

⊘ SIGNET  ONYX

SINFULLY SEXY READING

(0451)

- ☐ **WORTH WINNING by Dan Lewandowski.** An outrageously racy romp about love, sex, marriage—and the single male. The bet was the ultimate male challenge. All bachelor Taylor Worth had to do was woo, win, bed—and get engaged to—all three women chosen by his married best friend, Ned. What happens is a no-holds-barred battle of the sexes—and the heart.... "Exuberent sensuality!"—*Raleigh Spectator.*(400097—$3.95)
- ☐ **PROTEGÉ by Justine Valenti.** A glittering novel of scandal, sex, and power behind the glamorous world of TV—and the passionate men and women who reaped the joys of success and paid its ultimate price.... (400127—$3.95)
- ☐ **RECOMBINATIONS by Perri Klass.** How many men does it take to satisfy one wise and willful woman? Brilliant scientist Anne Montgomery researches the question in a wildly erotic, exuberantly witty sexual adventure that is no longer *for men only* ... "Wild, wicked, sparkling!"—*Kirkus Reviews.* (145550—$3.95)
- ☐ **THE SECRET LIFE OF EVA HATHAWAY by Janice Weber.** Eva has everything: A computer genius husband, two adoring lovers—and talents that range from composing church hymns to porno theater pieces. "Hilarious, sexy, raunchy!"—*Providence Journal.* "The book of the season!"—*John Barkham Reviews.* (145593—$3.95)

Prices slightly higher in Canada.

Buy them at your local bookstore or use this convenient coupon for ordering.

NEW AMERICAN LIBRARY,
P.O. Box 999, Bergenfield, New Jersey 07621

Please send me the books I have checked above. I am enclosing $_____
(please add $1.00 to this order to cover postage and handling). Send check or money order—no cash or C.O.D.'s. Prices and numbers are subject to change without notice.

Name_____

Address_____

City_____State_____Zip Code_____

Allow 4-6 weeks for delivery.
This offer is subject to withdrawal without notice.

PROTÉGÉ

Justine Valenti

AN ONYX BOOK

NEW AMERICAN LIBRARY

PUBLISHER'S NOTE

This novel is a work of fiction. Names, characters, places, and incidents either are the product of the author's imagination or are used fictitiously, and any resemblance to actual persons, living or dead, events, or locales is entirely coincidental.

NAL BOOKS ARE AVAILABLE AT QUANTITY DISCOUNTS WHEN USED
TO PROMOTE PRODUCTS OR SERVICES. FOR INFORMATION PLEASE
WRITE TO PREMIUM MARKETING DIVISION, NEW AMERICAN LIBRARY,
1633 BROADWAY, NEW YORK, NEW YORK 10019.

Copyright © 1986 by Justine Valenti

All rights reserved

 Onyx is a trademark of New American Library

SIGNET, SIGNET CLASSIC, MENTOR, ONYX, PLUME, MERIDIAN AND
NAL BOOKS are published by New American Library,
1633 Broadway, New York, New York 10019

First Printing, November, 1986

1 2 3 4 5 6 7 8 9

PRINTED IN THE UNITED STATES OF AMERICA

I

1 It was the nicest sort of December afternoon—cold but very dry, the deep-blue sky cloudless, and a low-hanging sun cast its pale winter glow.

As she stepped from her apartment building, Diana Sinclair dared to inhale a lungful of New York City air. A sudden gust off the East River whipped her raccoon coat open, sending a shock of icy air through her. She positioned the strap of her handbag over her head and one shoulder to hold the coat in place. Then, gripping her briefcase in one gloved hand, her tennis bag in the other, she walked briskly up Second Avenue.

As she strode across Fifty-first Street, the heels of her leather boots clicking on the pavement, her hair flying, two telephone-company workers emerged from a deep hole in the gutter and stared at her. The older man, unshaven and looking weary, doffed his hard hat with dirty fingers and said, "Here we are, darlin', take your choice."

It was a funny line, delivered with just the right amount of self-mockery. Not at all offended, Diana smiled as she continued on her way, feeling terrific.

She couldn't help stealing quick glimpses in shop windows, amused at the unfamiliar reflection of herself swathed in fur. It was her first, acquired only recently. She had been growing tired of freezing in cloth or looking dowdy in down, had seen the coat in the window of a Madison Avenue furrier, and had simply gone in and bought it. And why not? It was her own hard-earned money.

Independence was wonderful. In fact, everything was wonderful. Diana was feeling joyful and successful, and with good reason. She was one of a very rare breed—a writer/executive producer of a prime-time television series.

When she had started working at Coastal Television Studios in Los Angeles seven years before as a story editor—her first job out of college—the two things she had wanted most were to write scripts and live in New York. Within three years she had not only achieved both goals, but had done so in style, with Molly Abbott's help.

Molly had been the partner with TV expertise and the means to set them up in New York. Diana had created the concept for a drama series, and combining their talents, the women had formed Abbott and Sinclair Productions. They sold their first series, *Mom & Meg*, to Alpha Television Network. For the past four years, it had been one of the hottest prime-time dramas on the air. Not bad for a small-town girl from New Mexico.

Diana absolutely loved working in television, despite all the problems, excesses, and competitiveness. As a child she had been utterly enchanted by the world she saw on TV—intrigued by the dramas, delighted by the comedies. She had yearned to be a part of it somehow. Making up stories had seemed to her a wonderful opportunity to get people to say what she wanted and to have everything happen as she wished. So she had spun countless stories in her head and envisioned them being brought to life on the TV screen.

And now they were. It still gave her a deep feeling of satisfaction to be able to resolve certain problems in the space of an hour.

Even the collaborative effort, as tough as it could be, was very rewarding. Quality, good taste, and professionalism were what she most admired. The first two she had to fight for every inch of the way, but the third was abundant in the industry. Writers, actors, directors, producers, editors, stage managers, camera and sound technicians, set and costume designers—all played vital roles in putting a professional polish on every episode. When she watched the final tape on the studio monitor, it was like enjoying a finished painting while being aware of every brush stroke and subtle blending of colors.

Yet, much as she enjoyed putting *Mom & Meg* together, Diana had always felt that her special talent was comedy. She was dying for a chance to produce a sitcom series.

As she hurried to meet the director of East Coast entertainment at ATN, Oliver Feranti, she was more certain than ever she would be able to interest him in her newest project. Exciting news had broken that morning and as she had told Molly, Diana's enthusiasm grew.

"Noreen Sanders is interested in playing the lead in *Brownstone*. Isn't that marvelous?"

"Well, it's certainly interesting," Molly had replied, sounding her usual cautious note, "but don't get your hopes up. We have no track record in sitcom. Feranti's been sitting on your proposal for weeks, and it's a bad sign . . ."

Diana had tried to hold down her excitement—Molly had a point, of course—and yet she kept feeling wildly optimistic. She had spent a lot of time working on her proposal. Her idea was super, Noreen Sanders was practically in her pocket, and Feranti was giving her a hearing within the half-hour. The rest was up to her.

Diana could think of little else. In fact, she had failed to come up with a usable script for *Mom & Meg* all day yesterday and this morning. If only she could get some development money out of Feranti for *Brownstone*, she was sure she'd be able to go home and knock out the *Mom & Meg* script without any difficulty.

Then she remembered she wasn't going straight home but on to a tennis date.

Turning west on Fifty-fifth Street, Diana conjured up a picture of Dick Mann—tall and blond and blue-eyed, with good features, though they remained a little fuzzy. She had zeroed in on Dick at a cocktail party only a week ago, surprised that in spite of looking like an actor he was actually in the programming department at Continental Television. Well, it never hurt to have friends in programming. Especially as she had found Dick interesting during their brief though animated conversation. Before she went back to work at the studio, he had asked for her number. And he had called her the next day to arrange this date.

Diana hummed to herself as she entered the sleek, marble-walled lobby of the Alpha Television Network building, already hung with decorative holiday wreaths, and rode up to the thirty-fifth floor.

She often wondered when Oliver Feranti did his paperwork, because he was always on the phone or at a meeting. She had arrived fifteen minutes early for her four-thirty appointment thinking he might be available sooner and she would then have more time with him.

Evvie, his assistant—pretty, young, modishly dressed—was on the phone. She shook her head as Diana approached. Apparently Feranti wasn't free yet.

Might as well give her hair a quick comb in the ladies' room, she said to herself. Diana had spent many minutes earlier deciding what to wear. Something businesslike, of course, yet easy to put on and take off for tennis and romantic enough for dinner. Her dusty-pink two-piece cashmere dress was what she had finally chosen. Clinging softly to her figure, it suggested rather than revealed, and she felt very feminine in it, and pretty.

Well, maybe pretty was an exaggeration. Attractive. anyway, she thought, looking critically in the mirror and trying to see herself through Dick's eyes. With her fingers she puffed up her brown hair that fell almost to her shoulders in soft, layered curls. A noble brow, long-lashed brown eyes, which she hoped were warm rather than bovine. Her nose was straight and rather impudent, and she had a generous—well, very generous—mouth. When she practiced smiling, her face took on a pleasant glow, nothing more. Beauty, she was afraid, would have to be in the eyes of the beholder.

When Diana returned to the reception area, Evvie, looking a little uncomfortable, said, "I'm sorry but he's still tied up and will be until after five. Then he has a cocktail meeting, followed by a dinner meeting. He won't be able to see you today after all."

Diana felt her bubble burst. "But this has been going on for weeks—"

"I know. Everyone's frantic before the holidays. He's swamped." Evvie's phone rang.

Feeling hot with resentment, Diana sat down firmly and plunked her coat in her lap. Dammit, she wasn't going to let him push her around like this. It wasn't fair. *Mom & Meg* was making millions for ATN. Even if he didn't like her proposal, at the very least he could show her the courtesy of telling her so to her face.

Evvie glanced over at her nervously. "It's no use. He really can't make it today."

"Thanks, Evvie, I'll wait." He had to come out of his office sometime, if only to go to the men's room.

Diana sat with her legs crossed, swinging her top leg back and forth restlessly, remembering Molly's cautioning words. She was right again, dammit.

Molly had been right the very first time the two women had met, at Coastal Studios' commissary. Diana was just about to tuck into the lunch special when a small dark-haired woman of about thirty stopped at her table and said, "Hey, kid, you don't want to eat that crap. They call it chicken à la king but it tastes like rubber bands drowning in dishwater."

Diana had smiled, startled by the woman's colorful bluntness and amused by what she thought of as a typical New York accent.

"Have the roast-beef sandwich," Molly had advised, "with nothing but lettuce. Mind if I sit here?"

Molly had immediately appointed herself Diana's mentor and friend, helping her shake off the tinsel of her childhood dreams and get on with her career. Nobody was going to *discover* that Diana could write. She had to push ahead and prove it.

It was Molly, a senior writer at the huge television complex, who had assigned Diana her first script—and thrown it back at her to be rewritten. Diana had gone through her professional adolescence in the drama department because it was where Molly had a decade of writing and producing experience.

During Diana's second year with Coastal, Molly had talked of getting away from Never-Never-Land and moving back to New York. And the way back, she kept saying, was to come up with a show containing a dynamite role for a TV biggie who didn't want to leave the Big Apple. That was exactly what they had done.

Remembering their struggle to sell and produce their show, Diana grew angry all over again. Abbott and Sinclair had proved themselves with *Mom & Meg*. It was the first prime-time drama by women and about women who weren't Charlie's or anyone else's angels. They were a take-charge mother-and-daughter team of private eyes. The other networks had jumped in with imitations; women cops and detectives now jammed viewing time. Diana insisted to herself that such success was sufficient reason for them to have an inside track, for Feranti to recognize that they were innovators and give them a fair hearing. Christ, all she was asking was fifteen minutes of his time.

At five-twenty, two men emerged from Feranti's office. Before Evvie could react, Diana grabbed her gear and pushed past them through the door, shutting it behind her.

Oliver Feranti—forty-five, medium-tall, and dark, sprouting a Tom Selleck mustache—stared at her as she dumped her coat and tennis bag on his couch.

"Diana, for God's sake, Evvie told you—"

"Noreen Sanders," Diana interrupted softly. "She wants to play Selena in *Brownstone*." Studying his frown, Diana saw instantly that he hadn't looked at her proposal, didn't know what in hell she was talking about. Only the name of the actress had penetrated.

"Noreen Sanders, huh? Really?"

The intercom buzzed, and Diana cursed under her breath. She'd had him, almost. Thanks, Evvie, a lot.

Feranti opened his briefcase. "I'm late for a very important meeting."

"Sure. But on your way, just think about Noreen Sanders. Familiarity, the tops. Popularity, ditto. Her latest Q score was seventy-five. And *Brownstone* really excites her because it would be a departure—"

"Audience doesn't want a departure," Feranti mumbled, rummaging on his desk. "They want her to keep 'em laughing—"

"And so she would, that's the beauty of the role." Diana talked as quickly as she was able, wishing she could master that New York machine-gun delivery, because Feranti didn't seem to be taking much in.

"Right," he muttered. "Got to go."

"You have read my proposal, haven't you?"

"Diana, I've been up to my eyebrows."

"It's only six pages," she murmured, trying to keep her disappointment from showing, "and you've had it for more than a month. If you've misplaced it, I have another copy with me."

"Sitcom isn't your thing, hon," he said, slipping into his coat.

"It's not exactly sitcom, it's warmedy. You know, not

belly laughs but genuine humor, the kind that comes from the relationships between the characters—"

Feranti opened the door, shaking his head. "Not your speed, hon. Humor's hard to write—"

"*Mom & Meg* has plenty of humor. That's really what makes the show work as well as it does."

"The point is that the show works well, period. Let's stick with it."

"If all of us were happy to stick with whatever works, I'd still be twirling a baton in Santa Fe high school." And maybe he'd still be a station manager in Cleveland.

Diana followed him down the hall. "Let me give you a quick synopsis. The brownstone of the title is a house in the East Village. Noreen plays a rich girl fresh from finishing school in Switzerland. She's inherited the house from a distant relation. Comes to New York intending to sell it. Meets some of the tenants." Diana went on to describe the dancer, the artist, the Hispanic family with two cute kids, the Hungarian émigré widower. . . . "Noreen moves in and starts fixing up the place. . . . Her upper-class values collide amusingly with theirs. . . . She learns from them, and they learn from her. . . . The love interest. . . . Believable characters in believable situations. . . ."

At the elevator Feranti shook his head as if she were a naughty child. "Listen, hon, most indie prods nowadays don't even get one show airing, and you want to try for two." He waggled his index finger at her. "Greedy girl."

"Please, Mr. Feranti, all I ask is that you read the proposal, talk to Noreen—"

He stepped into a crowded elevator. "Waste of time, hon. I'll have to pass."

The elevator door shut in her face.

Anger bubbled up in Diana like lava. That fool! If independendent producers could have one hit show, why in hell couldn't they have two? Norman Lear had done it, and so had Aaron Spelling.

Had Feranti at least offered some reasonable objection to the idea itself, Diana could understand his rejection. But he hadn't heard a word she'd told him. What he was saying was, "Keep baking those apple pies, hon, you do them so well."

* * *

Diana sipped her beer at the crowded bar of the Midtown Tennis Club wishing she were anywhere else. The place was noisy, warm, with too many people milling around. A preholiday spirit was in the air but she felt grumpy and not at all festive after such a lousy afternoon.

Well, she supposed she could get rid of her frustrations by knocking the fuzz off the tennis balls. By dinnertime she might be feeling reasonably civilized.

Her spirits lifted the moment Dick Mann came toward her, looking handsome and elegant in his tennis whites.

"There's a fifteen-minute wait for a court, I'm afraid," Dick said, squeezing next to her at the bar. "Hope you don't mind."

"Nope. It'll give the beer time to settle."

"And us time to get better acquainted." They smiled at one another.

"I feel honored to have a date with the creator of *Mom & Meg*. Watched it again this week for the first time in a long time. You know, it's still damn good. I like the way Meg is so gung-ho, running down every lead, while Mom stays at home knitting sweaters and reasoning deductively. It's a class act, Diana."

"Thanks," she said, liking him more and more. He was a class act himself.

"It must be exciting to see your name flashed on a TV screen for millions of viewers to admire. Only thing my name is ever on is an interoffice memo."

Diana made light of her fame. "I was excited the first couple of times, but eighty-plus episodes later the novelty's worn off. Anyway, they flash the credits very quickly."

"Still. You're shown as co-creator, co-producer, and story editor," he continued, sounding a touch envious.

"Yeah, well, the more titles, the more work. Molly and I still write many of the scripts, and at least one of us is at the studio from nine in the morning to eleven at night most weekdays. Anyway, tell me what it's like to be a programmer. That sounds like quite a challenge, having to coordinate info from the research department, sales, standards and practies, business affairs. Knowing where to slot which program—"

"It's not easy," he acknowledged, sighing. "If anybody knew for sure why shows succeed or fail, Continental wouldn't be in third place. I'd like to work for number one, but at the moment ATN's sticking to the programmers they have."

"They're sticking to the programs they have, too. I've been trying to pitch them a sitcom but they 'passed.' Is Continental looking for material?"

"Not at the moment. Even though we're pulling most of our shows, we're filling in with big movies. Dead wrong, because that only boosts the ratings temporarily. What we need to do is invest in more original shows, maybe yours."

"Sounds good." Diana smiled at him. "Think you're in line for a promotion?"

"No, unfortunately," he replied, smiling ruefully. "That's not the way it's done at our shop. Phil Bannon doesn't move people up, only over. He wears too many hats himself. Not only president but also chief of programming. And he's just hired a honcho away from FAB to be in charge of East Coast entertainment, passing over our whole department—men who've been there for years."

"That's really too bad," Diana commiserated.

"You know, I never started out to be a programmer. I was more interested in the writing or producing end, but it takes so long to get started, and in the meantime I had to eat. And drink. Can I buy you another beer?"

"I'll get this round," Diana said, feeling a little uncomfortable at earning a great deal more than he probably did.

The second beer loosened them up, and their conversation veered from shop talk to the more personal disclosures of where they came from (he was from Michigan), whether her hair was naturally curly (it was), and if she would like to go skiing with him over Christmas (she'd love it). As they continued to talk and flirt, he put his arm around her shoulders and hugged her.

By the time their court was free, she was feeling pretty good. She hadn't met a man she liked as much in a long time.

Whap! Although it was a fine serve, the ball aimed precisely to catch her off-guard, Diana returned it so that it just cleared the net.

Surprised, Dick ran forward, lunged, and missed. "Lucky shot," he called out.

16 *Justine Valenti*

Well, not entirely. Skill had a lot to do with it, Diana thought to herself.

"You sure move fast for your size," Dick called, after winning the first game. "Better watch your backhand, though. I play to win."

She frowned, wondering what he meant by her size. She was five-seven against his six feet. Did size have to do with speed?

She sent Dick a slashing serve he returned wildly, then another he couldn't hit at all. But he returned her next serve beautifully, putting a topspin on the ball. She lobbed it out of play.

"Terrific shot, Dick."

As the ball bounced into the next court, she had a glimpse of a woman playing there who very much resembled the star of *What's Mine Is Yours*, ATN's long-running sitcom. In fact, the show had been slipping badly in the ratings. And no wonder. In her opinion the series had never been more than ordinary. Now it was simply coasting. Diana knew she and Molly could write rings around it. But they weren't going to get the chance to do *Brownstone* for ATN, thanks to Oliver Feranti's intransigence. Anti-woman bias was what it amounted to. *What's Mine* was male-written and male-produced, like most shows. In fact, all the TV execs with the power to pay out development money were males. And there wasn't a single female vice-president at any of the networks.

The defeat Diana had suffered that afternoon suddenly hit her with renewed force. The way Feranti had patronized her, shaking his finger at her, telling her she was a greedy *girl*.

"That's the set," Dick called, approaching the net to change sides. "You pack quite a wallop, but you're erratic. Need to do some work on that backhand."

Diana snapped back to the present. "You're right."

Dick, smiling indulgently, gave her some pointers for improving her game.

God, he must think she was a nitwit. She'd been playing tennis since childhood, and she was good. Usually. If you don't keep your mind on it, you lose, she told herself sternly. Okay, assume the stance, ready to receive your opponent's serve. This is it, Sinclair. Flushing Meadow. The U.S. Open. Navratilova facing McEnroe. Go get him.

Diana broke Dick's service with a bludgeoning forehand. When he went for her backhand, she was ready and whipped several shots past him. She won the second set, and would have called it even-steven, except that Dick insisted on a third . . . if she wasn't too tired.

On the contrary, she felt a tremendous surge of energy, of exhilaration, as she played with total concentration, pitting her skill and strategy against those of her opponent.

Double fault (his). Net ball (hers). Ace (hers). Break point (his). Deuce. Advantage (hers). Game (hers).

Diana ended their match 2-1 on a glorious backhand shot.

"Thanks for a wonderful game," she told him, pumping his hand enthusiastically over the net. "We have to do it again."

Dick nodded and smiled, but he seemed to be showing an awful lot of teeth.

After she had showered and dressed, she glanced fleetingly in the mirror. Her color was terrific. The flush of victory.

The Brazilian restaurant Dick suggested nearby delighted Diana with its soft lighting and fresh flowers. She was unfamiliar with Brazilian cooking so suggested he order for both of them.

When the food came, she tasted it eagerly. "Mm. Marvelous." She flashed him her best smile.

"Should be. It's the most authentic Brazilian place in New York, one of my special favorites."

"It could easily become mine," she replied suggestively, but he didn't react.

Diana, sipping her beer, began to feel a familiar anxiety. What had happened to the earlier spark between them? Dick was drinking a second margarita, and it seemed to be making him morose.

"Where do you usually go skiing?" she asked, trying to get him talking about something that had interested him earlier.

He shrugged and shoveled some food into his mouth. "Here and there." He didn't repeat his invitation that she join him.

Could he possibly be sulking because he'd lost a couple of sets of tennis? God, he probably would have won the next set; they had been pretty evenly matched.

"I imagine you're a good skier, Dick," she ventured. "Racing class, huh?" No response. "I'm not much good myself," she continued doggedly. "Haven't skied in years, but it would be fun to take it up again."

"It's an expensive sport, not that that should worry you," he said glumly, throwing her a hostile glance. "You're in the big time."

So *that* was it. Diana put aside her fork. "Well, yes, but it wasn't as easy as it sounds. My real piece of luck was meeting Molly." Diana went on to explain that Molly's wealth, left to her by her late husband, had enabled her to finance both of them while they put their series together.

What they had been trying to do had been considered undoable five years ago: to interest a network in a drama about women that wasn't simply jiggle, and to produce it in New York when practically all other drama series except soaps were taped in Hollywood.

"When I think of the false starts, delays, endless meetings, repeated refusals. It took more than a year—"

"But the fact remains," Dick interrupted testily, "that you're making it now, and you're still a baby."

"I'm twenty-eight," Diana said indignantly.

He snorted. "What I wouldn't give to have six years back."

That *was* a surprise. He didn't look thirty-four. Didn't act it, either. Drinking brought out his petulance.

In spite of her attempts to change the subject, Dick stayed with shop talk, bemoaning that Continental's new head of entertainment, Matthew Sayles, wouldn't be taking charge until January and would need a couple of months to get settled in. "Meantime, we're shifting shit around, nobody's got any clout to pay out development money . . ."

In margaritas veritas. Was this crybaby the same man who had flirted with her at the tennis club?

Diana made a mental note of the name Matthew Sayles. That appeared to be the only thing she was going to get out of this evening.

It all felt depressingly déjà vu. Men asked her out often;

she accepted seldom. Because sooner or later the evening seemed to come down to the fact that she outearned them and they couldn't stand it. Not that she would have dreamed of discussing it or flaunting it, but anyone in the business knew that she had to be taking home at least fifteen thousand per episode.

It did no good to explain that for ages she had lived off Molly and had been a partner in name only, or that it wasn't until the show had gone into syndication a year ago that Abbott and Sinclair had begun to make any money on the series. Diana had had to pay back thousands to Molly, and invest additional thousands in the partnership.

What really puzzled her was why Dick had bothered to ask her out if he resented her success.

He looked at his watch. "What time do you make it? Nine-thirty? No shit." He shook his wrist angrily. "The fucking thing's stopped. Not even a month old, and it's a Rolex."

While he mumbled about the unreliability of name brands, she saw that he couldn't wait to get away.

Which turned out to take longer than he expected, because the waiter gave him a hard time.

"But you've always taken credit cards," Dick argued, waving a selection. The waiter simply kept shaking his head.

"Please, let me," Diana said smoothly. "I have cash—"

Dick threw her a resentful glance. "But I invited you."

"That's okay. Winner buys dinner. A famous couplet. You can treat me next time." She meant to be funny but it was wasted on him. Clearly he just wanted out.

The words she was anticipating came, as he held the door open for her. "Listen, I have to run."

Work on a report . . . a meeting first thing in the morning . . .

Diana nodded. "You'll call me," she said wryly, fixing him with a challenging look. But he was already turning his head to locate a taxi.

A moment later she was standing on the sidewalk alone, flapping her hands against her arms to keep warm. She felt a rumbling sensation in her stomach. Too much rice and beans, with humble pie for dessert.

Brushed off by two men within the last four hours, she thought. Terrific going, Sinclair.

She began to walk east. When in hell was she going to learn not to cast herself as heroine in scripts never meant to be played out? She was angry at having wasted all this time; she should have been working on the *Mom & Meg* script that was due in two days.

When she reached Second Avenue she decided to go to the office. Although she usually wrote the first draft of her scripts at home, she occasionally opted for the office if nothing was flowing. There she wouldn't be tempted to clean out her closets or poke in the refrigerator.

The basement and parlor floor of Molly's town house, at Fiftieth and First, were given over to Abbott and Sinclair Productions. Each of them had an office, in addition to the reception area and a large conference room that also doubled as a work space for their assistant.

Diana used her key to the front door, careful to turn off the burglar alarm. For a moment she shivered in the vestibule, wondering whether or not to remove her coat.

A light went on in the upstairs hall. "Diana?"

"Yes. Don't mind me, Molly. I'm going to do some work."

Molly came quickly down the stairs. "Jesus, you look frozen. Come on up for a minute. I have the fire going."

In contrast to the offices, which were decorated in hi-tech modern—all chrome, black leather, and gray carpeting—Molly's living room was furnished lushly in New Orleans turn-of-the century style, with plush rugs, a red-velvet sofa, and damask chairs. Diana sometimes felt as if she were walking into a bordello.

Flinging her fur on a chair, she went to stand in front of the fire, as Molly handed her a snifter of brandy. "Here. You look like you need it."

"Thanks." Diana inhaled deeply before taking a swallow that warmed her down to her toes.

Molly sat down in a chair and continued with her knitting, an activity that relaxed her. As her needles clicked away, she kept glancing up with her sharp deep-blue eyes. Her straight, short black hair hugged her head like a cap. She was a very youthful thirty-eight, in her crisply pressed jeans and a sweatshirt that had a three-line legend in maroon and gray: *Mom & Meg/ Private/* and a picture of two long-lashed comic-strip blue eyes.

"You struck out with Feranti, huh? Yeah, I figured, when you didn't call."

Diana told her the story.

"He's a bastard, though no more than anyone else in this business. Nobody lets you cross over. You start in drama, you end in drama. Even if we had a firm commitment from Noreen—which we don't—a network wants proven comedy writers."

Molly got up and poked at the fire. "I'm sorry you're disappointed. Frankly, I'm almost relieved. I don't see myself writing sitcom—"

"You can write anything you want to. *Mom & Meg* has as much humor as most sitcoms I can think of."

"The humor's mostly yours, kid. Anyway, while we're on the subject, where's your script?"

"Wastebasket. Sorry, Molly, I'm drawing blanks. Every idea seems too tired, too old."

"Come on, you know there are no new ideas. It's all old wine in new bottles."

"Sure. Except I keep coming up with old bottles. I need some help with this one."

"Okay. Let's see." Molly picked up her knitting, reminding Diana of Mom herself. "In the last episode Mom gets romanced by a guy who turns out to be a swindler. And the one before that, Meg's on a bus that's held up by two gunmen—"

"Oh, shit, I wish Mom would go to visit her grandchildren or something so we could take a rest."

"Be careful what you wish for, Diana. It might come true. You're just in a shitty mood, not that I blame you. Feranti can be a pig. Are you hungry, by the way? I could whip up a salad or something."

"No, thanks. I've eaten, only it won't go down."

"Hey, tonight was the big date with the hunk, wasn't it? So what happened? Not the man you thought he was?"

Diana sighed. "Nope. And I wasn't the woman he thought I was, either."

"Are you sure? Are you giving him the benefit of the doubt?"

"It wouldn't matter. He's not interested. Anyway, I

give men the benefit of the doubt too much. You're the one who taught me not to. If it hadn't been for you, I'd still be a glorified gofer working for Barry at Coastal. And I've been giving Feranti the benefit of the doubt for weeks—"

"You're mixing up a couple of things. I'm talking man-on-a-date, not man-on-the-job."

"What's the difference? I screwed it up twice today."

"In business you win a lot of the time. Hell, that's why I backed away from pitching *M&M* finally and left it to you. You sashay into a meeting all smiles, looking deliciously feminine. And your voice. The word 'mellifluous' was coined with you in mind. Pure butter and honey—"

"Well, I'm from Santa Fe, not Hell's Kitchen. I don't do it on purpose."

"Of course you don't. And the way you talk is a definite asset. Throws people off-guard. By the time they get it through their beans that your words are a lot tougher than they sound, you've wiped the floor with them."

"So? What am I doing wrong?"

"In business, not much. But if you treat a guy on a date the same way, it's no wonder you keep striking out."

"Ouch."

"Sorry, kid, but I must be honest. A man has competition all day long. He doesn't want a woman who busts his chops. Who gives as good as she gets. A man wants to relax, to be giggled up a bit—"

"The way you giggle up Ted, I suppose. Not that it does you much good," Diana said unkindly.

"You're damn right it does me good. I don't care if he doesn't leave his wife. I don't want to remarry. Ted gives me what I need—"

"So you keep saying. But I'm not you. I can't drop my hankie and tiptoe on eggshells. I have to be able to say and do what I want to say and do."

"Jesus, what in hell *did* you say and do tonight? So tell me. You had dinner?"

"Yes, but he couldn't wait to get away." Diana filled Molly in.

"Wait, hold on a minute. First you played tennis, right? And did you go all-out?"

Feeling herself growing warm, Diana moved away from the fire. "We both went all-out."

"Aha. But you won, of course."

"It just happened I did."

"Surprise, surprise. Listen, don't blame what happened on Dick's envy of your job. He knew what you did and how much you earned. He was definitely interested—before the game, anyway. Why do you think he suggested tennis on a first date?"

"So he could check out my legs," Diana said flippantly.

"So he could shine, that's why. And did you let him? Like hell. Miss Fair and Square whipped his ass on the court. Did you expect that to be a turn-on?"

"He *wanted* me to improve my game, told me how, in fact." Diana poured more brandy into her snifter. "Where is the new man who's supposed to be out there? You know, tender/tough, understanding, wanting equality. He wins one, she wins one—"

"No man's that new, kid. In sports, especially. Couldn't you have missed a couple of shots? You'd be warming up in his arms right now instead of playing Cinderella by the fire."

"No, I couldn't," Diana said moodily. "If I have to lose the game to win the man, it's just not worth it. And I'm still not convinced that losing a lousy set of tennis was his only reason."

"No, you gave him another. He took you to his favorite eatery, and presto-chango, they suddenly don't accept plastic. You not only grab your wallet, you make jokes, in rhyme, no less. So while you're waiting for your change, it's going through his brain, 'Winner buys dinner, winner buys dinner.' Terrific. You expect him to end the evening on a romantic note, huh?"

Diana, realizing the absurdity of the situation, smiled. "Who says you can't write comedy? You'd be great. Hey, we're onto something usable here." She whipped out her notebook, but Molly grabbed her arm.

"Today, of all days, because you lost to Feranti you felt you had to win over Dick—"

"Okay, okay, Madam Freud. I get the point. I made him feel like just another dumb blond. Well, so be it. Scratch Diana and Dick. Sounds like a couple of fugitives from a first-grade reader. I'll survive as just Diana, thank you."

"Just remember that as you get older there are fewer guys out there."

Diana was silent, not wanting to point out that unlike her friend, she didn't have a desperate need for a man. Molly had claimed to adore her husband. Yet only two months after he had died of a heart attack, she had begun dating others.

Diana stood up. "I'm going. Maybe if I make this an early night inspiration will strike in the form of a dream. Then all I'll have to do is type it up."

Diana turned on the light in her living room and felt comforted. She liked the room, minimally furnished in simple modern and decorated in earth tones, which were accented by handmade Zuni rugs, pottery, and baskets. The ecru walls were hung with oils and watercolors, mostly by Martha Kent Sinclair, her mother.

Diana kicked off her boots, flopped down on the couch, and listened to her phone machine. One message was from Molly, another from the Red Cross asking if she could give blood. Hell. She'd been doing that all day. The final caller was her brother, inviting her to spend Christmas with them in Portland.

She switched on her stereo, remembering that when she and Kent were children he had relentlessly taunted her about her freckles, calling her "pie face with raisins." It had always made her furious, and she had pummeled him with her little fists—ineffectively, because he was three years older and big for his age.

Christmas in Portland. It might be a nice change from the hectic spectacle New York turned itself into. There was nothing to keep her here. And she had never been to Oregon. Hadn't, in fact, seen Kent since his wedding in Santa Fe more than two years ago.

Diana relaxed as the music washed over her. Soothing cool jazz. At UCLA she had had a crush on a senior named Scott and had learned to listen to the jazz he liked so much. Scott had gone the way of a number of other boyfriends but the jazz continued to be rewarding.

As she listened, she studied the only one of her father's

paintings she had hanging. Done in pastels, it was of a pueblo shimmering behind a cloud of dust, with the lone figure of an Indian boy in the foreground.

She had always admired the painting, imagining it to be a metaphor for her dad's feeling of being left out, and maybe a little lonely. It was understandable, because without a doubt her mother was the better painter. Her subjects were also New Mexican—mesquite, piñon, craggy mountain vistas—but her technique was very delicate, subtle, reminiscent of the Japanese. Her mother could have been a prominent painter, Diana believed, if she had been willing to show her work beyond the gallery the Sinclairs owned in Santa Fe.

Diana sighed as she thought about her parents and the difficulty of married people in the same profession. If ever she married, she would want a man whose business was unrelated to TV. She thought fleetingly of Dick and felt suddenly weary.

As she undressed in her bedroom, putting her watch on the night table, she remembered Dick's claim that his Rolex had stopped. An unlikely story. Unless it wasn't a Rolex but a fake.

Eureka. There it was, the idea she'd been searching for. Mom & Meg break up a ring distributing phony designer watches to unsuspecting retail outlets.

Wide-awake now, Diana flew to her den and typed steadily for a couple of hours.

By the time she got into bed she was exhausted, but pleasantly so.

Her eye fell on her Raggedy Andy doll slouching on top of her bureau. She joked about having found him in a thrift shop to anyone who inquired, but the truth was that the doll was hers from childhood. Her mother had carefully pushed his stuffing back and sewed up the seams many times.

Diana had never been able to give him up. She winked at him; Andy was still her best boy.

2

With a phone at each ear, Nikki De Paul leaned over her desk in the conference room. "Abbott and Sinclair Productions. I'm sorry, Miss Sinclair's not in. . . . This is her assistant. . . . I'll have her call you."

Nikki hung up one phone and spoke into the other. "We're casting two parts—couple of small-time perps—no, not him. We used him in an episode too recently. . . ." While she talked she punched figures into the computer. Actors' salaries.

The third phone rang. "No, Molly, not yet. I'll be surprised if she gets here before late afternoon. . . . No, I won't forget."

Stupid bitch. After more than a year Molly still treated her like a beginner. It was insulting; Nikki knew the operation from top to bottom.

If only there were a full time receptionist instead of a part-timer. You'd think Hilary was someone's daughter, the way she could come and go as she pleased. It was either exams or a workshop or winter recess. She was already on her way home to New Hampshire for Christmas.

When Hilary wasn't around, Nikki had to turn herself inside out to do two jobs. Sure, she'd complained. Molly would say that Hilary was so good she did more work part-time than her predecessors had done full-time. And Diana would chime in that they answered their own phones when they could, but they were always on another line or at the studio or on location.

It infuriated Nikki that a college degree earned her the same shit work as Hilary, who was only a college senior.

Not that Nikki hadn't tried to find another job. She'd been looking for more than six months, but it was rough.

Production companies got starry-eyed kids to work for almost nothing. Compared with other places, Abbott and Sinclair paid well. But her salary was still a joke, and she could barely afford her walk-up studio in the East Twenties.

When she thought of Molly rattling around in this town house, or Diana's two-bedroom condominium, she felt sick with envy, of Diana in particular. She hadn't inherited her money but was earning it, as Nikki wanted to, as an independent writer/producer. Diana had money to burn, terrific clothes, and a house in East Hampton.

The phones were quiet temporarily, and Nikki was finally able to get on with her statistics. God, she hated that bilious screen; it was so hard on her eyes which were large, hazel—some said beautiful—when they weren't red from fatigue. Her heavy, auburn hair was cut in a short swirl to one side of her head—a variation on a 1920's style. She kept touching it, wondering if she had done the right thing.

Diana walked in at two-fifteen and smiled at her. "Nikki, I love your hair. Turn around, let me see. Super."

"Thanks. It's the best I can do without perming."

"I'd swap you my curls any day to be able to wear mine like that." Diana opened her briefcase and took out her new script.

Nikki stared at it. "That's it? The whole thing?"

"Yes, but it's a very rough hundred-and-something pages. I hope it's readable."

Nikki scanned the first few pages quickly. "I can read it. But I don't know how you do it."

"Necessity. And practice. I've been churning this stuff out for enough years to slot the characters in easily. Getting the basic idea is the hard part."

"Oh," Nikki remembered, "problems. Terry was in a car accident. A real one, not during the shoot. He's got a busted nose so we'll have to write him out of a couple of episodes. I was just on the phone to Molly at the studio—call her immediately because she didn't want to interrupt you at home—and she's going berserk making changes while Ed's screaming and trying to block shots for the camera."

"Oh, hell. I'd better write Terry out of this script too, to be on the safe side. See if you can come up with anything. I want to look at my mail."

Nikki read rapidly, turning pages. The script was sloppy, with millions of penned-in corrections, but it was all there: plot, dialogue, directions. Counterfeit watches, such an obvious idea. Nikki knew that fake Calvin Klein jeans and Izod sweaters had been turning up all over town, mostly peddled by street vendors. Diana had simply toned up the scam by substituting expensive gold watches sold in stores. Why in hell couldn't *she* have thought of that? Nikki was dying to write her own script. That was why she had apprenticed herself to Diana in the first place, not to retype scripts and spend hours attending to production details. If she could write a script and produce it herself . . .

She chewed on the tip of her pen, wondering how to write out Terry, a street-wise former juvenile offender who worked undercover for Mom & Meg.

Diana returned. "How're you doing? Any ideas?"

"Yes. Terry's hurt in a fight so he sends a friend to take his place, someone sort of sleazy whom Mom doesn't trust."

Diana picked up her script and rapidly turned the pages, looking for Terry's appearance.

"Uh, that's a thought, Nikki. It's not bad, but maybe a little too complicated because we'd have to cast and rehearse another actor before Friday. It's Wednesday afternoon already—"

"But I know just the guy, Diana. I was talking to Kay over at casting a few minutes ago—"

"Wait, I've got it. We don't need a replacement for Terry. We get Mom off her ass for once to do the street work herself. In fact, it would add an element of surprise."

"Alice won't go for it," Nikki said glumly, adding that the star who played Mom hated to have to learn new lines this late in the week.

"Let's just try her." Diana called Molly on Nikki's phone.

Nikki was seething as she continued on the computer. Diana always did this to her—pretended to give her a chance at the creative stuff, then pulled it right out from under her. Nikki ended up looking like a nerd, even though she was sure her ideas were every bit as good as

Diana's. The trouble was that bitch wouldn't relinquish one iota of creative control, and *she* was the one who was supposedly on Nikki's side. Molly was at least honest in dismissing Nikki as a writer.

She tried to ignore the conversation with Molly, then with Alice, but Diana's treacly voice penetrated right down to her nerve endings. Diane persuaded the star to view the added dialogue as more exposure rather than a helluva lot of extra work.

After Diana had gone, Nikki began to put the script into the word processor. She was tired of doing all this shit. As she pounded noiselessly away, she reflected that Diana was only four years older than she was. It was humiliating.

Diana did go to Portland for Christmas. On her first day she got reacquainted with her sister-in-law, Patty, and delighted in meeting her year-old niece for the first time.

The second evening, Kent took Diana and Patty out to dinner and then to a club.

"Wait till you hear our jazz singer," Kent told Diana, propelling her to a table quite close to the stage in the densely crowded cabaret.

Through swirls of blue smoke, she could see a guitar-bass-piano trio softly playing innocuous music.

"Nellie is terrific, the best there is," Kent added as they sat down. "That's her over there—the black waitress."

Diana twisted her head. "Oh. You mean the waiters and waitresses make up the talent—"

"No need to sneer," Kent said defensively. "This isn't New York. People lead normal lives in Portland. They don't party every night, so the talent has to work at something else."

Diana put her hand on his arm and smiled. "I'm not sneering at all. It was just an observation, not a judgment. This seems like a very nice club and I'm really glad to be here. I'm enjoying myself altogether, seeing you and Patty so happy, and Jessica, is so adorable. Where is Patty?"

"On the phone with the sitter. We're still a little edgy about leaving Jess with anyone. Having a child's a responsibility. As you'll find out if you ever get tired of the rat race back there."

It sounded like "back Down There." Hell, in other

words. Diana wished he would stop sniping at her, implying that small-city living and marriage were the only options because he had chosen them.

As she observed her brother, she felt a mixture of affection and irritation. Since assuming the role of paterfamilias, he had acquired an unappealing smugness. Except for the brown eyes, he didn't resemble Diana at all. His hair was straight and dark, his face rather narrow, often pugnacious.

This was the first time she was spending time under his roof, and it was a bit of a strain. Sister and brother had fought incessantly during childhood. Only toward the end of their teens had they begun to get along better, partially because each had supported the other's wish to go away to college, over their parents' objections. The elder Sinclairs had hoped their children would become artists like them and remain in Santa Fe, eventually taking over the gallery.

Although Diana appreciated art, she rejected it as a career for lack of talent. Kent chose an allied field, architecture. After graduating from the University of Oregon, he had settled in Portland, married a local girl, and was hoping for a partnership in the firm that employed him.

Diana, more restless and adventurous, had always set her sights on a glamourous life and she felt that her brother couldn't quite forgive her for having done so well, even though he had what he wanted—a wife, a child, a prestigious profession with promise. Diana had made a few sacrifices on the way up. She had no husband, no child. Seeing Patty with little Jess made her envious, though she knew she could never put up with someone like Kent on a daily basis. Four days might even be beyond her limit.

Patty returned to the table, smiling. Jess was fast asleep, she reported to her husband, everything was fine, and she had promised the sitter that they'd be home right after the show.

Patty was Diana's age, small, fair, and a little plump. She was cuddly, Diana thought, and very sweet. She taught kindergarten, loved children, cooking, gardening, and always deferred to her husband. In short, Patty didn't cause friction.

Without consulting the women, Kent ordered three brandy alexanders. "You'll love it, Diana, they make the best in town."

PROTÉGÉ 31

She loathed sweet drinks but didn't think it worthwhile to make a fuss.

"Ah. Taste that, Diana. God, that's good," Kent pronounced after the drinks came. He sipped with his eyes closed, as if he were a connoisseur.

"It's delicious," Patty agreed.

Diana found it far too sweet but said it was very nice. Kent, by his standard, was putting himself out to please her. He had even arranged a date with a colleague for her tonight, but the man had gotten the flu at the last minute.

Diana had felt relieved, remembering from experience that the boys Kent thought appropriate for her had never remotely suited her taste. She wished he would finally realize she was an adult who could choose her own drinks as well as her own men. It was probably just as well that she and her brother lived at opposite ends of the continent.

Diana felt out-of-place as she looked around. Tonight she had worn the simplest dress she had packed—a plum-colored silk with a swingy skirt and a ruffled neck cut somewhat low. With a single strand of pearls and matching pearl-stud earrings, it looked understated and chic in New York. But this cabaret was mostly a hangout for Portland State students and she felt ludicrously overdressed.

Nevertheless she was determined to enjoy the evening. The audience was here to have a good time and they accepted the mostly amateur offerings with good-natured exuberance. The lookalike Woody Allen did an imitation which fell painfully short of the mark, and a cute little red-headed torch singer had too thin a voice and not enough style to carry her two numbers.

"Wait till you hear Nellie," Kent whispered for the third time.

Will the sun shine? Diana wondered, but didn't say so, knowing her brother hated her flippant side.

She finished her drink and threw herself into the spirit of the evening, feeling pleasantly lulled by all the goodwill. Being here was a welcome respite from New York work and worry. And when Kent ordered another brandy alexander for her, she offered no objection.

Her attention had been diverted momentarily; the next entertainer was now in front of the mike. He was a very tall man with an unruly mop of yellow hair. The waiter's outfit of black trousers, red vest, and white shirt, open at the neck, and sleeves rolled up, emphasized broad shoulders tapering to a narrow waist. He had presence, and his cheap guitar looked like a toy in his large hands.

Diana smiled and thought: "white bread." It was a stock type on TV, bland and wholesome-looking.

The performer, whose name she hadn't caught, began to talk while strumming rudimentary chords. He had a pleasant baritone voice but his drawl was so country it was almost a parody. Diana was amused and intrigued. Did he sing? Or was he going to try stand-up comedy?

It turned out he did a little of both. He began with a shaggy-dog story about a truck that "looked like last year's bird's nest with the bottom punched out," finally delivering a closing line that was so silly and anticlimactic that it had the audience groaning.

And yet there was something likable about the performer, as he stood there smiling, waiting patiently for the buzzing to subside. He had a surprising dignity about him.

During his next number, a little skit about picking apples, the audience became attentive in spite of his crude material and commonplace observations.

Diana studied him curiously. He had a nice smile but he wasn't really handsome. The nose was a little too long and pointed, the chin a little square. It was hard to tell his age—anywhere between thirty and forty—because his skin was so weathered.

His next story, about a determined woman who had "eight acres of hell in her," didn't have a plot; and the song that followed was pure nonsense but it didn't matter. Nothing mattered except the man himself, whose charm had obviously won over the cheering and stomping audience. Even Diana was impressed, although she couldn't quite figure out why. All she knew was that she kept leaning forward, as if she were trying to get closer to him.

Applauding with the rest, she asked her brother who he was.

"Don't know and don't care. Nellie's on next."

Through the clamor, Diana finally caught the name Luke.

A moment later Nellie walked in front of the microphone while the audience applauded. The singer was very pretty and her voice was pleasant, nothing more. After Kent's hype, Diana was disappointed, but the crowd loved her. Well, they were easy to please.

Diana's mind began to wander, and so did her eye. She thought she saw Luke at the back, leaning against the wall with his arms folded.

Nellie was given a huge ovation.

"How about that?" Kent prodded Diana as he clapped loudly. "Isn't she terrific?"

"Yes, very good," Diana said, not wanting to spoil his pleasure. "It was great fun. Thanks, Kent and Patty. A lovely show."

While her brother paid the check, Patty went for the car and Diana headed for the ladies' room. It was occupied, and as she waited, she observed Luke holding a tray of drinks and trying to move away from the service bar. It was hard going because of the knot of young women around him.

Luke suddenly looked over at Diana and threw her an engaging smile. "Enjoyin' yourself, ma'am?"

"I sure am," she called, smiling back.

He gave her a long look and another smile before lifting his tray and squeezing past the others, veering in her direction. "Excuse me, folks, comin' through."

Diana took a couple of steps forward. "You were very good, but if you're serious about being a performer, you need better material."

She was astonished at her boldness, not to mention her lack of tact. She hadn't meant to say anything at all. It was just the way he had looked at her, as if he had picked her out from the crowd as having something more important to give him than blind admiration.

He studied her for a moment. "Well, now, I thought my stuff was pretty good. But what do I know? Country boy like me. And you, well, you're somethin' special."

Diana felt flustered. Up close, his blue-gray eyes seemed bathed in an eerie light. Maybe he was on drugs. Whatever it was, his gaze reminded her of a sci-fi movie—eyes with the power to enslave.

She blinked. "Are you a farmer?"

"Used to be, sort of. But I got tired of stoopin' and

stretchin' so I come here. I like to entertain the folks." He threw her a knowing look. "You're payin' us a visit, right, ma'am?"

She nodded.

"Well, don't run off without tellin' me about this better material—"

"Diana," Kent said at her elbow, "we're ready to go."

"Oh. Uh, this is my brother," she babbled, while Kent scowled and repeated that Patty was waiting.

Luke kept smiling, shifting his heavy tray. "Well, it sure was nice to meet you folks," he drawled, his tone a trifle ironic. "And thanks for the kind words, ma'am."

Diana had the strangest impulse to yell get the hell out of this backwater, go straight to Hollywood, New York, get himself an agent, a writer, a professional photographer . . .

As Kent put his hand insistently on her elbow, she reached into her handbag for her card. "If you're ever in New York, look me up."

At least she had meant to say that but it came out: ". . . luke me up." She laughed self-consciously, unable to tell from his smile if he had noticed her slip. His eyes bathed her in their luminescence for a moment more. Then he glanced at her card, impressed. "*Mom & Meg*. Hey, you have somethin' to do with that there show?"

"I'm one of the writers."

"Luke!" the manager bellowed, nodding toward the tables.

"Well, good luck," Diana murmured, smiling quickly and moving past him with Kent.

"What in hell was that all about?" her brother asked, steering her hard by the elbow. "I told you we had to get home as soon as the show was over. And you disappear. I find you back there mooning over that guy—"

"I certainly was not mooning over him," Diana snapped. "For God's sake, the guy has talent, and he needs some encouragement—"

"Oh, sure, and you're inviting him to New York, just like that—"

"I didn't invite him. Really, Kent, you're too much. It was just a way of saying he should do something for himself, get away from this joint—"

Kent was vigorously shaking his head. "No way. You fell for that slab of beef. He's exactly your type—"

"You don't know what you're talking about." Diana angrily shook free of his hand as they got outside. "Stop telling me what I'm feeling. I know that better than you do. Okay, I'm here. You hustled me out and Patty isn't even back yet."

"She will be any minute. Frankly, I can't stand to see you make such a fool of yourself. You're old enough to know better."

Diana's ire rose. "And you're old enough to stop being such a goddamn bully."

Patty pulled up in the car and slid over so that Kent could drive.

As Diana got in the back, she said to her brother, "Let's just forget it now, okay?"

"Don't try to shut me up." Kent revved the motor, glaring at Diana in the rearview mirror. "What I hate is the way you fight me. You always have. It's a perverseness in your nature. I take you to the Viewpoint to hear a terrific jazz singer. The whole place goes ape over Nellie, but not you. Oh, no. You get the hots for some hick with a vocabulary of thirty-seven words. He can't talk, he can't sing. My infant daughter is better on the rattle than he is on the guitar—"

"Honey, please," Patty begged.

"Your credentials for judging singing talent are far from impeccable," Diana snapped, "considering you're utterly tone deaf, and further, can't tell jazz from the mooing of cows. Compared with a dozen or more jazz singers you never even heard of, your Nellie is okay, just okay. Certainly not world-class, not by any stretch of the musical imagination."

"Only because *I* said she was good. If *I* say day, you say night. You're impossible, Diana. No wonder you can't make it with a guy. You're one helluva ballbreaker."

"You think every woman who has an independent thought in her head is a ballbreaker," Diana retorted.

"Kent, please stop it," Patty implored. "I don't like that kind of language. He's had too much to drink," she added, turning around apologetically to Diana.

"You know what a man wants in a woman?" Kent shouted at his sister.

"I know what *you* want—total surrender."

"Softness, that's what. A little give. Do you think Patty's an oppressed female because she doesn't fight me every inch of the way?"

"Honey, please," Patty begged.

Diana took a quick breath. "Patty didn't grow up in your shadow, being told what to do moment by moment. Breathe in, breathe out—"

"What you want is someone who'll jump when *you* tell him to. Patty, keep out of this. Ever since you were a kid, Diana, the type you've gone for has been big, blond, and stupid."

"You haven't seen me in years. You don't know me, and you never did. God, can't we stop this argument? It's so idiotic, so childish—"

"Because you're the child. Kidding yourself. I'd like to see you settle down with someone worthy of you. But it's not going to happen while you're so contentious, so bitchy. . . . Believe me, I'm saying this for your good."

Kent continued to nag her and Diana felt a familiar aching in her throat. She was five years old again, and her big brother was able to outshout and outargue her—make her feel she was somehow in the wrong. The only things missing were the shoves and slaps he used to administer.

Hot tears suddenly blurred her vision. Stupid tears. She hated herself for being so emotional. Her brother could still push old buttons and get the same old response.

She was damned if she'd give him the satisfaction. As the car zoomed through the darkness, she sat in the back silently, tasting salt on her lips. She and her brother still had the same frustrating relationship of weak to strong, loser to winner.

3 "I don't think it's that bad," Molly said, looking down at a script through her half-glasses. "In fact, I think it'll play very nicely—"

"Oh, come on, Molly, it's more of the same," Diana groaned. "Mom & Meg are becoming boring." She sat down on her partner's desk, pencil in her teeth, and read the first few pages. "I've just had it with this show."

Molly, looked at her reflectively and murmured, "Yes, I can see that. But it's all we've got. We're lucky, in fact, it's doing so well. ATN hasn't had to pull a single series from the fall lineup, and they're waiting with quite a backlog, I understand."

Diana sighed. "I know, I know. You're right. But I'm so sick of Mom & Meg I keep having ideas for scripts in which one or both get knocked off."

Molly's phone rang, and Diana slid off the desk and went back to her own office. She flopped down in her chair and looked out of the window, which faced the wall of the next building. Up against the wall, she thought grimly.

She sneezed a couple of times. Her throat felt raspy, her nose twitchy. On top of everything else, she was getting a cold.

At the beginning of January she had tried selling *Brownstone* to First American Broadcasting but they had turned it down for the same reason as ATN: Abbott and Sinclair had no experience in sitcom.

Diana sneezed once more, as her phone rang. It was Noreen Sanders' agent, announcing that the actress had been offered a series in L.A. and she had accepted.

"Yes, of course I understand," Diana said moodily. A

show in the works was worth two on the back burner. She couldn't blame Sanders. As she hung up, Diana wrote in large letters on her *Brownstone* folder, "Aborted," and put it in her filing basket. She had dreamed up the show with Sanders in mind, and couldn't think offhand of another actress so perfect for the role.

As she wiped her running nose she thought wryly that things could get worse. Her cold could turn into pneumonia.

Molly stuck her head in. "I'm off to location. Are you up to it? Or do you want to send Nikki?"

"Oh, let Nikki go today," Diana agreed huskily. Her voice was failing. "I'm afraid we've lost Noreen Sanders." She explained.

"Well, it's still a good idea. Let's hang on to it. New actresses are always turning up."

"Sure. And there are bound to be a few mushrooms among the toadstools."

Molly smiled. "Hey, kid, ever think of being a writer?"

"Agh. Never. I'm sorry to be such a drag today, Molly."

"That's okay. We all have our bad moments. Stay in bed tomorrow. I'll give you a call."

Diana continued to sit at her desk out of sheer inertia.

Nikki appeared, her coat half-on, with a script. "I've gone over this. Came in yesterday. Say, you look a little droopy."

Diana wiped her nose. "I feel a lot droopy."

Nikki hesitated. "Can I get you anything? An aspirin? Maybe a cold pill?"

Diana shook her head. "Thanks, I'll wait till I get home before doctoring myself. That stuff really makes me groggy. I'd rather just deal with the script before I leave."

"Okay. Well, feel better."

Diana managed a smiled. "Thanks, Nikki. Do good work."

They were shooting in a deserted warehouse in Brooklyn, and Diana was glad she had opted out, in view of how she was feeling.

Her head began to throb but she ignored it and started to go over the script, from one of their best writers. She frowned as she deciphered Nikki's corrections and wrote "Stet" in the margin. In several margins, page after page. Nikki somehow managed to take perfectly readable lines and make them sound stilted. It was too bad, because she was so terrific on the production end. She had a fine memory and a real talent for detail, but she wanted badly to write. Diana, after encouraging her to stick to producing, was trying to help her, but it was hard to nurture what wasn't there, namely an ear for dialogue.

Diana looked up as Hilary came in smiling to herself. One of Barnard's brightest, Hilary was tall and slim with lank brown hair and a disdainful preppy manner. She made up for her essentially plain appearance with a self-assured style and a way of speaking that revealed her old-money background.

"There's someone to see you. No appointment. A Mr. Merriman."

Diana looked blank. "From where? About what?"

Hilary wrinkled her nose daintily. "I'd guess from a haystack in the hills, ma'am. And about what, I couldn't say, unless you've just acquired a farm."

Diana's memory clicked. "*Luke* Merriman? Oh, no! I don't believe it. Tall, blond—"

"Yup. You've got it. Do I send him in?"

"Christ. Today of all days."

"You look like you could use some coffee. So could your Mr. Merriman. Came in without an overcoat."

"Really? What's he wearing?"

Hilary's mouth twitched. "It's indescribable. Has to be seen to be believed."

Diana sighed. "Okay, send him in. And coffee would be great, thanks, Hilary."

Luke Merriman filled her office with his bigness. He was smiling, holding out a large red hand. "Miz Sinclair, pleased to see you again, ma'am."

Diana stood up and shook his hand across her desk, speechless for the moment as she stared at this vision in pastel polyester.

She felt as if she were back in Hollywood observing a walk-on from Central Casting. Either that, or the guy ought to be wearing an old-time sandwich board that said "Eat at Joe's."

Luke Merriman was done up like an easter egg. Lemon-yellow pants, pink shirt, lime-green jacket, and a white bow tie with lavender polkadots. His yellow hair was spiking around his head in all directions, and he was chewing an enormous wad of gum.

In a strained voice Diana told him to sit down. Her laryngitis was worsening.

He sat facing her, his crossed legs exposing gray work socks with red bands and what must have been the last pair of cardboard shoes ever stapled together. "I hope you don't mind me bustin' in here like this. But you give me your card, and I sure can use your advice. You know, 'bout me gettin' better material?"

Diana sighed. "I wish you'd phoned first. I . . . I mean . . ." She stopped, not quite sure how to go on. It had never occurred to her that her impulsive gesture, made after a couple of drinks in a smoky cabaret, would be taken literally.

Luke, seeing her expression, reached into his pocket. "You did give me your card, ma'am. But maybe you don't recall—"

"Yes, yes, I do," she said huskily, picking up a tissue. "Excuse me." She blew her nose.

Hilary returned with two mugs of coffee on a tray.

Luke stood up politely and smiled at her. "I thank you kindly, ma'am."

Giving him a look of tolerant amusement, she set down the tray and handed Diana her black coffee.

Both women watched, fascinated, as the visitor spooned four sugars into his mug and poured in as much milk as it would hold. Lifting it to his lips, he remembered he had something in his mouth. The brown wad he pulled out and deposited in Diana's ashtray wasn't gum. It was chewing tobacco.

Hilary whisked the ashtray off the desk, holding it out as if it contained an explosive, and left the office.

The only sound was Luke slurping his coffee.

Diana felt her head spinning. She kept throwing him quick glances, wondering about her moment of insanity when she had actually encouraged this man to leave the boonies.

But she had, and here he was. He was still holding her card with his free hand, rubbing his fingers over the embossing as if trying to draw life from it.

While Diana sipped her coffee and wondered how to

begin, he opened the conversation himself. "I never been in a place like New York City. Just what I can see is about as big as five Portlands all set end to end. It's disconcertin'."

Diana smiled. "Yes, I can imagine it would be. I felt the same way when I first got here from Los Angeles. And before that, to L.A. from Santa Fe."

He grinned at her. "Uh-huh. I didn't think you were a born New Yorker. You got somethin' real soft and western about you," he said in a low voice.

She quickly asked him how long he had been here.

"Got in last night. Come to see you straightaway."

"Uh, where are you staying?"

"The YMCA. Downtown a ways. Fella at the bus depot give me the tip."

Diana decided to level with this man. Simple he might be, but he hadn't done anything wrong. The error in judgment had been hers.

"Mr. Merriman, when I—"

"Hey, call me Luke."

"Luke, when I told you to get in touch I meant if you happened to be here anyway. I . . . I never expected you to come all this way especially to see me. I mean, getting started as a stand-up comic in this town is very hard. And I don't really know much about it—"

"Pardon me, ma'am, if I say right out that I'm not aimin' to be a stand-up comic. I'm aimin' to be on your show, ma'am. On *Mom & Meg*."

Diana's heart sank. That's what she was afraid of.

"Looks to me like the stuff you write is the best I could find anywhere. Your show's a hit, ma'am. Anyhow, I got no special call to make folks laugh—"

"Oh, but you do, Luke. That audience in Portland was quite taken with you. And dramatic acting is something entirely different."

"I realize that, but I know you can help me. I want to be an actor on TV and I want it real bad."

"I see. Have you ever acted? Had any training?"

He shook his head slowly and smiled. "No, ma'am. And no again. But I'm willin' to learn."

Diana swallowed her coffee, feeling terrible. "Luke, I steered you wrong. If it's acting you want, you'd be far better off in Hollywood." She went on slowly, as kindly as she could. "Very few TV programs are taped here because the film studios are out there, the equipment, the tradition—"

"*Mom & Meg* is taped here," he reminded her softly.

"Yes, but it would be impossible to get you a role on the show. I wish I could, but I can't. You'd have to go to acting school, and that can take years. Most of the male roles on our show change every week, so there are only bit parts. Even the pros in this town with years of experience work only weeks out of the year, sometimes on soaps—you know, daytime serials . . ."

"Sure, okay, I'll work for anyone who'll have me," Luke said eagerly, leaning forward and putting his hands on his knees. Some of the redness was beginning to fade, and Diana realized how cold he must have been.

She wished she could encourage him but she had to tell him the truth. "Even if you could get a job without experience, you would be typecast because of your accent. And there's almost no call for westerners here." Gently she continued to describe how many seasoned actors were working at odd jobs hoping for breaks that almost never came, and the casting calls, where two hundred actors would show up for one role.

Luke appeared to take in every word. "I know it's tough. But it's tough all over. Hell, my life's never been easy. I want to be an actor, ma'am. I want it bad. I'll go to school. Do whatever you tell me needs doin'. Hell, I'm twenty-six years old and I'm nowheres."

Only twenty-six. He not only looked much older, but also acted older. In spite of his rawness there was nothing immature about him. And he seemed so determined. Still, her impulse was to back away.

"I been wantin' to come east. Then I seen you. Somethin' special. And you give me your card. That sure was encouragin'. It give me the confidence to get on that there bus in Portland."

She sneezed and blew her nose, wishing he would get right back on it.

"Bless you, ma'am. Best thing for a cold is you take an old beat-up pot and put in a few drops of wintergreen or camphor. Fill it up with water. When it starts a-boilin', just put a towel over your head and breathe in the steam for ten minutes or so. Do that every couple of hours. Works every time. And if your throat's actin' up, a gargle with hot water, salt, and aspirin never fails." He smiled at her, and his eyes took on that glimmer that had struck her in Portland.

She smiled back, feeling a surge of warmth toward him. "Thanks. I'll try it."

When Hilary appeared to collect the mugs, Luke jumped to his feet. "That was real coffee, huh, not the powdery stuff. Best I had in a long time," he added, turning his luminous eyes on her.

Hilary's thin, disdainful lips widened into a smile, and she went into more detail about the beverage than was strictly necessary. Her tone was no longer patronizing, either.

Observing the receptionist's change in manner, Diana was reminded of the way Luke had overcome that cabaret audience's first impressions. Maybe it was his particular brand of innocence—his expectation that everyone would like him, the warm smile, those incredible eyes which looked at you as if you were the only person of any importance in the entire world and he would kiss you if you'd let him. And he was dignified, in spite of the hopeless clothes and stereotyped speech.

Diana was intrigued to note that snobbish Hilary was now totally engrossed in her conversation with Luke. Christ, they sounded as if they were doing a coffee commercial. Luke certainly knew how to draw people out. Or was it an effect he had on women only?

Diana sat back for a moment and scrutinized him, imagining him with decent clothes and a proper haircut.

When Hilary left with the tray, she threw Luke a last curious stare.

He sat down again. "New York folks are real friendly, not mean at all like they say out west."

Diana smiled wryly. She truly believed he had a way of making people want to be nice to him.

"I know of a good acting school, Luke," she found herself saying. "They have a number of courses that would be very helpful to you. Not only acting, but classes in speech, movement, and so forth. You would get an idea of what direction to go in. The thing is, it would take time and cost money."

"Well, I got two hundred and eighty dollars on me. That's it. I took it all when I left Portland for good. Look, if that ain't enough, I'll get me a job waitin' tables."

Not dressed like that, he wouldn't.

"Ma'am, from the moment you give me your card I been thinkin' over my life and how I got to do somethin' about it. So I come to New York—"

" 'Gave,' not 'give.' 'Came,' not 'come.' You want the past tense," Diana explained carefully, curious to see how he responded to criticism.

The answer was, surprisingly well. He listened, nodded, and said, "Uh-huh."

"And please call me Diana rather than 'ma'am.' "

"Uh-huh. Diana." He leaned forward enthusiastically. "Now, that's just what I need. To be set right on things. I don't want to be typecast as a westerner, like you said. I want to fit in here. I swear, I'll work harder'n a mule plowin' a field . . . Oh, hell, I'm doin' it again." He put his hand over his mouth.

Diana smiled. "Your background is part of you, and you don't want to lose it. In fact, it has a certain amount of charm. There's no reason not to be yourself off-camera." With a little polish, she amended silently. "As long as it doesn't stand in the way of learning to play another role, project another personality, another accent. Frankly, I don't know if you can do that. But if you're willing to try—"

"I'll work my tail off, I promise you that, ma . . . Diana. Hell, if you knew what a long way I come—came— already in three years. One day I got toothache, see, and I went up to Salem. For me, that was big city, and boy was I throwed. Thrown. I got me a job in a diner. Hell, I couldn't hardly hold a tray, but I learned. Couple of years there, a few months in Portland. You think I'm country now, you should've seen me then."

He held out his hands. "Them nails, for instance—black. I never heard of a nail brush, nothin' like that. Or deodorant. First time a waiter buddy brings it up, I says, 'Lookie 'ere, no man what ever worked the stream is gonna spray himself sissy with that stuff.' " Luke screwed up his face and raised his voice in a primordial whine that had Diana laughing.

"What's working the stream?" she asked.

"Oh, you know, goin' from farm to farm harvestin' the crop. Berry-pickin', mostly, but I've picked oranges and lemons in California, even dug potatoes in Idaho. . . ."

Diana stared at him. He had been a migrant worker. That really stunned her. She hadn't thought anyone but southern blacks and Mexicans did that nowadays.

"Did you go to school?"

"Yes, ma'am. Hither and yon. I done the—did—the best I could. I read pretty good. You got somethin' I can read?"

Diana handed him the script she had gone over.

Luke began to read, knowing enough to leave out the directions, and instinctively playing the parts. " 'Meg: Goddamm it, Artie, that psycho is holding Mom hostage, and you're asking me to wait it out when he's already gunned down his whole family . . . ' "

Luke read two pages without faltering, and Diana was amused to hear such New York dialogue delivered with his drawl. But at least he could read. He was a lot more intelligent than he had first appeared.

She picked up the phone and called the Herbert Berghof studio. A new term was about to begin. Luke could sit in on a few classes before he registered.

Diana hadn't made a conscious decision to help. It was more of an impulse. There was a quality about him she liked that made it difficult for her to let him down. And she couldn't ignore the fact that he'd almost spent his last dollar to get here; she owed him something.

"Okay, Luke, you can start tomorrow. Nine A.M." She wrote out the address. "It's only a dollar and a half to audit each class, but if you register for a full program—which I recommend—it will cost several hundred dollars. I'm willing to lend it to you. You'll pay me when you can. Now, I don't imagine you brought any warm clothes with you?"

He looked down at himself. "Nope. These ain't for winter, I reckon."

"Not for winter," she echoed, rising. "Let's get you fixed up for tomorrow."

She watched him uncoil from his chair. He was about six-three but seemed even taller because he stood so straight. It was hard to imagine him in overalls crouching over strawberry plants, though she never doubted the truth of his story.

"Hilary, I'm leaving for the day." Diana gave her some last-minute instructions.

"It sure was nice to meet you, Hilary," Luke said. "You take care, now."

It was damned cold outside. Fortunately, Diana's hairdresser was close by.

Luke's wide eyes revealed his thoughts. Diana was sure he'd never been in a unisex place before, nor had his hair cut by a woman.

Penny looked at him, then at Diana. "A cut to go with the outfit?"

"Uh, no," she said quickly. "An all-around modern cut, elegant, not too short."

Penny touched Luke's hair. "It's a little dry, but conditioning will fix that. I'll leave it long on top."

After it was washed, Penny styled it expertly, creating an off-center part. She blow-dried it in such a way that the longer, right side had a slight dip.

The rakish style gave Luke instant sophistication, far beyond Diana's imagining. In fact, as he sat in the chair, the smock concealing his garish clothes, he looked so terrific that several women walking by did double takes through the window.

Luke, admiring himself, smiled in wonder. When he saw Diana hand Penny thirty-five dollars, his mouth dropped open.

While they waited for a taxi, Luke fumbled for money.

"Keep it. You're going to need what you have, and a lot more. Don't worry about it. Part of being an actor is to present yourself well, and that really costs. So relax about it, okay? You'll repay me later."

"You bet I will. And I'll never forget what you done for me. Did," he amended, throwing her a warming look of gratitude.

Diana decided on Barney's. It was such a big store it would have a decent selection of large sizes.

Inside, people gaped at Luke's outfit while he looked around him at the clothes on the racks.

Diana picked out gray flannel and tan wool pants, a couple of shirts, a navy pullover, and a warmly lined leather bomber jacket.

"Just to start you off," she told Luke. "This is New York casual. Okay for going to work and school."

While he was trying on the pants she gathered socks, T-shirts, and some fashionable briefs, shuddering to think of what he might be wearing for underpants, if any.

When he emerged from the dressing room in the gray slacks, blue shirt, and sweater, the transformation was dramatic. He was a perfect size—the pants needed nothing but turning under. Diana slipped the tailor an extra ten to do it on the spot, improvising that her cousin from the sticks couldn't possibly wear the clothes he had come in. The tailor agreed.

Diana felt a surge of excitement, and without quite meaning to do any more buying, she chose a pair of good-looking jeans, some brown corduroys, and a natty tweed jacket.

"While we're here, you might as well get a suit, dark, I think, practical. Couple of ties. Oh, and you'll need a lined raincoat."

Luke looked unbelievably terrific in a Burberry. What the hell—in for a penny, in for a couple of thou. She was really enjoying herself. And she was touched by Luke's pleasure in his new clothes, and his attempt to hide his astonishment at the quality and prices. It was like buying toys for an orphan.

When the salesman asked about the clothes he had come in, Luke, who was examining himself critically in a three-way mirror, smiled at Diana and said, "I reckon I'm not goin' to need them anymore."

A couple of pairs of shoes and a rakish felt hat later, Diana and Luke stood in the street, their arms full of packages.

Luke peered down at Diana and said in a voice low with emotion, "Hell. And I thought Christmas was last month. Sayin' thanks just ain't enough."

"It will do for now."

"I'm goin' to live up to them clothes. You wait and see if I don't. Meantime, you ought to be home nursin' your cold and not traipsin' around doin' for me." He started to take his packages from her but they were more than even he could carry.

When a taxi pulled up, she told him to get in, she would drop him off. But as the taxi started, she began to cough and sneeze, and she ran out of tissues. Luke wasn't much help in that department, but he was concerned. "Look, you go straight home. Don't want you catchin' pneumonia as a reward for doin' me a good turn."

Diana really was feeling rotten, so she gave in.

"That's right. Don't you worry none about me. I'll be fine now I'm fixed up so's I don't stand out from the crowd."

Wrong. He still stood out a mile, and always would. He was not just striking, but handsome, she finally admitted.

Luke sat back in his seat and reached into his pocket for his tobacco.

"Please don't, Luke," Diana said. "Stains the teeth, fouls the breath. And looks bloody awful. Chewing gum is out, too, if you want to be taken seriously in this town."

He made a face. "Aw hell, I'm sure goin' to miss my chaw. But if that's what it takes. . . ."

As he opened the window, Diana perceived his intention and put her hand on his arm.

"Uh-huh. Don't be a litterbug. That's what them signs mean, huh? Okay. You know, nobody never paid me this much attention in my whole life."

Diana, reduced to a whisper, told him to go light on the double negatives and explained why.

He nodded and uh-huhed her without the slightest tinge of resentment.

Looking at him, so eager to learn, she had a stab of social conscience. There must be a lot of young people out there who had never been given a chance, who wanted to improve their lives but couldn't without help. During the last year of high school in Santa Fe, she had tutored Indian children in reading.

She suddenly felt glad that Luke had come to see her and was honest about needing her help. It wouldn't hurt her to put herself out for someone else for a change.

As they emerged from the taxi, gathering their packages, a group of noisy teenage girls came down the street, apparently on their way home from school. A couple of them looked back at Luke and began to giggle. They stopped, conferred, giggled some more. Then one girl peeled off and came up to Luke shyly. "You're an actor, aren't you?"

His face absolutely lit up. "Well, I'm tryin' to be."

"Oh. Aren't you on *All My Children*?"

"Uh, no, afraid not."

"Oh. Well, can I have your autograph anyway?" She stuck out her notebook at him, and without hesitating, Luke signed it, giving her his most dazzling smile. Her friends then rushed up, notebooks extended.

Diana watched, feeling a long, cool ripple down the length of her backbone, the sort of feeling she would have when hearing a wonderful jazz riff, or a rich, high note hit by Pavarotti. What she had dimly suspected in Portland now hit her full force. *Luke Merriman had star quality*.

Those little girls had picked him out, confirming an impression she had been reluctant to trust. She was going to trust it now.

"I see the folks are continuing to be friendly," she teased him.

"Thanks to you." He touched his hair, smiling sheepishly. Then he remembered where he was. "Hell, I'm messin' around here while you're freezin'. Is there a bus near here or a subway I can take?"

About to tell him to find another taxi and let her treat him, she said instead, "Come on up for a moment. I have a good map of Manhattan with all the transit information. And I'm getting hungry. You must be too. We'll have a bite upstairs."

She took some of the parcels and greeted her doorman, who helped them to the elevator.

Luke watched the rapidly changing floor signals over the door and shook his head with wonderment. "Never been higher than six floors in my life. But I ain't worried. Reason I ain't—I'm not—worried is this is my lucky day."

He looked around her living room, carefully walking up to each item of furniture, each picture, taking everything in. This gave her time to take him in. Clothes make the man—the phrase kept going through her head like a litany. And in spite of her worsening cold she felt very pleased with herself. She remembered having loved to make new clothes for all her dolls when she was small—except for Raggedy Andy. Diana's mouth twitched. She'd certainly dressed a live version of him today.

"I sure like your place, Diana. The way you've got it fixed up—not formal like some folks' homes, where you're afraid if you sit down you'll muss the material."

He insisted on preparing the lunch—canned soup and a couple of sandwiches, which they ate at the kitchen counter.

Except for slurping his soup—she gently called it to his attention—his table manners weren't bad at all. He had picked up a thing or two during his stint as a waiter.

"Now, Diana, Doc Merriman's goin' to get you all cozy. Got a beat-up little pot somewheres?"

"Not really. I don't have wintergreen either—"

"Well, then, I'm goin' right down to the dime store and get you some. No arguin', ma'am."

He wanted to repay her, and she decided to let him.

After a hot shower, she got into a flannel nightgown and a thick white terrycloth robe.

Luke returned with a white enamel pot and the wintergreen. While he was waiting for the water to boil he prepared a gargle for her.

Diana was touched. She tried—and failed—to remember the last time anyone had been so concerned with her well-being. Luke was really very sweet.

She gargled dutifully, then steamed her head according to his directions. She was surprised at how much better she actually felt.

"Now, you do that every couple of hours," Luke directed, putting on his jacket.

Diana suddenly didn't want him to go. When she thought of him in his new finery returning to his dreary room at the Y . . .

"How much are you paying for your room, Luke?"

"Twenty a night. But it's cheaper by the week. Sixty, I think. Once I get me a job—"

"I have a spare room," she said impulsively. "I mean, I use it to write in because my typewriter is there. But there's a couch that opens up for sleeping. You could stay for a few days. Until you find something affordable to share. And you could use the kitchen so you won't have to eat all your meals out . . ."

At the same time she was assuring him he wouldn't be inconveniencing her, she was amazed at the words that were coming out of her mouth.

Why am I doing this? It's totally crazy. He's a stranger. Maybe he's a very clever con man who knows how to get his way with women . . .

Yet he could get *that* on any street corner. And it was far less valuable than what she had already given. This was business, she told herself. Here was a man with tremendous potential. Why let someone else get their hooks into Luke when she had been the one to discover him? Star quality was rare. She'd be a fool to let him get away now.

4

When Diana turned up for work the next morning, Molly was surprised. "You could have stayed home for a day, with that laryngitis."

"I feel a lot better than I sound, thanks to a couple of folk remedies." She proceeded to tell Molly all about Luke Merriman.

Molly slammed down her teacup and began to sputter. "Are you out of your mind? You invited a man from out of the blue to be a guest in your home? Diana, I can't believe you'd be so stupid. That's how women get themselves killed. For Chrissake—"

"Calm down. He's a fellow westerner, and I can tell you that whatever his faults are, he doesn't go around strangling women. You may notice that I did survive the night." She threw her friend a wry smile.

"Don't tell me! He's another of your blonds—"

"Not one of mine—this is business, believe me. And if you don't, check with Hilary. She was utterly charmed, even before the sartorial transformation. Molly, this guy is a find. It doesn't matter if he can act or not. I'll think of something for him. Whatever it takes, he's got it. Christ, all he has to do is stand there—"

"Stop it right now, Diana, I don't want to hear another word." Molly stood up. "Aside from everything else, we don't need white bread on our show. Even if he could act up a storm, he'd be wrong. *And* with no experience. *And* a country drawl. It's out of the question—"

"Will you stop rushing ahead? I didn't promise him a role on *Mom & Meg*. And he's not just white bread, he has something much more—"

"Did you get in the sack with him too?"

"Oh, for God's sake!" Diana looked Molly in the eye. "I certainly did not. And no, he didn't suggest it, either. He's too ambitious to do something so silly."

"Okay, end of discussion. You're an adult and I can't tell you what to do. It exasperates me that you could be so blind to your own weakness, but there it is. I hope you don't find it out the hard way. Now, I have a lunch date and then I'm off to the studio."

"Fine. I'll meet you there later." Diana was unperturbed by her friend's outburst. She didn't blame her. If the situation were reversed she would probably react exactly the way Molly had.

The morning crawled. Diana had asked Luke to phone her between classes, but no call came.

She went over the script Nikki had edited, pointing out to her what needed changing and what was better as it stood.

"Remember that dialogue has to play," Diana whispered. "Say it to yourself aloud to see if it sounds natural."

"I do. But it's not a documentary. The writer is supposed to bring life to a situation."

"Yes, but it comes down to being able to distinguish between trite dialogue and pretentious dialogue." Diana had been over this same ground with Nikki many times. It was frustrating, because her assistant knew all the rules. She simply had a tin ear.

As the morning wore on, Diana grew annoyed with Luke. He was going to have to learn to be more reliable. She was glad Molly wasn't there to suggest he had run off with his new clothes.

When his call came at noon, he sounded excited but bewildered. He hadn't realized the time. He'd sat in on two classes and just loved it. But looking at the brochure was so confusing. Several courses were offered in technique and scene study, for instance. He didn't know which to chose, didn't know one instructor from another . . .

"Hold everything, Luke, I'll be right there." Diana grabbed her coat and told Nikki to go to the studio in her place. She jumped in a taxi and took it to Bank Street in the Village.

Luke was waiting for her, bursting with enthusiasm. "I learned more this morning than in the whole rest of my schoolin'."

Together they went to the office and had a consultation with the registrar. Then, over lunch in a chicken-and-ribs place nearby, they discussed the recommendations.

Diana suggested as full a program as he felt he could handle.

"I'm willin' to take everything in the brochure. I just love it. But the classes are so spread out. Two hours here, two hours there. There's classes seven days a week, and what about workin'?"

"Work is secondary," Diana said excitedly. They pored over the brochure and devised a program to include acting technique and scene study, comedy, speech, movement, and dance exercise. He'd be able to use some afternoons, evenings, and weekends for work and studying.

"This is a heavy load, Luke, but if you want to make quick progress—"

"You bet I do. Sooner I learn, sooner I get me a job as an actor instead of a waiter." He looked around. "Seems to me they could use help right here. Leavin' our dirty dishes in front of us after we're finished eatin'."

Luke got up and sought out the manager. Diana observed him talking to the man, turning on the charm.

Within moments, Luke had been hired as a part-time and weekend waiter, and he was going to start that evening.

He would be paid only four dollars an hour but Diana was certain he would do extremely well with tips.

After she had helped him register at the HB Studio, he went to work while she started home. On her way, she stopped at a jeweler's and bought him a watch—a Seiko with a leather strap, easy-to-read Arabic numbers, and the date.

She arrived home exhausted and went straight to bed.

At seven she awoke feeling better except for a crick in her neck, probably from lying in an awkward position.

She opened a can of chili and ate it in front of the living-room TV (she also had sets in the bedroom and the den). She made it a point to either watch several primetime shows a week or tape them on her VCR for later viewing.

Most of the sitcoms were terrible. And the few she liked—*Kate & Allie*, The *Bill Cosby Show*—only made her feel itchy to get her own comedy on the air. Diana toyed with the idea of tailoring the lead of *Brownstone* for someone else—maybe a man. An image of Luke floated in front of her eyes, but she quickly dismissed it. It would be a long time before he was ready to go in front of cameras in a lead role.

At eleven she switched off the set and decided to do a little work, forgetting that Luke was using the den until she had walked in. She was struck by the aura of masculinity—couch still open, pillows and sheets rumpled.

At least the rest of the room was neat, except for her desk, which was littered with papers.

She opened the closet, where his clothes were hanging, and then the bureau drawers. There were the shirts she had bought him, the underwear and socks.

What struck her was that he seemed to have no personal belongings. No letters, photos, mementos of any sort. As if he had sprung from midair. It gave her an uneasy feeling. She remembered Molly's warning, then dismissed it. What did his past matter? She knew what she needed to know about him, namely that he was smart and ambitious.

She should probably get him to help her move the desk into her bedroom temporarily.

As she was pondering this thought, she heard his key in the door.

Color suddenly flooded her face. She felt embarrassed to be in his room. But it would be even worse to be caught fleeing like a thief. After all, her typewriter and papers were in here . . .

Stop it, you idiot, she told herself. This is your apartment and you can be in any room you please.

She greeted Luke from her desk, where she was sifting papers. "I'll be out of your way in a moment."

"I'm the one in *your* way, ma'am. I tried to fold up this gizmo this morning but I couldn't get the hang of it."

She showed him, marveling at how fresh he looked, relaxed, hardly as if he'd attended classes and waited on tables for the last fifteen hours.

Luke was bursting to talk. Everything was new and exciting to him. His enthusiasm was so contagious that Diana's impulse to work left her. She just loved listening to him. New York, as seen through his eyes, was a revelation. She remembered how she had felt as a newcomer here, and they exchanged first impressions over a cup of tea Luke insisted on making.

He had an unusual recall of conversation and a fine ear, both of which would help him. Was it her imagination, or had he already modified the worst of his drawl in only one day?

It was very odd, but when she looked into his eyes she had the strangest feeling of being drawn in.

"How do you do that? I mean, I look at you and suddenly I feel sort of hypnotized."

He smiled. "Funny, you sayin' that. Fella workin' at the Viewpoint was a hypnotist. Wanted to teach me. Said I was a natural, but I wouldn't mess with that stuff. I'm still a down-to-earth sort of fella—even off the farm," he finished, pleased with his little joke.

Diana smiled and gave him the watch.

He was delighted that it showed the date, astonished that it didn't need winding. "That's real handsome, Diana, and I thank you kindly."

"It's for me as well as you," she said briskly. "So you'll call and get places on time. That's important. It's unforgivable to keep someone waiting. If ever you have an interview, be early."

"Uh-huh. Hey, you keep rubbin' your neck. Stiff, huh?

You know, I give the best damn massage west of the Mississippi."

Diana hesitated. Although the idea of a massage was appealing, she wasn't sure she wanted his hands on her.

"It'd loosen you up. Massage is somethin' I'm real good at," he persisted.

Okay, why not? It was to his credit that he wasn't only a taker.

She turned so he could massage her neck.

"If you pull back that thing you're wearin', I can get a better grip," he suggested.

She loosened her terrycloth robe so he could reach her shoulders.

"Mm. Feels good. Yes, right there. My neck really is stiff."

His hands were extremely strong, yet gentle, practiced. She could just imagine how many female necks had felt the benefit over the years.

Much as she hated to admit it, the massage was making her feel tingly all over. But then again, she hadn't been with a man in ages. It was no wonder that she was receptive to being touched. It's simply a physical reaction, she told herself.

"There now," Luke murmured at her ear. "You're loosenin' up. See, that tightness right here is going. Better, huh?"

"Much better. Thanks." As she started to move away, he suddenly reached for her breasts and squeezed them while he bent his head and nuzzled her neck with his lips.

"For Chrissake," she croaked, jerking her body and twisting away from him. Of all the crude, idiotic passes! Did everything have to be spelled out to this shit-kicker?

Diana suddenly imagined two berry pickers pawing each other in the fields, and she had to keep herself from laughing. This was not funny.

Pulling her robe tightly around her, she saw Luke's look of surprise. "That barnyard behavior is totally unacceptable, Luke." She wished her voice didn't sound so husky and strained. "Don't you ever do that again."

"I sure am sorry. I didn't mean to hurt you."

"You didn't hurt me," she said, exasperated. "It wasn't

pain, it was presumption. I agreed to the massage, that's all. Anything else is out of the question. Do you understand?"

"Uh-huh." He looked chastened. "I sure am sorry. I thought . . . I mean, usually . . . I guess I've been kinda spoiled—"

Diana snorted. "I'll bet you have. Okay, just so there's no further misunderstanding, my interest in you is strictly impersonal. That means *not personal*. I'm helping you because you *may* have talent. But if you can't be in the same room as a woman without—"

"Pardon me, ma'am. I didn't mean any harm. I mean, back where I come from, if a gal asks a fella to stay at her place he thinks . . . well . ."

"Yes, it's clear what he thinks." Diana took a deep breath. "You're in the big city now, Luke, and things are different here. The first rule is to assume nothing. A decent place to live is very expensive, and people make all sorts of living arrangements. And they don't include sex unless a woman indicates it's what she wants. Women in this town aren't particularly shy, either. You probably know that already. You don't need me to tell you how attractive women find you—"

"But *you* don't." He sounded chagrined.

"Luke, I'm two years older than you and years older in experience. Of life, not sex. If you want me to help you, you can't think of me as a . . . a girlfriend."

"Uh-huh." He looked at her balefully, utterly crushed. "I ain't good enough for you is what you're sayin'."

She sighed. "We're just . . . different. Come on, Luke, cheer up. I've seen the way women look at you. You can have your pick. Isn't that true?"

"I reckon."

"And so?"

He shrugged. "So nothing. I kinda like to make the first move. It's no fun to be caught before I even know there's a chase on."

Diana did her best not to smile. "Luke, when I asked you to stay, it was to save you some rent. But if you're used to having women and need a place you can be private—"

"No, ma'am. I have no time for that. I have a heap of studyin' to do. And what with my job and all . . . And I can sure learn a lot from you. So I . . . I hope you won't take offense where none was intended." He gave her an anxious look.

Diana smiled wryly. He didn't want to rock this particular boat, since it was in such a nifty harbor.

"Okay, we'll say no more about it."

He had been warned. If he tried anything like that again, he would have to go.

The next morning at eight sharp, there was a knock at her bedroom door. Luke appeared, dressed and shining from his shower, with a tray holding a mug of coffee, a fresh roll with butter, and one red rose in a bud vase.

Diana sat up sleepily and smiled. This was more like it. "Aren't you going to have something yourself?"

"Already did. I don't need a rooster to wake me. Up at dawn, just like always."

Diana sipped her coffee, luxuriating in her breakfast in bed.

It became a daily ritual.

Luke turned out to be an amazingly quick study. Within the next two weeks he changed before her eyes. The drawl lessened as the grammar improved. He began to lace his speech with the trendy expressions he was no doubt picking up from fellow students.

Luke asked Diana's advice about all sorts of things, from what shampoo to use to what he could do about his dry skin.

Diana found herself taking him on as her special project. She had a phone installed for him the day he helped her move her desk to the bedroom. And almost every day she came home with something for him: after-shave, cologne, a hairbrush, a blow dryer, half a dozen more shirts, an electric shaver.

With her help, he opened his first bank account and learned how to keep a checkbook. She directed him to the cleaners, Chinese laundry, shoemaker, and library. In addition to the *Times*, the *New Yorker*, and *New York Magazine*, she suggested books for him to read, to help him overcome a shocking ignorance of anything historical or literary.

He saw his first musical and his first Broadway play in her company and learned how to apply critical judgment.

She got him off junk food and acquainted him with tofu, sun-dried tomatoes, unprocessed cheese, and bakery bread, and cited nutritional reasons for eating more chicken, fish, and salads and less red meat and desserts.

Diana was so preoccupied with Luke that Molly began to come on strong, urging her to realize what she was doing.

"I'm helping him, that's what I'm doing. When I get through with Luke Merriman he's not only going to be a star, he's going to be a fully developed human being."

"Really? I've yet to meet this paragon, and I wonder why."

"Because he's been busy night and day, that's why."

However, Diana was now proud enough of him to want to show him off, so on the first Sunday Luke wasn't due at work until evening, she arranged for him to have brunch with her and Molly at a pretty little place on First Avenue, with brick walls, oak tables and chairs, and hanging plants.

The hostess took one look at Luke and led them to the best table, right in front of the window.

Diana nudged Molly. "You see?" she whispered. "We always have to fight for a window table."

"We're always two, not three," Molly replied, watching Luke hang up his raincoat.

When he gave his order to the waitress he really looked at her, conveying the impression that she was unique and necessary and he appreciated her.

Molly observed him, exchanged a smile with Diana, and then pounced. In her New York staccato way, she asked questions designed to put him on the defensive.

"You were born exactly where, Luke?"

"I don't know exactly. What my folks told me was in a bus somewhere between farms in the Willamette Valley. Home was whatever shack in whatever place in Oregon we were harvestin'. Spring, summer, fall. Winters we mostly went south to California."

Molly wanted to know about siblings, and if he had any photos.

"I had a sister and a brother older than me but I can't remember them. They got burned up with our house. I was real little. My folks, they got killed in a car crash when I was sixteen or seventeen. No pictures. We didn't have a camera. Pardon me, ma'am, but we hardly had food to eat."

The sadness in his eyes made Diana want to kick Molly for being so brutally nosy.

"I'd like to get me a camera, though. It would be fun to take snapshots of people and places in New York," he added, bestowing on an unresponsive Molly his contagious smile.

While Diana made a note to buy him a camera, Molly barreled ahead, and Diana had to bite her lip to keep from jumping in.

As it turned out, Luke didn't require her intervention. With his voice pitched low, the tone almost intimate, those glorious eyes fixed on Molly's shrewd, skeptical ones, he began fielding her questions quite adroitly. Finally he was interviewing Molly instead of the other way around.

By the time they were finished with their eggs Benedict, Molly had not only told him how she had started in TV but also allowed herself to be drawn into a discussion of the problems and intricacies involved in writing and producing a series.

Diana felt a surge of pride and excitement, marveling at Luke's brilliance. And he wasn't just putting on an act; he was really interested, really listened, as his intelligent responses proved.

Molly's guard had tumbled to her ankles, and understandably. Who doesn't want to talk about herself? Be listened to as if every word were a rare pearl of wisdom to be forever cherished? Molly drank an unheard-of third cup of coffee, finally responding to Luke's smiles with her own.

It was Luke who looked at his new watch and called for the check, pulling out the wallet Diana had bought him.

As he helped the women on with their coats, he had a friendly parting word for the waitress, who was fawning over him, and the hostess, who, Diana thought, was longing to fling herself in his arms.

Outside, Luke shook Molly's hand warmly, then bent and kissed her cheek. "It sure was nice meeting you, Molly. We'll be seeing more of each other. Well, I'm off home. Got to tackle that Sunday paper before I go to work."

Diana deliberately said nothing as she and Molly walked toward the office, where they had a script to go over.

"Okay," Molly began. "I have to grant that your Luke is attractive and probably photogenic. He's clever and the charm oozes out of him. But—"

"Never mind the buts," Diana broke in. "He had you, Molly, admit it. You were grilling him and he turned it around. Before you knew it you were giving him chapter and verse about the business. And what's more, you loved every minute."

"Yeah, I loved it like I love eating a box of chocolates, knowing I'm going to gain five pounds overnight. Your Luke is a charmer, but . . . *but* there's something not quite right about him. Something I don't trust—"

"Oh, for Chrissake."

"Something I don't trust because he's too quick, if you will, too ready to suck up information as if through a straw. He's not quite real."

Diana stopped in the middle of the street, exasperated. "Molly, you're too goddamn much! Did you see the hostess, the waitress, half the women in the place, giving him the eye—"

"I saw it, and it's fine. I'll grant you that Luke has possibilities for TV—"

"Hallelujah!"

"Possibilities for TV, I said, *not for you*. You sat there preening like some proud mama—"

"What's wrong with that? You should have seen him three weeks ago."

"I believe you. But will you slow down a moment and look at yourself? You're remaking the guy, okay. But you're also becoming involved with him."

"Bullshit. I'm not in any way involved with him. Believe me, Molly, mentoring is the least romantic connection I can think of. I have to make out reading lists for him. Teach him how to use a dictionary, an encyclopedia. Define almost every word I use, and spell it too. Give him an instant history or geography lesson, and he's hopeless in current events. When he arrived he knew zilch about New York, had never heard of the mayor or the governor—"

"You're not hearing me, Diana. Luke is getting to you, whether you realize it or not. When was the last time you had a date?"

"What's that got to do with anything? I go for months at a time—"

"No, you don't. You might not go beyond drinks or dinner, but hardly a week used to pass without your meeting someone new, at least putting yourself where the action is. You've been turning down invitations, I've heard you myself. Last week at the studio Al invited you to a party and you said no, even though you weren't doing a damn thing that Saturday night except waiting for Luke to get home."

"Al's nice, but not my type."

"Diana, you've made yourself unavailable to any other man because of Luke. Get him out of your house."

"That's absolutely ridiculous. It would be unfair to make him move now. He still needs my help. And he's helpful as well. Fixes things, does chores." As Diana spoke, she felt a little bit dishonest. She had never told Molly of the pass he had made. That, of course, hadn't been repeated, but Luke did continue to gently flirt with her. He paid her compliments about her hair or her clothes. Of course she didn't take any of it seriously. Molly probably would, and would have plenty to say if she knew about the morning coffee sessions in Diana's bedroom.

"I've told you what I think, Diana. Sooner or later you're going to pick your head up and realize that you're hooked on that guy."

"Even if that should happen, unlikely though it is, why would that be so terrible? He's kind, he's sweet."

Molly opened her front door. "He's never going to stick to one woman," she said placidly, hanging up her coat. "Not entirely his fault, of course. He'd have to be a saint or gay to ignore all the women who fall into his lap."

When Diana countered that Luke slept at home every night, Molly laughed at her. "That wouldn't stop him from screwing three women a day, you boob. Where? Anywhere. In the woman's apartment. In a quiet corridor at school. Behind the kitchen door at the restaurant. In the john. How can you be so naive? You, of all people, who are so critical and untrusting of most men. Frankly, that's why I'm worried. Because when it comes to Luke, you've suspended all common sense. Believe me, that's a guy who gets laid, and as often as possible. He exudes sex. It's not only his good looks; he radiates an animal earthiness, and he looks at a woman as if he can't wait to get into her pants. That's why the women are hot for him. And you too, whether you know it or not. To sum up: yes, I think we might be able to make a star out of him. I just want him out of your den and into his own pad. Think about it, will you? Please?"

"I'll think about it," Diana agreed sullenly.

Molly was projecting feelings onto her that she didn't have. Christ, she knew better than Molly what she felt about Luke Merriman. But arguing was pointless. Molly could be painfully stubborn.

Diana conjured up an image of Luke at home, with all his now-familiar habits. He sang in the shower, tended to comb his hair over the sink, liked to read sitting on the couch in the living room his legs on the coffee table and the TV going. His outfit around the house was jeans and a T-shirt, and he looked marvelous in both. He was lean, tan, and muscular, with wonderfully developed shoulders and arms. Nevertheless, her assessment was impersonal. She was a pro, for God's sake, and when she saw him looking so good she imagined him parading on a TV show in his casual clothes.

But he still had quite a way to go in his intellectual development. That was why it was important that Luke stay put, where she could not only continue to smooth away the rough edges but also observe his strengths, his weaknesses. He needed time to grow. Sophistication didn't come overnight.

If she let him get away now, he would without a doubt be swept up by someone else, and she would lose the chance to have first crack at his talent. She had already invested too much in Luke Merriman to let that happen.

Luke awoke at six A.M. and stretched luxuriously. It sure was a comfortable bed he slept on, even if his feet did hang over the edge.

It was Friday. Today he had a class from nine to eleven.

He would be working at the café from eleven-thirty to three-thirty, and then he was free.

He got out of bed, showered, dressed, and went down for croissants, Diana's favorite. Then he made some coffee in the special gizmo she had. It ground the beans, boiled the water, dripped through the grinds—hell, it did everything but pour itself out.

Everything was neatly arranged on the breakfast tray, especially the rose, for he knew how much Diana appreciated that little touch.

"Oh, no, not already," Diana grumbled sleepily when he knocked at her door.

"Good morning," he said brightly. She was sitting up in bed, covers up to her neck, her hair all mussy around her head, looking about twelve years old and as cute as a button. Remarkable that an hour from now she'd be dressed and dolled up, making deals, sweet-talking people into giving her whatever she wanted.

"You're so damn cheerful in the morning," she grumbled. "School going well?"

"You bet. It's a heap of work but I love every minute. Can't wait to get into a real production."

Diana grunted and swallowed coffee.

He was silent, waiting for her to get herself together. It was hard to read her sometimes, and he was careful not to do anything wrong, anything that would cause her to stop being so wonderful to him.

She had picked him out—him, Luke Merriman—from all those raggletaggle caterwauling nobodies at the Viewpoint and told him he had talent. Something he was born with. He likened himself to a strawberry seedling that just needed transplanting to some good soil, and careful watering. Diana had done that for him, and he was grateful.

"I'm gettin' through early today, Diana, and it's payday. I can't make a dent in what I owe you, but it would sure make me feel good if you'd have a meal with me."

"Oh, Luke, I appreciate the thought, really. But Friday is the worst. We do a final studio rehearsal and then start taping after lunch. Stop-and-go, until we've got it right. Might not finish until nine or ten. By then I'm bushed."

"Gosh, it sounds so interesting. In class we sort of prepare for the theater but not TV. It must be different to be in front of the camera," he added, putting a wistful note in his voice. "I've never even seen the inside of a TV studio."

She looked at him. "That's right, I guess you haven't. And you should. Tell you what. Come by this afternoon when you're through with work. I warn you, it means sitting around, watching take after take. It can be very boring—"

"No, ma'am, not to me. I'd be fascinated, really." He smiled at her. "I sure appreciate the invitation. And don't be concerned none. I'll be as quiet as if I was in church. No, you go ahead and get ready. I'll put the dishes in the washer. Hell, chores around here are nothing when you've got a gizmo for everything."

He felt absolutely terrific. Even the subway ride downtown had its good points. Dirty and noisy, sure, but he could look at the people, observe their mannerisms, as had been suggested by his teachers, and reproduce them later.

The thing he found disconcerting was the way people kept staring back at him. In fact, he had taken to wearing dark glasses even indoors.

Part of it was the jazzy clothes Diana had bought him, making him look rich and successful. That leather jacket, for instance, was a Perry Ellis, one of the best designers, he now knew.

His class this morning was modern dance, which was supposed to make him more aware of how to use his body to express a role. He found it the easiest of all his courses because his body had always obeyed him. In Salem and then in Portland he had worked out at the gym, trying not to go all soft, because waiting tables wasn't nearly as hard as stoop work.

At noon the restaurant filled up quickly. A group of ladies at his station were noisily discussing their tour of the local art galleries with the art historian who was leading the expedition.

They were from New Jersey, he gathered—housewives killing time. It was amusing, watching them trying to eat ribs with a knife and fork, finally picking them up with their fingers.

One of the ladies had strange hair. Sort of gray, but not really. It was nowhere near natural, anyway. She kept flirting with him. At one point she pushed a note into his hand. In the kitchen he deciphered her name and telephone number—daytime only, please.

Luke grinned and threw it away. That sort of thing happened almost every day. New York wasn't so different from Salem or Portland in the matter of ladies coming on to him.

Well, he wasn't interested in that one. She didn't compare to Diana. There was a lady with beauty and brains too.

Whenever he thought of the way he had pawed her that time he wanted to kick himself. But that was a month ago, when he still had grass seed sticking to him.

At any rate, he was learning. It took time, but if you looked and listened and copied, before you knew it you'd lost an old habit you didn't need. He didn't even miss chewing tobacco, for instance. In fact, he didn't miss anything about his old life.

All he knew was every day when he looked at himself in the mirror he saw a citified version of the old Luke. And every time some high-toned gal smiled at him or handed him her phone number, he felt real proud.

The good Lord had blessed him, and it was up to him to make the most of it.

When Luke presented himself at the studio door at four o'clock on the nose, the guard assumed he was one of the actors and asked to see his pass. Lord, it felt good to know he already looked the part. All he needed now was to get one.

Diana came out to fetch him, her morning grumpiness gone. She looked marvelous, her brown eyes and sweet smile warming him. From the moment he had first heard her speak he had felt comfortable with her. She didn't rattle on loudly and quickly like a wagon in a hurry. No sir, she talked real slow, and her voice sort of trickled out, like molasses. Only when she was riled or doing business (on the phone, for instance) did she give off New York sparks.

Like now, as she took him out onto the set and started introducing him to folks. Mom's name was Alice Dworkin and Meg's name was Ann Earle. And there was the director, the assistant director, stage manager. They were "staff," she told him in his ear, and the camera, lighting, and sound men, "crew"; the difference was between "creative" and "technical," and both were equally important.

Luke got it immediately. "Uh-huh. Don't worry, Diana, I got no call to look down on anyone. I sure know how it feels."

He was fascinated by the sets, which held real furniture, as in the theater. But when he looked up, the ceiling was pretty busy, what with wires looping and hanging down and those reddish-brown gizmos that looked like carpet sweepers or ladies' hair dryers from outer space. All that stuff was lighting, and off on the side were four cameras on wheels.

Then Diana took him into the control booth and sat next to him in the back. In the front were the director and assistant director, then the technical director, playing with an elaborate control panel. In front of everyone were several TV monitors.

Luke was glad Molly wasn't here today because she didn't cotton to him. Fortunately, Diana had a mind of her own.

He had missed rehearsal (he'd see that another time, Diana assured him), but the taping was real interesting.

Talking into his mike, the t.d. called the shots, in gobbledygook, which Diana explained from time to time, while the director spoke to actors on the floor, telling them to "stand on the marker," the place that had been especially designated so that one actor didn't block out another.

Diana said very little to the floor. "I did my stuff during rehearsals, Luke, so I leave it to them unless something just doesn't work. Oh, shit, like right now."

Everyone in the control room groaned as the cameras halted. Meg had dropped a contact lens, so the scene had to be reshot.

Luke asked no questions but sat there taking it all in, trying to memorize what he saw, just as, when introduced to someone, he would repeat the name to himself. Folks loved to be called by name.

Luke enjoyed watching Diana in action, and he felt proud that he was there with her, the lady everyone looked to, the one in "creative control," as she put it.

Yessir, he had sure been lucky the day Diana Sinclair had come his way and handed him a ticket out of nowhere.

For the duration of the following week, Carl Blayne, an actor in a *Mom & Meg* episode, flirted with Diana. He was darkly handsome, with glittery eyes. She hesitated to mix business with pleasure but there was no reason not to accept a dinner date with him for Saturday, after the taping was finished.

Carl suggested Amsterdam's, an Upper West Side restaurant he knew well. The place was jammed, and the noise and blaring music that bounced off bare walls made conversation impossible.

Diana didn't really care; she was content to exchange sexy looks with her date. After her predinner martini and a half-bottle of wine, she was, quite frankly, feeling horny. When Carl's knee touched hers under the table, she didn't move away. Over dessert, they held hands.

It had been a long time since she had been to bed with a man, and Carl seemed a very likely candidate for the purpose. He might even turn out to be someone she could occasionally date.

He was being careful not to come on too strong, possibly because she had been so reluctant to go out with him. That was sweet, and she smiled at him warmly, anticipating how pleased he would be when, after dinner, she kissed him with passion outside and invited herself to his place.

As they were leaving the restaurant, however, he suggested a short walk as an antidote to the heat and noise. He seemed a little nervous, and somehow the romantic moment seemed to have passed. It was strange.

Two blocks later he stopped in front of an apartment building. "Here's where I live. How about coming up for a nightcap?"

Of all the clumsy choreography! From the moment they had left the restaurant he had been cool and calculating. He wasn't interested in her at all, just in scoring.

"I'm sorry. I have to make this an early night."

Carl gave her a quick, resentful look. "I see."

"No," she contradicted, "I don't think you do. I don't like being manipulated. You pick a restaurant conveniently close to your house. Then you suggest a walk to the very place you live. You talk of a nightcap when what you really mean is sex. It's just too tacky—"

"Are you saying yes or no?" he asked tightly.

"I'm saying no."

He turned and stalked into his building without a backward look.

Diana hailed a taxi on Columbus Avenue, furious with him for being such an idiot. Men were impossible, especially actors, the most narcissistic of the bunch. She should know that by now. Dammit, she didn't have time for these silly games. The next time Molly quizzed her about why she wasn't dating, she would have her answer ready.

As Diana walked in the door of her apartment, Luke was coming out of the bathroom with a towel wrapped around him, his hair wet, and droplets of water still glistening on his skin.

"Oh, hi. I didn't reckon you'd be home so early."

"It's all right. No problem." She suddenly felt dizzy.

In a moment his strong hand was steadying her arm. "Are you okay?"

"A little woozy, that's all. Too much to drink, I guess. The room's spinning."

"Better get to bed. I'll bring you some milk and aspirin. Never fails."

She smiled wanly, feeling a little better.

When he knocked at the door, she was in bed.

"Here you go. This'll help you sleep."

"Thanks, Luke. That's very sweet of you." Diana took the aspirin and sipped the milk. The room was still going around, so she focused on Luke's bare chest, with its very sparse dark blond hair. His shoulders really were massive, and the color of his skin was such a beautiful golden brown.

"Better?"

His voice seemed to be coming from a distance.

"Yes. Thanks. Good night."

"Good night."

Did he brush her forehead with his lips before tiptoeing away? Or did she imagine it?

Within moments she was out.

5 "Abbott and Sinclair, good morning," Nikki said into the phone. "Yes, I sent it out yesterday. . . . Well, the mail is slow."

Ordinarily she would be fuming at the hundred and one extra things to do because Hilary was going to be out for a couple of days. But today Nikki accepted her drudgery with less impatience. Finally she was feeling a refreshing breeze of change, wafting her closer to her goal. And not because of talent and/or hard work, either. That didn't count for shit in this business. What counted was who you knew.

She wanted a chance to write scripts because that would help her become what Diana was, an independent writer/producer and her own boss. But she had little or no chance of writing for *Mom & Meg*. Molly treated her like a moron; and although Diana kept saying that as soon as Nikki came up with something good she would get the chance, Diana was a cheat. She kept turning down terrific ideas because she just didn't want any competition.

Her best bet, she felt, was to write an acceptable script for a soap. They aired daily and continuously, and moreover, every once in a while the producers fired all their writers and brought in a new team to freshen up the material.

For months she had been eating lunch in the office in order to watch the soaps. And if Molly and Diana were out, she kept the conference-room TV going all afternoon. By now she knew the plot lines of several of the soaps better than her own life; the characters had become her friends.

However, when she began sending out her own scripts,

they came back with polite rejection notes. She was sure it was because she had no credits; that was catch-22. How did a writer get experience if producers wouldn't accept a script unless you had experience?

The only way would be to connect personally with someone in a position of importance on a show, so Nikki began making the rounds of TV watering holes after work, observing, eavesdropping, trying to be noticed. After all, she was young and pretty. It ought to be a breeze.

Only a couple of days ago she had gotten lucky. She had overheard a conversation at the Ginger Man between two producers of the popular *Night and Day*, which aired on First American Broadcasting.

One producer, Herb Norman, was a man in his fifties, on the portly side, boasting both a wedding ring and an unmistakable eye for attractive women.

Nikki elbowed her way over to him at the crowded bar, introduced herself, talked with verve and intelligence about his show, and incidentally rubbed her breast against his arm at calculated intervals. She made it seem almost accidental but not quite.

Herb invited her to dinner; she invited him to bed.

He showed no inclination to merely get on top of her for a slam-bam-thank-you-ma'am, for his wife apparently served that purpose. Herb turned out to be a little kinky and rough. And Nikki didn't care.

She planned to get him sexually hooked on her so she would have power to negotiate, tit for tat. That was the way of the world, and Nikki remembered it from experience.

When she was fourteen and failing French on Long Island, her male instructor had kept her after school to give her a lecture on doing her homework properly. All the while, he was moving his hand up her leg to her thigh, and inside her panties, whispering that he would drive her home. She wanted to practice her French, didn't she?

Nikki had been desperate to pass so she could go to camp and not have to repeat the course at summer school. So she met her teacher several times in the parking lot. And even though she knew she didn't do too well on her final, she pulled a B in the course. She had passed her oral exam in the back of her teacher's car.

Nikki's reverie was interrupted when three phones began to ring at once. "Abbott and Sinclair, please hold," Nikki said, pushing phone buttons.

Just then the door opened and in walked the most gorgeous man Nikki had ever seen. He looked familiar; probably one of the string of handsome hunks who graced the soaps daily. When she heard the name she might recall who he was.

With a smile he said, "You must be Nikki. I reckon we've talked on the phone."

"*You're* Luke Merriman," she replied in wonder, her heart beginning to thump as he fixed her with a pair of extremely sexy eyes.

"Yup. Diana's not expecting me," he confided. "Just thought I'd surprise her."

"She's on the phone. Long-distance," Nikki improvised. "If you'd like to wait." She smiled seductively and indicated a chair.

"Thanks, Nikki, I will."

That gorgeous drawl gave her goose pimples. She couldn't wait to hear more of it. Pretending to be immersed in her work, she observed him put aside his camera and his *Times*, then take off his leather jacket. The navy knit sportshirt showed off magnificent shoulders and biceps.

Nikki was forced to return to her phones, but Luke continued to preoccupy her.

She knew all about him, of course, as she made it her business to know everything about Abbott and Sinclair. So this was Diana's "protégé," the lucky bitch. Of course she was paying for everything he gave her, and Diana could afford the best.

While he waited, Luke told Nikki that ever since he had gotten the camera a few weeks ago it had become his favorite toy. "I'd sure like to take your picture, Nikki," he said, smiling at her. "Your red hair is real pretty."

"I'd love that, but let me fix my face." She took a comb and mirror from her handbag, moving with deliberate self-consciousness as he watched. "Okay, ready." She smiled provocatively.

He leaned back, focused, and snapped.

Nikki would have to buzz Diana on the intercom, but not just yet. The longer Luke had to wait, the better Nikki could get to know him.

Just then an important call came in from Molly. Ann Earle was going to be leaving the show in June to make a film, and they would have to convince the network to replace Meg rather than let the show die.

Nikki talked rapidly and knowledgeably, smiling with animation while she suggested several replacements. She wanted to be sure Luke saw that she did a lot more around here than answer phones and greet visitors.

As soon as she hung up she buzzed Diana and told her to call Molly immediately. What Nikki didn't mention was that Luke was here waiting. In all the excitement over Ann's replacement, Diana would never remember.

Drawing Luke out further, Nikki heard all about his acting classes.

Too soon, Diana rushed out of her office and stopped short. "Oh, Luke. Is something the matter?"

"Nope. Just thought I'd surprise you. Take you to lunch."

"Oh, I can't, something's come up. I have to have lunch with Molly."

Nikki watched Diana get her coat, take Luke's arm, and walk him out.

But not before he had turned and waved, throwing Nikki a last enchanting smile.

God, he was gorgeous. No wonder Diana had somehow managed to keep him away from the office all this time. The smug bitch treated him as if he were her own private property.

Nikki smiled cynically to herself. Actors weren't anybody's property for very long. They went where the roles were. Luke's role, just now, was playing lover boy to Diana. But if he were offered something better . . . Nikki felt herself to be more than a match for Diana. The trouble was that her boss had the power to help Luke, and Nikki had no power at all yet.

But she was certainly working at it. In fact, she was due for a matinee with her producer.

She put on the answering machine and taxied to her apartment to wait.

After two days without her, Herb was horny as the devil and longing for satanic pyrotechnics. What he wanted was for Nikki to crawl around on the floor on all fours while he crawled after her, spewing a stream of obscenities.

"Wave it, you cunt, that's it, wave it at me."

Nikki gyrated her hips, and every time he reached for her she quirmed away, teasing him, working him up, turning over chairs to put obstacles in his way.

Glancing at her watch, she finally let him mount her from behind. It was bestial, and she hated it. The only good part was that she didn't have to look at his jowly face looming over her or watch his belly shaking.

Dammit, life sucked. While she was squatting on the floor with this pig, Diana was probably making love with Luke.

It helped Nikki to think of Luke, to imagine he was the one pounding into her. Those were Luke's powerful hands kneading her breasts, Luke's beautiful white teeth sinking into the flesh of her shoulder.

Just as she was getting close to orgasm, Herb began to bellow like a bull in a stall, puncturing her fantasy and forcing her to fake her cries of pleasure.

She lay on her stomach tasting rug nap and feeling sticky, violated, and unsatisfied. She did, however, have the consolation of believing that very soon she would be calling the shots and getting what she wanted.

She had just added something to her list: Luke Merriman.

"Tell me something nice before I go off to an indigestible lunch with Molly and a couple of casting execs from the network," Diana said as she and Luke stepped into the street. "In fact," she added, observing him closely, "you look ecstatic. What's up?"

"Ecstatic?" he repeated.

"As in ecstasy. The adjective form," Diana amplified.

"Uh-huh. Well, that's exactly how I feel. For no reason except March has come in like a lamb. It's real warm and sunny out and smells like spring. And I've learned how to use this gizmo." Swiftly he raised the camera and snapped her before she could protest.

"Oh, no fair. I wasn't ready."

"Yes, you were," he contradicted softly. "You look beautiful without primping. I want you just the way you are."

Diana's face grew warm at the double meaning. "Listen," she told him, flustered, "if you aren't careful you'll become so busy recording life you'll forget to live it."

Luke laughed. "Oh, no I won't. I was hoping we could go to Central Park. There's lots of folks who like having their pictures taken. Couldn't you play hooky just this once?"

"I wish I could. Tell you what. I have about half an hour, so I'll walk over with you. Might as well stock up on some fresh air. I'm gonna need it."

On the way to the park, Luke photographed things that interested him: a handsom cab overflowing with kids who were agitating the horses; a little doll-like Oriental girl with a noisy pull-toy; two greyhounds being walked by a tall young boy as skinny as they were.

Diana watched Luke snapping, his face animated. He looked so attractive, so dynamic. And in his small-town, ingenuous way he spoke to people, and they answered. Even frozen-faced New Yorkers relented when they heard his friendly drawl.

Just inside the park, a football some teenagers were throwing around came toward them. Luke kicked it back into play, hoisted his camera, and snapped. The sunlight glittered on his hair and bounced off his jacket.

An enthralled Diana suddenly had a brainstorm. "I have to make a phone call." Pulling Luke by the hand, she had him wait in front of the fountain of the Plaza Hotel, where there was plenty to photograph.

Inside, she found a phone. "Roy? Diana Sinclair. Look, a rush job for me. Good. Just grab your camera."

Diana fed another quarter into the phone and dialed the studio, leaving a message for Molly that she'd be late for their lunch and they should definitely start without her.

While she waited for Roy, Diana wrote rapidly in her little notebook.

Within minutes Roy pulled up in a taxi. "What's going on? You sounded as if it's life or death."

"It is. Of a new show, I hope."

While Luke was moving around the fountain photographing, Roy began shooting him. It took a few minutes before Luke realized what was going on.

Diana introduced the two men and explained to Luke,

"I just want to have you on tape. The thing is for you to ignore Roy and just keep doing what you're doing. Can you handle it?"

"Yes, ma'am, I reckon I can."

Luke was eclectic in his subjects, without any prompting from Diana. In the park once more, he photographed a well-dressed elderly man reading the *Wall Street Journal*; a young mother in mink thumbing through *Esquire* while her infant twins slept in their expensive pram; a couple of black boys on roller skates; a bag lady eating a slice of pizza. And he kept whirling and shooting Diana—always when she least expected it.

As discreet as Roy was being, it was obvious that something was going on, and a crowd began to gather.

Luke was amiable in fielding questions. "I'm just having fun, sir. Got me this new camera. Roy, there, he's having fun too."

Diana lost track of time, and it was Luke who finally said, "Hey, I have to be at a class in twenty minutes."

"God, that late already?"

Hand in hand, Diana and Luke ran to Fifth Avenue, waving frantically at taxis until one pulled over for them.

"First stop, Forty-eighth, then down to Bank Street," Diana said, getting in first.

She and Luke were out of breath and laughing. "I can't wait to develop the pictures of you," he said huskily. "Wind blowing your curls. In that furry coat you look like a model or something. How about we go out and have a real good supper somewhere."

"Dinner," she corrected. "Supper is a late meal."

"Supper is what I meant, because I have to work until eleven. Gotcha."

Diana laughed with him but said she would have to take a rain check.

When the driver stopped to let her out, Luke quickly kissed her cheek and gave her a hug.

For some stupid reason her legs were all tangled up and she had a hell of a time getting out of the cab. The goddamn things were slung so low it was impossible to be modest in a skirt.

The meeting at Charley O's was in progress when Diana

joined Molly and two male execs she didn't know, and Kay, from ATN's casting department.

Judging from the loud voices, and Molly's querulous tones, they were working on a second round of drinks.

The gist of the argument was that the network wanted to scrap *Mom & Meg* in spite of the good ratings, and Molly was fighting to save the show.

Diana felt guiltily disloyal for being more concerned with her new idea for Luke.

"No matter what you say, Molly," one of the men was insisting, "Ann is so identified as Meg that the audience won't go for a substitution."

"Sure they will," Molly contradicted, "if it's someone good. Hell, it happens all the time on the soaps. We'll just send Meg on vacation for a couple of weeks and when she comes back—"

"Who do you have in mind?" the other man asked. "And she'd better have tits."

While Kay accused him of being sexist, Molly began to suggest names.

"Dammit, Diana, come up with someone, and quick," she whispered. "Your Nikki, by the way, is a cretin. Suggested stars, would you believe, when we obviously need an unknown. And I don't appreciate your waltzing in so late, either. What was so fucking important it couldn't wait?"

"Tell you later." Diana sipped her beer and prepared to edge into the fray, but it wasn't easy. She felt at a disadvantage among people to loudness and vulgarity born—namely New Yorkers.

Finally there was a silence, and the others looked at her.

"Uh, how about Cindy Thomas. Played a small part on the show a couple of years ago and stopped working to have a baby, I think. She's the same type as Ann. What if Meg rushes into a burning building—a fire started by an arsonist, say—to save someone. She gets facial burns, needs plastic surgery. When the bandages come off, Meg looks different. She looks like Cindy Thomas."

"Hey, that's not bad, that might work." They all began to talk at once.

"I forgive you all your trespasses, kid," Molly said, hugging Diana and kissing her cheek.

She smiled and tried not to remember that Luke had recently done the same thing.

"This had better be worth it," Molly said grumpily, eyeing the seafood salad Diana had ordered.

It was several days later, and they were sitting in the control booth at the studio during the lunch break. Roy was about to run a tape.

"I hate to eat where I work, Diana. I feel like a mole subsisting on worms and never seeing the light of day. I also hate surprises. At least give me a hint."

"Too late. It's starting."

There was a long shot of Luke in the park wielding his camera. He was smiling, his yellow hair ruffling in the breeze, and all the people around him were smiling too. Children followed him, women beamed, young girls giggled, and one crusty old man broke into a big grin and waved.

Roy had done a terrific job, Diana thought, and so had the editor.

Luke was shown front and profile, and there was a final closeup of him smiling, with that irresistible intensity in his eyes. The shot froze. The screen went blank.

"That's it?" Molly asked.

"That's it."

"Whew." Molly turned to look at her partner. "I'm impressed. Even if you set it up—the people gawking at him, and so forth. He's unbelievably photogenic. Makes you want to reach out and touch him. And I don't even like him. Diana, this guy is pure gold."

"He sure is. And no shots were set up. The reactions to Luke were spontaneous."

Reflectively Molly took a bit of salad. "Thing is, kid, what are we going to do with him? Giving him a bit part on the show—if we're still gonna have a show—won't work. I think he'd steal every scene—"

"Exactly," Diana cried with excitement. "The thing to do with Luke Merriman is write a show for him. Listen to this: Luke is living in a brownstone in the East Village, maybe, or SoHo. He's a widower, three kids—eleven, seven, four. Wife died maybe two years ago. Accident."

"He's kind of young to have an eleven-year-old—"

"Not really. He can pass for thirty-five, even thirty-eight. And he married young. They do in Oregon, where he was a farmer. Might as well make it authentic. Photography was his hobby, and he came east for some reason—"

"He won an amateur photography contest. First prize was two weeks in New York—"

"Wonderful! And he decided to stay, brought his family, got a job at an ad agency—that can be worked out later. So he has decent money, a fair amount of success, and he's raising his own kids."

"His name is Pete Winston," Molly supplied.

"Oh, Molly, I love it!"

"But can the guy act?"

"If we write it properly, he won't have to act, he can be himself, more or less, and just turn on the charm. All he has to do is learn his lines. Just think of it: Luke as young widower and father. Available yet committed to his children. Handsome and virile, yet tender, nurturing. Every female in his neighborhood flipping over him, women all over America, ditto."

"Yeah, yeah, I like it," Molly reflected, "but we'll have the same problem as with *Brownstone*. Where are you going to pitch it? Feranti probably won't bite . . ."

"Probably not. Let him have first refusal. The one to try is Continental. They haven't any sitcoms to speak of. And Matthew Sayles, the new veep in charge of East Coast entertainment, has to be looking for stuff."

"Maybe, but what makes you think he'll be receptive to an unknown and untried actor?"

"We won't bring Luke in right away, we'll sell the concept first."

"A man raising his own kids isn't exactly new—"

"The networks don't want new, they want proven, with a twist. Not just any father, but a masculine father, like Matt Houston, like Magnum. Luke is similar enough to be familiar, different enough to be interesting. He's western but he's made it in New York, has a glamour job—"

"Which conflicts with the demands at home—"

"Yes, yes, exactly. Is it manly for him to stay home with a sick child, et cetera."

As they went back and forth, exchanging ideas, Diana's excitement grew.

"Hey, before we go overboard, kid," Molly finally said, "hadn't you better talk this over with Luke? Maybe he doesn't feel ready to put himself on the line."

Diana gave her partner a knowing grin. "Wanna bet?"

6

Diana sent her proposal to Oliver Feranti by mail, and by mail he rejected it. She refused to be discouraged. She had high hopes for *Pete Winston* and was sure that Feranti would regret his decision. At least she had his refusal in writing so that he couldn't claim at a future date that he hadn't had his chance at it.

Now Diana felt free to approach Matthew Sayles at Continental. As she had explained to Luke (who was awed at the prospect of playing a lead in a comedy), they would have a better chance if they took their idea to a major production company and let them sell to the network. But if they did that, it would mean giving up ownership, money, and a large amount of creative control. Abbott and Sinclair wanted to remain independent, yet their very independence could cost them the show.

Luke had assured Diana he never counted his chickens before they hatched, and she hoped he meant it.

Matthew Sayles's assistant, Jill Murray, sounded brisk and competent on the phone. Of course she screened all calls, so Diana told her she had an idea for a new show but declined to give any details. Jill assured her she would relay the message. However, her boss was busy attending meetings and it might be a while before he got back to her.

While she was waiting, Diana put her time to good use. She knew that because most TV series failed, the only way a network could attract popular actors and actresses was to make commitments to them. So if a program was canceled, the network would be obligated to find the out-of-work actor another property.

"Nikki, I'd like you to compile a list of Continental programs that have gone down the tubes within the last year or so and indicate whether they were drama or comedy. Also, get me a list of all the actors and actresses involved and what roles they played, putting the stars first, and so on down the line. Include kids."

After Nikki had done the research, Diana blocked out several characters—including two women and three children—who could reasonably be cast from the roster of possible commitments. She knew that dangling parts for these actors would be an important selling point and would also mitigate the fact that Luke was unknown and inexperienced.

Next, she gathered as much information regarding Matthew Sayles as she could, but not much was known about his personal life. He was apparently something of a recluse, and although he was invited everywhere, he accepted few nonbusiness invitations. Nor was he romantically linked with anyone, in spite of his apparent eligibility. It was rumored that he was about forty years old and divorced.

As far as his career in television was concerned, it had followed a fairly routine path. He had gone straight from New York University to the research department of First American Broadcasting in Hollywood and moved up to head the department. To Diana, that signified a heavy reliance on numbers and audience pretesting. From research he went over to prime-time development and became the head of West Coast entertainment. He was part of the team that helped move FAB from third to second place in the network hierarchy, increasing FAB's profits by millions. What advertisers paid for was numbers, *i.e.*, how many people were tuned in to a specific program. During the "sweeps" months of November, February, and May, audiences were measured in more than two hundred cities by means of audimeter boxes placed in representative households. The way the three networks ranked determined the advertising rates that could be set by local affiliates.

FAB rewarded Matthew Sayles by appointing him vice-president and director of programming in the New York office, and for the next two years he had continued to do wonders for the network.

Yet he suddenly left FAB to take charge of East Coast entertainment for Continental. Had they made him an offer he couldn't refuse? Had he had a falling-out with the new president of FAB? Or did he simply like the challenge of turning an underdog into a top dog? Second dog, anyway. ATN was indisputably in first place.

Diana did learn a couple of things that were going to help her. Since Continental's execs on the Coast had more clout than their counterparts in New York when it came to series development, Diana was gambling that Sayles would try to strengthen his own position here by backing strong programs to originate in New York. She also knew that he had consistently promoted quality material, and that was why she was confident he would go for *Pete Winston*.

She spent a Saturday working up a new proposal with Continental in mind and tried it out on Luke when he got home from work that night.

"Hey, I like this real well. I mean, it sounds right, seems a lot like me, taking photographs and all. And I could talk like myself, too."

"How do you feel about being a TV father?" she asked.

He grinned. "Fine with me. Don't know that much about kids, but if you write the lines, I'll be happy to learn 'em."

As he handed the proposal back, she noticed a long dark hair on his shirt and discerned the faint odor of scent. A woman's scent. The thought that Luke had been with a woman irked her, quite unreasonably. Diana was ashamed of herself. What Luke did about women was none of her business because she didn't want him for her lover, period.

"The only thing is, Diana, it says here thirteen episodes. Is that a good number? I mean, some folks might be superstitious."

"There are thirteen weeks in a TV season. Though to expect that much of a commitment from a network at this point is like wishing for the moon."

She explained that the networks dealt in "step deals," which meant a series of cutoff points. "For example, if Continental is interested in the idea, they may agree to step one, the go-ahead to write a treatment—they call it a bible—and one or two scripts. Only if they liked the result would we get a chance to write, say, another four scripts. In other words, the network could always drop the project after each step they agreed to."

Luke smiled. "I'll bet on you. You're a very persistent lady and I reckon you usually get what you want."

For a moment their eyes locked. Diana was the first to look away, uneasy at the feelings he was stirring within her.

"Well, I'm gonna take a shower and go to bed." His voice held just a note of teasing.

She avoided looking at him as she answered, "Fine. Good night."

The living room seemed very quiet after he left. Diana poured herself a large glass of wine and sipped it slowly. She felt restless, jumpy.

She suddenly thought of Brad, an old friend and former lover, one of the first directors of *Mom & Meg*, who had gone on to form his own production company. For the life of her, she couldn't recall why or when she and Brad had stopped seeing each other. They had worked well together; in fact, Brad had been a very nice man.

Her glass was empty, and she suddenly felt the same way. As she shut the door of her bedroom, she had an impulse to hear a friendly voice, and she picked up the phone and dialed Brad's number.

As soon as he answered, she realized that it was almost one A.M.

"Brad, it's Diana Sinclair. Sorry to be calling so late. Did I wake you?"

"No, no, that's okay. How're you doing?"

"Just fine. And you?"

"Oh, just fine. It's been a long time, Diana. Two years, just about."

Had it really? During the long pause that followed, Diana felt foolish. I'd like to sleep with you tonight, Brad. How could she possibly say something of the sort to him after all this time? And if not, what did she have to say to him? And calling at this hour . . . Christ, he knew damn well what she wanted.

"Uh, I'd like to have a long talk sometime, Diana, but

this isn't the best moment. Matter of fact, I'm living with someone. . . ."

Diana hung up feeling like an idiot. What in hell did she expect? The world didn't stand still, even if she did.

She lay back on her pillow with her arms folded under her head. Maybe she ought to ask Luke to move. At the very least, his presence reminded her of the possibility of being with a man more than she wanted to be reminded—especially with nobody on the horizon.

Yet, for practical reasons, she couldn't ask Luke to go yet. Maybe after she had sold the show, and Luke was acting and earning good money . . .

As she looked over at her Raggedy Andy she had to resist her impulse to take him to bed to cuddle with her. She turned out the light and told herself not to be so damn silly.

Monday morning they started rehearsal of the last *Mom & Meg* episode. Just before they broke for lunch, Ann Earle received a call from Hollywood that her film had been canceled.

During the flurry of excitement, Ann phoned her agent and Molly phoned ATN. The result was everyone willing to work out a new contract to carry them through one more season.

"Well, that's certainly a morale booster," Molly told Diana over lunch. "Especially since Cindy couldn't make up her mind to play Meg. I guess we'd better start thinking about next spring."

"Molly, I need time for *Pete Winston*. Maybe Nikki can take over as story editor—"

"Over my dead body. She's fine on some production details but she has less creativity in her whole body than an octopus has in one section of one tentacle. And she's a lousy writer, so forget it."

"I won't be able to come up with enough scripts, or the time to read what does come in—"

"For the moment I can take care of things while you pitch *Pete Winston*. If you succeed, we'll go on from there."

* * *

After a couple of weeks without word from Matthew Sayles, Diana tried to reach him again. She called once at noon, once at one-thirty. His assistant would no doubt be out to lunch one of those times, and maybe he would pick up the phone himself. But no, Jill apparently ate lunch at her desk.

Another time Diana called at nine A.M. precisely, hoping Jill got to work after her boss. No, she was already on the job. Then Diana tried at six-thirty. Surely the assistant would have gone home. Wrong again. The peerless Jill was still at her post. Jesus, did the woman sleep in the office?

Jill was always very polite to Diana, assuring her the messages had been given to Sayles and he would get back to her. "Yes, he's looking for new material. If you could tell me a little more, it would help."

Diana hedged, feeling that Jill had enough clout to turn down a sitcom from Abbott and Sinclair without checking with her boss.

As the days continued to roll by without a word, Diana became more and more impatient. Finally she tried at eight in the morning. This time Matthew Sayles answered his phone.

She just had time to introduce herself before he said, "It will have to wait, Miss Sinclair. California on my other phone. Sorry." And then a click.

Diana slammed down the receiver so hard she hurt her hand, adding injury to insult. That lying bastard! It was five A.M. in L.A. Did he think she was that much of an imbecile?

Dammit, it was the middle of March already, and Diana was feeling so frustrated. With *Pete Winston* stalled, she agreed to do a script for *Mom & Meg*. The hardest one ever, as it turned out. Page after page wound up in the wastebasket. Everything sounded trite, boring. She spent hours typing decorative lines of X's on blank paper. Finally she succeeded in pulling together a script, but the fun had gone out of it.

Luke picked that moment to tell her he had landed a little acting job, a commercial to be shot in Atlanta over the weekend. She tried to share his excitement. Yet, when he packed his bag and left that Friday morning, she felt bleak and out of sorts. For a couple of hours she slopped around in jeans and a shirt, switching the TV dial, looking at her watch every fifteen minutes.

Then she wandered into Luke's room, for no particular reason. She was surprised to see his snapshots all along one wall, and they were damn good, too. She wondered why he hadn't shown any of them to her.

As she turned she noticed that the wall facing the couch contained the photos he had taken of her blown up to eight-by-tens.

She had a funny sensation in the pit of her stomach as she walked slowly toward them. Most photographs didn't look like her at all, she felt, but these did. He had captured something nobody else ever had, amateur or professional: her vulnerability. God, she looked like a little kid caught trying on her mother's fur coat. How had he done that? Restraining her impulse to tear them off the wall and rip them up, she left his room feeling worse than when she had entered.

Maybe she just needed a change. This would be a good time to open up her house in East Hampton. An actress friend of Molly's had moved to Hollywood a year before and sold the house to her for a good price. Molly, in fact, had lent her money for the down payment.

Having grown up inland, Diana was still awed by the ocean and loved having it practically at her feet. Georgica Beach—a little away from the hub, the crowds, and the tourists—was often deserted. The houses were built far apart here, and many were more like mansions, lived in year-round. Diana's house, of course, was just a modest little saltbox with weathered siding.

She arrived quite late on Friday in her rented car. The house smelled musty and a little damp, and she opened the windows for a while, although a cold wet wind was blowing off the water. At least there was firewood, supplied by a local handyman who maintained the place through the winter.

Among some local mail was an invitation from her neighbor, Tom Ryan, to his annual St. Patrick's Day cocktail party the following evening. Well, maybe she'd go, maybe not. What she really came out here for was a rest.

Diana lit the fire and lay in front of it until the place was warmed up and she was feeling drowsy.

She had decorated the house with white wicker furniture and flowered chintz curtains and pillows—what she thought of as country Victoriana. She completed the look with ferns and palms planted in several genuine Victorian cachepots. The style suited the simplicity of the house and was a nice change from her modern apartment. In fact, it was very comforting to be back here, quiet and by herself. Luke's continuing presence, she saw clearly, wasn't entirely relaxing.

She fell asleep in her canopied bed, lulled by the music of the waves breaking on the beach.

"Diana, my love, glad you could make it. I assume you know everyone," Tom Ryan said, drawing her into his huge living room, crowded with people. "But first, have a drink. Irish whiskey, cream, or mist. No foreign stuff like wine on St. Paddy's Day."

Tom, a bright, expansive man in his forties, was divorced and involved with a different woman every few months. He ran a very prosperous real-estate business, and as a year-round resident he knew just about everyone, and just about everyone came to his parties.

Diana accepted a glass of Irish whiskey on ice and stood sipping it, leaning against a wooden beam a little off to the side of the festivities.

This was the second party at Tom's she had attended, and undoubtedly she had met some of the guests, but nobody stood out in her mind. Scattered among them were several notable writers, painters, and designers. There was also a decorative selection of young women, very fashionably turned out. Almost everyone wore something bright green; in fact, several punkishly dressed guests had dyed their hair in honor of the day.

Diana hadn't any green clothes so she had settled for her gray silk pants and white silk tunic blouse, with a Zuni silver chain belt slung low around her middle. The only green she sported was in her Chinese jade earrings.

She felt a little shy and awkward at the moment. Her social persona was very different from her business one. No matter how many people were at a meeting, she was able to join in because she had something to say. But just making party chitchat of the and-what-do-*you*-do variety made her feel foolish.

A young waiter in green suspenders was offering canapés. As Diana reached toward the tray, she bumped hands with a man who had suddenly materialized beside her. Only his larger fingers succeeded in securing a canapé before the waiter, oblivious of the little tableau, melted into the crowd.

"Oh, sorry," Diana said, a little flustered.

The man looked soberly at her. "I'm the one who should apologize, since I came away with the prize. Please, you have it." He dropped the canapé into the palm of her hand.

It was a tiny quiche. Diana bit off half and extended the other half. "It's only fair to share it. I have no diseases that I know of."

"I'll trust you." He popped his portion into his mouth.

"What's in it?" Diana asked. "Chicken? Lobster?"

"I'd say crab with mayo and a touch of dill," her companion replied knowledgeably.

"Aha. A man who not only eats quiche but knows what's in it."

"Even worse, he can cook it." His tone of resignation made her smile.

He was about thirty-five, not more than a couple of inches taller than she, with wavy brown hair. High cheekbones and a rather flamboyant Edwardian mustache gave his face an exotic foreign cast. He was dressed in an oxford blue shirt, a maroon pullover, dark slacks, and a gray buttery suede jacket.

She noted that he was studying her as intently as she had been him, and there was something sad about his eyes.

"Are you holding up that beam or is it holding you up? You haven't moved from that spot since you got here."

So he had noticed her before approaching. "Let's just say we're a mutual-support system. I'm a little shy at parties." She discovered she had imbibed enough of her drink to feel loose.

He nodded wisely at her confidence. "You prefer to go into the ocean inch by inch, though it's even colder that way."

She made a face at him. "How did you know?"

"Just a guess. I'm sort of the same way. And we have another thing in common. We're the only two here, I think, who aren't flaunting green."

Diana playfully jiggled her earrings at him.

He nodded. "Very subtle." Then he brought his face closer so that she could see that his eyes were green.

She smiled. "That's carrying subtlety to its ultimate."

He drew his face back. "Oh, do you think so? Okay, how's this?" He snatched a piece of parsley off a passing tray and stuck in comically in the collar of his button-down shirt.

"Diana! Diana Sinclair." A statuesque woman with streaked frizzy hair rushed up to her and took her arm. The woman was outlandishly dressed in a two-piece emerald-green satin outfit, the top of which tied in a side bow like a diaper.

"Tom pointed you out to me. I'm Paula Taft, the photographer, of course. I'm doing a book about women in the entertainment arts. *Mom & Meg* is my all-time favorite show. . . ."

As she went on and on rapidly, she kept flashing predatory teeth that had Diana cringing.

"Thanks, but I'd rather not be photographed for a book," she said in her soft voice.

Her words went unheeded. Paula Taft barreled ahead, even grabbing Diana's chin and turning her head to see her profile.

Diana moved her head back and kept declining, but the din had increased, aided by music blaring on the stereo.

The man beside her said, "I believe this is our dance, Diana." Taking her hand, he danced her away to the disco rhythm, his deadpan expression and exaggerated motions vastly amusing to her.

When they had made it to the other side of the room, Diana thanked him. "Some people are incredibly persistent."

"Yes, some people are," he agreed. And then he smiled for the first time. An attractive smile. She wondered why he was so stingy with it. His green eyes were twinkling in a knowing manner, and she suddenly had a funny feeling about him. "I don't think you've told me your name."

"Matthew Sayles."

"Oh, God!"

"Well, it's not that good. Or that bad, depending on the way you look at it. You've been wanting to talk to me, Miss Sinclair. Well, here I am."

Feeling quite embarrassed, she realized she must have seemed as obnoxious to him with her endless calls as Paula Taft had seemed to her. "Did you know who I was before that woman—"

"No, I didn't. But when she said your name I remembered I hadn't returned your phone calls. I'm sorry about that. I really have been busy."

Diana had pictured Matthew Sayles as older and crabbier. She remembered the way he had brushed her off on the phone and knew she had to take care how she handled this unexpected and possibly profitable meeting.

Before she could formulate her next words, he said, "I want to compliment you on *Mom & Meg*. It's one of the best. Character development, rather than just plot piled on plot. I especially like the relationship of mother and daughter and the way they work together. There are generational differences, of course, and competitiveness, but also affection. Damn. It's so noisy here. Do you want to step out on the deck for a moment?"

"Yes." She didn't care if she froze to death. This she had to hear.

"I gathered from my assistant that you had an idea for us, Diana—if I may call you that. Actually, I can't be very encouraging because we don't need drama at the moment."

"It's not drama, it's sitcom."

He looked slightly surprised. "I see. What do you have in mind?"

Diana told him, in her soft voice and measured tones that were supposed to be so soothing and unthreatening. "I see Pete Winston as the quintessential new man—so secure in his masculinity that he can dare to be sensitive, so truly tough that he can dare to be tender. A man determined to keep his family together."

Diana could see by Matthew Sayles's thoughtful expression that she wasn't boring him. As she paused to take a breath, he asked if she had anyone in mind for Pete Winston.

PROTÉGÉ 91

"Uh, I'm sure we'll find someone wonderful. I mean, if you like the basic idea."

"I like it, but frankly, I was thinking in terms of a female lead. I was thinking of Gemma Lopez."

Gemma Lopez! Dammit, Nikki hadn't included Lopez on the list of possible commitments, no doubt because her series had ended quite some time ago. But not, apparently, Continental's commitment to her.

Thinking on her feet, Diana said brightly, "Gemma Lopez would be a perfect costar for Pete Winston. She's dark and intense, so we can make him fair and a little laid-back. And I see her as more than just jiggle. Maybe she's a feminist, despairing of the Latin macho man, but comically so. Some dude sucks his teeth at her and she throws him a pack of floss and a one-liner about dental hygiene. Her name is Lola, she's Pete's neighbor, and she has plenty of bucks. ironically from alimony. She'd love to be Pete's one and only. At the same time she comes on strongly political."

Matthew Sayles was almost smiling. "For instance?"

"Uh, for instance, she finances a clothing designer—say, a woman who's also a feminist—who's designing a line of menswear to raise their clothing consciousness so that they'll realize what women have had to cope with for years. Imagine how a bachelor would get dressed in the morning if his shirt buttoned up the back."

Now he *was* smiling. Encouraged, Diana went on. "Or maybe Lola's trying to get women to lobby for more booths in the ladies' rooms of theaters and movies. She once complained to an usher, who agreed that ladies' rooms could use more urinals. . . ."

Diana was deliberately being outrageous to keep Matthew Sayles a little off-base.

"The thing is, Diana, that we're inundated with suppliers, all thinking they have winning shows, most of them wrong."

His tone held a challenge, and she suddenly realized that he was playing devil's advocate. He was interested in *Pete Winston* but he needed more amunition to convince others at the network.

Taking a deep breath, she launched into a discussion of programming; of which sitcoms had succeeded against all odds, and which had failed. She was careful to present many of her statements as rhetorical questions. "Does anybody really know in advance what will make a given show succeed or fail? Isn't it all a lot of guesswork? Surely a proven record of success is what counts, and Abbott and Sinclair has a such a record."

"Only in drama. That's not going to impress the bright boys in research. I know because I was one of them. They go by track records, statistics, demographics—"

"Let's start with demographics," Diana allowed warmly, having done her homework. "*Pete Winston* will fall into the yup-com category. You know, young, upwardly mobile, urban professionals et cetera who badly need a laugh after a hard day."

The appeal, she went on, would be even wider. Children would watch it, and so would their grandparents as well as parents. Young men would identify with Pete, young women would fall for him, kids would find in him the ideal father. This wouldn't be like the outmoded cartoon type of sitcom. These situations would be real, the people would be real, the dialogue would be believable, with comic overtones.

"For the past two seasons," Diana went on, "hasn't Continental had a chronic eight-P.M. lead-in problem on Tuesdays and Wednesdays?"

Matthew's raised brows indicated surprise that she was so well-prepared.

"On either night," she went on, "*Pete Winston* will be the perfect audience-grabber because it will be light, it will be gay—in the old meaning of the word—but not inane."

"You're used to a one-hour format. Twenty-two minutes and thirty-seven seconds goes very fast. It requires different pacing."

"Yes, you're right. We have to nudge the audience from one everyday crisis to another, each one happening just before the commercial. And each little crisis has to have a satisfying solution. And it will, I promise. One-parent families are increasing, and a man caring for his children will definitely appeal to the main target group—women of eighteen to forty-nine—who of course do most of the product-buying."

"Do you have any children of your own?"

"No, not yet," Diana said quickly, "and neither does

Molly Abbott, but isn't that irrelevant? Lewis Carroll had no children, Louisa May Alcott had no children."

Matthew looked at her sharply and changed his tack. "Do you think a father raising his own children is particularly funny?"

"Not at all; in fact, I think it's deadly serious," Diana said truthfully, "but seriousness—tragedy, even—is the source of most genuine humor. In *Pete Winston*, as in life, there would be amusing times and sad times, when Pete remembers his wife, the kids remember their mother."

"What kids did you have in mind?"

This time Diana answered specifically, naming the three possibles she had already chosen. "They're adorable but not sickening. The seven-year-old, Kelly, misses having a mother so is trying to get Daddy to date . . . but Sharon, the eleven-year-old, cherishes the memory of Mommy and sabotages every effort. . . . I can get a written proposal to you Monday afternoon."

By the time they went back indoors, Diana's lips were blue with cold and her bones felt brittle but she was still overflowing with enthusiasm.

The crowd had thinned out, and the remaining guests were leaving.

"We can talk some more over dinner," Diana suggested as Matthew helped her on with her jacket.

She regretted her words when his face tightened and he drew back. "Some other time. I . . . I have to be getting home. Didn't realize it was so late. Can you really have something for me by Monday?"

"It will be on your desk without fail."

He nodded at her and quickly left.

Diana took several deep breaths, feeling a little anxious. By the way he tore out of there she feared she had sounded as if she were coming on to him, which was the last thing on her mind. Her idea was terrific; that was all she was offering, and he could take it or leave it. He had certainly seemed interested. He had asked to see the proposal, after all, so why was she worried?

"Well, Diana, I see you didn't let any grass grow under your feet," Tom Ryan said at the door, winking slyly at her. "Matthew's time is expensive. Did I detect a little pleasure mixed in with the business?"

"It was *strictly* business," Diana said crisply. She kissed Tom on the cheek, thanked him, and slipped away.

Alone, in front of her cozily sputtering fire, she reviewed her conversation with Matthew Sayles.

She hadn't really flirted with him, and certainly not after she had learned who he was. The dinner suggestion had been businesslike, and if he had misinterpreted it, that was his problem.

The more she thought about their conversation, the more excited she became because it was clear that he wanted a vehicle for Gemma Lopez. The actress had become popular as a result of *Bubbles*, in which she played a teacher of English to adult foreigners, mostly male, who, of course, were continually trying to date her. The show had run its course, and Lopez hadn't done anything big on TV since. Then again, major comic roles for fiery Latin females didn't come along every day.

Diana felt confident that if Lopez liked the idea of *Pete Winston*, the network would be willing to give Abbott and Sinclair a development deal.

Diana returned to New York Sunday evening with a good first draft of her proposal.

As she entered her apartment, she heard Luke's voice coming from his room. It sounded as if he was on the phone to a woman.

To be sure she didn't overhear anything intimate, she waved at him through his doorway on the way to her bedroom.

Almost immediately he hung up and followed her.

While she unpacked, he stood in her doorway, telling her how well the taping of his commercial had gone and how much he liked being in front of the camera.

"Thought it would scare me half to death, but it didn't at all. Heat of the lights felt sort of like the sun warming me, making me feel real good. Remembered my lines, too."

"Good for you, Luke. Congratulations." She decided not to say anything about Matthew Sayles until there was something concrete to report.

While she put away a few things, she could see him from the corner of her eye. Jesus, did he have to walk around half-naked like that! He was standing with his hands in his jeans pockets, his muscles rippling. She supposed she could tell him to put on a shirt, but he would smile and tease her.

In fact, he was looking at her in a way that was doing unwanted things to her breathing. Dammit, he was going to have to move, and soon.

"I'm glad things went so well, Luke. Good night," she said firmly.

Slowly he unpeeled from the doorjamb, saying good night in a suggestive voice, as if hoping she would change her mind.

She did no such thing.

7

Monday afternoon Diana delivered her proposal to Jill Murray, who would give it a first reading, the usual procedure.

Jill was a no-frills woman in her early thirties, efficient, sharp, and with an opinion on every subject. Diana rather liked her, and she reflected that some men would find an assistant like that intimidating. Apparently not Matthew Sayles.

Prepared to wait a week or more for a response, Diana was stunned to be invited to lunch with Matthew two days later.

Riddled with excitement, she dressed for success in a wine-colored suit and a navy blouse with a bow for what she suspected was going to be a crucial meeting.

They were lunching at the Four Seasons' cozy Bar Room, by reputation a place reeking of money and power, where the high and the mighty negotiated important deals, and the acoustics were such that they couldn't be overheard.

Although Diana arrived five minutes early, Matthew was already at his table. He looked much more formidable in business clothes—a double-breasted gray flannel suit, gray-and-white-striped shirt, and subtly patterned silk tie—than he had at Tom's party.

He stood up. "It's nice to see you again, Diana," he said pleasantly, his sharp eyes taking her in at a glance.

Diana thanked him, smiling nervously. She was actually shaking with anticipation. While she drank her Perrier (she had to be alert), she glanced around the wood-paneled room, recognizing people from publishing, advertising, real estate, politics. Surely Matthew Sayles hadn't invited her here to reject her idea, had he?

Well, why not? He lunched here regularly, and looking at it another way, treating her to a meal might be his way of compensating her for saying no.

If only he would say something. Because she found herself unable to utter a word, sure her voice would falter.

He drank half of his martini before saying, "*Pete Winston* looks good on paper. I like it. So does Jill, but she suggests some changes. . . ."

Diana listened and was impressed. Jill had come up with several valid criticisms. Finding her voice, Diana expressed her agreement and willingness to make changes.

It was only then that he told her Gemma Lopez was interested (she had read the proposal in L.A.) and Continental was willing to go ahead on development of a bible and a pilot script—provided Diana could work quickly.

Like the wind, she assured him, and tried not to get carried away into fantasyland. The network would be parting with only about fifty thousand dollars, which was peanuts to them. Even if they hated the pilot script they would have lost very little.

"What do you think of Chris Forman to play Pete Winston?" Matthew asked.

"Uh, that's a thought," she said slowly. "He's a good comedian. Of course, he's very much associated with the *Jensen Brothers Show*, and this would be such a different role. Plus he's on the dark side. Don't you think someone less well known but highly charismatic, maybe blond, would be better with Gemma?"

Diana trod softly and carefully, feeling twinges of conscience on two counts. She disliked having to deceive Matthew at this point; he was being very decent. On the other hand, she wouldn't have thought of the idea if it hadn't been for Luke. But what if an unknown was totally unacceptable to the network? Could she agree to another actor and disappoint the man who had been her inspiration? Or would she allow the show to fizzle?

As she suffered an acute anxiety attack and her whole body became suffused with warmth, she left most of her salad uneaten.

She had to concentrate to keep her voice tentative and her manner receptive. After all, she kept telling herself, this was only step one. Continental would have to approve the pilot script before the role of the lead male would be considered in earnest.

It was not a long lunch, but Matthew looked at his watch twice. He was a busy man, and she didn't take it personally.

He signed the check as soon as their coffee arrived, and she pondered on what a strange man he was. That deadpan quality made him seem to be holding back, as if he feared to reveal his true feelings, whatever those might be. Maybe he was simply uncomfortable doing business with women.

She thanked him for the development deal and the lunch, told him her agent would be in touch to negotiate the details, and went directly to the office to discuss everything with Molly.

"Good for you, kid. You've done wonders with old Sayles. I'd heard he was hell on wheels, like most guys who come up from research. Yeah, they like quality, sure, until it rubs up against the facts and figures."

"He's not like that. More complex, I think. I don't quite know how to read him. So far, though, he's in our corner." Diana sighed.

Molly picked up on the "so far." "Of course the stumbling block is Luke. You may have to put that dream aside. I mean, the guy's a novice. Why should the network go for him?"

"Only because he'd be terrific. Looks the part. Acts the part. Of course, is the part. And he's unknown enough to make Gemma feel she's the star attraction. Apparently nobody else had come up with anything for her, and my impression is that she really wants this. In fact, Molly, the more I think about it, the more sure I am that we should hold out for Luke."

"Well, I'm not. Added to everything else, I'm not convinced he could carry the show. In fact, I think you should tell Sayles about Luke now. If he finds out later you've been conning him—"

"I can't tell him now. And I haven't been conning him exactly. Christ, when did you become Honest Abe? I seem to recall a lot of maneuvering back in the days when I was still sucking my thumb, listening to my mentor working up a deal."

"This is different, because you're saying the show hinges on the acceptance of one actor. If you withhold that little piece of info, it will backfire later."

"I'll take that chance," Diana said firmly.

"Okay. I won't argue. This is your baby. Incidentally, is this guy Sayles interested in you as a woman, do you think?"

Diana stared at her and then laughed. "On the contrary. I suggested dinner after Tom's party, and he nearly fell on his face refusing. Had to get home, et cetera."

"You think he has a babe stashed away? If so, I wonder why he approached you at that party."

"Look, I don't know and I don't care. This is business on both our parts, nothing more."

"I wonder."

"Well, don't. Take my word for it."

Diana went to her typewriter and worked away nonstop for several days, leaving the office only to go home to sleep. First she worked out the bible—the detailed treatment of the series, describing the lead characters, giving the back story, and outlining the five episodes that would follow the pilot, as well as pinpointing in one sentence the story line for an additional six episodes. Then she and Molly went over everything, and they wrote the pilot script.

While the bible and script were being considered, Diana learned that Gemma Lopez had come to New York and wanted to meet her. It was rapport at first sight. The two had a spirited discussion about the character of Lola, and

Diana came away from their meeting convinced that Gemma would be a wonderful partner for Luke.

Matthew seemed in a tearing hurry to get the project under way, because everything proceeded with incredible speed. The program board met, the director of standards and practices asked for changes, and Diana and Molly made them satisfactorily. The network then began to discuss a half-hour pilot, to the tune of five hundred thousand dollars. At this point, Abbott and Sinclair would no longer be able to stall regarding the lead actor.

"This is all yours, kid," Molly told Diana. "You're so keen on Luke, you'll have to pitch him. Personally, I think Chris Forman would be fine."

"Oh, no he wouldn't, and what's more, Continental doesn't think so either or they'd be shoving him down our throats. I've done a little more digging and I've turned up something interesting. Gemma detests Chris. Apparently they're both difficult to work with, and that augurs well for our side. Because Luke is going to charm the ears off her—"

"If she gets the chance to meet him. How are you going to break this little piece of news to Sayles?"

"Well, I thought I'd invite him here. And with both you and me sort of doing our routine—"

"Not me. Sorry. You've spun this little spider web on your own, kid, and it's a sticky one. The spider may catch the fly; on the other hand, the fly may spread its little wings and get clean away, and I don't want to be there."

Diana did feel more secure on her home ground. She was seated at her desk, and Matthew Sayles, in the visitor's chair, looked much more approachable.

She began by softening him up, telling him how appreciative she was of his help, how happy that he was considering a pilot for *Pete Winston*.

He frowned. "But. There's a 'but' in all this, isn't there?"

She took a deep breath. "Not a but, exactly. An 'and' would be more like it. I have a small favor to ask of you. If you wouldn't mind looking at a short tape—"

"Let me guess. You have someone in mind to play Pete Winston and I'm not going to like him."

Diana smiled guiltily. "I think you will. Just eight minutes is all I ask," she finished appealingly.

He fidgeted. "It doesn't appear that I have much choice."

He sounded annoyed, but Diana remained confident as she led the way to the conference room and slipped her tape into the VCR.

For the umpteenth time she watched Luke's good-natured interplay with the people in the park.

When the machine clicked off, Diana stole a glance at Matthew and found his face stony.

"White bread," he said disparagingly.

"Oh, no, he's much more, believe me—"

"Why? Why should I believe you?" Matthew asked sharply. "I've never seen him or heard of him. What's he done on TV so far?"

Diana felt chilled by Matthew's angry tone. "Nothing yet," she admitted.

"Jesus Christ!"

She made a split-second decision to tell Matthew the whole story, as briefly as possible, including the fact that Luke was boarding with her.

By the time she was done, Matthew was furious, "Do you expect me to believe that you've practically adopted the guy with no other motive than to help him 'develop his talent'?" He stood up. "You must take me for an idiot."

"No, I take you for a very clever, imaginative TV expert who wouldn't let prejudice keep him from recognizing star quality. I'm leveling with you, Matthew. I'd like you to meet Luke, talk to him. He takes people's breath away—"

"Does he take your breath away, Diana?"

She looked him in the eye. "Only as a spectator. I give you my word on that."

The question had been impertinent but not totally uncalled-for. Matthew didn't want to put up network money for an actor she might be pushing only because he was her lover. She didn't blame him.

For a moment they stared each other down, and then Matthew shifted his gaze and sighed. "Run the tape through again."

Afterward, he sat quietly for several minutes, tapping

his fingers against the arm of his chair, studying Diana soberly with sharp eyes.

"All right. I'll show the tape to Gemma. If she likes it, I'll meet this guy, but I have strong reservations." He stood up.

Diana stood as well and smiled. "Thanks. Luke really is the best candidate," she offered mildly. "Quick to learn, takes criticism well, is grateful for any opportunity. Not one ounce of temperament."

Matthew's eyelids flickered, and she gathered that the rumors about Chris Forman were probably true. He and Gemma would create the wrong kinds of sparks, and Matthew knew it.

As if he had read her mind, he said irritably, "Chris isn't the only possibility. There are half a dozen others with years of experience—"

"Maybe, but they wouldn't be as good as Luke. I wrote the pilot with him in mind." She knew very well who else there was, and as far as she was concerned, they weren't even in the running.

Matthew put on his raincoat. "This may be out of my hands entirely, you know. There's the program board to consider, and Phil Bannon. Suppose nobody else goes for your Luke? Then what?"

"Then there won't be a pilot," she said softly.

There. The words were out. And what was more, she was glad. That's how strongly she felt, how sure she was that she was right.

Matthew stared at her, his face registering disbelief. "You don't mean that."

"Yes, I do mean it."

"You're quite the little manipulator," he said angrily. "Goddammit, I've spend so much time on this fucking project! If I had known this from the start—"

"You would have passed. I know that. In fact, if it weren't for Gemma you wouldn't even have considered comedy from Abbott and Sinclair—"

"I liked the idea from the start, I said so, goddammit. I also told you about Gemma right off the bat, which is more than you did with that guy of yours!"

Diana, flinching away from his anger, took a deep breath and nodded. "Yes, to be fair, you did mention

Gemma, and I'm sorry if I wasn't completely straight with you. I was afraid you'd turn me down flat. I was remembering that bullshit about a call from L.A. when you hung up on me."

"It wasn't bullshit."

"Oh, come on, at five A.M. their time?"

"That's right. Phil Bannon got on the horn at dawn because he had something that wouldn't wait. I wasn't home so he tried the office. I'd stayed in town overnight and happened to be there." He looked angry enough to be telling the truth.

"Well, if I was wrong, I apologize. This is a rough business, and total honesty has to be measured against the possibility of failure."

He snorted. "I'd say that total honesty is not one of your problems, Miss Sinclair."

"Maybe I deserve that, Mr. Sayles. I told you I was sorry. But don't you really see Luke playing Pete Winston? Honestly, now."

Matthew clenched his teeth. "Possibly, but only because I don't underestimate the female weakness for a . . . a hunk."

Diana thought he sounded bitter but she avoided asking why and opening another can of worms. "Will you meet Luke?" she asked softly.

"If Gemma agrees, I'll meet him, but this is far from settled. This pilot may go down the drain, and you'll have nobody to blame but yourself."

"I know. I hope it won't go down the drain for everyone's sake. Continental's, too. Because I'm convinced that *Pete Winston* will put your network back in the running."

Diana walked him to the door. "Whatever happens, I want to thank you again. I hope we're still friends."

He grunted and hesitated. As he held out his hand to say good-bye, Diana handed him the tape.

Finally Matthew's face cracked into a smile, albeit a sardonic one. "I see how you've gotten where you are. So when am I going to meet the other lady of this partnership?"

She grinned. "When we have a deal. And, by the way, Molly's the tough one."

Diana pirouetted back to her desk and dialed the studio. "Molly, hi. It's your favorite spider, licking her chops."

PROTÉGÉ 103

* * *

At the end of a very trying week, Matthew Sayles got into the back of his limousine, pulled down the flap in front of him, and positioned a sheaf of papers that demanded his immediate attention. But he was interrupted by the phone.

Phil Bannon was having second thoughts about allowing a pilot to be made for *Pete Winston*.

Matthew gazed out at the Long Island Expressway as he listened. "I know the actor's unknown, we've been through all that, Phil, but he has something. People respond to him. More important, Gemma went bananas over him, and you know what a bitch she is to work with. Win or lose, this show will get her off our backs."

While he listened to his boss's harangue, Matthew poured himself a Scotch and belted it down. Then he reiterated his position. "The pilot script was great, you loved it. And Abbott and Sinclair are young and bright and enthusiastic. We need fresh talent badly."

Jesus, they had gone over all of this for the entire week, and Matthew was exhausted. "The pilot stands, Phil. The contract has already been negotiated. Yes, if it's lousy the responsibility is mine." Who the fuck else's? he thought savagely as he hung up.

He tried to get back to his papers but his concentration faltered. The whiskey had given him a slight headache, and he was feeling depressed. At this moment he deeply regretted ever having joined Continental, in spite of his dissatisfaction with FAB at the end. The address of Continental was different but the place was the same.

He had helped push FAB to second position with his less-than-orthodox methods. Such as not trusting only ratings and audience surveys to decide the merits of a show. Several times Matthew had let a quality slow starter stay on the air even if it was doing poorly in the ratings, in spite of the way his superiors had howled that the programs had to come off. Matthew had proved to be right, and in more instances than not, the programs had gradually built audiences and become hits.

FAB had treated him handsomely, had promoted him, and had sent him to New York at his request, after his personal life had collapsed and he had needed to get away from the Coast.

All had been well at FAB until the president had died and Raymond Trask had moved into the spot. Matthew had locked horns with him from day one because Trask liked trash. He would allow any garbage on the air, whereas at the drop of a rating point he was ready to pull a quality show out of prime time.

So when Phil Bannon came knocking at Matthew's door, offering him the moon and the stars, he had been ready to accept. What intrigued him, in part, was Continental's lowly state. It was doing so badly, in fact, it had become a joke in the industry. It was said that the best way to end the conflict in the Middle East would be to air it on Continental because without a doubt it would be canceled within two months.

So going with Continental had seemed a challenge. But Matthew didn't think the network was entirely hopeless, even if it had been floundering, unsure of its target audience. He felt strongly that the yuppie market was the one to attract, and initially Phil had said yes to everything, if only Matthew would do for them what he had done for FAB.

Unfortunately, things had changed in TV. Nowadays there was simply no time to let a show develop an audience. Costs were too high, competition was too great, and advertisers wanted instant results. All they cared about was how many people were watching a show then and there, and Phil was under pressure to deliver what the advertisers wanted.

The question was, would they want *Pete Winston*? In his heart, Matthew wasn't as convinced about developing the show as he had sounded to Phil. And the reason was partly personal.

He looked at his papers, said to hell with them, and put a tape in his stereo. Then he leaned his head back, closed his eyes, and as the Bach drowned out the whir of traffic, he thought about Diana Sinclair.

When he had approached her at that East Hampton party, he had been attracted by the way she was standing there, looking a little scared, a little amused. He had found an appealing silky softness about her, in her curling hair and the clingy outfit she wore. Then, her sweet, slow drawl had confirmed an impression of femininity, the old-fashioned variety.

Even when he'd learned who she was, his first thought had been that Molly must be the force behind the partnership and Diana the creative one. Even though he knew that any successful independent producer had to be wily and aggressive, even more so if she was a woman.

Yet he hadn't been able to connect those traits with soft-spoken, smiling, warm-eyed Diana, who had the same sense of humor he did.

Dammit, her attractiveness had caught him off-guard, and her gentle manner had seeped behind his defenses. Her idea had grabbed him, too. Not because a father raising his children was anything new but because he was such a father himself.

Listening to Diana talk so glowingly of Pete Winston had warmed his cold and aching heart. He knew from personal experiences that many women really gave out double messages. Yes, it was admirable for a man to be a single parent. But wasn't there something a teensy bit wrong with him? Where was his wife? Why had she abandoned him? How was it that he hadn't found someone else during the past three years?

The whole subject was still terribly painful both for him and for his daughter. It was one reason only a few trusted relatives and friends were even aware that eight-year-old Andrea was living with him in the modest old house in Sag Harbor. At the network, only Phil and Jill knew that he left at four every day (if he had no meetings) so that he could be home in time to have dinner with his daughter, and that he spent most weekends with her as well. She needed one parent to believe in and rely on. He was all she had, and she was all he had.

For a long time after Lorrie had gone, Matthew had been a zombie. Gradually his interest in women was coming back but he remained extremely wary. An occasional date was all he was capable of. Certainly he didn't want to get involved with anyone while Andrea was still recuperating from her hurt.

And yet he had already developed such a soft spot for

Diana that it was affecting his business judgment. This had never happened before and it bothered him.

Diana was so enthusiastic, so inventive, so sprightly, so sure of herself, and with good reason. Her bible had been as impressive as her pitch, and the pilot script was fresh and snappy. He had recognized its ring of truth.

But he still couldn't forget her duplicity with regard to Luke Merriman, and it was without much joy that he remembered his meeting with the actor.

In addition to Diana, Jill, and a couple of people from entertainment, Gemma had been there, and Molly Abbott. Although Abbott had looked much as Matthew had imagined, she had taken a back seat, saying very little, letting Diana carry the conversation.

Diana. Matthew had grudgingly admired her style. The same woman who seemed genuinely shy at a party was remarkably strong in a business meeting. There, in fact, her soft-spoken presentation gave her words added impact.

She had been right on target in her dissection of the roles and her way of infusing everyone with her enthusiasm. It would be Lola who was obsessive and riddled with ideology—in this case feminist—while Pete would be more emotional, more impulsive. A clever role reversal with comic overtones. Yet Pete was supposed to be unequivocally masculine, too. Matthew wondered if Luke could carry it off, but Gemma had been bubbling with joy and enthusiasm. On his part, Luke had kept up that dazzling smile that didn't indicate whether or not he understood a damn thing that was being said.

The truth was that Matthew loathed the type. The old aw-shucks routine made him sick, but Gemma ate it up, and Gemma was the one the network was trying to please because they were paying her a fortune while she was idle. This was the first show in two years that was remotely right for her—so much so that she was willing to share top billing. It was a miracle and a tribute to Luke's appeal, damn him.

Matthew, observing the interplay between Diana and Luke, had come up with nothing conclusive. She seemed to take maternal pleasure in her protégé, which was perfectly natural. And Luke had scarcely looked at her; he had been directing his charm mostly to Gemma.

Matthew felt in his bones that this shit-kicker was shrewder than he looked and probably more unscrupulous, too. Was his feeling true prescience? Or simple jealousy?

Matthew was forced to ask himself several important questions. If Diana had been shrill or ugly or even a man, would he have stood out on that freezing deck in East Hampton for almost an hour? And would he have seriously considered a proposal for a sitcom to be written and produced by independents whose track record was in action drama?

The honest answer: not in a million years. And that's what was bothering him.

8

"Nikki, terrific news," Diana announced, bursting into the office, coat already half off. "We've gotten the okay on the pilot."

"Oh, wow, fantastic," Nikki jumped up, smiling brightly, and gave Diana a hug of congratulations. But the moment her boss's back was turned, Nikki's smile vanished.

Shit. As if she weren't already feeling like death warmed over, this was the topper. While she had been striking out all over town, Diana had had the good fortune to meet Matthew Sayles at a fucking party. Wasn't that always the way? The somebodies always hung out together. In L.A. they'd be sitting hip-to-hip in a hot tub or whatever. Here it was East Hampton or a charity ball. The insiders' inside track.

Diana emerged from Molly's office looking so happy that Nikki felt like punching her in the face.

"Nikki, how would you like to be assistant executive producer on the pilot?" Diana asked her, beaming.

"That would be wonderful." Nikki followed Diana into

Molly's office, her mind clicking over the pros and cons. Mostly cons. Just the thought of what needed to be done, and in a very short time, made her feel ill. Gathering a staff and crew, finding a rehearsal hall and a studio, getting sets designed, and costumes, casting the roles . . . it was going to be a bitch.

A half-million in network money was involved, and though it seemed like a lot of bread for a half-hour pilot, Nikki knew what could go wrong. A couple of people out sick, for instance, a strike or a slowdown, an unseasonal blizzard, a problem with delivery of materials, a power failure—the list was endless.

"Nikki, you'll have to drop everything else and get on this," Molly told her briskly. "I've put up the completion bond myself, so if we don't come in on time and under budget, heads will roll."

You mean my head, Nikki thought. Since Abbott and Sinclair were unaffiliated with a major production company, they had to offer the network some guarantee that the pilot would be completed satisfactorily and not run over the stipulated cost. Molly's private fortune was the source of that assurance.

The one really positive aspect of this pilot was that Nikki would be working closely with Luke. That would suit her very well, and she intended to profit from it.

She needed a new course of action anyway, because her last plan had fizzled. She had been screwing the ass off Herb Norman in order to get hired as a writer on *Night and Day*. Then she would have been in a position to help Luke get started. But she had been too eager; Herb had gotten huffy the moment she dangled a script of hers in front of him. It turned out that he was a very proud man who thought she was screwing him because she really loved his cock. When he realized she wanted quid pro quo the creep pulled out of the affair.

So Nikki had dropped back to square one while Diana had advanced a giant step with a pilot for Luke. It was infuriating.

Well, at least Nikki's association with Herb hadn't been a total loss. She had come away with an interesting piece of gossip about Gwen Van Ryck, his head writer, a woman reputed to be the best in the business.

That afternoon, when Nikki was alone in the office, she phoned Gwen Van Ryck's home and asked to speak to her.

"Speaking," the strong, low voice replied.

"Miss Van Ryck, I represent the Elizabeth Arden beauty salon, and I would like to invite you to come in for a consultation and makeup session—"

"Thanks, but I'm a customer of Georgette Klinger's, have been for years."

That was all Nikki needed to know.

Three weeks later Luke sat in the makeup chair in a hole-in-the-wall dark little room at the studio Abbott and Sinclair were renting for the pilot.

There was hardly room for Marty, the makeup specialist, to maneuver, but he was managing somehow.

Luke didn't care how cramped they were. Better that Abbott and Sinclair should skimp on studio rent than on his salary.

Marty talked an awful lot but he was an expert at his job, and mostly Luke didn't have to pay full attention to the conversation. It was like listening to the crickets chirping in the field—restful, not really requiring any response.

Marty was about as gay as they come, but that was okay with Luke, as long as he kept his hands on Luke's face and out of his lap.

Luke smiled to himself, remembering the first time Diana had taken him to the male cosmetics counter at Bloomingdale's, where they were waited on by a gay man. Not only gay, but an absolute swish. Hell, if you'd put a skirt on him you could have taken him anywhere. Luke had felt foolish and uncomfortable. Then he had noticed several other male customers, looking not only like he-men but rich he-men, who were buying the place out. So he'd changed his opinion of cosmetics for men, and of gays, too, once he'd gotten to know some as fellow actors.

As Marty worked on his face, Luke remembered what he had been only three months ago. How he had dressed and talked, what he had eaten, what he had thought of as big money. Now he even had an agent, just like Diana. It was sure worth ten percent not to have to befuddle his brain with all that legalese in a contract.

Incredible as it seemed, Luke Merriman was going to

star on television with Gemma Lopez. He had watched Gemma on TV years before, finding her so attractive, adorable. And now she was playing opposite *him*, flirting with *him*, unable to keep her hands off *him*, and not only on the set.

Luke grinned to think of it and winked at himself in the mirror. He couldn't really see what all the fuss was about. Okay, he was good-looking, but so were lots of guys. California beaches were loaded with men like him. True, in New York he seemed to stand out. Women stared at him wherever he went, not only because of the clothes but also his height and coloring. Well, you used what you had going for you. Every bit totted up.

He worked out at a gym, sweated in the sauna, and sat under a sunlamp to keep his tan looking good.

Even with the tan, Marty had a lot to do because the harsh TV lights picked up every wart and wrinkle. Marty covered over his real lines and blemishes and then put some back where he wanted them. Today was dress rehearsal, and the makeup man was taking special pains because it was going to be taped. Tomorrow there would be two tapings in front of a live audience. Diana was insisting that the actors work for their laughs. That was okay with him. He was used to playing to a lively crowd. Diana and Molly, working with the editor and director, as well as the technical people, would take a scene here and a scene there, as he understood it, and put together the best footage for the final tape.

Luke wasn't as nervous as the first day at the rehearsal hall, when he'd been shaking in his boots, even though he knew his part backward and forward. Fortunately, everyone had been wonderful to him—Gemma, the director, Diana, of course, Molly, even the kids, who were cute little tykes. It had worried him that they had much more experience than he; yet, they hadn't known that and he had tried not to show it.

Actually, being on a stage rehearsing was almost like being in class. The trick was to remember to call everyone by their fictional names and to pay close attention to the director and the a.d. and Diana and Nikki. To stand where they told you and smile when they said smile, and never miss your cue or forget your lines, and they would be happy.

Shit, he had said to himself, this was the chance of his life and he certainly wasn't going to blow it. He hadn't, either; he'd done just fine.

The plain truth was that he loved being an actor. And he still couldn't get over the fact that Abbott and Sinclair were paying him fifteen thousand smackers for a couple of weeks of playing a part. It sure wasn't work as he knew it. Now he could understand why so many actors were breaking down studio doors to get on TV. He had been one of the lucky ones, thanks to Diana, his fairy godmother, who had waved her wand and made magical things happen.

His admiration for Diana grew with every day, as well as his curiosity. Aside from an occasional date, she didn't seem to click with any man. He had a hunch that she worked so hard not only to make money but also to avoid making love. That really pleased him. It meant that no man had ever really gotten to her. He had suspected that the first time he met her. She might not be a virgin, technically, but he doubted that she had ever been fully turned on to the pleasures of the flesh.

He could tell from the look in her eyes that he got to her sometimes, especially when she caught him walking around without a shirt. She would stare at him, and her lips would open just a bit. She would look away, maybe smile shyly at him. . . . Lord, she was sweet.

He remembered how she had looked that morning, sitting up in bed, as sleepy and grumpy as usual, until she got some coffee into her. And then she had said, "Thanks, Luke. I'm beginning to come alive."

Luke had smiled, and he smiled now as he imagined repaying her for everything she had done for him by making her come alive fully, inside and out.

"Okay, Luke, all finished," Marty said, beaming at him. "Now, you go on out there and show them that you're not just a pretty face."

Standing up, Luke smiled and gave Marty's shoulder a friendly squeeze. "Thanks. I'll do that."

Matthew sat in the executive screening room alone, watching the pilot of *Pete Winston* on his seventy-two-inch screen. Assuming nothing, refusing to anticipate, he pretended he was an ordinary viewer.

From the opening scene, he was smiling. Then he was genuinely moved, and then smiling again. He marveled at the way Diana and Molly had taken the bare bones of a story and brought it to life. Pete's seven-year-old daughter, ashamed of being the only one in her class not to have a mother coming to open-school week, asks a new neighbor, Lola, to pretend to be her mother. The show examined the effect this had on Lola as well as all the Winstons.

Just before the spot where the third commercial would appear, Matthew's eyes blurred. Afterward, the show lightened and drew more smiles from him. At the end, what he felt was smiling emotion. And even though he identified so acutely with the situation, this pilot excited him as nothing had in years.

He sat quietly for a few moments, reviewing what he had seen and making a few notes. He had expected Gemma to be dynamic and the kids appealing, but he had been unprepared for the impact of Luke Merriman. The guy projected a manly vulnerability that really got to Matthew and overcame his prejudice.

How brillliantly Diana had tailored the role to Luke, drawing forth his best and downplaying his worst—what Matthew thought of as a basic superficiality.

He felt a surge of heightened respect and admiration for Diana. She had been absolutely right, not only regarding Luke, but even in her insistence on taping in front of a live audience and not allowing canned laughter. This soundtrack certainly needed no sweetening.

Matthew got Jill into the screening room along with several execs from the entertainment divison. They laughed in the appropriate places and applauded at the end.

"This is dynamite," Jill told Matthew. "Not much can make *me* laugh and cry on the same show. Who in blazes is this Luke Merriman, and can I have one for my very own?"

It was interesting that Jill, the only woman present, was wild about Luke. The men gave most of the credit to Gemma and the kids, mumbling cynically that Luke wasn't really acting at all.

Next, Matthew pulled in secretaries, computer operators, and general personnel from the accounting department to get their reactions. Unanimously favorable. The women loved Luke instantly. And whereas the older men said they "didn't mind him," the younger men tended to identify.

Matthew carried the pilot home with him and suggested that Andrea invite a few friends to the house for a viewing.

After the children had demolished the milk and cookies furnished by the housekeeper, half a dozen nine-to-ten-year-old girls and two younger brothers, five and seven, clustered in front of the conventional twenty-one-inch set.

Matthew didn't remain in the living room, guessing that his presence would inhibit their spontaneous reaction. He did, however, stand right outside so that he could listen.

The kids howled and genuinely liked the show. They picked up the name Pete's children called him, "Pops." In fact, Andrea called him "Pops" for the rest of the day. If these were at all representative, children all over America would be doing the same thing, and their fathers, as well as their mothers, would be inclined to watch the show. Advertisers would really go for that.

Matthew was confirmed in his belief that he was onto something terrific. He was so excited he got on a plane that Sunday and delivered the tape to Phil Bannon by hand.

Sitting in on the Monday screening, Matthew took pleasure in the reception it got, not only from Phil but also from the v.p.'s in charge of West Coast entertainment, who tended to be negative about all programs originating in New York. In this case, they seemed to be mollified because Pete was western himself.

On the plane trip back, Matthew was very pleased, yet unable to stop thinking about Diana. Visions of her kept appearing to him: her beautiful, understated clothes, her warm smile, her gentle voice. Now he could forgive her for holding back about Luke Merriman.

The plain truth was that Diana intrigued him in every way, but he intended to go very slowly on this one. Yet he looked forward to seeing her face when she learned the network's decision.

He called Diana himself to make the lunch date, for the only day he had free.

"You mean I have to wait until Friday to find out what you thought of the pilot? That's really cruel, Matthew."

Her voice, with its wistful sweetness, hit him in the solar plexus. "Okay. I like the pilot. In fact, I like it a lot. The rest will keep."

He hung up thoughtfully, wondering whether she was as tough as she sometimes seemed, or as vulnerable, or both.

Unfortunately, Phil Bannon turned up on Friday morning and called an all-day emergency meeting about something else, so Matthew had to tell her on the phone that the network was airing the pilot and willing to go to series.

9

Luke raised his tulip of champagne. "To you, Diana, who made all my wishes come true."

Diana smiled. "And to you, Luke, my talented protégé and inspiration."

They were having a celebratory dinner at the Acute Café, a place Luke had chosen. In fact, he had insisted on making all the arrangements for tonight, even though everything had been last-minute. She'd only heard the news from Matthew that morning, and here she was, dressed for a gala evening with Luke, in the most stylish restaurant in Tribeca, a warehouse area rapidly developing into a popular new dinner oasis.

"You've never been here, have you?" Luke asked, observing her looking around the restaurant, crowded with chic diners.

"No, though I have heard the name. I'm afraid I immediately thought of acute indigestion."

Luke laughed. "No, ma'am. It gets its name from the acute angle of the plot it sits on. I just love this place—the white pillars, these rattan chairs, the palms, the soft colors. And look at that painting, just over there. Famous folks are painted in it like Richard Pryor and Jackie Onassis."

"I see you know this place well," Diana said, as a waiter brought them oysters on the half-shell.

"I sort of know it, but only from the bar. I've had some drinks here after work. Never ate here before. I was saving that for when I could afford to take you here. I've quit my job, by the way. I've got better things to to do now."

"I hope so. We still haven't settled everything. The network wants a run-of-the-series contract but your agent is asking for more money than we can afford—"

"Don't worry about it, I'll take less. I've already talked it over with Harriet. But I won't sign an r.o.s. just yet. The way I figure it is if the show gets cut off at the pockets—you know, flops, is canceled—I've lost a few thousand up front. But if the show's a winner, then my contract will be renegotiated for next year. Then if they still want an r.o.s. everyone will have to shell out a lot more than ten thousand an episode."

Diana listened with astonishment to the way her country boy had caught on, and she couldn't help laughing.

He grinned at her. "Hey, I bet I know what you're thinking. 'Listen to him, talking big bucks when he's been working for four an hour plus tips and a meal, and glad to get it.' Yeah, I know. And I also know what you told me. That even if we get on the air, the audience has to be crazy about us right off the bat or we're dead. But you know what? I'm sure we're going to make it big. I feel it, don't you?"

She did. She had never been so thrilled about anything in her life. In a way, this was more of a coup than *Mom & Meg*. This was her *dream*, a sitcom, and with Luke as the star. It was heady stuff, and she was bursting with it, and with pride over Luke.

At rehearsals he had been a paragon. Smack on time and on cue. Hardly flubbed a line, and when he did, was so devastated that everyone jumped in to reassure him. He had been a delight, his remarkable professionalism a model for everyone else. Especially Gemma, who was so smitten with him she walked around purring.

The live taping, which Diana thought might make Luke

nervous, had actually brought out his best. Of course, he was no stranger to an audience.

When Diana saw the final tape, she felt repaid a thousandfold for her faith in Luke.

He leaned over now and said, smiling, "Remember me, back in Portland, and look at me now. If it hadn't been for you I'd of been hanging around at the Viewpoint making bad jokes until I was too old to do anything different. And it wasn't only the confidence you gave me to go to acting school and such, but all those other little things. Little tips that only a guy's folks tell him—only mine didn't know any more than I did, and anyway, weren't around long enough."

The intensity of his gaze, and his words, delivered in a low, intimate tone, were making her feel tingly.

The waiter kept filling their glasses. Diana hardly noticed when their champagne bottle was empty and a second one appeared.

"Diana, you're the kind of gal all boys dream about meeting when they grow up. I'm one of the lucky ones. As soon as I first saw you, I knew. That's why I had to say something to you, even if it sounded dumb. You know, I'd have followed you clear to the ends of the earth. So when you got out that card of yours it was like a miracle."

Diana tried to look indulgent but suspected she wasn't carrying it off because every word he uttered struck a responsive chord. Was it his voice? His smile? Or his hypnotic eyes, drawing her to him like the churning waters of a whirlpool—intriguing yet dangerous.

She excused herself, and in the ladies' room dabbed a few drops of cold water on her face, vowing not to drink any more champagne.

It had been very nice of Luke to take her to dinner. She considered herself thanked. It was time to go home, and never mind the coffee. Even better, she would say she had to stop by at Molly's. Any excuse would do.

Suddenly, absurdly, Diana didn't trust herself to be alone in the apartment with Luke. Surely it was only the champagne talking, she kept assuring herself. As soon as she sobered up, everything would fall back into place.

When she returned to the table, two young women were leaning over Luke, one redhead, one brunette.

Diana decided to be amused. "Pardon me," she said wryly to the brunette, who was blocking her seat.

"Oh, sorry." She and her friend looked Diana over quickly before saying good-bye to Luke and moving back to the bar.

"It seems I can't take you anywhere in this town without attracting groupies," she said with a little laugh.

"They're not groupies. I sort of know them, but not their names. They work in a boutique on Astor Place. Come into the café for lunch sometimes."

His smile conveyed that he thought she was jealous. Of course that was preposterous.

Before she could ask him to get the check, he was ordering dessert and coffee for them both. Then, when he looked at her with luminous eyes, she automatically lifted her glass and took one more sip of champagne. And then another last sip. Until the glass was empty.

"I've been thinking, Diana, about the really big difference between the old me and the new me. It's not only talking better. Not just the clothes. The hair. The shined shoes. That's important, sure, but it's all outside. What really knocks me out is the way you've helped me way down deep to broaden my horizons. Do you remember when you told me way back then, 'Luke, you have to broaden your horizons'? Hell, I figured you were talking about my shoulder pads or something."

Diana laughed and laughed, as he not only told her, he acted it out.

"I mean it, Diana," he said, serious now, looking at her intently. "You helped me to let more things into my life. Strange foods and books and other folks who were different than me—"

"Different from me," Diana corrected automatically.

"Uh huh. From me. I learned not to run away from stuff I don't understand. Instead, I try to take it in, to see if I like it or not. I'm always going to be a little bit of a country boy but that doesn't mean I have to be wimpy about it. There's folks from all over in New York. So what counts is where you're at, not where you've been. And that's my existential point of view."

Diana, staring at him, was suddenly moved and warmed

throughout to think that he credited her with all that. She was bursting with pride.

And then he took her hand across the table and murmured softly, "I love you."

She didn't move; not a muscle. Her hand didn't even feel like hers. And she certainly wasn't breathing. Only her heart was stubbornly, disobediently pounding away in her chest. She forced herself to say quietly, "I know, I love you too. You're a great guy, we're good friends, and we're going to have the best sitcom ever—"

"I mean more than the sitcom, more than friends," he interrupted softly. "I love you. *You*, Diana. Sweet, wonderful Diana. I want to be good enough for you. Maybe I'm not, yet, but I sure am trying."

She had a dreamlike feeling of euphoria tinged with fear. This wasn't happening, it couldn't be, it was all wrong. . . .

Not expecting an answer, Luke called for the check, while Diana sat utterly still, trying not to feel so wonderful.

When he helped her into her coat, his touch made her tremble.

The limo he had hired for the evening was waiting for them. As Diana got in, her confused brain tried to come up with some reason to stop at Molly's, but before anything materialized, Luke announced that they were going dancing. "I'll bet you've never been to Limelight. I'd like to show it to you."

Okay, why not? Tonight was his party, and she had no reason to spoil it. They were headed for a public place, and she suddenly felt in the mood to dance. It would sober her up.

When the limo pulled up on Sixth Avenue and Twentieth Street, Diana recalled having heard about a church that had been turned into a fashionable club frequented by pop-music and film people as well as by celebrities.

"Will we get in, just like that?"

He grinned at her. "Just watch us."

As they stepped up to the door, she realized that simply arriving in a limo was enough to merit entrance. Aside from the fact that Luke carried himself like a show-biz VIP.

In the small Gothic chapel that was now a bar, Luke persuaded Diana to drink a brandy.

"This is super, Luke. I'd never have thought of coming here. It's really delightful to see something new." As she smiled up at him brightly, he leaned over and kissed her forehead.

She buried her nose in her snifter, suddenly afraid to look at him, afraid of how vulnerable she was feeling.

But they had come here to dance, and dance they did, in what had once been the sanctuary. It was dark and noisy and crowded and wonderful fun.

In theory, Diana loved to dance but was generally a little shy to start off with. However, by this time she was awash with booze, and her body simply began to move quite naturally to the music.

Luke was a superb dancer, easily the best on the floor, graceful and rhythmic. Diana felt so proud to be with him, so thrilled that his smile and his gaze were for her alone.

Glancing at the various people who were admiring him, she felt an urge to shout, "This is my discovery, and I want the whole world to know it." Well, the whole world would, when *Pete Winston* became a hit.

Diana threw herself into the dancing, glad that her little black crepe dress had a full skirt, and that her sling-back pumps were low-heeled enough to be comfortable.

The music was compellingly sexy, and the pounding rhythm made her imagine she was at a bacchanal. It felt wicked and exciting to be flinging her body around with such abandon in a church.

As she moved, and watched Luke move, she became utterly swept away by his grace, his beauty. He was one gorgeous man, and she marveled at how she could have lived under the same roof with him all these months and not really noticed.

When a slow number was played, Diana moved dreamily into Luke's arms, where she fit magnificently. It seemed natural to be pressed against him, her cheek against his neck, his powerful arms holding her, while they undulated, thigh-to-thigh.

She had never danced with anyone this way, and when he bent his head to kiss her, she opened her lips in acquiescence.

He drew back first, as the music quickened again, and released her. He resumed dancing as if the kiss had never happened.

But he was smiling, and she had the weird feeling that the strobe lights were beaming from his eyes.

Diana danced sinuously and unselfconsciously, her body attuned to his, turning, dipping, swaying. The music was pulsing, and so was her heart. The floor got more crowded, the music grew louder . . . Suddenly they were on the side, then off the floor.

"Had enough?" he shouted in her ear.

No. Yes. Christ, she couldn't think. Her body felt stuck halfway to fulfillment, reaching for sensation, yearning for something more. . . .

Luke held her coat, led her outside, and guided her into the limo. He got in beside her wearing a look that seared her flesh.

Now he was going to take her in his arms. He was going to kiss her, caress her. . . .

"I love you, Diana," he whispered. "I want you to love me."

Her answer was to turn toward him and slide her arms around his neck. He didn't respond, and it spurred her to press against him and kiss him. She felt his body tense, and then his arms tightened around her, and his lips opened.

What a kiss it was. Eyes tightly shut, lips and tongues meeting, licking, probing. As waves of desire radiated through her, she wanted to be closer, wanted to be incorporated into him.

When they came up for air, he asked, "Do you love me?"

"Yes," she murmured.

Gently disentangling himself, Luke rapped on the glass and spoke to the driver.

Diana didn't hear, couldn't concentrate. She didn't want to think, only to feel, and what she felt was her body's urgency. She trusted it as never before.

His hands moved under her coat, and he fondled her waist, rubbing it sensually, moving lower to her hips, then back to her waist.

Moaning, her mouth glued to his, she touched his hair, his face, his neck, his ears. He was so fragrant, so appealing. "Luke, oh, Luke," she whispered, squirming under his fingers. She slid lower so that for a moment they rested on her breasts. But he quickly moved his hands to her waist once again, tantalizing her beyond bearing.

Suddenly he drew back. "We're here."

She got out without recognizing where she was. It wasn't her building at all; it looked like a hotel.

She didn't care. She hung on to Luke's arm, not aware of stopping at the desk. One moment she was in an elevator, the next moment in a dimly lit room with an enormous bed in its center, and red roses everywhere.

Diana let her coat fall to the floor and watched Luke put his suit jacket on a chair. He turned and stood quietly, waiting.

She suddenly felt afraid. She remained motionless and gazed at him uncertainly. What she saw was a very handsome man, six-foot-three, with sun-streaked hair tumbling over his forehead, magnetic blue-gray eyes, and a sensual mouth that slowly curved into a seductive smile. He seemed to be saying, "Take me, I'm yours."

He *was* hers. She had discovered him, shaped him, and she wanted him. Oh, God, how she wanted him!

She surrendered to her impulse to walk toward him slowly, while he stood his ground, and his smile became a challenge. Come and get me, if you dare.

Diana's whole body was on fire. She had never wanted a man as much as she wanted Luke at this moment.

But when she reached him he pulled back.

"What's wrong?"

"I want you to love me, Diana."

"I do," she whispered. "Oh, Luke, I do."

"Say it," he requested, his expression an amalgam of longing and uncertainty.

"I love you, Luke." As she said the words—for the first time ever—she believed them. What was love if not an overwhelming urge to join one's body to that of another? To be as close as two people could possibly be to one another? To lose oneself in the flesh of the beloved?

His smile of joy dazzled her. "Show me," he murmured.

Diana moved into his arms, squeezing him to her, pulling his head down so she could kiss him, explore his mouth with her tongue. She put her palms against his chest and unbuttoned his shirt with trembling fingers.

"Kiss me, Luke," she whispered. "Kiss me everywhere." She thrilled to the sensation of his lips on hers, then on her cheek, her neck, her ear, as he flicked his tongue over the delicate shell, darting in and out, and causing ripples of heat throughout her body.

She reached for his hands and clamped them to her breasts, crying out as soon as she felt his touch. "Oh, please, please," she begged, undulating beneath his fingers as he fondled her, kneading her breasts sensually.

Diana pressed closer, her arms locked around his waist, her fingers digging into his muscular back and moving down to his buttocks, then his thighs, until she could feel the growing hardness of his erection.

"My dress," she whispered, unbuckling his belt.

He undid the satin tie around her waist and lifted the dress and petticoat over her head. Then he bestowed feathery kisses on her chest and bare midriff.

In a frenzy, Diana unhooked her bra and brought his face against her naked breasts, moaning as she felt his lips and tongue on her stiffened nipples. At the same time, she guided his hands to lower her panty hose. His fingers lightly grazed the insides of her thighs and moved higher, to her panties.

She parted her legs, wet with desire, shaking while his fingers crept under her crotch and he slowly rotated his tongue around first one taut nipple, then the other.

Her knees buckled, and she staggered against him, feeling him suddenly lift her up in his arms, thrilling her with his strength as he carried her to the bed.

"Let me," she demanded hoarsely, sitting up on the edge and undoing his trousers. Gasping at the bulk of him straining against his bikini shorts, she pulled them down and fondled him, rejoicing at the way he hissed and caught his breath.

Diana wanted to gobble him up alive, but he gently drew back. "Tell me you love me, Diana. I need to hear it."

"I love you. I love you, my darling," she murmured, coaxing him down beside her.

She lay on her back, her legs apart, and brought his face

to her breasts, and then to her belly, and then lower, between her legs.

His touch was exquisite—and his lips—and his tongue. Through the frenzy of her own passion she detected his, in his hoarse breathing, and the way he drew back when she tried to caress his swollen flesh, as if afraid he wouldn't be able to wait.

She couldn't wait. Diana lifted her legs. "Come to me, oh, please, Luke. I love you. Please, now, oh God, now!"

He straddled her, lifting her buttocks, and slowly entered her.

"Oh, Luke," she cried. As she felt the exquisite sensation of their joining together, she surrendered herself completely, body and soul, for the first time in her life. "Luke, Luke, Luke," she cried, as an incredible spasm shook her from deep inside to the tips of her fingers and toes.

"I love you," she cried, straining against him, experiencing a profound thrill as she felt him thrusting rhythmically inside her.

Mesmerized, she gazed at him above her, his eyes wild, his teeth bared, perspiration dripping off his forehead onto her face.

His motion quickened, and her excitement increased. As she felt him explode within her, moaning hoarsely, she had another orgasm.

"Oh, Lord," he breathed. "Christ Almighty."

Diana wrapped her legs around his back and with her arms held on to his neck. She wanted to keep him within her forever.

For a while they lay inert, and then she felt him growing again. It was impossible. Surely he couldn't again, so soon. . . .

He could, and he did, urgently pounding into her, his face supremely handsome in its passion. "I love you," he shouted as he came. "Diana, I love you."

"And I love you, my darling Luke. Oh, God!" It was true. She did love him. How could she not?

Finally they lay damp and exhausted in each other's arms.

"I can't believe this is me," she said. "I've never experienced anything like this. Not even close. I mean, it always took me so long to come, and then it was over pretty quickly."

Luke smiled and kissed her cheek. "That makes me feel real good. I've been waiting for this night, Diana. I knew the first time I saw you it could be like this."

"But how? How could you know? I didn't flirt with you, did I? I mean, I was thinking of your talent. Really. It never remotely occurred to me that we could be lovers."

"You may not have been thinking about it but it was inside you all the same. And I saw it. You're a very sexy lady. I bet you scare lots of guys away because they're afraid they can't handle it."

She looked at him startled, then impressed. "Yes. Yes, that must be it. I've wondered, but I never understood why before."

He smiled and kidded her again.

"Luke," she said, sitting up and looking around her. "Where are we?"

"The garden of Eden, I reckon." he grinned at her.

She made a face at him. "I mean what hotel?"

"The Vista. At the World Trade Center. Since I met you at the Viewpoint, I thought I might as well love you at the Vista." He sounded so proud of himself.

"How did you know I'd come here with you tonight?"

"I didn't. I hoped you would. And I took a chance."

Diana smiled and kissed him before lying back. "I'm glad you did. You know, you're very smart, Luke, and you have the right instincts. You should stick with them."

He grinned. "Yes, ma'am."

They fell asleep.

Several hours later, Diana awakened. Propping herself on one elbow, she studied Luke and reveled in his godlike form. No wonder the ancient Greeks had so deified the male body.

Luke was perfectly made, from his splendid head to his narrow, aristocratic feet. Even in repose, he was magnificent.

Diana was sober now, yet still euphoric, marveling at herself, at the way the evening had turned out.

She was touched by Luke's love and his honest need for her love. Now she understood his casual attitude toward the women who flocked around him. What mattered to him was not what he could have, but what he wanted. And he wanted her. Even more remarkable, he was able to give her what she wanted. He didn't worry about technique, about performance, about proving himself.

Diana smiled to think of her disappointing skirmishes with other men—those who were as conversant with the Kama Sutra as with sex manuals, who had a drawerful of French ticklers and battery-operated vibrators (not to mention porno films that were more amusing than arousing). The men she had been with had sought to please her by showing off just how experienced they were. And not one—until now—had been artless enough to ask for her love.

For the first time tonight she had really seen Luke's sensitivity and recognized it as being like her own. He didn't want to feel that he was a woman's plaything, that just because he was handsome and well-endowed he had to be content with being objectified. No, he wanted to be loved for what he had learned and how he had grown.

Tears of joy suddenly rose to her eyes, and she leaned over and gently kissed him. She really did love him. She loved his sweetness, his unspoiled delight in his new fortune, his gratitude, and the way he loved her.

Diana suspected that Luke didn't say such words lightly. And until now, she had never said them at all. It was all so wonderful.

She couldn't resist kissing him lightly on the shoulder, then moving her lips down to his chest, his belly, smiling when he began to stir and grow, though still feigning sleep.

She took him in her mouth and caressed him with her lips and tongue until he was fully erect, and fully awake.

They made glorious love again.

All day Saturday they remained in the hotel room, having their meals sent up.

Sunday morning, when they came back to the apartment, Luke moved into the bedroom with Diana.

10 Gwen Van Ryck sat at her typewriter at home doing breakdowns for *Night and Day*. Once she had worked out the plot lines, summarizing the daily episodes was almost mechanical. However, these last couple of months had been murder, and she felt herself slowing down. Here it was Saturday and she was still not finished.

She began to type act two, putting in the scene settings, the characters, and the story line, but leaving out any actual dialogue because Linda, the writer who would do the script, was excellent at providing her own.

"Deena overhearing Mort talking to Prince about the merger, which will only take place if—"the ringing phone shattered Gwen's concentration.

It was Perry calling from Boston, and of course he needed money. When didn't her son need money?

While she listened, Gwen lit a cigarette. Perry wanted to move off-campus with a roommate, pointing out that they would actually save money by doing their own cooking. . . .

"Yes, okay. I'll send you a check. I can't talk now. No, I'm not annoyed, dear, and I do want to hear about it. Let's talk tomorrow night."

At the end of act four, she stood up, stretched, and went out on her terrace to run in place and do a few knee-bends.

Still trim, even at forty-four. God, how had so many years crept up on her? Perry had bought her a digital watch for her recent birthday. Only a kid of twenty would describe such a watch as "real cool." To him every minute was a new adventure, not sixty seconds closer to old age, to loneliness.

A stiff breeze from the west was blowing some noxious chemical over from New Jersey. She had the benefit of the fumes but not the view: her eighteenth-floor Eleventh Street apartment faced south, overlooking Washington Square Park. When she squinted she could see skaters and cyclists circling the fountain.

She glanced at her watch, relentlessly changing from one-forty-eight to one-forty-nine, and remembered she hadn't even stopped for lunch. Well, only act five to go. Half a page, single-spaced, and she would be finished.

The library seemed somber after the bright sun of the terrace, but it suited her. She deliberately kept the curtains drawn because it was easier to write *Night and Day* if she didn't know which it was in reality.

Tying a headband across her forehead, Gwen zipped up the jacket of her gray warm-up suit and left the apartment. As she jogged down west Eleventh and up Fifth Avenue, she realized that she hadn't been out of her house since Wednesday afternoon. She had been feeling so down she just couldn't face getting out of her robe, and there had been no real need. The *Times* was delivered, and she ordered food from Gristede's. Her secretary picked up her breakdowns and delivered them to each dialogue writer, then brought back their finished scripts for her to go over.

Gwen was feeling so rotten, in fact, that she was grateful for her weekly appointment at the Georgette Klinger salon, because without it she might have stayed at home for several more days. She was feeling like Oblomov, the fictional Russian character who had had difficulty getting out of bed each morning. Maybe someone would write a novel about Van Ryck who couldn't think of one good reason to leave the house.

After two turns around the block she felt winded, and her knee was acting up, too. Jogging was taking it out of her. Of course she knew she ought to give up smoking, but she was terrified she would gain twenty pounds.

After a shower, Gwen slipped into silk-lined pleated dark purple slacks and a rainbow-colored hand-knit sweater. She looked at her face in the mirror and grimaced, musing that she had been born to be a nun. Fine, limp brown hair, brown eyes, finely chiseled nose, thin lips, sallow porcelain skin that was beginning to crack from age.

Trim and prim. That's what Bobby said had first attracted him to her. She had believed him, at twenty, but by twenty-two she had realized Bobby had married her for money. Mistakenly, it turned out, because little was left of the fortune the earliest Van Rycks, settled in New York in the 1670's, had amassed in commerce and banking. It turned out that too many Van Rycks had been married for their money by people who either invested it badly or gambled it away.

Gwen *had* been prim when young, but thirteen years of marriage to Bobby had knocked it out of her; indeed, she had discovered herself to be quite the opposite.

She looked at herself in the full-length mirror. Five-five was her height, and one hundred and fifteen pounds was her weight. She had weighed that for twenty years, but she feared that her all-too-solid flesh was gradually melting into mush from sitting on her ass all day long writing. And for the last few months there had been nobody to look pretty for.

Even though she would be having a facial, she applied makeup because she didn't dare be seen in the street or even in a taxi looking so naked. Even light makeup created the illusion of long lashes, high cheekbones, tawny complexion, and a sensually etched mouth. Only her thin hair was hopeless, but she put on a dashing gray fedora that covered it and suited her very well.

The receptionist at Georgette Klinger's was arguing with a young woman when Gwen arrived.

"I'm sorry but you made the appointment for Monday, not today."

"But I didn't, I know I didn't," the woman said, distressed. "I couldn't have made it for Monday. I can't take a whole afternoon off from work. It has to be today—"

The receptionist looked past her to Gwen. "Good afternoon, Mrs. Van Ryck. Go right in."

"Oh." The young woman turned to stare at her and then smiled, an intriguing, contagious smile. Gwen hesitated and smiled back, looking under a shock of auburn hair into large, clear, beautiful light brown eyes flecked with blue, or was it green? . . .

"Excuse me, but you couldn't be Gwen Van Ryck, could you? I mean, it's such an uncommon name. And *Night and Day* is my absolute favorite. I never miss an episode."

Feeling a delicious shiver, Gwen nodded, pleased. "As a matter of fact, I am Gwen Van Ryck. But I'm amazed that you made the connection."

"Oh, yes. You were mentioned as head writer in a piece about the show in *Soap Opera Digest*."

Gwen was curious enough about the young woman, called Nikki De Paul, to persuade the receptionist to fit her in.

"Oh, thanks a million, that's really sweet of you," Nikki said as they went into the dressing room together. "Like, being here is a gift from my aunt. Makeup consultation, facial, massage, the works."

As far as Gwen was concerned, the girl was perfection as she was. Her hair was gloriously thick and shiny, her complexion peaches and cream, with just a few residual freckles across the bridge of a pert little nose.

And she was slender, about Gwen's height, and nicely dressed in a navy skirt and pale blue silk shirt. Like many of her contemporaries, she wore no bra.

"My aunt believes in preventive cosmetics." Nikki confided.

Gwen quickly averted her gaze. "Your aunt is wise, and you'll be glad you took her advice a long time from now." She saw to it that her manicure and pedicure would coincide with Nikki's so they could spend some time together. This was not a chance to be missed.

It was amazing that such a random encounter could alter Gwen's mood so completely. Gone was the feeling of heavy despair, the hopelessness, the terror of aging. She suddenly felt charged with energy and with joyful anticipation. Not that Nikki had indicated any overt sexual interest in her, but she had awfully flirty eyes. She also gave off teasing signals a little along the lines of "You attract me but I don't quite know how or why."

It was up to Gwen to show her. Especially as she truly believed that every human being was bisexual and that only cultural taboos caused concealment and denial.

Hadn't Gwen denied this side of herself for years?

And even if she was wrong about this girl, at the very least she would spend the afternoon pleasantly. And later, in her lonely bed, the fantasies she wove would have at their center a slender auburn-haired girl with teasing eyes and ripe red lips.

During their conversation while their nails were being done, Nikki confirmed that she was a soap-opera freak to the extent that she had scrimped to buy a VCR so she could record her favorite series while she was at work, dismissing her job as boring and dead-end. Gwen gathered that she mostly operated a word processor.

Nikki kept switching back to her. "You have children of college age? I don't believe it. Gosh, I guess Aunt Sue knows what she's talking about. I mean, if I can look as good as you when I'm a little older I'll be thrilled."

Gwen smiled. "You don't have a thing to worry about. I suppose you have a date tonight with that special someone," she ventured.

'Oh, no. There is no special someone," Nikki said glumly. "Honestly, the men in this town just make me sick. I've about given up."

Gwen could hardly contain her growing excitement. "Well, if you're free, would you like to have a drink? I don't have too much time, I still have work to do, but—"

"Oh, I'd love it," Nikki said enthusiastically. "I'd love to hear how it works. I mean, how everything comes together for the show to be so riveting. I can hardly wait for Monday's episode. Maybe I can get you to give me a hint," she finished, smiling with every part of her beautiful face—those full, sensual lips, made for kissing, and those eyes, like dancing lights.

Gwen smiled back, thrilled that Nikki had given her something tangible to entice her.

Nikki turned out to be a sweetheart. She bubbled with enthusiasm over the view at the Top of the Sixes, where they went for a drink. And she was far from stupid. In fact, she had a college degree and was fairly well-read. Gwen gathered that she was interested in acting but hadn't made any serious moves in that direction.

The girl could certainly hold her liquor. She downed two vodka martinis without showing a flicker of inebriation, whereas Gwen felt as if she was flying after one glass of wine. Of course, her euphoria had something to do with the company. Nikki was an utter delight, and such a tease, trying to find out the substance of the next episode of

Night and Day. Gwen teased her back, giving her what purported to be a hint but was really a red herring.

"Oh," Nikki said, looking at her watch, "it's getting late. I don't want to keep you from your work."

"Well, I have to eat dinner anyway." Gwen remembered she had had no lunch. "Do you like Spanish food? There's a nice place in the West village. . . ."

Nikki loved Spanish food. She chatted animatedly in the taxi, answering Gwen's questions about her background. Her father was dead and her mother lived in Huntington, Long Island, with Nikki's two sisters, nineteen and sixteen, who were both in school. No, Nikki didn't see her family often, wasn't very close to them. Her mother was in real estate and did pretty well. Nikki had moved away from home after college because Manhattan was the place to be.

Nikki sounded ashamed of her studio in the East Twenties, so Gwen didn't press for details. She understood that the girl's life wasn't satisfactory and that was why she escaped into the glamour and intrigue of the soaps. It was too bad. God, if Gwen looked like that, and were twenty years younger. . . . Well, things didn't work that way. Nikki needed more self-confidence and some attention paid to her. Attention that was possibly given to her younger sisters.

Gwen often ate at El Faro, and they were led to a nice table in a quiet corner. The dim lighting, Gwen hoped, softened her face. Nikki, of course, would look beautiful even under the glare of fluorescence.

Although Gwen didn't mean to linger over dinner, time seemed to be suspended because of her enchantment with Nikki. The girl had charm to burn. If Nikki really was interested in acting, Gwen knew a lot of people in the theater—playwrights, scenic designers, directors. . . .

Nikki fairly jumped out of her seat with joy and eagerness to meet Gwen's friends, to accept any help Gwen could offer, any suggestions she might have.

"Right now," Gwen said huskily, blowing out smoke, "I suggest we get out of here." The place had become noisy and packed with people waiting at the bar for tables.

She offered to drop Nikki off in a taxi.

"Fine," Nikki said, but she was suddenly subdued. Did she not want to say goodnight?

Gwen lit a cigarette, trying to keep her excitement at bay. She knew from painful experience that too quick a move on her part might result in a scathing rejection. She had experienced them all. The exclamations of disgust, of denial, of outrage that Gwen would dare to think the girl in question was "*that* kind of person." All evening Gwen had been careful not to touch Nikki—not even a friendly hand on the arm, that sort of thing. Now she sat in the taxi a little distant. Nikki was silent, and Gwen was too. As she became accustomed to the darkness, she could see Nikki's hand resting in her lap, delicate, smooth, and unveined. Her skin would be silky, her fingers sinuous.

Gwen shivered involuntarily and stubbed out her cigarette.

Nikki glanced at her. "Are you cold? It's so damp, and you're wearing such a light raincoat. I'm always warm myself." For a moment Nikki covered Gwen's icy hand with her own.

Expelling a gasp she tried to turn into a laugh, Gwen mumbled, "You certainly are," and forced herself to keep her hand absolutely still during their brief contact.

"Look, why don't you just drop me off at your place," Nikki suggested. "I can walk the rest of the way. I sort of feel like a walk. I'm in no rush to get home."

Feeling jubilant, Gwen redirected the driver. She sat back in her seat, biting her lips to keep from saying or doing the smallest thing to spoil the moment.

God, it had been so long since she had met anyone who remotely appealed to her. A casual affair was rarely a possibility because she tended to get too involved, so it was useless to hang around lesbian bars. She had always preferred to wait for the private gathering, hosted by someone trustworthy, which drew women like her. Women who were, at least theoretically, capable of deep affection and commitment. Meeting someone like Nikki at a beauty salon, of all places, was almost too good to be true.

Gwen paid the taxi driver and fumbled in her bag for the keys. "I'm not in a working mood at this point. There's nothing that can't wait until tomorrow. Why don't you come up and have a drink?"

Nikki immediately perked up. "Oh, are you sure? I mean, I'd feel terrible keeping you from your typewriter."

"No need," Gwen said, daring to look straight at her. "I never did tell you about Monday's episode," she finished teasingly.

The look she got back caused her to lower her eyes and be glad it was too dark for Nikki to see how affected she was.

Nikki was enchanted with the apartment—so large, so beautifully furnished with wonderful antiques.

Gwen enjoyed Nikki's pleasure, realizing that she had lived here for so many years she took her place for granted. Both her children had been brought up here, and when they had gone off to school Gwen had turned the dining room she no longer used into a library. Nikki walked around it, fascinated to see where Gwen worked, teasing her by trying to catch a glimpse on her desk.

"That's not nice," Gwen admonished softly, daring to take Nikki's arm and lead her into the living room. She poured Kahlua for herself, Drambuie for Nikki. "I've been divorced for fifteen years," she said, in answer to Nikki's question. "No, I never considered remarrying. One husband was enough."

"Yeah, I can imagine," Nikki nodded her head. "I've thought of getting married, mostly to have kids, but I find men like from another planet. They want different things. I have had nothing but disasters with men. Anyway, it's possible to get pregnant without a man nowadays, not that I'm ready for that yet. I'd like to do something with my life first."

Nikki's glass was empty.

"Help yourself, please, Nikki," Gwen said, relaxing on the couch. "Make yourself at home."

"Thanks." On her way to the bar, Nikki passed the baby grand and stopped to look at the framed photo sitting on it. "Is that your daughter?"

An empty feeling of sadness hit Gwen, as it always did. "No, my sister. She died many years ago. Leukemia. That was her piano."

"Oh. I'm sorry." Nikki refilled her glass, but in replacing the bottle she spilled her drink. "Oh, no, not all over your carpet." She knelt and tried to mop it up with a napkin.

"It's okay, don't worry about it." Gwen knelt beside Nikki, making a joke of it, saying that what really made old Oriental rugs so valuable was the hundreds of exotic drinks that had been absorbed into the fabric.

Nikki was too upset to laugh, repeating that she had ruined it, that she was sorry and hoped Gwen would forgive her.

As they stood up, Gwen repeated that there was nothing to forgive.

Nikki suddenly leaned against her, murmuring that she must be a little drunk.

Putting a firm, protective arm around her waist, Gwen soothed her and dared to brush her cheek against Nikki's, feeling the girl's arm encircling her waist.

Gwen eased them onto the couch, her heart pumping madly. She embraced Nikki and kissed her lightly on the lips. She met no resistance. Indeed, Nikki put her arms around Gwen's neck and kissed her back. "Your lips are so soft," Nikki whispered, sounding surprised.

Gwen stroked her silky hair, breathing in her intoxicating fragrance, greatly excited by the certainty that Nikki had never before kissed a woman. Gently she fondled Nikki's neck, that young, firm, unlined skin, those slim, fragile shoulders.

Nikki leaned back on the couch, making small noises of pleasure. "I'm so warm," she whispered.

With practiced fingers, Gwen unbuttoned Nikki's silk shirt, exposing two small but perfectly shaped breasts, firm, jutting out proudly. She caressed them lightly for a few moments, and then bent her head and sucked gently on one nipple.

"Mm," Nikki moaned, "that feels so good."

Gwen moved to her other nipple, while she deftly undid Nikki's skirt button and zipper. Then she eased the skirt and half-slip down and removed them, doing the same with the girl's panty hose, and exposing lushly curving hips, pink microbikini panties, and slender, shapely legs.

Catching her breath sharply, Gwen caressed the smooth skin of the girl's thighs and calves—skin as soft as rose petals. "You're incredibly lovely," Gwen murmured between soft kisses. "Simply perfection."

Lifting her legs onto the sofa, Nikki lay on her back, both arms flung over her head. Her body arched lazily under Gwen's gentle exploration.

Nikki was like a feline goddess, stretching and purring, delighting in the pleasure she was giving, as well as receiving. Her motions were so sensual and unselfconscious, so graceful, so naturally wanton.

After a while, Gwen took Nikki by the hand and led her into the bedroom.

Gwen sat propped against the pillow with a cigarette, feeling giddy with fulfillment and tenderness. Nikki was as much of a delight in bed as out.

Take it slow, take it easy, Gwen kept telling herself, terrified she would frighten Nikki away.

The girl was lying on her back, appearing relaxed and pleased. She turned her head and smiled at Gwen shyly. "I've never done anything like this before. Like, it was strange but wonderful. I mean, it just seemed to happen so naturally."

Gwen, overcome with emotion, nodded a few times and then said huskily, "I'm glad, Nikki. I'm very, very glad."

They began to talk, and Gwen was relieved that Nikki confined their conversation to Gwen's work. It took her time to become intimate with someone, even Nikki, who she now felt certain was going to be very important to her.

"I can't imagine how you can come up with so many ideas, week after week, without any help."

"I do have help. FAB owns the soap, you see, and I work with their production company. We have story conferences. The dialogue writers make suggestions, and the producers, the directors, the actors, who get a sense of the characters they're playing."

"I see, but most of the plots are yours, aren't they? You're remarkable, Gwen, you really are."

"Thanks, my love, but I'm no more remarkable than real life, as reported in the newspapers every day," Gwen said. "Love, hate, envy, greed, power, anger, obsession, compulsion. Using reality as a basis, we dramatize for soap audiences what they want to have happen in their fantasies. And when these wicked and exciting things are happening to the rich and powerful, it gives the audience a special satisfaction. . . ."

A wellspring of emotion hit Gwen. This was what she had been missing—an intelligent, responsive listener who was genuinely interested in her, beyond the satisfaction of the flesh. Someone she could really talk to afterward.

Gwen had so much love to give to Nikki, so very much, and time was running out. She wanted to establish a loving relationship before she became an old woman and the Nikkis of this world wouldn't want her.

Nikki sat back in the taxi, yawning, for it was almost four in the morning. Gwen had wanted her to stay the night, of course, but she had begged off, claiming a family gathering on Sunday in Huntington. But she would be seeing Gwen after work on Monday evening.

Nikki yawned again. The experience hadn't been as bad as she had feared. Gwen was better than most men, in fact, who were such rough pigs. At least Gwen was soft and gentle, and God, was she smart! Nikki would take full advantage of that. Not to write soaps, though. She had changed her mind about that. It was too obvious. If Gwen caught on, she might drop her just as Herb Norman had, and she couldn't afford to take that chance.

Of course the whole number was a little nutsy. The picture of that sister, for instance. When Herb had once mentioned in passing that Van Ryck was a dyke who favored redheads, Nikki had stored that away for future reference. But seeing a photo of the redheaded sister, who resembled Nikki somewhat, had really thrown her.

Well, it didn't matter. Nothing mattered except getting her name on a script. She smiled as she remembered how she had twisted Gwen around her little finger, persuading her to tell her the substance of Monday's episode.

Men, women, they were all the same, as long as you gave them what they wanted.

11

Diana lay on her towel on Georgia Beach in East Hampton under the warming rays of the sun. With her eyes shut against the glare, she could nevertheless see little pictures before her. Pictures of Luke in his swimming briefs, looking marvelously tanned and muscular, diving into the waves.

She smiled as she remembered that he had only recently learned to swim, yet he was about as good as any California beach boy. How she admired his fearlessness, his willingness to learn.

She sat up, stretching lazily, and applied sun lotion to her shoulders and the backs of her legs, and then lay on her stomach.

The last three months had been pure bliss. In fact, she often wondered how she had ever gotten along without Luke. It wasn't only the lovemaking, superb though that was, but having his warm body wrapped around hers in sleep. And then awaking each morning and seeing those eyes beaming love at her.

His love had helped, because things had been difficult, starting with the first Monday morning she had walked into the office.

Molly took one look at her and said, "Uh-oh. You've fallen for Luke, haven't you?"

Refusing to be treated like a little girl caught with both hands in the cookie jar, Diana said, "No, I haven't fallen, I've been uplifted. I feel like a whole woman at last."

"Diana, Diana" Molly shook her head. "I hope you know what you're doing."

"Of course I do. Why are you so opposed to Luke?"

"Because I have a gut feeling that he's not to be trusted. There's something feral about him, and I feel he's liable to revert to a wild state at any time. I just don't want to see you get hurt, that's all."

"If you're so concerned with my feelings, try accepting him as my lover, okay?" Diana sank into a chair and grinned at Molly. "What a weekend we had."

Molly listened to the general details, smiling skeptically. "You've invented Luke, can't you see that?"

"So what? Don't we all invent our love objects? Men do it all the time. Filmmakers and playwrights fall for their leading ladies—"

"Sure, and we've always had a good laugh at male blindness. Now you go and do exactly the same thing. . . ."

Diana was too happy to let her partner's negative reaction get to her. "Let's face it, Molly, the only way for a woman to get the man she wants is to fashion him out of raw material."

"That's fine, if the diamond in the rough doesn't turn out to be paste."

Diana shot her a glorious smile. "Listen, I can tell the difference, and believe me, I've got a gem—the real thing. I won't hear another word against him, Molly."

She shrugged. "Okay. Anyway, we've got other things to think about. Like having two shows in full production."

They would have to expand their office space. Molly suggested installing a small elevator so that the top floor of her brownstone could be made into offices. Instead of continuing to use other people's production facilities, they planned to rent their own studios and to put writers, producers, and directors on the payroll. And Molly would continue mostly on *Mom & Meg* while Diana remained in charge of *Pete Winston*

Of course, we're taking a tremendous gamble," Molly said. "I've heard that Continental is struck with more series for the fall than they can program. If the pilot doesn't do as well as Bannon wants, he'll pull the plug so fast—"

"It won't happen," Diana interrupted. "I have confidence in the pilot and in the audience's readiness for *Pete Winston.*"

Although Diana had hoped to keep her connection with

Luke a secret, that turned out to be impossible. From the moment they began rehearsals for the thirteen shows ordered by the network, everybody took one look at the two of them and knew they had to be in love.

The reactions varied from disappointed coolness on Gemma's part to giggling from the children and knowing smirks from some of the cast and crew, though romances on the set were nothing new or startling. It was just that Diana had never approved, and it was embarrassing to go from being above that sort of thing to being smack in the middle.

And she saw that she had to break the news to Matthew before he heard it elsewhere. She did it over lunch, and very clumsily, too. "Uh, Luke Merriman and I—that is, before the pilot, when I said I was only helping him, that was absolutely true. But since then . . . well, we've gotten together.'

Diana looked at Matthew a little guiltily, finding no encouragement in his ironic frown. "It was a total surprise to me, in fact, Matthew. But I was telling you the truth, at that time—"

"As far as you knew," he interjected sardonically.

Diana blushed. She could hardly blame him for thinking she was a flake.

"I'm glad you told me yourself, but in fact I've already heard. Good news travels quickly," he finished, the same mocking note in his voice.

Diana's heart started pounding. The fate of *Pete Winston* was very much in Matthew's hands, and if he was totally disgusted with her, there was no telling what he might do.

Enduring his sardonic scrutiny for a few moments more, she was vastly relieved when he remarked that he felt the pilot should be aired in August, during rerun time, when it was likely to do well in the ratings. They could start the series early in September, before the fall season got under way, and build some audience support.

"Our prime-time slots are all filled, as you probably know. But if *Pete Winston* does well, it will have a chance as a replacement."

Her anxiety lifted. It was wonderful news—even though it was far from a promise, of course—and her respect for

Matthew as a reasonable, scrupulously fair person was greatly enhanced.

Now it was July, and she and Luke were taking two weeks of vacation, just lazing in the sun and enjoying each other. Diana dozed off, awakened by a sprinkling of icy water on her back.

She jumped and rolled over. "Hey, stop that," she cried, as Luke, laughing and dripping, shook his wet head at her.

"It'll cool you off a little, babe, so you can dive in with me instead of hunkering at the edge like a cat that'd rather lose seven of its lives than get one paw wet."

Diana jumped up and purred at him, nuzzling his cool, wet flesh in her most provocative feline manner.

"Hey, you better quit, 'cause if you're playing that kind of pussy I'm gonna hoist you over my shoulder and carry you home this minute."

"Not before my swim," Diana cried, breaking away and running toward the ocean. She really meant to brave the water, but as soon as she was up to her ankles she began to shiver and reconsider.

"Come on, scaredy-cat, in you go," Luke cried, scooping her up, protesting, and carrying her out. He lowered her into the water, while she shrieked and splashed as much as she could.

He dived under her legs and emerged with her sitting on his shoulders. She held on to his neck and yelled like a cowboy busting a bronco, not caring that people within earshot looked a little startled. What the hell, it was a glorious Sunday in summer and she was in love.

They dried each other off, sensually reapplied tanning lotion, then lay on their stomachs, holding hands.

"Time to roll over," Luke said, tugging on her hand.

"Not yet," she murmured. "I was almost asleep."

"Please, babe. You'll be glad you did."

Groaning, she eased herself on her back, and he handed her her sunglasses.

"Now, you just look up over there. Keep looking. Tell me if you see anything interesting."

Diana did as he suggested, using her hand to shield her eyes from the glare. In the distance she saw a small plane approaching, flying low, and trailing a banner behind it. It drew close enough for her to read, in huge white letters, "Luke Loves Diana."

She melted and looked at him, resting on one elbow, enjoying her surprise. "What a beautiful thing to do," she whispered, moving closer and hugging him. They were sticky with lotion but she didn't care. This big, lean, muscular, exquisite man was hers, and she was his, bound by such love.

Tightening her arms around him, Diana glued her mouth to his, feeling an incredibly strong arousal throughout her body. She pressed against him, her fingers entangling his damp, matted hair, and rubbed her breasts and belly against his bare flesh. Moving one thigh between his legs, she probed his mouth with her tongue, drinking in the deliciousness of him.

"I've had enough of the beach," she murmured against his mouth. "You?"

"Yup. Enough beach, not enough Diana."

They walked slowly toward the house, staying close to the water where the sand was wet and cool, and stopping every few moments to kiss.

Diana could hardly believe the feelings Luke aroused within her. The minute she was alone with him she wanted to drag him to bed. It was excessive, to say the very least. Even in the studio, sometimes, when they had been rehearsing or taping, she would feel love juices flowing in her body. Everything Luke did was simply adorable, and she had fantasies of being marooned with him on an island and doing nothing but making love all day and night.

Luke seemed to like her that way. He was always ready for a romp, though it bothered her slightly that she almost always made the first advances. Well, Jesus, when did he have a chance? Hardly a day had gone by that they hadn't made love at least once, even when she had her period. That hadn't been a sexy time for her in the past, but with Luke it was wonderful. With Luke she was another woman, a sensual woman.

He knew that, too. "It makes me real proud, Diana," he would say, whenever she told him how he had awakened her passion.

Now as they strolled along the wooden walkway to the

house, Diana had to force herself to keep to his pace and not pull him by the hand, so urgently did she want him.

They peeled off their wet suits and hosed off on the deck, squealing and squirting each other. Diana wouldn't let him reach for his towel. She simply couldn't wait. Grabbing his hands, she pushed him into a beach chair and began to devour him with her lips and tongue, stroking him and licking him until she had him aroused. Then she lowered herself on him and teased him with her breasts, letting him nibble at her, then drawing back.

She gyrated her hips, dancing on him, feeling like a sex goddess enacting a primitive ritual in an ancient civilization.

Luke's eyes were open, his face was flushed, and he was sucking in his breath, biting his lip, holding back.

"Give it to me," she hissed at him. "Give it to me now. Oh, God, I want it now." She loved this position because even if he refused to move she could bounce on him and whip up the froth of his desire until he could hold back no longer.

"Now—I'm coming now," she yelled, jumping up and down with such vigor that at her moment of orgasm the chair broke beneath them.

Diana didn't even realize what the shattering feeling was beneath her. She was screaming, vibrating, as wave after wave assaulted her at her body's core.

"Oh, God, darling," she moaned, burying her head in his neck. "Didn't you come?"

"No, ma'am. I was just working up to it when the chair gave way. It's sort of sticking my backbone."

"Oh, Luke, I'm so sorry." Diana disengaged herself, laughing at how oblivious she had been. "Let me see. Oh, you're cut. Let me put something on it."

She went inside, feeling embarrassed. Luke was really hurt, and she had been so single-minded she hadn't even noticed. She simply had to control herself better. This was crazy.

He was lying on the mat on the deck, and the sight of his naked buttocks, so perfectly formed, did something to her breathing.

Stop it, Sinclair, she lectured herself. You're turning into a sex maniac.

She knelt beside him and wiped his cut with cotton and

peroxide, then applied a Band-Aid. When she was through, she couldn't resist kissing the back of his neck, then his shoulders. He wiggled his buttocks appreciatively. "Keep going, babe."

Diana inched her way down his back, rubbing her breasts against him while she bestowed feathery touches up the backs of his thighs. Then she moved her hands between his body and the mat, as he grunted and turned over.

"You're so gorgeous," she murmured, so irresistible—"

"Then don't resist," he said, pushing her on her back. He leaned over her, kissing her neck, her breasts, her belly, and using his tongue between her legs in a way to make her quiver and strain toward him.

Finally he straddled her, smiling like a mischievous god who knows he wields superhuman power. Although he was fully aroused he was able to hold back, to tease her. "What do you want, babe? You tell me, now. Say the words."

"I want you inside of me," she moaned. "I want you to fill me up."

He entered her slowly and pushed back and forth, then stopped and drew back a little, smiling at her, his eyes hooded with desire.

"Oh, please, Luke, darling," she begged. "Please."

"Well, now, I just might, if you really love me—"

"I love you, I adore you, I worship you," she moaned, her fingers digging into his back.

"Maybe we ought to stop now," he suggested, teasing her.

"No! No, don't stop, oh, please, don't ever stop. I love you, Luke, forever. I want you forever—"

"Like this?" he asked, plunging into her. "Is this what you want? Is this the way?"

"Yes, yes, yes," she screamed, and lost herself in ecstasy.

They had drinks on the terrace of a seafood restaurant where they could watch the magnificent sunset—when they could take their eyes off one another long enough.

"You sure are a beauty, Diana," Luke said softly, touching her hair. "You look real good with a tan. It's cute, the way it brings out your freckles."

"Oh, it doesn't," Diana said, dismayed. She had hated her pie face with raisins when she was a kid.

"Freckles," Luke insisted, smiling, "and I love them."

She didn't care if he loved them, freckles bothered her. Reaching for her mirror to see, she caught a glimpse of Tom Ryan right behind her.

"Your face is perfect as it is, doesn't need a thing," Tom joked, kissing her cheek, "How are you, Diana?"

"Wonderful." She beamed, and introduced Luke.

Tom shook Luke's hand and nodded with approval at Diana. "Well, you seem to be having a good summer." He had just returned from Europe and was throwing a party the following week. "Hope you two can make it. In fact, why don't you join me for dinner? I'm over there, with those people."

"Thanks, Tom, maybe for coffee. And we'd love to come to the party."

After he had walked away she told Luke it was at Tom's house that she had first met Matthew Sayles and set everything in motion.

"Uh-huh. Well, I'm glad you said no to eating dinner with a bunch of folks. It's nicer just the two of us."

Diana lifted her glass. "To the two of us."

"Amen," Luke replied, winking at her. He leaned back in his chair, glancing at the orange-purple sky and the other people sitting around them.

"What are you thinking, darling?" she asked.

He smiled. "You know, this is the first time in my life I've had a real vacation. I went to Santa Monica for a couple of weeks once but I was filling in for a buddy, a waiter and comic rolled into one. And when I was down the valley, not working meant not eating, so 'vacation' wasn't exactly the word. I'm not complaining, mind you. No, ma'am. On the contrary. It feels real good to see myself moving up from the bottom."

She smiled back at him. "You're going to go all the way to the top, but you won't forget your friends, will you?"

"Not this friend," Luke said, squeezing her hand.

"Andrea, for God's sake, pull your feet in, "Matthew shouted at his daughter. "That's where the propeller is. I've told you ten times—"

"But we're under sail, Daddy," she complained, while doing as she was told.

"That doesn't matter. You can't develop bad habits on a boat, because if you forget—"

"—no more feet," she finished gaily. Too gaily. She sometimes exhibited a breezy self-destructiveness that worried him.

Beth Blackman emerged from the galley with a tray of sandwiches. "Lunch, you guys."

Andrea, as well as Beth's twin daughters, who had been sitting with their feet over the side of the boat, came whooping and crowding around her, both hands out and grabbing.

While Beth admonished them, Matthew dropped anchor and pulled in the sails, suddenly aware of not having a woman in his life.

Beth was not only a terrific mother but also admirable from every point of view. Her laughing dark eyes and softly flowing hair glowed beautifully in the sunlight. She was a competent lawyer, an excellent cook, and a good wife to Lloyd Blackman, with whom she shared a law practice in Sag Harbor. In fact, the Blackmans had become Matthew's closet friends.

Although he could sail his thirty-footer single-handedly, he usually invited the Blackmans along. Lloyd was a fine sailor, and Beth whipped up delicious edibles in the galley, while the kids had a wonderful time together. Today Lloyd wasn't with them because at the last minute he had been called upon to get a client out of jail.

Matthew joined the group for a sandwich and reflected on how much he owed the Blackmans. When he had first moved here more than two years ago, he had been overwhelmed by everything. Furnishing a new house, hiring a competent housekeeper, getting Andrea into a decent school. He was worried about her making friends, and plagued with anxiety at being the only person close to her.

In Beverly Hills his mother had been a big help, and he had agonized about separating Andrea from her grandparents. Yet he had truly felt his daughter would be better off away from the place that depressed her and reminded her of her mother.

For hours the small girl had sat at the window looking

out, waiting, unable to accept that her mother wasn't coming back. She had resisted going to bed, and even after she was tucked in, couldn't fall asleep. Matthew had sat with her, read her stories, talked to her, played soothing music—nothing had helped.

He hadn't been able to bear the pain of his daughter's sadness, so when he had a chance to come east, he jumped at it. He missed New York. He also didn't want Andrea growing up in Hollywood. She wasn't beautiful like her mother. Andy was like him in appearance and temperament—quiet, reflective, and far too sensitive. She gave off a waiflike impression, unlike the golden girls of Hollywood. Even her contemporaries were already self-involved and self-possessed, ambitious to make it big as actresses or as wives of producers or directors, with the final goal of being able to shop without concern on Rodeo Drive. His daughter showed signs of being a misfit out there; at least in New York more choices were open to her.

He had chosen Long Island over Manhatten, feeling he needed a small, safe community and a place that would be less of an overwhelming change for his daughter. And he had opted for Sag Harbor because it was an old whaling town and had struck him as having a stable community life all year round.

Fortunately, during his first week there he had run into Beth at a store with her twins, who had immediately gravitated to Andrea. They were lively and appealed to his daughter in a way that none of her previous friends ever had.

Beth had been an invaluable friend ever since. He had been embarrassed to ask anything of her, but she had understood his needs and volunteered her services in her casually thoughtful way. "I'm taking the girls shopping. I thought Andrea might like to come along. Does she need a winter coat, by any chance, Matthew?"

It was Beth who invited Matthew and Andrea to her home for Thanksgiving and Christmas dinners, and that was now a tradition. Matthew had found Lloyd as likable as his wife, a man who participated in raising his daughters. The Blackmans had moved to the area from Manhattan because they couldn't see themselves working endless hours for their respective law corporations and leaving the raising of their children to strangers. They earned less money in their mom-and-pop law firm, as they dubbed it, but they had the kind of family life they wanted.

Andy had made a pretty good adjustment at school and she now had other friends besides the Blackman twins. Although she no longer talked about her mother, she expressed her longing through her artwork. She loved to paint animals—birds, cats, dogs, usually in families—two adults and one baby.

And she still suffered from insomnia. Matthew felt that on some deep level she was afraid to go to sleep. Maybe she feared that she would dream of her mother and wake up to the pain that it had only been a dream. Or it might have been the fear that her mother would return just when she was asleep, and then steal away again.

He felt he should remarry, yet Matthew knew Andrea would have great difficulty accepting a stepmother. Certainly there was no shortage of divorced women around, and he had met several at the Blackmans' home. But his daughter, he noticed, always made it a point to avoid them, even though many of them were very nice. It was as if Andy could relax only with someone like Beth precisely because she wasn't stepmother material.

After lunch on the boat, the girls played Monopoly, and Beth took a nap. Matthew relaxed in a deck chair with a gin and tonic and found himself thinking about Diana Sinclair and wondering why he had such lousy taste in women. After his experience with Lorrie, you would think he would never again be attracted to the kind of woman who went for a Luke Merriman. Yet, at odd moments, Diana's smiling softness would float stubbornly in front of him.

It made no sense. She was attractive, but not beautiful in the way that had men's heads turning. She had never given him the slightest encouragement. But he had still been furious and hurt when he had first heard from Jill (who had heard it from Gemma) that Diana and Luke were mooning at each other on the set—furious because Diana had recently looked him in the eye and sworn she had no personal interest in the guy. Hurt because—hell, he felt rejected, stupid as it was.

In those first few angry moments of digesting Jill's

bombshell, he had fantasized about airing the pilot when nobody in his right mind would be watching TV, and in spite of the financial beating the network would take, seeing to it that Diana's series was canceled.

But that vengeful thought had been only momentary. After all, Diana had been shaping Luke into her masculine ideal for months, so it wasn't really surprising that she was now reveling in her own handiwork.

You ought to be relieved, you idiot, that you didn't show your hand, Matthew told himself. Nothing ventured, nothing lost.

And even if there were no Luke, what would you have told her? I'd like you to be my woman, Diana, only it will have to be now and then, and in secret. No, I'm not married anymore but my daughter—that's right, I have a daughter—won't accept a woman friend as yet. . . . It was totally absurd.

Fortunately, when Diana had called him soon afterward and invited him to lunch, he had himself well under control. And in the end, he was glad he had listened to his professional instincts regarding *Pete Winston*. The pilot had gotten a surprising twenty-four share of the audience, even though Luke was an unknown and Gemma not that well remembered.

The reviews had been good, too. "Promising" was the word for *Pete Winston*. The program board had perked up, and Phil with it. Especially when it seemed likely that some of their scheduled programs were going to bomb, based on the reception of those pilots.

Matthew had appeared at a couple of rehearsals of *Pete Winston*, finding the byplay between Diana and Luke, subdued as it was, disturbing. So he found excuses to see her alone at lunch, even though he supposed he could have talked to her in his office or even on the phone.

Was he secretly hoping he would like her less as he got to know her better? That she would pick her teeth at the table or yell at the waiter, or do something else to show him how mistaken he was? It turned out that the opposite was true, and he found himself liking her more all the time.

Matthew was suddenly aware that Beth was awake and smiling at him. It was growing late, and they would have to be getting back.

He started the engine, feeling sad, and wondering if Diana and Luke could possibly last. They didn't have much in common, as far as he could see. Perhaps it was the same sort of obsession he had once had about Lorrie. He sighed, remembering all the early warning signs, and how little attention he had paid. One is always inclined to make excuses for the beloved.

Still, any relationship was bound to cool off in time, especially when the two people involved came from such different backgrounds as Diana and Luke.

Sara Coles lifted her eyes from the carton she was trying to pack, to see the naked light bulb swinging on its wire overhead, while her children screamed and fought with each other, flinging things around the cabin.

Sara moved over to separate them. "You quit that now, you hear?" She smacked Daisy across her bottom. Her six-year-old daughter flinched and then screamed, "You always blame me. He's the one who started it, Mama."

"I d-d-didn't either," four-year-old Joey yelled.

"Did too."

"D-d-did not."

"Quit it, you two. I've had just about enough. Daisy, you're older, you're supposed to know better." Seeing Joey stick his tongue out at his sister, Sara ran over and shook him. "What'd I tell you about doin' that, huh? You quit right now. If you got so much vinegar in you, help me pack up our gear. Time's a-wastin'. Daisy, put them things in this box.

"No. I don't wanna move again. I like it here, Mama. I got friends to play with."

"We gotta move. All the blackberries in Gresham's been picked. No work, no money and what're we gonna do then, huh? Use your head, girl."

"I'm not goin'." Daisy deliberately picked up a cup and smashed it viciously against the wall of the cabin.

Sara lunged for her daughter but the girl was too quick; she veered sideways and ran out of the cabin, leaving the door open.

"Hey, w-w-wait for me," Joey stammered, going after his sister.

Sara decided to let them be. They weren't much help anyway.

She picked up the broken cup wearily and saw that it couldn't be mended. With a straw broom she swept up the shards and put them in the garbage.

It was pretty cool but she was sweating as she folded faded jeans and shirts and laid them in the carton. She felt weak, but then she hadn't had much to eat that day. Money was real low, and she needed enough for gas to fill the car so they could get from Oregon to California.

It was too bad they had to move so far away. She'd heard on the migrant grapevine that hop pickers were wanted near Salem, but she didn't dare, because she knew Walt was getting out of prison right about now.

Walt. Just the thought of him made the little hairs on Sara's thin arms stand on end. She must have been out of her head to take up with him. Well, Joey had been a handful, at two. A real nervous boy, with quick-blinking eyes, making all kinds of noises but not able to talk proper. In fact, both kids always had something wrong with them. Daisy was as skinny as a branch, and her nose ran all the time. And Joey kept breaking out in rashes. He was finally able to talk, but not without stuttering.

Sara said her prayers and believed the good Lord would pay her some mind. She was a decent, God-fearing woman most of the time. Walt had been a mistake, as well as a sin. But it wasn't her fault that she had been left with two-year-old Daisy and infant Joey. She'd managed on her own for more than a year, but she'd been desperate because keeping Joey with her while she picked was real hard. He could tear through a berry patch and destroy more fruit in five minutes than she could pick in an hour.

Walt had seen her at work and taken a fancy to her. He wasn't much to look at with his short squat body and funny face. And he must've been forty, while she was only twenty-four. But Walt kept saying if they all lived together and pooled their money she could pay an older kid to watch Joey and Daisy.

So she'd given in, even though she didn't fancy Walt much. He was okay at first, but then he had stepped up his drinking something awful, especially when he'd broken a leg and couldn't work. Drinking turned him mean, and he beat her and the kids. She'd packed up and moved on but he found them. Wherever she went, he kept finding her. He'd say he was sorry, that he wanted them back and would never hurt them again, but each time he broke his promise.

He was a drunk, pure and simple, and she wanted no part of him. They'd gone down to California to pick oranges just to get away. Then she'd heard from someone else working the stream that Walt had gotten himself into a fight, knifed a guy, and was sent to prison for a year

They'd come back to Oregon and lived in peace until a couple of days ago, when Doris had warned her Walt was getting out on parole. She had heard the news from her cousin, who was kin to Walt on his mother's side.

Sara finished packing the carton and dragged it outside. "Daisy," she yelled into the darkness. "Daisy, you come here. I need you to help me."

"No, I won't. Not movin' nowheres," her daughter called from nearby.

Sara decided to do without help rather than to drag and force her daughter.

The Dodge had been left to her by Lucas, and Sara took the best care of it she could. It meant she could go where she wanted instead of having to depend on trucks and buses taking migrants to this place or that like they transported cattle. It was also because of the car that she had taught herself to read—slowly, laboriously—so that she could get a driver's license.

As she tinkered with the engine, she knew the Dodge was coming to the end of its days. There was only so much she could do herself. The generator needed replacing, the spark plugs were dull, and the brake lining was shot. In fact, if Lucas could see her now he would be amazed that the car was still operating at all. It hadn't been in good shape way back then.

She didn't think much about Lucas nowadays. He had simply vanished. No telling where he had gotten to in three years. One thing was sure: he no longer worked the stream or she'd have heard.

An hour later, Sara was ready. It was after ten, and she was so tired she could hardly stand. Well, she'd be sitting in the car. She figured they'd have to drive most of the night to get a good start. She wanted to be clear out of the state by morning.

Taking a last look around the cabin, she marveled that they had been able to spend three months there at all. When it was cleared of their things it looked so poor and shabby. The one bed was sagging, the table was missing a leg, and all the chairs were rickety. The kerosene stove had smoked badly, and there was no refrigerator.

Hell, she was glad to be getting out.

"Daisy, Joey, get over here," she shouted. "We're goin'."

There was no answer. Sara felt a surge of fury as she stalked the bushes near the cabin, looking for them. They weren't with the Garcias or Isabel Perez. In fact, nobody had seen them.

Time was wasting. Sara got back to the house and heard a commotion. The little sneaks had returned and brought a box of berries with them. Blackberry juice was all over the floor and smeared on the walls.

"Ow," Daisy screamed when her mother grabbed her. "I'm not leavin' nohow."

"You're leavin', like it or not. And you stop sassin' me," Sara shouted, giving the child's arm a pinch. "That hurt, don't it? Well, that ain't the worst you're gonna get. Cause Walt's comin' lookin' for us. That's right. He's out on parole. And if we don't get a move on he'll be beatin' the shit out of you like he used to."

Daisy began to cry as she rubbed her arm, while Joey opened his eyes in fright and tried to utter something but failed.

Sara suddenly drew the two children to her in a fierce embrace. She hadn't meant to tell them about Walt because they'd start having nightmares again. All she'd wanted was to get them into the car so they could clear out. But seeing the shack dirtied up again, after all her efforts. . . .

She couldn't leave it that way: her pride wouldn't let her. She released the children and began to clean up their mess. This time Daisy helped her without saying a word, and Joey, as usual, copied his sister.

The kids got into the back of the car and fell asleep almost immediately. As Sara drove down the bumpy road of the farm leading to the highway, she glanced at them in her rearview mirror and felt awful.

Poor little tykes. It wasn't their fault. They needed a daddy. Sara loved them the best she could, but it wasn't enough.

She was getting to the end of her rope.

12

"I've missed you, Nikki," Gwen told the younger woman over dinner in a quiet little restaurant in the West Village.

"Not as much as I've missed you, Gwennie," Nikki responded, smiling suggestively.

Gwen had just returned from Provincetown, where her son had a summer job in a restaurant. Although the two women had been separated for only a few days, Gwen was almost tearful over their reunion. Nikki noted it and thought of the best way to profit from her friend's emotion.

"I've been fine except for this heat," Nikki said. "I'd love to get away to someplace cool. Any chance of us doing something together?" She watched Gwen's eyes glitter with pleasure.

"Of course, love. Let me make the arrangements. It will be my treat."

Gwen insisted on paying for everything, and Nikki, feigning reluctance, was happy to let her. After all, the woman was loaded. What Nikki did do was buy Gwen a little something every couple of weeks: a bottle of wine, some fancy soap. Inexpensive but thoughtful gifts. It was important for Gwen to believe that Nikki loved her as much as she loved Nikki.

Gwen suggested Scandinavia for two weeks, and Nikki was greatly pleased. She had never saved enough money to travel, and she deserved this for giving Gwen so much of her time. They were almost always alone. Nikki had, of course, pretended eagerness to meet some of Gwen's theatrical friends, but socializing with gays wasn't her idea of fun. She feared, too, that people who weren't blinded by love as Gwen was would guess she was actually straight. And if Nikki should run into people she knew from TV, it would blow everything. Although Gwen didn't particularly look or act masculine, when she gazed at Nikki with such love, even a child would be able to guess.

Nikki discouraged Gwen from phoning her on workdays, claiming she had no phone at her word processor and no privacy. But Gwen needed some way of reaching her, so Nikki arranged for an answering service to take her calls in the name of a fictitious company and relay Gwen's messages to her at Abbot and Sinclair. Fortunately, Gwen wasn't at all suspicious. She was too besotted by Nikki not to believe every word she uttered.

In bed that night, Nikki went to particular lengths to please her lover, though she was also careful to watch the clock. Afterward, while Gwen was in the shower, she switched on the TV to a rerun of *Mom & Meg*. Tonight's episode, luckily, wasn't one of the best.

"You ever watch this, Gwennie?" Nikki inquired, when Gwen reappeared in a robe. "I used to like it a lot but I haven't seen it lately."

Neither had Gwen. She rarely watched anything but the soaps.

Nikki slipped her arm around Gwen's shoulder, snuggling close. At the halfway mark, Nikki yawned. "It's becoming awfully boring. Same old stuff. A crime is committed, for some reason the cops can't make any progress. Then Mom & Meg get on the job, one or the other of them is in danger, et cetera. Like they need something new to beef up the series. I'll bet you could think of wonderful ideas, couldn't you, Gwennie?"

Gwen lit a cigarette. "Probably."

While the commercials were on, Nikki could practically hear Gwen exercising her brain, and she smiled to herself. She had gathered early on that Gwen was horribly sensitive about her age and went to great lengths to compensate for it—which meant trying to live up to Nikki's expectations.

"I'll bet I know how this episode is going to end," Nikki said, venturing a guess that was deliberately way off.

Gwen looked doubtful. "I don't think so, love."

When Gwen turned out to be closer to the mark, Nikki praised her and speculated that Gwen could outplot any other writer.

And as she had hoped, Gwen took up the challenge. "If it hasn't been done, something might happen to Mom or Meg that could threaten the partnership. A serious illness, say. Maybe Mom needs an operation, that kind of thing, just as a change of pace—no, not Mom, Meg. That would be better, more unexpected."

Nikki nonchalantly probed for details; Gwen unsuspectingly gave them to her.

Later, Nikki initiated another bout of lovemaking. She knew that Gwen sometimes held back for fear of offending her, but now the older woman loved it when Nikki was the one overcome by passion.

Nikki sensed that Gwen was feeling more intimate than usual tonight, and during their pillow talk she gently probed to find out about Gwen's initiation into lesbianism.

"Ironically, Bobby, my ex, started me off in that direction."

Gwen had had the usual schoolgirl crushes on her women teachers but it had never occurred to her that she could be homosexual. Indeed, it wasn't a subject she knew much about. When it came to sex she had been a late developer. She hadn't really dated until college, and Bobby had been her second or third lover. Handsome, dashing, and very popular, he had been noted for his womanizing, so Gwen had been greatly flattered that he had not only picked her out, but also proposed marriage. Actually, he had knocked her up—purposely, she realized much later. He had been disappointed to learn that her family's wealth was less than he had supposed. In any case, he had continued to have affairs. Gwen hadn't been jealous. Sex with her husband was more of a duty than a pleasure.

Gwen lit a cigarette. "About ten years into the marriage it really began to bug him that I was so indifferent to something that meant so much to him. He fancied himself a great lover, so what was wrong with me? He gave me alcohol, pot, coke. I used to get pretty high but I never wanted sex."

One night he brought home a pretty young redheaded girl he worked with. The three of them had dinner, drinking wine and snorting cocaine. For the first time Gwen felt stirrings of sexuality and allowed herself to be involved in a threesome. The girl was bisexual and she knew just how to get Gwen going.

"It was a shock, I can tell you," Gwen said huskily. "I suddenly realized what I was, and so did Bobby."

"He must have been furious," Nikki mused. "Lots of guys think the opposite is true. That if they could somehow put their big cocks between two dykes, as they would say, both women would turn on to them."

"Yes. Bobby certainly thought that and he freaked out when the truth hit him. He went straight to Reno and then moved to Boulder. I didn't try to stop him. And I managed without child support. I was too afraid he would fight me in court. That was about fifteen years ago, and I'd certainly have lost my children."

"Do they know you're gay?"

Gwen shrugged. "Liz may suspect but she's never asked. And Perry is oblivious of everything but his own concerns. Just as well. Talking about stuff like this isn't easy for me."

"I'm glad you told me," Nikki whispered, kissing Gwen and snuggling next to her. "Wasn't your sister a redhead?" she asked a few minutes later.

Gwen immediately stiffened. "No, not really. Her hair was more of a strawberry blond. She was a beauty, a lot younger than me. I was in college when she first got sick, and I didn't know. She wanted to be a pianist." Gwen paused and swallowed. "It's really too painful to talk about it, if you don't mind, love."

"Of course not, Gwennie." Nikki kissed her good night and rolled over, reflecting that the woman's obsession with young redheads was some sort of twisted way of coping with the death of her sister. But it had worked to Nikki's advantage. She had played it exactly right, she thought, satisfied with herself.

What Gwen would remember about tonight was confiding her secrets, not being tricked into providing an idea for *Mom & Meg*.

"Diana," Molly exclaimed, bursting into her partner's office, "I was right about Nikki. Her script is hopeless."

Diana, immersed in her own script for *Pete Winston*, looked up foggily.

"You remember Nikki's idea, surely. God knows you twisted my arm to let her write it. Meg isn't feeling well, won't see a doctor. When he does, it turns out to be a tumor."

"Oh, yes, of course. It was a terrific idea—"

"Sure. But at the time, I suggested buying it and getting someone else to write it. Remember, I bet you all my assets in one lump sum that your tin-eared wonder wouldn't come up with one speakable line of dialogue? Well, I was right. It's the pits."

"Be kind, Molly, be kind. Give the kid a break. She's trying so hard—"

"A for effort, F for talent."

"Okay, let me have the script. I'll go over it with her."

Molly plopped it on her desk. "I really don't know why you bother."

After Molly left, Diana skimmed through it. The idea was super, no doubt about it, with tension generated to wire-tautness. Mom always joked about her health, about getting older, but Meg was only in her twenties. For her to have a possible life-threatening illness had never occurred to either of them. In Nikki's script, Mom stretched herself to do both of their jobs on a tough case, running back and forth to the hospital, and not until a few seconds before the penultimate commercial break did the viewer learn that the tumor was benign.

It was really a departure, a chance to show Mom & Meg falling into old roles of mother and child. What really excited Diana was that Nikki hadn't missed a moment of the tension, and the relationship between the two women had been dealt with head-on.

However, Molly had been absolutely right about the dialogue, and Diana thought of running the script through her typewriter, but knew that wouldn't be fair. She spent hours that evening going over the script with Nikki, while they nibbled Chinese takeout food.

"Oh, I see what you mean," Nikki kept saying. "Yes, that's much better." She sounded sincere and willing to learn; Diana fervently hoped something was finally penetrating.

When they left at ten-thirty, Nikki asked Diana if she would be willing to persuade Molly to let her be co-executive producer on her own script. Diana promised to try.

"Oh, thank you for everything," Nikki cried, throwing her arms around Diana and hugging her.

As Diana walked home she shivered in her light jacket. There was a nip in the air, a preview of autumn. It was the weather she associated with her birthday. I'm going to be twenty-nine tomorrow, she thought. She smiled, trying to remember a time when an upcoming birthday had been a pleasant prospect.

She turned on a warm shower as soon as she walked in the door. Luke would be home by eleven-thirty.

In the living room Diana ran her Betamax to check out an FAB sitcom pilot. It didn't compare with *Pete Winston*. She knew her series would be a smash if it was aired in prime time. But even if Matthew was willing—and a spot became available—Phil and the program board would have to agree.

Diana had met Phil only briefly. An attractive gray-haired man in his late fifties, he had been pleasant, even courtly, and quite pleased by the reception of the pilot. How smart Matthew had been to suggest airing it on a Monday in August. A rainy Monday, as it turned out, so more people were at home. And even though the series was slotted in on Wednesday at seven—a bit too early—in the three weeks it had been airing, its share of the audience had picked up to a twenty-seven. She was convinced that at eight it would do much better. That was early enough to keep the children and late enough to pull in their parents.

When the bell rang at midnight she was startled. Had Luke forgotten his key?

It was Luke. Dressed in full western regalia, with boots, a fringe suede jacket, and a broad-brimmed Stetson, he was delivering a singing telegram, and the message was "Happy birthday, dear Diana, happy birthday to you."

Inside the door Luke began to do a slow dance, moving his shoulders and hips slowly and seductively, removing his jacket, string tie, western shirt, and suede pants. "I thought you might want a little special something on your birthday, ma'am."

Diana watched his magnificent muscles rippling as he worked his body out of his pants. Underneath he wore the merest loin covering, held up by a G-string. God, if he hadn't once been a male stripper, he certainly knew how to fake it. She found his performance particularly arousing because he was still wearing his hat and his boots, making him look familiar, yet like a very sexy stranger.

He did bumps and grinds, then whirled and let her see him from behind, the buttocks completely bare and terribly tempting. He faced her again, smiling that irresistible smile, challenging her to discover what was beneath his flimsy covering, drawing closer. She leaned forward and slid her fingertips over his shoulders and pectorals in a gossamer touch, then moved them down to his lean belly and thighs. He retreated slightly and turned his back, drawing away as she reached for him, teasing her.

She stood up and untied her terry robe, letting it fall to her feet. She was nude, and she stepped up behind him and pushed her breasts into his back and rotated them. He moved forward and stopped, and again she grazed him with her taut nipples.

In this way they inched from the living room into the bedroom. As Diana pushed him forward onto the bed, his hat fell to the floor. Slowly she turned him over and knelt to remove one boot, then the other, while her breasts caressed his thighs.

He was growing large underneath the loin covering. "Well, now, ma'am, I've just about finished delivering my telegram, but if you want a little more—"

"I want a lot more," she whispered, whipping away the G-string.

Luke continued to play the reluctant stranger, while Diana took the role of the experienced woman crazed with desire for him. The lovemaking was exquisite.

Afterward, Luke produced a bottle of champagne and two glasses.

Diana was so delighted. "How did you know it was my birthday?"

He smiled and winked. "Oh, we have our sources, ma'am."

Diana fell asleep locked in his arms, brimming with love for him.

She awoke to find a pile of gift-wrapped boxes all around her. Feeling stupidly teary, she admired the beautiful wrappings.

Luke appeared with coffee and croissants. "Aren't you going to open them?"

"They're so splendid I don't see how," she murmured, smiling radiantly at him, and letting him persuade her. The boxes were from Bendel's and each contained a Scottish cashmere sweater, a dozen in all—crewneck, V-neck, turtleneck, cardigans and slipovers, in beautiful colors for mixing and matching.

"You told me you needed a new cashmere sweater," he explained, "and every one the gal showed me I knew would look terrific on you so I bought one of each."

"Oh, Luke, I do love you," Diana cried, kissing him.

But that wasn't all. He produced a small, exquisitely wrapped box from Cartier, and as she undid it, her fingers trembling, her heart pounding, she couldn't help visualizing a diamond.

It turned out to be two diamonds—stud earrings, and very beautiful. She would wear them proudly.

When she got to the office she found a huge bouquet of roses from Luke, and on her desk were gifts from Hilary (a lovely china coffee mug), Nikki (French soaps), and Molly (a Saint Laurent wide belt in white leather and brass).

"I feel like a kid," Diana said as she thanked everyone. "I haven't had this many presents since my sixteenth birthday party, too many years ago."

She put the belt on the lime-green cashmere sweater she was wearing over a white wool skirt and it looked stunning.

Just then she had a phone call from Matthew in L. A. to say that *Flanagan's Army* was being shifted, which would leave an opening at eight on Thursday. Continental was going to give *Pete Winston* a try in that spot.

Diana was thrilled. "Thanks, Matthew, I really appreciate it. Yes, lunch next week. Wonderful."

Diana hung up and told Molly the good news. "Not only that, they want nine more episodes, so we'll have a full season."

"All right!" The two women hugged. "Let's have lunch," Molly said. "It can't be long but it sure can be liquid. I've got to drink to this."

They ate at a little French place and grinned idiotically at each other over a bottle of wine.

"I never thought we'd make it, even though we've been doing much better than Flanagan's Shenanigans."

"Well, I did. Have to have faith, Molly. It's also a question of program flow. Matthew didn't say so but I think they're afraid of bad ratings for *Turning Tides* at eight-thirty. That soap, I gathered from Jill, is Bannon's special baby. With *Pete Winston* as lead-in, *Turning Tides* will have a chance. Matthew couldn't have given me a better birthday present. I can't wait to tell Luke."

She did that night, over dinner at Windows on the World, at the top of the World Trade Center.

Luke shut his eyes for a moment, saying, "Thank you, Lord. And thank you, sweetheart."

Diana was practically floating on a cloud. She had lived for this moment—fantastic career and a wonderful love, the two held together by a glorious man. Every woman in the place envied her.

After dinner, Luke took her to the adjoining lounge. As soon as they sat down, the trio played a cool jazz version of "Happy Birthday," smiling in their direction, and Diana knew that Luke had arranged it.

"Luke, I love you forever," she murmured, holding both his hands, while his eyes beamed love at her. After a while, the jazz trio left and a combo took over, playing dance music. Diana and Luke danced to the slow music until closing time.

The limo was waiting to take them home but they couldn't wait until they got there. Under the cover of darkness, and shielded from the driver by the curtained window, they made love.

Diana rated her twenty-ninth birthday as the happiest day of her life.

13 "Phil, oh, Phil, it's so marvelous to see you," Gemma Lopez shouted, throwing her arms around Phil Bannon's neck. He was in New York for the Christmas party Continental was throwing for the cast and crew of *Pete Winston* in the executive banquet room of their penthouse.

Matthew, clutching his glass of Scotch, was wishing he were elsewhere. Gemma's famous throaty laugh rose insistently above the din.

Phil Bannon—tall, urbane, charming, dressed for New York in a three-piece pinstripe with a carnation in his buttonhole and a cigar in his mouth—was seeing to it that the half-dozen execs from the Coast were meeting and mingling with all the guests of honor: Luke and Gemma, Diana and Molly, the directors, scenic and costume designers, and the three children of the show. The kids were a little overexcited, and their parents followed them around and tried to keep them from overeating the goodies or wrecking the joint.

Gemma's laugh kept resounding, and Matthew cringed as he watched the actress behaving as if she were the star attraction tonight, as if it were primarily her doing that *Pete Winston* had become one of the top ten shows on prime time over the last two months.

Her performance had helped, of course, but it was undeniably Luke Merriman who had catapulted to stardom. In an incredibly short time the actor had amassed a loyal following. And the network's publicity department hadn't missed a beat. From the first airing of *Pete Winston* on prime time, when the show attracted an amazing thirty percent of the audience, Luke had been interviewed on all of Continental's talk shows and written up in newspapers and magazines. Ads had appeared in papers nationwide and on buses and billboards.

Gemma got some of the attention, of course, but she was clearly second to Luke. Matthew thought she was probably aware of it and that was why she was acting like number one, as if pretending would make it so.

Luke certainly wasn't competing for the spotlight by sounding off, but then he didn't have to make a big noise. Casually but expensively dressed in Italian gray slacks, black blazer, and a white silk shirt, he was lighting up the entire room with that dazzling smile of his.

Matthew finished his drink and observed Luke at the crowded bar. He was talking to some young thing, probably a production assistant, who was hanging on his every utterance.

Both Jill and the p.a. were served their drinks at the same time, and almost as if it had been rehearsed, each woman turned and offered her drink to Luke.

Matthew had a feeling of desolation as he watched the actor diplomatically take each offering and say, with a certain show of wit, "Thank you kindly, ladies, I sure have a thirst tonight."

"I don't believe this," Molly murmured at Matthew's ear. "You'd think Jill would know better than to confuse the actor with his role."

Matthew smiled wryly. "You'd think so. Well, it must be true that blonds have more fun."

Molly howled, and he was pleased to find one female who wasn't taken in by Luke.

"I've tried to warn Diana," Molly said in a burst of confidence, "but she's blissfully oblivious." As if suddenly realizing she was talking out of turn, Molly hastened to change the subject.

While Matthew listened to her, he reflected that he liked Molly quite a bit. She came on tough sometimes but he respected her honesty and loyalty.

After another drink, Matthew forced himself to circulate, make introductions, and see to it that nobody was being neglected.

He tried not to keep staring at Diana, though it was hard to avoid. She was absolutely stunning this evening—

one of the few women Matthew could think of who looked better in casual clothes than in glitter. She was wearing a long pale aqua cashmere sweater over a slightly darker-hued skirt, slim and long, with buttons down the side. Did Luke really appreciate her? Could a man like Luke really care for anyone? It must have been hard to live up to the Pete Winston who spoke the sharp, comedic lines that Diana wrote for him. Although Molly and others also wrote scripts, Matthew was pretty sure that most of the humor was Diana's.

He had seen it first-hand at rehearsals. She would sit on the sidelines, scanning the script, watching how it played, and then she would replace a word here, a phrase there, with such comic precision that the actor, the director, or even the original writer rarely had grounds to argue with it.

"Hi, Matthew. We've met a couple of times. I'm Nikki De Paul," the young woman said, pumping his hand.

"Yes, I remember you, Nikki. How're you doing?"

It was only a polite question but she insisted upon telling him in detail, launching into a discussion of how wonderful it was that *Pete Winston* had become such a hit. She had predicted it, of course, from the moment Luke had set foot in the office. She was hoping to write for the show herself but was at the moment producing her own script for *Mom & Meg*. . . .

Why is she telling me all this? Matthew wondered as he studied her curiously. She was certainly very pretty, with regular features and lovely coloring. And she kept smiling provocatively as she talked, yet he wasn't fooled into thinking she had a genuine interest in him as a man. No, she was just another ambitious supplier trying to make a useful connection with a buyer, nothing more. Matthew had met dozens of this type in L.A., though usually at the other end of the camera. This one called herself a writer/producer, but from the banality of her conversation he doubted that she was anything special.

When Dick Mann, of programming, interrupted, Nikki wandered away. Matthew listened impatiently to Dick for a moment. The guy was competent enough, but as soon as he downed a couple of drinks he became whiney and argumentative. Matthew wasn't in the mood for nitpicking.

"Why don't you write me a memo, Dick," he suggested, excusing himself to go to the men's room.

The trip wasn't strictly necessary but it did give him a breather from the crowds. He had once liked parties, but now they reminded him of Lorrie, of the way she would circulate, holding her head a certain way, and the look in her eyes, especially when she was talking to some attractive young man.

Matthew became aware that Luke had stepped up to the adjoining urinal.

"Hey, Matthew."

"Luke," Matthew acknowledged. He turned his head away quickly, resisting a terrible urge to compare himself with the actor. He didn't want to imagine him with Diana, holding her, making love to her.

As the two men rinsed their hands, Luke grinned at him in the mirror. "I thank you kindly for this shindig."

"You're welcome. I take it you're enjoying being a star," Matthew replied, trying to keep the irony from his tone.

"I sure am. It beats being a nobody. But you know, I can hardly believe it's me everyone's fussing over. Funny. Back in Oregon I was just another country boy, about as common as flies around the garbage. Here I'm still a country boy, only you spell it capital C and B and you pay me big bucks to be myself. I love it but I reckon I still can't get over it."

Matthew flicked his dripping fingers over the sink. The paper-towel holder was empty.

Luke, following his eyes, hardly had to reach up for the stack of paper towels on the holder.

"Thanks," Matthew mumbled, self-conscious about being a few inches shorter.

Luke held out his hand. "I don't know if I ever thanked you proper, Matthew, for giving me this chance."

Matthew shook his hand briefly, feeling embarrassed.

"You know, when I first acted in the pilot, I thought, hell, this is going to be easy. I didn't realize what a full season meant. I reckon it's the hardest work I've ever done. Not physical but mental. You know, memorizing, and standing around. Of course it's worth it, but I'm sure looking forward to taking a break—"

"Have a good one, Luke," Matthew said, patting his arm as they rejoined the party. "Excuse me, there's someone I must say hello to."

Matthew felt irritable. He knew damn well that Luke and Diana were going to L.A. for a few days. Phil was going to fete them out there. Matthew disliked himself for not being able to accept Luke and Diana, but he wasn't going to make a pal of Luke when that was the way he felt. He was fair and businesslike, but that was where it had to end.

Phil suddenly grabbed his arm. "Why the long face, Matt? This isn't a wake, it's a celebration."

Matthew roused himself. "So it is, Phil, and I'm having a whale of a time," he said, forcing a smile and smacking his boss on the shoulder.

"Good, good," Phil said, moving on,

Matthew could have kicked him. After having busted his chops and trying to pull out of *Pete Winston* initially, Phil was acting as if he himself were the force behind the show. Phil never admitted a mistake and always presented himself to the best advantage. He was a chameleon in his dress as well as his manner. In L.A. he wore flowered shirts and affected a laid-back delivery; in New York, it was pin stripes and clipped yuppy talk. If Matthew was right about something, Phil took the credit. If he turned out to be wrong, Phil crucified him.

Right now Phil was floating amid the angels because *Pete Winston* was this season's miracle. Continental had nudged out FAB for second place in the prime-time ratings, and *Pete Winston* was the principal reason. Not only had it garnered critical as well as popular praise, but it had proved a successful lead-in to *Turning Tides*, which was getting a bigger audience than it deserved although it was as trashy as any other soap.

"I hope you're feeling happier than you look, Matthew," Diana said, coming up to talk to him. "This is your triumph as much as anyone's. I remember another party where this whole thing began."

He remembered too—remembered having turned down her dinner invitation that night because his daughter was waiting for him. "I'm not much of a party person, Diana, so don't feel you have to cheer me up. This is about as cheerful as I get."

"Good God, that's terrible. There must be something I can do." She sounded a bit high from drinking, and altogether charming.

With a mischievous grin she snatched a canapé off a tray and held it out to him. "It's not quite quiche but it looks interesting. Can I tempt you?"

You can, you can, he thought glumly, and as she was still holding out the canapé invitingly, he leaned over and bit off a piece, making her laugh.

"Just be careful not to bite the hand that feeds you."

"Why not? It probably tastes better than this."

"You may be right; this isn't wonderful," she agreed, nibbling a bit of the remains. "What in the world is it?"

"I haven't a clue. Tastes very veggie. A yup-veg probably concocted by our esteemed research department. Where, oh, where are the cocktail franks of yesteryear?"

She grinned. "Probably en route to the third world, which gets all the stuff we think is bad for us. Oh, I meant to ask you for your favorite eateries in L.A. Luke and I are going out there for a few days—"

"Hey, babe, calling me?" Luke asked, moving up beside her.

"As always, right on cue." Diana linked her arm in his before turning back to Matthew. "Of course we'll eat at the Polo Lounge and Chasen's and Morton's, probably. Where else?"

"You mustn't miss the Taco Bell," Matthew replied with a straight face.

'Hey, that's a Mex chain, isn't it?" Luke asked. "I think I tried it a couple of times but it was pretty ordinary—"

"Matthew's only joking," Diana interrupted, looking at him resentfully.

"Un-huh," Luke replied with good humor and a shrug. "Well, what did I know way back then?"

Matthew took another swallow of his drink. This was his fourth Scotch on an empty stomach, but he felt as sober as a funeral director.

I wish I could get the hell out of here, he thought. But he couldn't yet. He was supposed to be co-hosting this "shindig."

Fortunately, Jill came up then to ask him something, and he was spared more Diana-and-Luke chitchat.

A while later, however, Matthew regretted his response to Diana, and taking out a few white index cards—he called them "idea cards" and always carried some with him—he jotted down some restaurant names and a sentence or two of description.

The moment he caught Diana by herself he approached and handed the cards to her. "Sorry for being so flippant. These are the places to be at the moment, and bon appetit."

He walked away quickly, her thanks making him feel guilty because he wasn't being entirely altruistic. He knew that if she referred to his notes at least she'd be thinking about him.

When Diana and Luke left, Matthew began to relax. At least he no longer found himself looking around for her, compelled to know exactly where in the room she was standing at every moment.

He observed that Gemma was delighted to be number one at last—even though it was only during the tail end of the party. Luke's departure, it seemed, had hastened everyone else's.

Matthew was certainly glad to turn in his glass. He had actually managed to advance from sobriety to hangover without ever having gotten high.

Diana felt a particular pleasure in coming back to L.A. more successful than when she had left it. No more boarding in creaky-floored attics of widows' houses or eating in cheap diners or getting around town in an old heap.

Diana and Luke were staying in a two-room suite Phil kept for visitors at the Beverly Wilshire, and he provided them with a car and driver.

The first thing they did was to shop on Rodeo Drive.

"That's ro-*day*-o, not *ro*-de-o," Diana corrected. "It's the most concentrated selection of expensive boutiques in the world, I think."

Luke, browsing through shirts, couldn't find any price tag.

"If you have to ask, you can't afford it, so just hand them your American Express card."

"Yes, ma'am." He grinned.

She taught him the difference between pastels in polyester and in these shimmering gossamer wools, Irish linens, and Egyptian cotton, pointing out the ingenious designs, the careful hand-finishing.

Luke purchased a suit, slacks, jackets, and shirts, then helped her pick out shirts, skirts, and dresses. They kept whispering to one another as they paid, "It's only plastic."

With their new wardrobes, they certainly looked like VIPs, and one hour in the sun near the hotel's swimming pool took away the worst of Diana's winter pallor.

They toured Continental's offices and studios and were introduced to everyone of importance at endless meetings, many of them in restaurants. Phil gave them breakfast at the Polo Lounge, where executives in jogging gear were already making deals before going off for their morning run, and of course there was dinner at Chasen's. It was big and sprawling, and Phil seemed to know every other diner. Table-hopping was a necessity, and so was ordering hobo steak—not on the menu—which was pan-fried at the table.

They didn't have too much time to themselves but they managed to snatch an hour here and there so they could see some of Hollywood's tourist sights. They scrutinized old time stars' footprints and handprints in the court of what used to be Grauman's Chinese Theater, pored over memorabilia of Old Hollywood in the Larry Edmunds shop, and admired the eclectic architecture of the Golden Age—Spanish, Tudor, art deco—among other buildings that still remained on Hollywood Boulevard.

Diana chose places for meals according to Matthew's scribbles. They ate lunch in the Ivy even though he had dubbed it "An adobe showplace, everything grilled on mesquite, if you like that kind of thing."

Diana did, and flashed Matthew's card at Luke. He made a face. "So he came through after all. The guy simply doesn't cotton to me, for some reason."

Diana, knew that was true, but dismissed it, characterizing Matthew as a man of private sorrows.

Matthew had noted all the chic places even if he didn't think much of them, and when Diana was out with Phil and company, she would glance at Matthew's notes in the ladies' room, amused to find his comments apt. About Spago he wrote, "A pizza joint for celebrities jaded by the real thing but craving pizza quacking with duck sausage or wild mushrooms still atwitch."

She found his slightly jaundiced comments a refreshing antidote to all the extravagant adjectives that natives out here applied to everything and everyone.

"This is Hollywood, Luke, not to be taken literally or even seriously. 'I love you' can mean 'You're not too bad.' "

They were at Spago waiting for Phil and his guests.

Luke laughed and looked into Diana's eyes. "When I say I love you I mean I adore you," he finished in an intimate tone that caused her to brush her knee against his and smile back at him intently. "I'll get you later."

"I reckon you will, if I don't get you first."

Diana found it remarkable that after all these months they were still so hot for one another. No matter where they went, whom they met, what they did, there was always the arousing thought that they would return to their suite and fall upon each other as if they hadn't made love only the previous day—or even that afternoon.

"The chambermaids must think we're bonkers," Luke said after one of their bouts, when their king-size bed looked as if it had hosted a sheik and his harem.

"We are bonkers, about each other," Diana answered.

Molly phoned her as their trip was drawing to a close. "I'm glad you're having fun, kid, but I'm even more glad you're coming back. Christmas was the usual. The weather was miserable, and so was I, having to watch Nikki putting on airs and making herself generally obnoxious."

Diana's spirits fell. She had been trying to convince Molly to let Nikki remain as executive co-producer on *Mom & Meg* but saw that it simply wasn't going to happen.

"Do me a favor," Molly continued. "Let Nikki co-produce *Pete Winston* if you're so enamored of her. I just can't put up with her anymore."

"All right." Diana sighed. "I think she's better on *Mom & Meg*, but I can't force her on you."

"Good. So much for business. How's pleasure? You two living it up royally?"

"And how." Diana filled her in. Luke was in the shower, so she could be blunt.

"Sounds as if between you and Phil you've planned every second down to the last detail. Doesn't Luke ever want to do something his own way?"

"I don't know what you mean. I don't force him to do anything. I make suggestions. After all, I know this town and he doesn't. Anyway, the reason we're together is that we like the same things."

"Mm-hm. Except he doesn't know what to like until you tell him."

"So what? He's learning, like any intelligent Frankenstein's monster," Diana joked.

"Just remember," Molly cautioned, "that the monster got away from Frankenstein. Sooner or later Luke is going to have a mind of his own."

Molly was just sounding off, feeling forlorn, as she generally did during holidays, because her married guy had very little time for her.

As Diana hung up, Luke walked out of the bathroom in a towel that looked like a made-to-order toga for an Olympian god.

"Come here," she demanded, beckoning.

His smile was even brighter than the California sunshine. "Aren't we due at a shindig round about now?"

"Yes, right here in bed. Phil's shindig can wait."

And wait it did. Diana and Luke made a fashionably late entrance to the final blowout being given in their honor, and it was a lulu. The party was held at Phil's elaborate mansion in Bel Air, and there were crowds of guests milling around, indoors and out, and there was food and drink everywhere.

As soon as Diana and Luke stepped from the car, Phil grabbed them and pushed champagne tulips into their hands. They were led here and there, introduced to hundreds of people, or so it seemed to Diana, and pressed to try the smoked salmon, the sushi, the chilled shrimp, the hot chili.

Diana knew she and Luke would be separated within a matter of moments, and of course she was right. Every gorgeous star and starlet within hailing distance was there trying to get close to Luke.

Hollywood was infinitely worse than New York as far as hype was concerned. The mere fact that Phil had flown

Luke out here and was throwing this bash was enough to convince people how important the new star was.

Diana recognized all the elements of a successful Hollywood party. It had been organized by a large public-relations firm with thirty years' experience in party-giving. The gimmick for this one, she could see, was "launching the hottest new TV star in Hollywood," and launched he was. They did everything but crack a bottle of champagne against his ribs.

She was relieved to linger in the shadows and observe the spectacle, never having cared for the limelight, and since she wasn't recognizable as the writer/producer, people left her alone. She did have a few bad moments when she became trapped into an inane conversation with a couple of the "dress extras"—people invited to help the hosts get over the embarrassing early period before the real guests turned up. Diana thought the extras had overstayed, since the place now resembled a zoo. But the animals were the most important in the kingdom: at least a dozen famous TV actors and actresses, as well as top producers and directors, plus several influential journalists were in attendance.

Luke was the perfect guest of honor. He looked magnificent and smiled with a brilliance that eclipsed other carefully cultivated smiles. He didn't say much, but whatever he said seemed to be appropriate because it drew cascades of appreciative (mostly feminine) laughter.

As she looked at him, Diana reveled in the knowledge that all this was her doing. Luke was her creation, and no creator had ever been more proud or more in love.

What did it matter that all the women out here were super glamorous and flawless, stunningly dressed, permanently tanned? After all the smoke and Giorgio perfume had cleared, Luke would be going home with Diana, and it would be in Diana's arms that he would sleep all night long.

II

14 The call from East Hampton came at seven-thirty on a Thursday morning, waking Diana moments before the alarm.

"Oh, no," she groaned. "Yes, I see. I'll be there as soon as I can. And thanks for everything, Joe."

Diana turned to Luke, lying motionless beside her. "Luke, wake up," she murmured, leaning over to kiss his temple. "Please, darling, I have to talk to you."

He didn't budge, apparently in a deep sleep.

Diana felt a touch of annoyance, wondering how late he had stayed at the Odeon restaurant the previous evening. She had left at midnight, quite exhausted. It was impossible for her to stay up half the night and be able to get to the studio to do a day's work.

In fact, it wasn't easy for Luke, either, and most mornings she had to prod him to get out of bed.

"Luke. . . ." She raised her voice close to his ear, making him jump. "I'm sorry but you have to wake up."

"Mm," he groaned, rolling over onto his back. "Whatsa matter?"

"A pipe's burst in the house, and it's a mess. I have to go out there to clean it up and supervise the repairs."

She got out of bed, threw on some warm clothes, and phoned Nikki to tell her she'd have to take over rehearsal today. Although Nikki assured her she'd be fine, Diana also called Molly and asked if she could possibly look in on the set. Molly, busy with rehearsal for *Mom & Meg*, said she'd try but was caustic about Nikki's value as a co-producer if she couldn't take over on her own.

Diana, seeing that Molly had a point, didn't respond.

She certainly wanted to trust Nikki but she kept feeling it was too soon.

Luke was lying just as she had left him, although it was after eight. She set the alarm again and moved the clock across the room. "I'll call you later," she told him on her way out, doubting he could hear her.

She couldn't recall another February quite this cold, and driving on the icy streets was hazardous. The wind kept whipping around the car, making an ominous whining sound. It would be even worse out on the island.

She drove slowly, carefully, with the radio on, glad that she was moving against the traffic coming into the city. At the same time, she felt a little strange and out of synch. She had been feeling that way since they had returned from L.A.

Production on the series was under way for the spring season, and it was a tough schedule. But what was really bothering Diana was Luke.

It began with invitations for them to dinner parties and charity balls all over town. At first Diana was pleased to be a part of the VIP scene in New York and mingle with novelists and theater people, clothing designers and architects, rock stars and restaurateurs, preppies and punks. It was fun to stay out almost all night at a party or a restaurant. The cold, gray days were so short and gloomy anyway, she was content to stay in Saturdays and Sundays with Luke, alternating sleeping with lovemaking.

But after a few weeks that routine began to bore her. There was a lot of eating and drinking and dancing but not much connection or memorable conversation. Besides, she couldn't take the physical strain of so little sleep, especially on top of too many exotic meals and alcohol to get her drunk, then coffee to sober her up, followed by a tranquilizer to get her calm enough to sleep. She wasn't meant for that kind of treadmill, and with their production schedule it was impossible.

But Luke had not had his fill; on the contrary, he seemed to want more and more. Diana could understand it, of course. From obscurity to celebrity in a few months was bound to be exciting. He would tire of it soon enough. But she worried that before it happened he might have second thoughts about being with her exclusively.

Wherever they went, women buzzed around Luke enough to turn any man's head. And to someone as young and as unused to such attention as Luke, it might prove irresistible. What mere mortal man could resist such a feminine onslaught? Diana had always been able to understand why stars found it so difficult to settle down and make one relationship work when there were hundreds of possible mates out there just waiting for a chance.

Diana was attractive, yes, but hardly extraordinary. There were women who were younger, prettier, richer, wittier, and they all seemed to be panting to get a crack at Luke. When she left a restaurant early or didn't go on to the all-night party, she wondered exactly what she might have missed. Several times recently he had rolled in at dawn and not bothered to come to bed at all, simply showering, changing, and going to work. He might be able to get away with it once in a while, but his all-night sessions were increasing, and she feared his performance would suffer.

When she brought the matter up, however, he refused to take it seriously. "Stop worrying, babe, I feel fine. Hell, I slept away my first twenty-six years. I have it all stored up. Folks sleep too much anyway. The ones that make it hardly sleep four hours a night."

"That's true for some, but others who've made it need seven or eight hours."

"Really?" he grinned. "Like who?"

"Like me," she replied, kissing him.

But behind the jocularity her anxiety persisted. He had begun to pepper his conversation with quotes from Gay (Talese) or Jerzy (Kosinski) or Yoko (Ono Lennon) or Mike (Nichols). Diana remembered Molly's warning about the monster getting away from Frankenstein. And Luke was such a gorgeous monster, too.

As she had feared, her house was a shambles. Diana had left the heat on to prevent the pipes from freezing, but a storm had knocked out the power at her house without the caretaker's being aware of it. The pipes had frozen, of course, and one of them had burst.

Joe had called a plumber, who was repairing the damaged pipe, after having drilled a hole in her living-room wall. Water had soaked her carpets and totally ruined some of her wicker furniture.

Diana hadn't been in the house ten minutes before Molly called from the studio to report that Luke hadn't yet turned up for rehearsal.

With a sinking feeling Diana fibbed that he hadn't been feeling too well that morning but she was sure he'd be there any minute.

"Wait, he's just walked in," Molly confirmed. "I don't want to be the one to chew him out, Diana, but he's held up the works for almost an hour—"

Diana had her put Luke on the phone. "Didn't the alarm ring?" she asked, trying to keep her tone even.

"It rang. Listen, I'm here now, babe, so what's the problem?"

Diana let him go but she was disturbed and a little angry. He had sounded short with her, as if she were the one who had kept the cast and crew waiting.

She spent most of the day mopping and sponging and wiping. It would be some time before things dried out, and the pervasive smell of mildew depressed her. So did the cold, the gunmetal sky, and the ocean waves, looking black with anger and crashing like cannon shot.

She went into town to replace some cleaning materials, depressed at the deserted look of East Hampton in winter. The trees were barren, the tourist shops closed, and the sidewalks and gardens encrusted with ice and snow.

Unable to find the particular things she needed, Diana drove to Sag Harbor. She had better luck at the hardware store there, and decided to pick up a few staples in the supermarket nearby.

She was just maneuvering her shopping cart around the bend in an aisle when she saw Matthew Sayles slowly pushing a cart in her direction.

He didn't see her immediately, so she had a few moments to observe him in his khaki parka and fur hat with the flaps up. He stopped to consult a shopping list and then picked several packages of toilet paper off the shelves.

Such a mundane purchase made him seem acutely human to her, and she smiled to herself, wondering who had written the shopping list and why he was here on a Thursday afternoon instead of at work.

Matthew would have walked right past her if she hadn't called out his name.

He looked stunned and then embarrassed. "Diana, good grief, I didn't recognize you. I'm so sorry. My. . . . my housekeeper's sick today. . . ."

Diana had never seen him so flustered. It was hardly her business even if he was playing hooky. "That's okay. You were busy squeezing the Charmin, and I'm not exactly the last thing in fashion," she added, realizing that she probably did look unrecognizable in her gray down jacket and a red wool hat. Self-consciously she whipped it off.

"Aha. That's the Diana I know and . . . and admire. So, do you shop here often?"

She smiled and told him what she was doing in his neck of the woods. "I'm almost finished in here. Can I buy you a cup of coffee?"

His face clouded. "Uh, ordinarily I'd be delighted, but just at the moment—"

He was interrupted by a little girl in ski pants and a white jacket running up to him holding a box of dried cereal in each hand. "Daddy, I'd like to try both of these—" She stopped, suddenly seeing Diana.

"Uh, Andy, this is Diana Sinclair, the lady in charge of the *Pete Winston* show. My daughter, Andrea."

Diana swallowed her surprise and smiled at the child. "Hi, Andrea. Nice to meet you."

"Hi," the girl said shyly, appearing uncomfortable.

She was eight or nine and looked remarkably like her father, down to the sad green eyes and unsmiling mouth.

"Do you ever watch the show?" Diana asked, to fill the awkward silence.

"Sometimes."

"I see. You don't like it too much, huh?"

Andrea made a face and shrugged. "I don't like Lola. Because she's always telling the kids what to do and acting like she likes them but she really doesn't."

"Oh, do you think so? Why doesn't she?"

"Because they're not her kids. All she wants to do is marry their Pops."

"That's a very shrewd observation, Andrea," Diana said, impressed. "Is there anything you like about the show?"

'Uh, I guess I like the kids. I mean, the way they have fun and things, even though their mother is dead and never coming back.'' Andrea suddenly looked stricken, as if identifying, and Diana could have kicked herself for asking.

At that point Matthew intervened, telling his daughter that she could try only one of the new cereals.

After adding her choice to their cart, Andrea went to return the other box as her father had requested.

"Matthew, I'm sorry if I upset her."

"No need to apologize," he assured her briskly. "Her mother is alive and living in Europe." Abruptly he changed the subject to a business matter.

Andrea returned and hung on to the cart, shifting her feet restlessly, then kicking at the cart with her boot.

"Stop that, please Andy, we'll be done in a moment."

"Well, I have to go to the bathroom," she said plaintively.

"Ah, some things just can't wait," Diana agreed, smiling at the girl. "Anyway, I have to go too. Home, I mean. Nice to have met you, Andrea."

The girl stubbornly lowered her eyes and wouldn't answer or say good-bye in spite of her father's prompting.

Diana felt a surge of warmth for Matthew, and she touched his arm in a friendly gesture. "It's all right. I'm cutting into her time with her father, and she doesn't like it. We'll talk on Monday."

She quickly wheeled her cart to the express counter and didn't look back. Her head was whirling as she rearranged her image of Matthew to include his being a single parent. Jesus, no wonder he had reacted so favorably to the series. Had his wife left him? Was that why he often looked so sad? And why was he so secretive about his daughter? Maybe, she answered her own question, to keep people from making just the assumptions she had made.

One thing Diana had seen during the brief contact was that father and daughter were very closely and lovingly attached. Andrea didn't like Lola. By extension, she probably didn't care for any real-life woman she thought might be after her father.

The plumber was finished by the time Diana got home. With dry wood she was able to light a fire and take some of the dampness out of the house.

After eating a sandwich she drove back to the city and went straight to bed. That long drive always took it out of her, especially having to be so careful on a slippery road. Luke had an acting class and wouldn't be in until at least eleven.

Although she fell asleep quite quickly, she awakened to find that it was almost three and Luke wasn't yet home. She thought of calling some of his hangouts around town and immediately rejected it. She didn't want to give him the idea she was checking up on him. She was being ridiculous. She knew that he loved her. He told her so often, and the way they made love proved it.

But doubt nagged at her all the same. The one day she hadn't been at rehearsal he had come late, had been terse on the phone, and now he still wasn't home.

Stop being so silly and possessive and suspicious, she told herself. These feelings were new to her, and she didn't like herself in this role. What was the matter with her anyway? Just because he was out late didn't mean he was with another woman.

Diana heard the key in the lock and all her anxiety evaporated. As soon as Luke walked into the foyer she was in his arms.

"Hey, babe I thought you'd be fast asleep by now." He pecked her on the lips and moved back immediately to take off his coat.

"I'll bet I know where you ate tonight," she said, forcing gaiety. "An Italian, Mexican, or Chinese joint, right? You absolutely reek of garlic."

"Oh, sorry." He seemed tired as he hung up his coat.

"Well, which was it?"

"Which was what?" He was irritable and a little drunk. "Listen, let me take a quick shower, okay?"

Diana was having difficulty catching her breath. He was so cool, so distant. Wasn't that the first sign that a lover was straying? Isn't that the way she would write it into a script?

She had to be very careful. Now wasn't the time to talk about anything. Let him have his shower (was he washing away traces of another woman?) and then just enfold him in her arms.

Although Luke had brushed his teeth and used mouthwash, the garlic odor was still pungent and a little sickening, but she ignored it. She kissed and fondled him, feeling suddenly very aroused.

He apologized for not being responsive. "It was a murderous day, babe. Molly was bitchy from the word go. Just because I was a few minutes late."

"Do you want to talk about it?"

Luke sighed. "Not really, but maybe we'd better. 'Cause we won't have a chance in the morning. I mean, Molly is hardly ever there and yet she just barreled in and took over, especially when Sid had a tiff with Emily about the kids in the second scene. . . ."

As she listened, Diana began to feel much better. This was reality, this she could deal with. The director and stage manager had had a dispute, and Nikki had been trying to mediate when Molly had stepped in and made the decision.

"Molly was right," Diana told Luke. "Producer has to exercise control."

"But what about the director? Doesn't he get any say?"

"Not over the producer," Diana patiently explained, though she knew they'd had this conversation several times before. Luke had difficulty understanding that a TV director was mostly a technical person, different from a movie director, who assembled the film in the cutting room afterward. It was the producer who planned TV camera setups and the shot sequences before the taping even began. TV was a writer's and producer's medium; the director was secondary. Diana gathered that Nikki had been trying to please everyone, and she felt disappointed in her assistant. Producers didn't win popularity contests, they got the job done. Nikki should have known that by now, and Diana was sorry Molly had had to be the one to step in. She could almost hear her partner telling her, "Nikki stinks. Dump her."

"I sure am tired, babe," Luke said in Diana's ear.

"Let's go to sleep." Diana curled up in his arms.

"G'night, babe. Love ya."

"MM. Me too." As she was drifting off, she realized he had never told her what had kept him out so late. She would find out tomorrow. He was here, and he loved her. That was all that mattered.

* * *

"Luke, wake up, darling," he heard in his ear.

"Mm. Soon, soon, stop nagging, will you?" He rolled over to the other side of the bed.

His head felt like a balloon from too much vodka. He had to watch the way that stuff crept up on him. One minute he felt terrific and the next he had a thick head.

Diana stirred in the room. He had to get up, put on coffee, heat that damn croissant—shit, enough of that. He couldn't wait on her forever. He was done with being a waiter; he was an actor now.

He had just drifted into a lovely dream when he felt his shoulder being shaken. "Luke, please. It's almost eight-thirty. I've made the coffee."

Big fucking deal. She sounded like a martyr when all she had done was press a couple of buttons in the machine. She had heated the croissants, too, and the smell was making him sick.

"Today's going to be rough, darling, unless we get an early start." She had such a sweet voice. If only she'd stop badgering him.

He made a supreme effort to roll over and open his eyes. "Yeah. Okay. Be right with you." He couldn't remember having been this tired or hung-over. He propped his head against the pillows and watched her getting dressed, while she sipped her coffee and chewed on a piece of croissant.

Seeing him awake, she smiled. "I know it's hard, darling, but try. I've brought you a couple of aspirin. Today we're taping the first show of the season and it has to be really good."

She babbled on. Luke knew that when she babbled like this she was nervous about something, and she wouldn't quit until she felt better. And he could make her feel better with very little effort.

He put his legs over the side of the bed and took a gulp of his coffee, swallowed the aspirin, then enfolded her in his arms. She felt wonderful, her soft body next to his bare skin, her fragrant hair in his nostrils. But best of all, she had finally shut up.

That was much better. He kissed her forehead and cheek, then her lips. Suddenly he was aroused.

"Oh, Luke, not now. I mean, I'd love to, but first—"

"First, ve must vork," he finished. It was a line from some play or other, maybe something from Chekhov. Whatever it was, it made her laugh and improved her mood.

He was feeling a little better too; he still couldn't eat but at least he was able to get into his clothes.

Just as they were leaving, Diana gave him a big hug. "Oh, Luke, I do love you. Let's have dinner tonight. Alone, for once."

When she looked at him with those come-hither eyes he found it hard to resist. "Yeah," he agreed, smiling his special smile, and seeing her absolutely light up. "Dinner alone, and what happens afterward is nobody's business."

The taxi driver careened through the streets like a maniac but he got them to the studio on the dot. Anyway, Molly wasn't waiting with a pinched mouth to look at him like he had taken time out to murder someone.

In fact, it was a pleasure to have Diana back. Everyone was immediately relaxed with her there. She sat on the sidelines as they went through dress rehearsal, interrupting every once in a while with a suggestion or a question. "Wouldn't it be better if. . . ?"

Luke admired her way of getting things done without ruffling feathers. Molly made you want to do the opposite simply because she was so positive, acting like nobody else knew what they were doing.

Diana was talking to Gemma. "What if you delivered the line with a smile instead of shouting it? If you get it just right, she'll know you're angry but it will also be funny. Okay, try it again. That's it, Gemma. Great."

Luke had to be prompted a couple of times—his head really wasn't on straight yet—but he managed. Then he ad-libbed in the last scene, making Diana laugh. "That's marvelous. Let's write that in," she called out to the p.a., sitting in the booth and annotating the script.

By the time they were ready for the live taping, at four, he was really into the episode. The "warm-up" man, a stand-up comic, was talking to the audience, introducing the cast to enthusiastic applause. Most of them were female tourists. They had come to see Luke, and it made him feel great.

"Okay, quiet, everyone," the stage manager called. "Here we go."

This was the best part for Luke—acting in front of an audience. Even though they were cued to laugh and applaud, he felt their genuine enthusiasm, their love, directed at him, and he always surpassed his rehearsal performance.

It took about an hour to tape twenty-two minutes. They had a rest and taped again at six-thirty. Tonight both tapings were extra-special, and everyone was delighted. Diana couldn't stop giving him the eye.

They had dinner in a quiet Italian restaurant in the West Fifties, and it was like old times, the two of them mooning over each other. Except for two little bumpy moments, first when she asked him what had kept him so late the previous night. He resented having to tell her but knew from experience that if he tried keeping it back she'd never let up. In that sweet way of hers she'd poke around until she knew where and with whom he'd been.

It seemed to Luke that women thought they owned you as soon as you told them you loved them.

He said he'd had dinner with a couple of guys at class who wanted to go dancing at Area, and he went along. No, he hadn't danced. Just had a few vodkas and enjoyed the new theme the club had devised, science fiction. He described the lunar landscape, and all the weirdos in the place fitting right in. "I thought I'd take the opportunity, babe. I know Area's not your favorite place."

"You're right, it's not. So you stayed there until almost three?"

He nodded and talked a little more about the club to avoid telling her the truth—which was that he'd gone to Area by himself. He'd been recognized, and gals had come on to him all over the place. He'd had a few too many drinks and wound up in some gal's pad and just about passed out. She'd been real nice about him having to leave. Anyway, he didn't have to tell Diana every single thing he did. And nothing had happened beyond a couple of kisses. He'd been too bombed.

The second bumpy moment came when he told Diana he was dropping acting classes altogether. "Enough is enough, babe. I got out of it what I wanted. My show's one of the top ten, so I must be doing something right."

"Yes, but however good the show is, it's not going to go on forever. And when the time comes, you want to have developed as an actor, to have some range. This isn't like the movies, where the actors are more important than their roles. In TV the opposite is true. The characters are the most important, probably because of the weekly format. What happens is that the characters become real to the viewers, and the actor is so much identified with the role that change is very hard. Think of Telly Savalas after Kojak, and Carroll O'Connor after Archie Bunker. . . . ."

Diana could certainly talk a man's ears off. She was smart, but she didn't know everything, like what a difference it made when you were somebody. *Luke Merriman was somebody*. He couldn't go anywhere nowadays without women throwing themselves at him. Luke had learned that being a celebrity was the most important thing in the world. If people knew your face and your name, doors opened magically all over town. Nothing could stop him now. Memorizing a lot of dead old plays in a dreary old schoolroom on Bank Street wasn't going to help him anymore.

He leaned forward, took Diana's hands in his, and kissed the tip of her nose. "Now, sweetie, I know what I'm doing. Trust me. Hell, I can always start up the lessons again. But just now, I'm enjoying being Pete Winston and loving the gal of my dreams. How about we go on home and do a little more of that?"

He smiled as her face softened and all that blah-blah went right out of her head. She had such pretty lips, meant for kissing, not reprimanding.

In bed, he could read her like a book. He knew when she wanted him to touch her and where, and when she wanted him to be a little standoffish so she could take the lead. And what thrilled him was that he really turned her on. Lots of women just pretended because they wanted to feel pretty, or be cuddled afterward, or wanted their friends to see them with a handsome guy on their arm. Not Diana. She really wanted the sex itself, bless her, and it made him feel marvelous.

Just as long as she didn't think she could run his life for him. What he hadn't told her was that he'd actually quit acting lessons at the Christmas break.

15

Diana sat in the back of the audience listening to Luke lecture to a Westchester women's group on the changing roles of men in today's society. During the past couple of months he had been asked by a number of women's organizations to speak on similar subjects.

Diana and Luke would confer, and then she would write his speeches, covering such points as the need for men to relinquish macho behavior and relate to women as human beings, and the way that would benefit men, women, and their children. Yet, while she listened to Luke saying that women had no special biological equipment for raising children, that men could learn to be as nurturing as women if they weren't afraid of that side of themselves, that stereotyped sex roles were old-fashioned and there was no reason a man couldn't be both masculine and tender, she had a nagging feeling that he was playing the character much as he did on the show.

It was complicated. She wrote his speeches with Pete Winston in mind, since it was that character the audience loved and came to hear. The speeches were also, of course, good publicity for the series. However, she felt uneasy because the character was idealized as well as fictional, and Luke Merriman was only an actor.

Diana sighed as she listened to Luke now answering questions from the audience. He looked gorgeous standing up there, beaming at them, his sexuality and charm so palpable Diana had an urge to rush up to the stage, grab him around the waist, and shout to the female audience, "He's mine! You can look and admire, but keep your grubby fingers off him. I created him and he belongs to me."

But did he? Diana felt the lump in her throat that had been bothering her for weeks. She had originally thought it was indigestion from too much rich eating and drinking. But no matter what stomach remedies she took, or how lightly she ate, and even if she drank nothing alcoholic for days, the lump persisted.

Her doctor hadn't found anything wrong and had asked if she was feeling tense or emotionally upset. Diana had denied it, but in fact both guesses were correct.

Luke had changed, and it had begun that night a month ago when he had told her he was giving up acting classes.

He had opposed her for the first time, refusing to even briefly discuss it. Nor would he talk about his late hours. He had turned cold, avoided looking at her, and had finally mumbled something about needing more time to himself.

She had been afraid to make him angry enough to . . . to what? Leave her? She couldn't bear to think of such a possibility, yet it had been with her intermittently ever since.

Hundreds of fan letters arrived for Luke every week, including dozens of marriage proposals, and not only from star-struck groupies. Women of means proposed to him: a Texas oil heiress, and professional women—lawyers, executives, college instructors.

Being out with Luke had become nerve-racking. Public transportation was out of the question, so they went everywhere by chauffeured limo. Even a walk in the park together, once such a pleasure for Diana, became impossible. Not just because the women were flinging themselves at Luke but because he appeared to accept it as his due—to believe that Pete Winston's persona was his own, that *he* had become every woman's fantasy man. And Diana had nobody to blame but herself. She had created the character. It was ironic because she had based it on Luke—the old Luke, that is. For example, Pete often cooked for his children, took care of them when they were sick, brought them meals in bed, on a tray, with a rose. . . . When Diana remembered the way Luke had once brought her breakfast in bed she wanted to cry. That hadn't happened in ages. If his fans could see him at home, lolling in front of the TV, flinging his clothes everywhere, saying breezily that he'd done enough dirty work to last him three lifetimes, and now he could pay someone else to do it for him. . . .

Luke had endured such a deprived youth that Diana couldn't blame him for wanting a little luxury, now that he could afford it. But his change in attitude was still an utter shock.

Luke's meeting was coming to an end. Diana always felt the most insecure at public gatherings, when she saw how women adored him. Things were better when she and Luke were alone. They had become a little cooler to one another—no, he had become cooler to her—but the infatuation stage of any relationship eventually had to end.

Diana had to admit that she would feel calmer if they were married, although the issue had never even come up. Living together was modern and chic. It enabled each of them to preserve a certain amount of independence, but if they were married it would be a public statement. She would be his wife and he would be her husband—very different from live-in lovers.

Good God, was this really *her*, thinking along such conventional lines? Cut it out, Sinclair, you sound like your grandmother, she scolded. If a man's going to stray, marriage won't hold him. In fact, it might have just the opposite effect.

Diana looked at her watch. The lecture was at an end but the women were swarming around Luke with further questions, holding out papers for his autograph, while he was smiling, basking in the attention, yet easing his way toward the aisle.

Diana slipped out of the meeting room to wait for him in the limo. She had learned not to be visible on these occasions, because for every woman who smiled at her with frank admiration, about fifty threw her hostile, envious glances. Besides, Luke seemed embarrassed at having to publicly acknowledge her. Diana, deeply hurt, kept rationalizing that preserving his public image of the young widower was good for the show, to keep up the audience's interest. Any TV show was only as good as its latest rating. As in sports, there was always another potential star waiting in the shadows for an opportunity to soar to the top.

It was something of which Phil Bannon, through Matthew, was constantly reminding her. Diana was glad that Phil spent most of his time on the Coast because Matthew was a pleasure to deal with. He was straightforward with her, and she had learned to be the same with him.

A loud noise in the street told Diana that Luke was finally emerging from the hotel, followed by members of the audience.

"Thank you all kindly," he said, laughing as he opened the door and got in. As instructed, the driver pulled away immediately.

"Well, how was I?" Luke asked, smiling engagingly at her. The question was rhetorical, of course. He knew damn well how he had performed but he wanted to hear her praise him.

"You weren't bad at all, but then, you've got pretty good material."

"Geez, the way some of those gals grab a fellow makes you wonder what their husbands are doing besides watching the ballgame," Luke said, either not understanding her joking reference to the first time they had met or not caring to acknowledge it.

The lump in Diana's throat ached. Again she reached for humor. "I hope they didn't grab away anything we need."

She so yearned to touch him that she couldn't contain herself. Slipping one arm around his neck, she leaned toward him and kissed his lips, feeling him tense. "Oh, Luke," she breathed. "I love you, darling."

He relaxed, grinned, and kissed her back, putting his arms around her. "I love you too, babe."

And then he did what she had silently willed him to—moved his hands up from her waist to cup her breasts. Diana pressed against him, her body on fire, wanting him so much she thought she would burst with desire.

And he responded—oh, god, how he responded—kissing her, caressing her, his arousal apparent.

It didn't matter that they hadn't made love in a couple of weeks, for they would tonight.

Diana felt the lump in her throat dissolving under Luke's passionate kisses.

It would be all right. Everything would be all right, as long as they loved one another.

*   *   *

Nikki sat in the control booth at the studio—a converted Broadway theater—flanked by the director and the assistant director, while they did the six-thirty taping on Friday. Diana had been there for the earlier taping and then cut out because she had a stomach bug, leaving this one to Nikki.

Watching the first segment of the show, she thought that Luke was surpassing his earlier performance. For one thing, they had a terrific audience out there. About twenty of them belonged to a Pete Winston fan club in Ohio, and the women not only laughed and applauded on cue, they whooped and carried on like lunatics. Which of course helped the actors, especially Luke.

Actually, the audience was always responsive, every seat filled. Not only were droves of people turned away every week, but the producers knew that women hung around the studio on Fridays from early afternoon, offering money to ticketholders (who had written in for the free tickets). Selling the tickets was illegal, of course, but there was no stopping sellers from finding plenty of buyers.

Nikki was thinking less about the taping than her dinner with Luke later that evening. When Diana had left to go to the doctor, then home, Nikki had immediately taken advantage of the opportunity to ask Luke if he'd like to have "a bite" right after the taping. She wanted to talk over some aspects of next week's show, and since Diana was indisposed. . . . He had agreed without hesitating.

Nikki was elated. She had been carefully planning this little tête-à-tête for a long time so as not to arouse Diana's suspicions.

She even had the restaurant picked out—Luigi's, a neighborhood Italian café in the East Twenties, the kind of place married men took their lovers. It was dimly lit by candles, with checkered tablecloths, discreet waiters, tables well separated, soft, romantic music—the perfect setting for Nikki's purpose.

She wanted Luke more with each passing day, just as she longed to escape from Gwen. Nikki had begun to feel like a canary in a cage with a vulture. It was really sick, the way the older woman was trying to enslave her. Yet she didn't dare make a break until she came up with a script for *Pete Winston*. The trouble was that comedy wasn't really Gwen's thing, and it was taking time to worm a good idea out of her. Every suggestion Nikki made, Diana shot down, and it was already the middle of March.

At least Luke was finally getting tired of Diana, but there were many other women trying to claw their way into his affections. Gemma Lopez, for one. She had to be forty, under that obvious face lift. And though she seemed to eat as much as anyone else, she managed to stay as slim as a snake. Nikki had the spiteful thought that Gemma probably kept her weight down by purging herself after every meal. The way that bitch hung around Luke's neck, smiling at him, flirting with him, made Nikki sick.

Yet, it helped the actress play the role. Nikki watched Gemma on the monitor and had to admit she was damn good, able to show anger and yet be funny about it. The audience was roaring. This was one of the best episodes, but Nikki couldn't wait for it to be finished, when she would be sitting across the table from Luke and giving her own performance.

An hour later she was doing just that. She had slipped the maître d' a ten when they arrived and requested a "quiet table in the back," which he had given them with an unctuous smile.

Nikki had taken off her suit jacket so that Luke would be able to see her breasts, straining unfettered against her tight shirt, with as many buttons undone as she could decently get away with. An additional attention-grabber was her silver Coptic cross, Egyptian, very unusual, a present from Gwen. Luke was staring at the cross dangling between her breasts, merely inches away. Though they were not particularly large, they were nearly perfect, she knew—high and firm, with long nipples that stiffened when she had a sexy thought. She was having one now, as she looked deeply into Luke's eyes and smiled at him with as much sexual challenge as she dared. "Your performance tonight was terrific, Luke, and I say that as a producer not a fan."

Luke smiled. "Thank you kindly, ma'am. That makes me feel real good."

Over their Campari and soda, they read the menu, and the maître d' hovered, making suggestions and treating

Nikki like a princess, understanding exactly what she was trying to achieve.

As they ate, Nikki turned the discussion to the show. "I'm not quite sure about something, Luke, and thought you could clarify it for me." Of course, Diana would be going over it on Monday, but the one thing she wouldn't do would be to ask Luke what he thought.

Luke told her, at first hesitating, then with more confidence. Nikki was hoping he would realize how Diana treated him like a puppet.

Nikki had already established rapport with the waiter. It was wonderful, the way Italians understood women without having to be told. The waiter knew he was to keep pouring wine, and to bring them a second bottle.

Nikki leaned closer to Luke, her breasts grazing the tablecloth, and she noted how often Luke's eyes went to them. She also made a show of sharing dishes, giving him a taste from her fork so that her smooth hand was close enough for him to smell her perfume and to brush his skin lightly.

She was thrilled that Luke's famous, breathtaking, sexy smile was now beaming on her alone. Between bites she said, "I thought the scene tonight where you were trying to find out from Sharon what had happened at school was just perfect. Like, your ad-lib really made the scene. Even Diana had to admit that, at yesterday's rehearsal. She's so professional, of course, that it's sometimes hard for her to see that an actor has a special feel for a line because he's deep into the character, while the writer is only looking at it from the outside."

Luke ate up the flattery more eagerly than his veal. Nikki felt a surge of elation, knowing she was exactly right about how fed up he was to be dangling at the end of Diana's string.

Nikki was careful not to say anything directly against Diana, but she got the point across that her need to be in charge of the production caused her to be blind to some of the ideas of others on the show—especially Luke's brilliant perceptions.

"Like, the writing is important, of course, but let's face it, Luke, that show is Pete Winston. Your character is the pivotal one and you know Pete better than anyone else possibly could."

Luke seemed content to let Nikki do most of the talking. She got around to describing how she had once dated her college math instructor, who had become possessive and jealous if she as much as spoke to a male classmate. Watching Luke's face, she saw her arrow hit its target.

"Yeah, I can understand how you must have felt."

Nikki stirred impatiently, waiting for him to utter just one small complaint about Diana, but he didn't, though all the wine seemed to be getting to him.

Nikki herself was a prodigious drinker. She could consume a vat of alcohol without showing a flicker of inebriation.

No, Luke wasn't yet ready to talk against Diana, but since the subject of possessiveness versus freedom seemed to interest him, she stuck to that.

"I wanted to be with my math professor freely, not because he felt insecure or something. Independence is very important to me. But, like, he wanted to know where I was all the time. It wasn't really his business, but if I told him, he got hysterical. So I had to keep things back, tell little lies, you know."

Luke knew, all right. He was looking at her intently. "So what happened?"

She smiled and shrugged. "I had to call it quits. It was tough. I really liked him a lot, and after all, he did help me pass math. It was almost as if he had made an investment in me, like I was his special project or something. It was so claustrophobic. I felt a little bad at first. He called me constantly, wouldn't give up. He finally did. Found another student, I guess."

They were now drinking Sambuca with their coffee, and Luke's eyes were on Nikki's bosom.

"Do you like my cross?" she finally asked, giving him her most seductive smile. "It's solid silver." Touch it, touch it, she silently prayed

At last he did. As she felt his fingers against her hot skin she grew tremulous with longing. "You have such beautiful hands," she murmured huskily, touching them lightly. "Very expressive. You use them brilliantly."

For a moment their eyes locked, and Luke smiled,

holding his seductive look until her juices were flowing. It was an exquisite moment, but it passed.

He sighed, removed his hands from her neck, and looked at his watch. "I'm enjoying this, Nikki, but it's getting late," he said apologetically.

Nikki nodded and signaled for the check. She was disappointed, of course, yet heartened by the way he seemed to regret not being able to do more tonight. At least he didn't make a fool of himself by saying he had to get home to Diana.

Although Nikki offered to pay for dinner (she had invited him, after all), he wouldn't hear of it. She was relieved when she saw they had eaten and drunk (mostly drunk) their way over a hundred dollars.

She was hoping he'd offer to drop her at home in the limo but he didn't. Instead, he put her in a taxi, telling her how much he had enjoyed their dinner.

It was something, but not enough. Shit, it was only nine-thirty, and she felt like a cat in heat. She needed a man badly.

The phone was ringing as she opened her door. Gwen, probably. Nikki took off her clothes, letting it ring.

Three minutes later it began to ring again. When it stopped, she called a guy she knew. No answer. The next one she tried, she got a machine. It was almost ten and getting too late to reach anyone on a Friday.

When her phone rang for the third time she answered.

"Where the fuck have you been?" Gwen's agitated voice came over the wire. "We had a date tonight, and I don't appreciate being stood up."

Nikki tried to placate her, without much success. Gwen was really raging. Nikki had never heard her like that, and it worried her. She still needed Gwen. In fact, only this week an unsolicited script for the series had crossed her desk. Nikki had read it quickly and sent it back, but not before making a note of the idea. It was pretty good but she couldn't totally steal it because she needed some help.

Nikki lied through her teeth about having to work late and trying to call Gwen but getting a busy signal each time. Then she suggested meeting her lover in a West Village gay bar she knew Gwen favored because it was one place women could dance together.

"Please, Gwennie. I'll make it up to you, I promise."

Gwen finally agreed.

Nikki knew it thrilled her to be able to mingle publicly with others of her persuasion and not feel either guilty or stupid. In a gay place she could show off that in spite of being middle-aged she could attract such a young, fresh beauty. Nikki didn't care who saw her in this sleazy joint.

Dressed in becoming tight pants and a sheer frilly blouse, Nikki was by far the prettiest femme in the place, and a proud Gwen relented after a couple of dances.

At their table, Nikki began to discuss TV, turning to humor, and asking Gwen what she thought really made people laugh.

"Well, recognition, for one thing. People laugh when they see other people acting in the same ridiculous way they might, or have, in a given situation." She expanded, while Nikki, her chin in her hands, listened raptly.

"Yes, I see what you mean. Like, do you ever watch that sitcom *Pete Winston*? I sometimes find it amusing. Gemma Lopez really makes that show. She's terrific, dark, gorgeous, very funny."

Watching Gwen's expression of jealousy, Nikki continued to tease, then switched, saying she had seen an episode that wasn't too good. Pretending that her new idea was the one in question, she summarized it and asked Gwen her opinion.

After thinking about it, Gwen said, "Well, if I had written it and I wanted to show Pete's children trying to get Lola to drop their father, I'd have had them acting up in uncharacteristic ways to drive her crazy."

"Oh, Gwennie, that's terrific, but how?"

"Well, one of them, say, shoplifts and gets brought home by the police, and another one maybe spills something on the woman's best dress."

It was wonderful, perfect.

"I'd like to dance again, Gwennie," Nikki said.

On the small dance floor of the smoky, dark place, reeking of pot and booze and perversion, Nikki danced cheek-to-cheek, breast-to-breast, until she felt Gwen trembling with desire.

Later on in bed, Nikki was also worked up, but she was thinking about Luke.

* * *

"You two get in the car, and I don't want to hear another peep out of you!" Sara shouted at her children, yanking them hard by their hands.

Joey was crying, while Daisy resisted, hanging back and digging in her heels.

"Ow, you're hurtin', Mama, stop that pullin'," Daisy yelled.

"Just shut up, both of you," Sara snapped, slamming the car door shut. She ground the gears as she shifted into first and maneuvered out of the parking place in front of the school.

Sara drove angrily to the end of town, and when she reached the road she floored the accelerator, her mouth set in a tight line.

How dare that high-falutin teacher make her feel like a criminal just because she was only a temporary resident of the school district. All Sara had done was bring the kids to school and try to get them accepted. They were clean and shiny. Daisy was even wearing a dress.

As for the school, it was awfully tiny, but the teacher had put on airs, doing Sara a favor by saying the kids could "sit in," while the others gawked and giggled.

However, when Sara had returned, just before lunch, she had found the schoolroom in an uproar.

Daisy was sassing the teacher, who was red in the face and yelling at her that she was retarded, while Joey was crying because the boys were taunting him and mimicking his stutter.

The teacher took one look at Sara and began to bawl her out in front of the whole class, saying it was the middle of the term and everything couldn't stop because of Sara's "unruly children." Joey, she went on, was too young for school and couldn't sit still, while Daisy, at seven, couldn't even read.

"But that's why I brung them here—to learn," Sara had argued.

The teacher had shaken her head, snapping that Sara would have to wait until September.

Mortified at being reprimanded like another one of her kids, Sara had taken her anger out on them. She had missed a day's work to bring them to school, and it had all been for nothing.

"Mama, I feel sick," Daisy called out from the back seat.

Sara slowed down, realizing she had been tearing around the curves at fifty and shaking up the children.

Pulling off on a shoulder, Sara got out and opened the back door. She helped Daisy out and held her head while she was sick. Sara was sorry she had yelled at her.

By the time they had returned home, Sara was feeling much calmer. She hugged the children and told them not to worry, promising they would go to a nicer school in the fall.

But her words sounded hollow in her own ears because she had no more idea than the children did where they'd be six months from now.

Later, Sara tried to interest Daisy in learning how to read, as she had been doing for months, without success. Daisy just didn't seem to get the hang of it, and Sara was sure it was because she didn't know how to teach her. The children needed to be in school every day, and the only way that would happen would be if they could get off the stream. Working the land was no good anymore. Even rich farmers were going broke. Everything was big, big, big, and mechanical pickers had begun doing more of the work. Sara knew it was time to quit the stream, but she didn't see how she could. No matter how much she tried to save, she could never get ahead.

What Sara really wanted was to live in town, go to beauty school, and be a hairdresser. Maybe she could even get her own little beauty shop and live upstairs or something. She prayed for it every night, but awoke every morning to the reality of stoop labor.

"Well, I'm never goin' to school again," Daisy proclaimed as she helped dry the supper dishes.

Sara didn't answer, knowing her daughter was only saying that because she had had a couple of bad experiences at school. Daisy didn't like to fail at things; in that way she was like Sara.

Long after the kids were asleep, Sara stayed up, racking her brains for a way to stay put long enough to keep the kids in school for a whole term.

On Saturday she left Daisy and Joey with a neighbor and drove to a couple of nearby towns, asking in diners and markets if anybody needed help. Several places did, but not one store owner was willing to hire Sara because she had no retail or restaurant experience.

Well, how the heck was she supposed to come by experience if nobody would give her a crack at it?

16

"I'm sorry to have to pull you away from the studio," Matthew told Diana when she was seated across from him at his office.

"It's okay." She smiled at him, a little nervously, he thought.

He hesitated, hating what he had to tell her. She looked so lovely, in a beige wool knit dress, her hair falling softly around her face.

In fact, he had noticed her increased respect for him ever since that meeting in the supermarket in Sag Harbor. At the time, he had been embarrassed. Andy had been at her worst, as if sensing that she was meeting a woman who was important to her father.

Diana and Luke, Luke and Diana—Matthew said that to himself whenever he had a surge of hope that she could possibly care for him as more than a friend. He did feel they were friends. The first time he had seen her, after Sag Harbor, he had not only apologized for Andy, but had told Diana that his wife had left him and her child some years ago.

Diana had looked at him with compassion and said she was sorry. She hadn't pressed him for details, like most other women, because she wasn't romantically interested in him. Still, Diana's friendship was something he valued.

He sighed and tore his eyes from her face to the papers in front of him—the first script for the fall season and a summary of the plots for the next twelve episodes to be approved for production.

Diana zeroed in on the problem. "Phil doesn't like what we've submitted?"

"Yes and no. Most of it's fine. But there's material in the script and a few of these stories that he's having trouble with." Matthew translated his boss's harsh words so as not to offend her. The gist was that Pete Winston's children were showing too much sexual precocity for Phil's tastes and for what he insisted was the morality of their viewers.

"Oh, for God's sake," Diana interjected, leaning forward impatiently. "Kids *are* precocious nowadays. Isn't your daughter?"

"She is, yes, and I'm not saying I agree with Phil. Clearly, he wants to be as universally appealing as possible because he feels Continental is ready to challenge ATN for first place next season. And continuing this series as a hit is vital." Matthew kept his eyes on his papers as he detailed the changes Phil wanted.

"But that means the first script and four of the episodes would just about have to be scrapped! I mean, if we take out the controversy, there's nothing left."

"I understand, Diana. Well, you're so inventive, I'm sure you can come up with something acceptable—"

"No, I can't, and what's more, I won't. Because within the context of the Winston family, certain questions would normally arise. Sharon is twelve and biologically a woman. And Kelly tries to keep up with her sister. Max, because he's a boy and the youngest, makes sure he's not left behind, yet his precociousness is mostly pretend and terribly innocent. The oldest, anyway, would be interested in her father's dating habits—if he goes to bed with any of his dates, and if casual sex is sometimes okay."

"Here in New York people are more sophisticated. What Phil's afraid of, Diana, is the viewers who want a return to old values and have threatened to boycott products advertised on programs opposed to their views."

"I disagree. If we go for the lowest common denominator we might pick up conservative viewers but we'd certainly lose the ones who've made the series a hit. It's so popular because it takes chances. Don't tell me you agree with Phil."

He sighed. "No, of course I don't. I think the opening script is terrific and I've said so. But it's not only Phil. He's met with the program board, and they agree."

"He hasn't met with me," Diana said testily.

"No, he was hoping that wouldn't be necessary." Matthew looked at Diana soberly. "And so do I. Phil is a formidable adversary. The worst. He's devious, tricky. Shoots point after point until you're angry and frustrated because his argument can be logical although the premise is flawed—"

"Then why not start by attacking the premise?"

Matthew smiled wryly. "Because by the time you've caught up to him you've usually lost the argument. I'd rather face a debating society on some arcane philosophical point than argue with Phil over whether to wear my red tie or my blue one. He's really very, very difficult."

Diana shifted in her seat. "So you've been saying. Well, I'm going to have to find out for myself. Because frankly, Matthew, I'm not going to give in on this. Pete's kids have to develop. They're a year older next fall. They're taller, they're wiser, and it has to be shown in their behavior as well as their appearance. This isn't a cartoon Orphan Annie who stays the same age for thirty years."

Matthew's intercom buzzed. "Yes, thanks. I have a meeting, Diana. Why don't you talk it over with Molly?"

"In effect you're asking us to throw out the first script and four episodes—"

"Not throw out, exactly. Maybe tone them down. In any case, at least change the order. Put the approved stuff up front and air the ones Phil objects to later on in the season. By then we'll have a fix on the ratings, and if the show is still top-rated maybe Phil—"

"No, Matthew," Diana interrupted, her voice low but firm. "I'm sorry. I don't want to be difficult, but I feel strongly about this. If the children remain infantile, it will destroy the series."

His intercom buzzed again, and he was forced to stand up. "I've really got to run. Think it over, Diana."

She stood too. "I already have. I'll discuss it with Molly, of course, but I'm sure she'll agree with me."

Matthew gathered his papers. "You know, Phil can be awfully stubborn. I don't want to imply any threat, but I can't ignore the fact that he's capable of cutting off his nose to spite his face."

"You mean he'd cancel the series? Well, there are two other networks."

Matthew walked with Diana to the door, annoyed with Phil for putting him in this position and annoyed with Diana for failing to understand. "Yes, but they wouldn't be right for *Pete Winston*. ATN, as you know, is going for more violence and musical-video stuff, and FAB has an older entrenched audience. Having worked for them, I can tell you first-hand that they would never buy those episodes as they stand."

Diana turned to face him. "I would like to speak to Phil myself, even if I have to go out to the Coast to do it. I think I'll be able to convince him."

"All right. He'll be in town next week, as it happens. I'll set it up, once you're absolutely sure—"

"Yes, I am. Absolutely sure."

Matthew shrugged. On the way to his meeting he felt anxious and irritable. Diana had integrity and guts but she didn't know what she was letting herself in for. Last season Phil had been rather mellow, grabbing at any program that would lift the network off the bottom. But now he saw a chance to compete with ATN and he was prepared to be ruthless with anything and anyone standing in his way.

Diana was no pushover, certainly, yet Matthew felt she had a deep-down vulnerability. It was the thing about her that touched him the most. And he wondered if she would really be able to fight Phil when he turned mean and dirty and went for her jugular.

It was unusually warm for early April, and Diana was sweating in her gray winter suit as the elevator at Continental carried her to Phil Bannon's office on the fortieth floor.

She was quite nervous, though she'd gone over everything with Molly, including how far to push her luck.

"Remember," Molly had cautioned, "negotiating means giving in a little, especially on the less important issues. Are you sure you don't want me there to do the giving in, if it comes to that?"

"No, I don't, and it won't."

Prepared to confront Phil and possibly Matthew, Diana was stunned to be greeted by the entire program board. About a dozen men got to their feet—mostly West Coast vice-presidents from sales, research, affiliates, business affairs, and standards and practices. Some names and faces were familiar, but Diana felt a little silly having to smile at each one in turn as they said hello. When she threw Dick Mann a special smile of recognition he merely nodded coolly at her. She remembered having caught a brief glimpse of him at the network Christmas party, but he had vanished before she could say hello.

As Phil led her to a seat in the huge office, she felt her heels sinking into the thick deep-blue carpeting, and she caught a glimpse of the Hudson river from the floor-to-ceiling windows.

She disappeared into the leather of a chair much too big for her, noticing that the men deployed themselves intimidatingly. Only Matthew and two others sat on the leather sofa to her left, while the rest stood or leaned on the chairs to her right.

When Phil was seated behind his massive mahogany desk, which dominated the room from its position in front of the windows, he was at least a foot higher than she was in her "hot seat," as it seemed to her. She felt trapped in the folds of leather, deceptively smooth and buttery.

Her heart was thumping stupidly, and her mouth felt dry. This kind of confrontation was a first, yet she hated being frightened of it. If only Matthew had warned her that she'd be going up against the entire board. Maybe he hadn't known.

Phil lit his cigar. "Let me start by saying, my dear, how pleased we are to be finishing second for the season, in spite of some rough competition. And I want to acknowledge that *Pete Winston* was one of the reasons for our success. Am I right, gentlemen?"

Noises of agreement rumbled through the room, and

Diana smiled as best she could, while her mind raced on anxiously. She was definitely being set up.

Phil's tone was courtly and a touch patronizing, as if he were saying, "I'm trying to be nice and patient with you but I don't appreciate the trouble you're causing."

He rehashed the objections she had already covered with Matthew, except that he backed up his statements by having several of the others quote their own departmental statistics purporting to show what the public wanted and did not want. And what they did not want—especially Continental's affiliate stations—was controversial material, such as children's sexual curiosity.

After the parade of statistics there was a momentary silence. Diana surmised that everyone expected her to be so overcome by the numbers that she would immediately cave in.

She was going to disappoint them. Although she had come prepared with her own statistics, she decided to leave everything in her briefcase. She would make a spectacle of herself struggling to reach it on the floor and then fumbling through papers. Not in front of this assembly.

Looking Phil squarely in the eye, though she had to tilt her head up to do so, she said, in her soft, sweet voice, and without irony, "I appreciate all the trouble you've gone to in order to convince me of the rightness of your position, Mr. Bannon, but . . ."

While not being foolish enough to dispute the statistics, she countered Phil's interpretation of them, first by quoting from memory bits of reviews of *Pete Winston* which stressed that it was the innovative quality of the material, the risk-taking, and the believability of the characters that were the primary reasons for the popularity of the series.

Diana watched Phil's face harden; the patronizing smile became a frown of annoyance.

He interrupted her to say that he couldn't possibly endorse programming that would cause the network's affiliates to refuse to run certain episodes. "What will happen is our affiliates will bump *Pete Winston* in favor of a locally produced program or something they've bought from an independent syndicator. That will rob our network of ad revenues and lower our ratings. In fact, if a quarter of our affiliates choose not to air the show, the rating will come down as much as six points."

Diana pointed out that their refusal was based on mere speculation. Had the affiliates actually seen the script? No, but the vice-president representing them agreed with Phil.

Diana tried to reassure them that the way the episode was acted would show the essential innocence of the children's questions, and amusingly so. With a smile, she went on to cite precedents—previous sitcoms that had dealt with children and yet succeeded in breaking new ground.

As she heard a dissenting rumble, she held up her hand for silence and noted that fewer and fewer TV watchers were tuning in to network television. Instead, viewers were switching to independent stations, cable, and videorecorded material.

Diana knew very well that alternative media was a sore subject with the networks, and she could sense the men bristling at her boldness in rubbing their noses in it to make her point. She stressed that only by continuing to grow and being receptive to change could network television compete with alternative media.

Phil concealed his obvious anger behind a mirthless smile. Then he slugged her below the belt. "My dear, our children have lost the protection they used to have when their mothers cared for them. Now their mothers go to work, and so their children are in day care centers and schools and camps where child molesters can get to them. . . . It is our children who have become the true victims of the sexual revolution."

He went on in this vein, implying that the new material for *Pete Winston* was an invitation to child molesters by assuming children knew a great deal more than they actually did.

Matthew hadn't exaggerated. Phil was willing to make her look not only cheap but also dangerous. Moreover, he now spoke without pausing, one snide accusation after another so there was no way Diana could deal with each point without interrupting him.

In spite of the anger welling up in her, she kept silent, waiting for him to finish. However, when he ran out of steam on child molesters he switched his attack. Citing a new survey, he said it was time for Pete Winston to marry Lola, and the first episode of the new season should deal with Pete's proposal of marriage.

Diana stared at Phil, stunned, and then glanced questioningly at Matthew. He looked as surprised as she, and shrugged. Apparently this was news to him, too.

As Diana started to object, Phil turned the floor over to Dick Mann, who spewed more statistics, and she gathered that he was the one behind this particular idiocy.

She shut her eyes for a moment, beginning to feel the leather of her chair pulling her deeper into its embrace.

The atmosphere in the room subtly began to change. Diana could sense an aggressive spirit of male connivance and anticipation of the kill.

"Research shows," Dick Mann went on smugly, "that the audience views Lola's feminism primarily as a way to protect herself from rejection. What she really wants is the domestic fulfillment that marriage to Pete would bring. . . ."

Diana knew well enough that researchers could come up with any kinds of statistics they wanted, to prove a point. Had they interviewed people watching *Pete Winston* or those tuned in to the football game?

As Dick was winding up his argument, Phil zoomed in on his last words. It was like a verbal relay race designed to leave Diana at the starting line.

Before she could say a word, Phil brought up the fact that Luke had been speaking to women's groups. "You should know, my dear, since you no doubt, er, collaborate on his speeches about the joys of marriage and the family. Well, it's time Pete, at least, backed up his words by proposing to Lola."

Diana's face reddened as the nasty innuendo caused fleeting smirks on the faces of the other men. Everyone knew, of course, that she and Luke were lovers. They were implying that Luke might not think enough of Diana to marry her but Pete ought to think enough of Lola to do so.

By the time the floor had been given back to Diana she felt that every man in the room—with the possible exception of Matthew—was mocking her. She was burning with fury but refused to give them the satisfaction of reacting to the slur in a personal way.

Her voice sounded so soft to her own ears—soft and weak—that she was surprised at its lack of timbre. "'If Pete marries Lola,'" she began slowly, "it would get a favorable response. Naturally. Everybody loves a wedding. Especially if, as you suggest, Mr. Bannon, we show it taking place. We could work up lots of publicity, with many product tie-ins. . . . We could keep the excitement building for weeks," she continued, turning her head to look at the others, and watching their faces soften and turn indulgent.

"Aha," their expressions seemed to say, "every woman is a romantic at heart, even this tough cookie. All we have to do is get her all weepy over the idea of a wedding on camera and she'll forget the reason she even walked into this room."

When Diana felt her audience had been sufficiently disarmed, she pounced. "However, the wedding would not only be the climax, it would effectively destroy the show. Because the whole point of Pete Winston is that he's a *single father*. With Pete married, we'd have just another domestic comedy—"

"The hell we would," Phil interrupted angrily. "Marriage is the goal of most *normal* single people, widowed or divorced or whatever. It would give the children two parents instead of one—"

"Absolutely," Dick Mann chimed in. "The pendulum has swung away from the single life toward marriage. Away from abortion and toward pro-life. Away from sexual promiscuity and toward commitment. . . ."

Jesus, he sounded like a pop psychologist in the pay of the Moral Majority. Why was he doing this? Diana asked herself.

While Dick paused for a breath Diana quickly turned back to the president. "I seem to remember another series some years back, Mr. Bannon, called *Rhoda*. It was a spinoff from the *Mary Tyler Moore Show* and very popular at the start. . . ."

Diana had been at college then and hadn't watched it more than a few times. But subsequently, in the course of trying to write her own comedy series, she had read reams of material and monitored dozens of tapes to determine why some shows had succeeded and others failed.

"The new series had been airing only about eight weeks when Rhoda married her boyfriend, Joe Gerard. If I recall correctly, about forty million viewers smiled and wept their way through the wedding ceremony. Rhoda ranked sixth at the end of that season. Yet the show went downhill unhappily ever after. The point of it—that Rhoda was kind of a flaky *single woman*—was blurred in domestic bliss. The series lost so much popularity that the producers tried putting Rhoda through a separation and then a divorce. Well, the audience hated the divorce, and the series died."

Diana smiled pleasantly at the scowling faces all around her—all but Matthew, who, in fact, smiled back—while Phil chewed ferociously on his cigar.

Of course, he was furious at not having done his homework, at having taken Dick Mann's argument more seriously than he should have.

Diana wondered fleetingly why Dick had come up with something so ill-thought-out as that projected marriage. He was far from stupid. Had he been so eager to spite her, out of continuing jealousy, that he had risked making a fool of himself? Since they had last talked, she had devised a top-rated sitcom, whereas he was still the bright young man in programming at Continental. He hadn't made it into the creative end, as he wanted, hadn't made it to vice-president, hadn't even been able to make a move to another network. All he could make, apparently, was trouble.

Matthew, who had a handbook with him, spoke for the first time, backing up Diana's points with some statistics tracking Rhoda's drop in popularity. "As Miss Sinclair has indicated, we can take it as a given that when a show loses its reason for being, the audience falls away. If Pete were to marry Lola, she would become a stepmother. With that change alone the focus would have to move from Pete to Lola. And judging from the fan mail, Luke is what makes the series such a hit, not Gemma."

"All right, all right," Phil finally snarled ungraciously, amid the buzzing in the room. "I'll think about it. But in the meantime, I'm not going to approve the first script or those four episodes as submitted."

Diana took a deep breath. Phil clearly had backed down on the marriage. He'd given something, and now she had to give something.

"I could tone down the first script somewhat—"

"No way!" He shook his head vigorously. "The material is controversial no matter how it's handled, and I want it dropped."

Diana felt a shock of dismay, because what he wanted was out of the question. She knew she was right on this, and she tried to convince Phil by citing her own statistics, in round numbers, on single-parent households. Millions of children like Pete's had parents who dated. All sorts of questions and feelings were bound to crop up.

"As long as the material is handled delicately, Mr. Bannon, as long as the dialogue is tasteful and the scenes aren't played leeringly—all of which I think is so in the opening episode—the audience will be charmed rather than offended."

"You don't know what you're talking about, little girl!" Phil shouted, losing his temper. "I was in this business when you were in pigtails, and believe me, there's no way to put a good face on a father screwing around, goddammit!"

It took an enormous effort for the "little girl" not to raise her voice or lose her cool. "I think that remains to be seen, Mr. Bannon. The audience has a right to be the final judge. If they don't like the show, they'll change the channel."

"Are you crazy?" Phil shouted. "Millions of dollars are at stake here. We can't possibly take such a gamble. It's taken us ten years to climb out of the cellar—"

"With the help of *Pete Winston*," she broke in smoothly. "We must be doing something right, and the report card proves it."

"You think this is some kind of fucking game, don't you?" Phil roared at her. "Listen, I'm accountable to my shareholders, and believe me, Middle America is incensed to the point that anything can happen." He thumped on what appeared to be her submissions on his desk. "This script is fucking offensive, no question about it."

Everyone began to talk at once—except for Matthew, who sat back tapping his pen against his mustache and gazing at Diana steadily.

When the din had lessened, Diana said, "I don't think the script is in any way offensive, Mr. Bannon. There's no nastiness, there's no vulgarity, there's no foul language...."

Blinking angrily but offering no apology for his own language, he stashed his cigar in an ashtray, where it smoked and smoldered and gave off an awful stench.

Phil Bannon was pale, and his eyes had closed to angry slits. Diana clearly understood how enraged he was. His previous meetings with her had been social, pleasant, and uncontroversial. He had expected her to smile and simper and give in to him. Instead, he had been forced to back down on Pete's marriage and now he had lost his temper.

The men were shifting restlessly, waiting for their leader to deliver the coup de grace. Diana's breathing turned ragged as she realized that Phil was going to have to tough it out so as not to look like a complete idiot.

She tried to forestall an ultimatum by giving him an out. "Why don't you and I sit down with the opening script, Mr. Bannon, go over it line for line, and see if we can come up with something acceptable to both of us."

She realized her mistake from the way his eyes took on a sheen of victory when he saw she was willing to negotiate.

'No point in going over it, my dear, because it just won't work. Pete Winston's sex life is not going to be discussed by his children on *my* network to open the fall season. He has dinner dates, and that's all he has. Now, we're going to start with this episode here," he continued, consulting her bible.

I'm sorry, but I can't agree to that, Mr. Bannon."

Phil jumped to his feet. "And I can't agree to broadcast any one of those offensive episodes, period!"

Slowly Diana peeled herself out of the leather chair, feeling a nerve pounding in her temple. "In that case, you don't have a show."

Was that *her* voice, so deadly calm?

For a second or two there was a choked silence, and then a low murmur from around the room.

Diana's voice grew stronger. "I can't agree to destroy my own creation, Mr. Bannon. It would be wrong. I'd rather see *Pete Winston* die than turned into mush. I'd feel ashamed, and what's more, the audience would feel betrayed."

Phil, white around the lips, glared at her in fury and disbelief. "You don't mean that."

"I'm afraid I do."

Diana had endured enough. Picking up her briefcase, she added, "I simply won't put my name on a series that lacks integrity."

Without waiting to be dismissed, she turned and walked firmly to the door, opened it, and closed it behind her.

Nobody came after her, even though it took several minutes for the elevator to arrive. By the time she got in, she was shaking. Oh, God, what had she done?

In Phil's office, there was an explosion—men shouting back and forth, several spewing streams of obscenities that had been held back while Diana was present.

Only Matthew sat perfectly still, his head lowered so that nobody could see his smile.

Diana was one hell of a woman.

17

"You did *what*?" Molly screeched. "I don't believe it."

"Believe it," Diana muttered. They were in Molly's living room. Diana had needed a place private enough to tell her what had happened.

"Christ, Diana, that's *your* career, *my* career, Luke's career, Gemma's—you took all that on yourself, without even asking—"

"There was nothing else I could do. To give in—"

"You didn't have to give in, you boob. You could have played for time. 'I'll check with my partner, I'll get back to you, I'll sleep on it!' "

Diana shook her head. "I didn't have an option. It was

either-or, I promise you. He was forcing me, daring me. It was an exercise in pure macho blackmail—"

"Oh, shut up, just shut up," Molly said angrily. "I don't want to hear it. *Of course* Bannon was provoking you. The man's a total prick, everyone knows that. Matthew warned you. I asked you if you wanted me at the meeting but you said no, you could handle it. This is supposed to be a partnership, not a one-woman show. Listen, you want all the power and all the glory, but the one thing you're willing to share is the defeat!"

Diana couldn't blame Molly for being furious, and she stopped arguing. Molly talked herself into such a rage she threatened to dissolve the partnership.

"Okay, I guess I shouldn't have let him goad me," Diana finally conceded, "but the way he was grandstanding got me so mad—"

"—that you had to go him one better. Talking of grandstanding, yours was a dilly. God, I'd like to pound some sense into you," Molly said, shaking her fist. "The thing that really gets me is that you've left us no way out. Given the kind of bastard you're dealing with, even if I called him and you called him and we both called him to back down, he'd tell us to fuck off. You've humiliated him in front of his program board. Do you think he's gonna forget that?"

"No. But I don't think he's going to let the series die, either. He needs it at least as much as we do. When he thinks it over, he'll see that. He never expected me to brazen it out—"

"Not surprisingly," Molly snapped. "Nobody in their right mind would throw away a successful series."

"I think he'll back down. He had to save face in front of the board. But he's so tricky, he'll find a way to come out of it smelling like a rose. I don't think anyone in that room was happy to see me walk out."

"Oh no? Then why the fuck hasn't anyone been on the horn telling you different? Even Matthew. Have you heard from him?"

Diana shook her head. "No, but I haven't been home or checked my machine. I've been walking around awhile." Three hours.

"Check your machine now," Molly challenged. "Go on."

Diana looked guiltily at her partner. "Well, it's too soon. Phil's going to let me sweat it out for a few days, probably—"

"I doubt it. Besides, the news will be all over town by morning. It's hard to keep a secret in this business. Someone will talk. One of those creeps will tell his wife, his secretary, his bimbo. And what are we going to say to the cast and crew, huh? Sorry, folks, we've pulled the plug on our own show. No, not because of money, because of a principle, for Chrissake. A point of integrity! You explain it to them, kid, and bring your bodyguard, because the shit is gonna hit the fan, I can guarantee it. Listen, I've got to go. Dinner date with Ted, and I'm late. Though why bother? I'll probably choke on it."

Diana remained seated and put her head in her hands. She felt terrible, and her emotional barometer kept going up and down. One moment she had convinced herself that Bannon needed *Pete Winston*, the next moment she was equally certain that he'd drop the series just to make her squirm.

She was afraid to go home. How could she face Luke? He had become so identified with Pete Winston that there would be no other role for him for a long while, except an occasional commercial. But that was nonsense. Even if Phil didn't come through, ATN would pick up the series and be happy to get it, wouldn't they?

Every time she anticipated the look of astonishment on Luke's face when he heard, and then the hurt, she felt like weeping.

And there were other ramifications. Luke spent his money as fast as it came in. She had been forced to provide more drawer and closet space for his wardrobe, and he'd just bought a 1953 red Jaguar convertible, a wildly expensive classic, from a collector. Diana had been dismayed that he would make such a purchase without even consulting her. But there he was, one Saturday afternoon, sitting in it in front of the house, looking so proud of himself.

The enormity of her confrontation with Phil Bannon finally hit her, and she remained in Molly's living room in a semistupor.

Finally she dared to dial her home number to check her machine.

There was no message from Matthew; that was a bad sign. He'd been on her side up until the end, but she had backed herself into a corner.

Jesus, she had tried to bluff the president of Continental. Molly was right, she must have been crazy.

Finally she rose wearily and let herself out of Molly's house. It was almost ten. People were out strolling, enjoying the clear, balmy night, a preview of spring. How carefree they looked. Nobody in the whole city was carrying her burden. Except, she thought ruefully, maybe Phil Bannon.

Diana felt empty in every respect, and she realized she hadn't eaten dinner. She wasn't really hungry so she bought an ice-cream cone. She needed something sweet.

How she dreaded going home. It was so hard for her to conceal things. Luke would take one look at her and realize something was terribly wrong. Should she tell him what had happened so he wouldn't hear it from someone else? Or should she wait, hoping it wouldn't be necessary?

By eleven she was exhausted and her feet hurt so much she dragged herself home with a sense of impending doom.

Luke wasn't there, and for once she was glad. She would take a shower, go to bed and pretend to be sleeping when he got in.

She took a stiff drink before retiring, and as it happened, she really was asleep when he made it home, whenever that might have been.

Both of them overslept, so there was no time for any sort of morning discussion. They were a half hour late to the studio, and Diana had a million things to think about. But running through her head all through rehearsal was that today's episode of *Pete Winston* might be one of the last.

No, she refused to be so negative. At the very least, wouldn't another network pick up the series? In spite of what Matthew had said, she felt that *Pete Winston* was too good a series, too proven a money-maker, to be allowed to die.

"Diana, do you think this is all right?"

Nikki's insistent voice cut through her obsessive thoughts. Turning a blank face to her assistant, she said, "Sorry, can you repeat the question, please?"

Nikki did, and Diana answered it, but the younger woman hovered. "Yes, what is it?" Diana asked irritably.

"About my new script—"

"Yes, yes, I'll get to it, but not just now." Goddammit, she could hardly concentrate on rehearsal. Last thing she needed was to be pressured to go over Nikki's script. It was an excellent idea but as usual the dialogue was horrendous and needed a complete rewrite. And she would have to get to it soon because the episode was next to last of this season's shows.

Rehearsal was particularly trying and she had to interrupt scenes constantly to make changes. But it was her own fault. She hadn't been at rehearsal yesterday. Nikki had been in charge and virtually every piece of dialogue she had tampered with had to be altered. The actors were resisting and arguing over every change because they hated to have to relearn anything.

Molly had been wrong about one thing, anyway. The news of that meeting hadn't traveled. Certainly nobody on the set seemed to know anything was wrong. And Diana's heart ached to think that all these people were proceeding on the assumption that the series would be going into another season.

At lunchtime she fled, muttering she had some shopping to do. Her fingers itched to ring up Matthew and see what was going on, but she resisted the impulse. He would call her when he had something to say.

The dress rehearsal that afternoon went much better, and Diana's depression lifted marginally. Luke's performance was fine, but she was dreading the end of the day, having dinner with him and pretending that everything was normal when it was anything but.

Diana hung around the studio, and Nikki accosted her, again with that damn script. Diana finally went over it with her. Luke had slipped out without saying where he was going, and Molly hadn't been in touch either.

Diana went straight home and spent the remainder of the evening in front of the TV watching but not seeing a thing.

For the second night in a row, she went to sleep alone, lulled by alcohol and wondering how much more suspense she'd be able to take,

She awoke early but Luke was in such a deep sleep that

she could barely rouse him. Clearly he had been out half the night. She didn't have the heart to call him on it this morning because he soon might be at liberty to sleep as long as he wished, thanks to her.

The morning dragged because dress rehearsal had gone very well and there wasn't much to do. At lunchtime she didn't even think of eating; nothing would have gone down. As she walked up Broadway she found herself envying the plainest, most ordinary women she passed, simply because they weren't going through her own particular kind of hell. She would have to call Matthew. When she thought of sweating this out over the weekend she knew she'd never last.

As she returned to the theater, her pulse began to race. In three minutes she'd be there, in two more minutes she'd be on the phone to Matthew. She'd know the worst. If there was anything to know.

As soon as she walked in, the p.a. told her there was a call for her.

When Diana took the phone she could barely say hello. It was Molly. "Any word yet?"

Diana exhaled sharply. "No. Not yet. I'm about to call Matthew.".

"Listen, kid, I've been thinking it over. You should have consulted with me first, of course, but I think I would have come to the same conclusion you did. What the hell. I don't want my name on a piece of shit either. So whatever happens, we'll deal with it together. At least by some miracle everyone's kept their mouths shut. I think it's a good sign."

Diana's mood lightened. "Yeah. Maybe Bannon's got the board locked up in his office like a hung jury."

"That's right. And they can't stand eating take-out Chinese food for one more meal so they've shot the bastard right through the heart with a paper clip and a rubber band."

"Molly, I love you."

Diana put in a call to Matthew but was told he was at a meeting for the rest of the afternoon.

During the six-thirty taping, Matthew appeared at the studio.

Leaving Nikki to take over, Diana hurried him into the nearest private space, the wardrobe room.

As usual, she learned nothing from the enigmatic expression on Matthew's face.

"Okay, I'm ready for the verdict," she said calmly.

"The verdict is you've won." He gave her one of his rare smiles. "Phil will agree to changes in the script."

"Oh, God," Diana breathed, shutting her eyes for a moment and saying a silent prayer. "What about the program board?"

"Sworn to secrecy. There was quite a flap, of course. Phil was foaming at the mouth, and half the board backed him up. The other half, led by me, felt we needed the series more than Phil needed to salvage his pride."

Eventually Phil and Matthew had thrashed it out. Matthew had dredged up some other statistics from Middle America that Phil could cite to prove that as long as the material in question was "toned down considerably" it would not offend. Since nobody besides Phil, Matthew, and Jill had actually read the first script, nobody would know what changes were made. It had taken Matthew until noon today to convince his boss that Diana was not going to back down.

"You weren't, were you?" Matthew asked, looking suspiciously at her.

"Absolutely not," she said, "but it cost me. I've been agonizing as much as anyone. I took a lot on myself."

"I admire your guts, Diana, and your integrity. Molly went along?"

"Yes, she did," Diana answered loyally.

Matthew nodded, looking around him. "Let's have a drink, for God's sake. This place makes me feel I have to climb into a skin diver's wet suit or something."

Diana thought she should go back to the control room and then decided to hell with it. She needed a drink. And she wanted to thank Matthew properly. She was sure he'd moved boulders to change Phil's mind.

They needed a quiet place to go over changes in the script, so she suggested the Landmark Café, on Eleventh Avenue. It was a nice old-fashioned wood-paneled bar that served terrific martinis.

In fact, after only a few sips she felt as if she were levitating.

Matthew brought out her script and bible. When she noted the changes Phil and Matthew had worked out, she saw they were minor at best, nit-picking at worst. She smiled and okayed them, feeling a tremendous surge of euphoria. She had done it, by God. She had outbluffed Phil Bannon, president of Continental Television Network. Now that it was all over, she was feeling very proud of herself.

Matthew observed her with his shrewd, strangely lit green eyes, and she smiled self-consciously. "I'm sorry, I know I'm looking smug, but I can't help feeling absolutely terrific. It's not just my personal triumph, it augurs well for the show. Because I'm convinced we're going to have a great season."

"You're probably right. Anyway, you deserve to feel good, after a couple of sleepless nights."

Her hands flew to her face. "That's what happens when you're pushing thirty. Everything shows, dammit."

"Not a bit. You look wonderful, as always. I was speaking metaphorically. The only thing that shows is that you certainly like winning."

"Why shouldn't I?" She smiled defensively. "Do you find that unfeminine?"

"You could never be unfeminine," he said quickly, looking at her with an intense expression she had never seen in his face before.

As if aware of having given something away, he added, "Wanting to win is simply very human. I like winning myself."

There was something personal in his tone that puzzled her. She studied his face for a few moments, and to her surprise, saw him look uncomfortable and chew his lower lip.

A sudden insight into his strange behavior struck her. He found her attractive. You look wonderful, as always, he had said, and now he was embarrassed by his slip, because, of course, she was not available.

Feeling a little flustered herself, Diana impaled her olive with a toothpick and chewed it thoughtfully. Did she like the idea or not like it?

Don't be coy, Sinclair, you love it. Who doesn't want to be thought desirable by someone as impressive as Matthew?

She kept looking at him and allowing herself to speculate on how she would feel about Matthew if there were no Luke. Very much interested? Somewhat interested? Not at all interested? She teased herself with all three responses but the only thing she would grant at this point was her curiosity to know Matthew better.

However, she wasn't curious enough to accept a second drink now. Besides, she wanted to phone Molly and tell her the good news.

"I have to run, Matthew," she said, putting down her glass. "Thanks for the drink and thanks most of all for your support. I realize you had a considerable influence in all this and I want you to know how much I appreciate it. You're a real friend." And nothing more than a friend, she finished silently.

Yet, she couldn't resist pecking him on the cheek before grabbing her jacket and taking off.

Diana invited Luke to have dinner with her but the evening didn't go quite as she had anticipated. Of course he had no way of knowing why she was suddenly in such a good mood, after her noncommunicative depression for the past two days. Although she did mention that she had been worried about acceptance of the fall episodes, she hadn't dared to tell him the whole story.

In truth, he seemed uninterested in anything she was saying, much preferring to look around the restaurant, preening and smiling and wanting recognition from everyone there.

They were dining at Le Cirque, where every other patron was a celebrity. Yet Luke got much more than his fair share of attention—feminine attention, to be precise.

Diana couldn't blame women for going bonkers over him. To her he seemed more handsome than ever, and it worried her. Luke had very little to say to her over this dinner, yet he was receptive to any female who stopped by the table and cooed over him.

Diana began to feel the euphoria of her triumph evaporating but she put a smile on her face and reached for his hand across the table. "Let's do something special tomorrow night, darling. See a play, maybe go dancing—"

"Oh, I can't tomorrow, babe," he said, slowly pulling back his hand. "Drinks with Harriet at five. Couple of Hollywood people she wants me to meet. I think it's going to extend into dinner. You're welcome to come along, of course. . . ."

She was "welcome" to come along to a business dinner? And on a Saturday night? He'd made plans without consulting her and without even including her? Indeed, he was now actively discouraging her, hinting that she would probably be bored and might prefer to see a friend. "It's your opportunity to go to the ballet. I've tried to like that stuff but my mind wanders and the music puts me to sleep."

Diana didn't like the shaky feelings she was having, and she held back saying anything. At least next weekend they would be begin spending time in East Hampton. She couldn't wait. Last summer had been so idyllic, the full flowering of their love.

"Next Friday," she said, "let's have the car rented and our bags packed. We'll park it in midtown, and right after the taping, we'll take off and have a full weekend—"

"Oh, I meant to tell you. I can't make it next Friday. There's a benefit on Saturday, at the New York Public Library. Some disease or other. I told Gemma to put me down for a ticket—"

"One ticket? Gemma's selling tickets but not to me?" Diana asked before she could stop herself.

Luke didn't look at her as he replied smoothly, "Well, you weren't around at the time. Anyway, I knew you wanted to get out to the house—"

"But I assumed we'd be going out together," she cried, feeling a panic rising.

"Well, I know you don't like those charity affairs. You want to leave almost as soon as we get there. So why don't you go out to the house and I'll drive out later in the Jag."

"But that means driving back separately Sunday night!" she cried. "What's the point in having two cars—"

"Oh, Lord," he said in an exasperated tone. "You can return your car out there and drive back with me. I mean, what's the big deal?"

Diana swallowed. She hated the way he was speaking to her. This was something new, and it worried her. She tried to see the issue from his point of view. Okay, he owned a car now—a fancy one at that—so it was natural that he wanted to drive it. And it was true that she didn't enjoy charity balls, whereas he loved them. So they would meet at the house afterward. Surely there was nothing terrible about that.

Then why was she so upset that she couldn't finish her dinner? Why did her hands tremble every time she reached for her wine glass? Why did she feel rejected and abandoned when he excused himself to talk to someone at another table?

All she knew was that she had the most awful sensation in the pit of her stomach, in addition to the lump in her throat.

Diana ordered coffee for them both, then sipped hers while his grew cold in the cup because he remained at the other table.

Diana felt too embarrassed to turn around and look. Instead, she pulled her mirror from her bag and applied lipstick, using the mirror to see behind her.

Luke was leaning over a beautiful, regal brunette with a fur draped over her chair. She was smiling up at him as if he were the love of her life.

Diana forced herself to say and do nothing. She asked for the bill and paid it, having the feeling that everyone was staring at her, witnessing her humiliation. But it wasn't true. Not a soul was paying her the least attention. In that room full of well-known people, she was nobody.

Diana forced herself to remain calm. She didn't want to start something with Luke that she would not be able to finish.

On the way home, in the limo, she leaned against him, turning to kiss his lips. They were cool, unresponsive. He didn't push her away, but neither did he kiss her back. He began talking about Joni somebody or other, a model who was married to a famous racing-car driver, the ones he had been talking to with such animation at the restaurant.

Diana made a valiant attempt to show interest, and Luke warmed up a bit. But not enough to make love to her, even though the last time had been more than a week before. In bed, he pecked her on the forehead, told her he was exhausted, and simply rolled away from her.

She lay on her side facing his back and felt tears welling. She didn't understand what was happening to them. She and Luke had been so much in love.

The honeymoon is over. The phrase stuck stupidly in her head. How could there have been a honeymoon when there had never even been a marriage? Luke was free, and she was going to lose him.

She couldn't lose him. She loved him. He was everything she had ever wanted. She had seen to that. The trouble was that he had risen to stardom too quickly. Celebrity hounds were all over the place, ready to take up new stars, and equally ready to drop them the moment a newer one presented himself. Luke didn't know that, the poor innocent. He didn't realize that he was everyone's newest trivial pursuit and nothing more.

Over a drink on Saturday she had occasion to discuss Luke with Molly, because in the end Diana hadn't been able to bring herself to tag along with Luke and his agent. She had invited her partner to the ballet.

Molly, studying her face, saw something was wrong.

"No, nothing's wrong. I'm tired, that's all. It's been quite a week."

"Oh, cut it out, you don't fool me," Molly said. "You were over the moon when you phoned me yesterday. It's Luke, isn't it? The bloom is off the romance."

Diana compressed her lips and swallowed. "It's nothing, really. He's more independent and . . . and we're not mooning over each other so much. Well, it was inevitable, I guess. I just wish he'd realize how ephemeral success can be."

"How can he realize it, kid?" Molly asked softly. "Thanks to you, he didn't have that long struggle to get where he is. He reminds me of some of those lottery winners. Poor working stiffs who go from rags to riches because of a few magic numbers. They've got the loot all right but not the slightest idea of what to do with it."

Molly was right about Luke but Diana felt too loyal to discuss it further.

She came straight home after the ballet; Luke wasn't there. As the hours ticked away, she realized he was having one of his late nights. She never knew when he came in, because she fell asleep sometime after four.

When she awoke Sunday at ten, Luke was asleep beside her. She leaned over and kissed his temple lightly so as not to wake him. Was there an unfamiliar perfume in his hair, or was she imagining it?

Feeling like a fool, she went to his clothes, flung on a chair, and sniffed them also.

Stop it, Sinclair, stop playing the jealous female. He was bound to break out a little, sooner or later. Be glad you've noticed and can take steps.

At noon Diana ordered up an elaborate brunch and served it to Luke in bed, chatting amiably all the while, and wearing nothing but a sheer white silk negligee.

Diana avoided asking where he had been so late or showing any resentment whatsoever. She wanted him to make love to her, but she didn't initiate anything. She simply smiled, flirted, enticed.

And after about an hour at her labors, she got what she wanted.

Diana felt wild with passion, but she made an effort to let him take the lead and give her as much as he cared to give without showing disappointment that their lovemaking was so brief. In fact, her one orgasm left her ravenous for more. She yearned to stay in bed all day but told herself not to be greedy.

Luke turned on a baseball game and she watched with him, rooting for the Yankees, asking Luke to explain certain plays, trying to share his enthusiasm.

Yet, right after the game, Luke began to dress, and her stomach turned over. He wasn't going out, surely?

She joked with him about where "they" were going, and if he was going to surprise her. He hesitated, glanced at her, then glanced away. "I dunno. Got any suggestions?"

"Yes. Roseland. I'll bet you've never been there. It's not trendy or anything. In fact, it's so far out it's almost in. It's been around for fifty years at least. On Sunday they have a big band and a Latin band. When I first came to New York someone took me there and it was really a howl."

It was a brilliant stab in the dark on her part. She knew he had sampled all the trendy rock-video places, most of which were closed on Sunday anyway, and she talked on, adopting a tone that indicated he was missing out on something.

Luke waggled a finger at her. "Okay, you've got it."

She was sure he made a phone call from the den to cancel a date. But that was what she had wanted, wasn't it?

Most of the people at Roseland were refreshingly ordinary. Although Luke was recognized, he danced only with Diana and paid attention only to Diana.

When they got home she poured them nightcaps, but before they were through with their drinks she had half his clothes off and was pulling him down on the living-room rug.

It was wonderful, glorious. All her anxiety and sexual starvation caused her to be on a hair trigger, and she experienced the ecstatic orgasms she'd been missing lately. And for the first time in a long time, they slept in each other's arms, and Diana felt content.

However, Luke's behavior at the studio the next day completely wiped out her contentment.

While the cast sat around reading the new script, Luke and Gemma whispered back and forth incessantly, until Diana told them sharply to cut it out. But she couldn't prevent them from slipping out together at lunch.

In the afternoon, both of them argued with Diana over everything, backing each other up and drawing the director to their side. Diana overruled them, feeling like a tyrant.

Luke vanished before Diana could even suggest dinner. And he was out until after midnight.

She was waiting for him. "What's going on with Gemma?"

"Hey, let me take my jacket off, okay?" Luke had been drinking. "Nothing's going on," he said sullenly.

"Don't tell me that," Diana objected sharply. "The two of you are like a couple of kids at school, bzzz bzzz bzzz. It's very distracting and I want it stopped."

Luke looked at her coldly. "It gets boring sitting around while you worry tiny little points like a dog with a bone. And your director is a pain in the ass too, repeating everything—'

"Because you and Gemma don't pay attention, you're too busy with your private jokes—"

"Listen, quit nagging, will you? I'm beat. I need a shower." He stomped out of the living room.

Diana was too hurt and angry to say anything more. When Luke came to bed, she was over on her side as far as she could get, and she stayed there.

He stayed on his side as well.

Things were no better the following day. Gemma not only whispered to Luke, but also had her hands familiarly all over him—his arm, his hand, his shoulder. Diana pretended to ignore it but her tension and irritation increased.

Molly's series was finished so she came to the studio in the late morning, and she was the one to put a stop to the buzzing between Luke and Gemma.

Then Molly dragged Diana to lunch. "I've been hesitating to tell you this, kid, but maybe I'd better. It's not only Gemma Luke is fooling around with. I saw him having dinner with Nikki one night not too long ago."

Nikki! Diana felt her heart lurch. It had been the evening of the day Diana had been feeling crummy and gone home early. Molly had spotted Nikki and Luke at the back corner table of what she described as an off-limits place. "I should know. I go there all the time with Ted. That's the clientele it gets, married folks sneaking a meal and you-name-it afterward."

"Not necessarily," Diana murmured, wanting desperately to believe it.

"Not necessarily," Molly echoed, "but suspicious all the same. They didn't see me because they were too wrapped up in each other."

"You've never trusted Luke," Diana accused her partner, "and now you're making a mountain out of a molehill."

"Two molehills, to be exact. If you'd seen Nikki flaunting her tits at him, and Luke smiling and enjoying it. . . ."

Diana felt chilled to her marrow. Even if Molly was exaggerating. . . . Jesus, she'd been sick that day. Luke hadn't phoned to find out how she was feeling. Still, he hadn't gotten home very late. Questioning Molly about the time, she pieced together that he had come straight home after leaving the restaurant.

"Yeah, maybe he did. That night. I'm not trying to be cruel, Diana. Just don't be an ostrich. See what's happening—"

"What's happening? He's having an affair with Nikki *and* with Gemma?"

"I don't know. I just think if he hasn't yet, it's only a matter of time."

Diana felt shaken, and she was quiet all afternoon, making a point of telling Luke not to leave the studio without her. "Do you have plans for tonight?"

"Well, sort of. I can get out of it," he finished, apparently seeing something in her face, or hearing it in her voice.

"Please do."

She suggested dinner at home, ordering it up from a good Italian restaurant nearby because she knew she wouldn't be able to hold his attention in public.

She thought of tricking Luke into telling her where he had been the night she had been ill, but was too ashamed to play such a game so she told him straight out that he had been seen with Nikki.

His eyes flickered momentarily, and he looked puzzled. "I was?"

Diana refreshed his memory, adding the name of the restaurant. She waited, simmering. Had he dined with Nikki so many times he couldn't recall that particular instance?

"Oh. . . . oh, yes, that's right. I do remember. It was a Friday, yeah. And she wanted to talk about the next week's shoot. You were sick, she didn't know if you'd be in on Monday." He shrugged and smiled innocently. "So we had dinner. So what?"

When he put it that way, Diana felt foolish. Luke didn't look or act guilty. But he was an actor. Was he acting for her benefit now?

She knew very well that the worst thing she could do was to show suspicion and jealousy, and let him see how much she needed him. So she let the matter drop.

The next day she cornered Nikki at the office in the morning to question her about the dinner with Luke.

Nikki's eyes widened. "Oh, yes. I hope you don't think . . . Gee. I asked him to have a bite because I was a little worried about the following week." Nikki went on rapidly, describing which episode they were working on, and having excellent recall of her conversation with Luke. Too excellent, Diana thought, searching her assistant's face for any sign of guilt or deception, but not finding any.

Neither Luke nor Nikki asked who had seen them, a fact that reassured Diana more than anything else. She was probably silly to worry. Nikki was so ambitious, so dependent on Diana's good opinion of her, that she would never be so foolish as to go after Luke. Molly was just a suspicious person, reading more into a situation than was actually there. And yet Diana's fears were not put at rest, because day by day, it seemed, Luke was slipping away from her.

She drove out to East Hampton on Friday because she was ashamed not to, after he had told her he would join her there Saturday night.

As it turned out, it was a cool, rainy Friday and Saturday. She missed Luke. The community still had that shut-up winter air about it. She wondered where he had been Friday night, then began to imagine him arm in arm with Gemma at the charity ball that evening. . . . .

Dammit, she thought I have to snap out of this mood. So she spent Saturday afternoon preparing for Luke's arrival. He'd get out late, no doubt, tired from the long drive, and would probably go right to sleep.

But Sunday she'd bring him coffee and juice in bed. They would have a leisurely brunch.

By late afternoon she was feeling her usual optimistic self. As she was driving her car into the parking lot in town, she caught a glimpse of Matthew Sayles driving out. His daughter was with him, laughing and looking very pretty.

Diana honked, and he stopped and rolled down his window to say hello.

She invited them back to have some tea, to warm them before they drove back to Sag Harbor. Matthew looked as if he wanted to accept, but Andrea made a face and said she wanted to go home.

Matthew wisely didn't force the child to pretend a friendliness she didn't feel.

She had tea alone and a long soak in the bathtub. Then she read a book in front of the crackling fire. Later on, she relaxed with a brandy and listened to music.

By midnight she was wishing Luke would get there. At

one-fifteen Luke phoned to say he was too tired to drive out after all.

Disappointment rushed over her but she tried to keep it out of her voice. "I'm not tired myself, so why don't I just drive on home. It's supposed to rain tomorrow anyway—"

"No point, babe," Luke said. "I'll be long asleep by the time you get here. Might as well wait until tomorrow."

Diana hung up, shaking, feeling as if she was losing her grip. What was wrong with her? He wasn't really being unreasonable. He couldn't have arrived before three in the morning, and the weather was lousy. Yes, but in the past wouldn't she simply have said she was coming home, instead of agreeing with him meekly to wait until tomorrow? It was absurd. She wasn't behaving like herself but like some frightened kid.

Slipping into jeans and a shirt, she flung a few things into a bag and was speeding home within ten minutes. Traffic was very light, and she made excellent time.

But when she got home, Luke wasn't asleep. He wasn't there at all.

18

When Diana awoke on Sunday, after about three hours of restless dozing, the apartment was still empty. Like an automaton she got up and made the bed, then systematically erased all traces of having been there at all.

She grabbed her bag, got her car, and drove through the Holland Tunnel and into New Jersey, aimlessly following one road after another. The pain in her chest and throat was acute, and she was gripped by the fear of not knowing what to do.

Luke had spent the night with someone. He was tired of her. She should kick him out without a second thought.

Yet she found herself closer to tears than to anger. Her head told her that she had enjoyed the best of Luke, that she should let him go, but her emotions were too overwhelming. She missed him and she was scared. Jesus, he'd been with another woman, and all she could think of was wanting to be in his arms. She felt crazy. It wasn't only the lack of sleep and the worry—it was her inability to recognize herself.

As she drove over hill and dale, the low-hanging mist seemed like a metaphor for her very being, befogged and lacking its usual clear vision. She kept obsessing about Luke, imagining him first with Gemma, then Nikki, then that model Joni.

Yet, after carrying each image to its extreme in her imagination, she kept shaking herself and saying it couldn't be true. Maybe he simply had stayed late at the charity thing, then gone on to one of those all-night eateries.

Did Luke really crave sex with other women, or was it the admiration he wanted?

She drove until her arms felt stiff, and she found herself in Princeton. She was feeling a little wozzy and extremely hungry, even though she had no appetite.

In a diner near the college campus she ordered scrambled eggs and toast. It was noon. Surely Luke was home by now.

Diana rang his number before leaving the diner and he answered his phone. She hung up. Since she was supposed to be coming from East Hampton, she preferred not to have to lie.

When she returned, Luke was in the living room surrounded by the Sunday papers. Diana came up to him as if nothing was wrong and kissed him. He was unresponsive so she moved away and picked up a section of the *Times*.

She turned the pages but very little was sinking in. Her heart was pounding, and she kept feeling panicky every time she glanced at him. He appeared too rested to have been out all night. He'd bedded down somewhere, and with someone.

"Well, East Hampton was boring," she ventured, as if he had asked her a question. "It's too dull out of season. I should have gone to the charity ball with you. How was it, by the way?"

"Fine."

"Sorry I missed it. I need to start going out again. All work and no play. I mean, there's no point sitting by the fire just because I've reached the wrong side of twenty-nine—" Diana stopped, flustered, feeling like an idiot. Why the hell was she reminding him that she was older than he was?

He was so wrapped up in his reading that he hadn't heard her. Diana grimaced, how ironic it was that she considered thinking it good fortune that he no longer paid attention to her. He now had power over her because of her love for him.

The period that followed was very painful for Diana. Dressing up and going out with Luke almost nightly exhausted her. At the end of an evening her face muscles would ache from the forced smiles, the pretended animation, although she thought she carried her pose off well. She was as bright and amusing as she had ever been. And if the women in Luke's crowd resented her reappearance, they managed to hide it quite well—except Gemma, who dropped out altogether. Diana felt a triumph of sorts, though there were dozens of other women she imagined in Luke's arms. After all, Diana couldn't be with him every moment of the day and night. All she could do was try to keep him as happy with her as possible.

But the strain was terrible. All her life Diana had behaved with honesty, doing what she wanted without giving it another thought. And now, in order to keep Luke, she was living a pretense, if not an outright lie. She felt like a bystander in her own life, watching her pathetic clone going through the motions, and being ashamed of her.

Her tension was evident on the set, too. Night after night of very little sleep made her irritable and easily upset.

And Luke didn't help. They were coming to the end of the spring season, and everyone felt pressured. Almost every day of rehearsals Diana left the house first. Luke was either still sleeping or just staggering dopily into the shower. And she was afraid to say a word or he'd accuse her of nagging.

She would stalk into the studio, almost daring anyone to complain that Luke wasn't yet there. And if anyone even hinted at it, she would snap her head up and say, "He's on his way."

While waiting, Diana made a great show of going over points with the other actors, getting as much done as possible until he loped in, closer to ten than nine-thirty.

The dress rehearsal of the season's last episode was particularly bad. Luke was late for makeup, and when he got on the set he was a walking zombie.

Sally Fein was one of the most genial and experienced directors on the show, and her episodes were usually the best. But today there was all sorts of trouble.

"Luke, please stand on the marker," Sally called to the floor through her microphone. "We just blocked that shot. What happened?"

"It's a stupid shot, that's what happened," Luke said breezily. "It's awkward standing there. I'm trying to see around Gemma's head—"

"Hey, are you blaming me?" Gemma yelled, glaring at Luke, "You've got a fucking nerve!"

"Oh, for God's sake." Sally stood up, looked at Diana, sitting next to her busily turning pages of the script, and went out on the floor.

Diana felt hot with humiliation. Sally was right, of course, but if she took her director's part over Luke . . . Gemma had gone from being Luke's flirtatious conspirator to his vicious enemy, and one extreme was as worrisome as the other.

The argument continued on the floor, while the cameramen and technicians watched and waited. Nikki was trying to step in, unsuccessfully, and in the end, Diana was forced to go out herself. Suddenly she was in a fury. "I'll handle this, Nikki," she bellowed. "Goddammit, we've been over this all week. Sally, move the goddamn marker if it's such a problem. Gemma, stop taking everything so personally. Let's get on with it!"

Later, back in the booth, she apologized to Sally.

If the morning was bad, the afternoon was even worse.

The young production assistant, Thea, was obese. It was easy to see why, because she sat gorging herself in the control booth. After downing a few doughnuts, she munched virtuously but loudly on some carrot sticks, then drank a large soda.

The scene they were shooting was a mess. Luke never stopped yawning, and Gemma kept making asides, such as, "The guy's dead on his feet. Anybody got any speed?"

The actress who played Kelly, the middle child, upset by all the hostility, was confused and kept asking, "Which way do I go?"

"Into the sunset," somebody quipped, drawing a laugh. However, the eight-year-old actress burst into tears and had to be comforted.

"All right, settle down, everyone," the a.d. called into the mike. "Let us know when you're ready on the floor. Camera four, stop waving to your mother."

"I'm adding, 'Let me ask you something,' " Gemma said. "Okay?"

Diana nodded, and Sally told her okay.

When Diana saw Thea eating an apple, she exploded. "Jesus, can't you stop shoveling in the food long enough to do your job? This isn't a fucking restaurant, we're trying to finish this taping!"

Thea cringed trying to swallow her apple along with the humiliation.

Diana suddenly felt absolutely terrible. "Forgive me, Thea. I'm sorry. I'm not myself today."

The trouble was she hadn't been herself for several weeks. It was so unlike her to lash out at people. Poor Thea had enough troubles without having her weightiness called to the attention of everyone in the control booth.

Molly, who had spent the morning elsewhere, joined Diana at that point. "How's it going?"

"Don't even ask," Diana said irritably. Suddenly she caught a glimpse of Matthew on the monitor. He was sitting on the sidelines, quietly watching, taking a few notes. Spying, Diana thought resentfully. Christ, was everyone going to pick today to turn up, just because it was the worst dress rehearsal of the season?

Well, maybe nothing else would go wrong, but that was too much to hope.

During the next scene, Luke nearly collided with camera two.

"Watch it," the cameraman warned.

"You watch it, bozo," Luke retorted sharply. "You drive that thing like it was a tank or something."

"Shit," the technician yelled back. "If you were standing on your marker you wouldn't be in my way."

Luke was ready to punch the guy in the face.

The taping went on. Luke missed a cue, then flubbed his lines.

"Cut. No, no, no," Sally called, exasperated. "Not 'You only think so because you're not experienced.' It's 'You think so *only* because you haven't *had* the experience.' "

"Whatever. What's the difference?" Luke drawled, shrugging. "What I said is quicker and to the point. 'You haven't had the experience,' " he mimed derisively. "Nobody talks like that. I don't mind stopping for something important, but that's chicken-shit."

Diana went out on the floor. "What's the trouble?" she asked Luke tightly.

"Trouble is the line sounds phony the way it's written." He was staring coldly at her, knowing very well that it was her line.

Diana was trying to control herself. "I see," she said. "And how would you fix it?"

"Diana, for Chrissake," Molly called into the mike. "Why are you encouraging him to write his own dialogue? This show *has* writers. You're supposed to be one of them."

Diana felt defensive but she said, "If Luke has a way of saying the line that seems more natural to him—"

"Bullshit! since when does the piano compose the music?"

To keep peace, Diana herself altered the line to make it more readable, but it didn't help. It was as if Luke had been holding back all season and now he was letting out all his hostility.

In the script, Kelly was going to her favorite aunt's for the summer, and Pete was afraid she would choose to remain because her aunt and uncle had no kids of their own and she would be special instead of just being the middle child.

Luke interrupted the action to disagree with the concept. "I feel dumb worrying about a thing like that. Kelly would never want to stay out there."

Molly, Sally, and finally Diana took issue with him.

Only Nikki hovered at the sidelines, too timid to take a stand.

Then Matthew piped up, pointing out that now was hardly the time for them to make a structural change in the script.

Luke suddenly turned on him. "Who the fuck invited *you* to get into the act? The trouble with this show is there are too many sidewalk superintendents. How many people do I have to take orders from, anyway? I've had enough of this shit!"

He whirled and walked off the set.

Though she felt like a fool, Diana ran after him, biting back her fury at his infantile tantrum.

"Please, Luke, try not to be upset," she coaxed. "Everybody's on edge because it's the last day. . . ."

She succeeded in getting him to finish the dress rehearsal.

But immediately afterward she laced into Matthew. "I don't appreciate it when you turn up here unannounced and put in your two cents."

Matthew's expression indicated he knew exactly why she was being so bitchy today—because she was trying to hold on to her lover.

Matthew's tolerance only made Diana angrier, and she fled to the ladies' room feeling panicky. Everything seemed to be collapsing all around her.

She had been looking forward to the end of the season, but now she dreaded it. Luke would be at liberty. What hold would she have over him all summer?

Nikki left the studio feeling elated. A lot of what had been happening was her doing. She had been getting to Luke, fanning the flames of his dissatisfaction over the occasional drink, and even on the set. Today, for instance, while Molly and Diana had been having a catfight over Luke's line, she had sidled up to him and whispered, "If there were no piano, the composer would have to sing his own tune and do the harmony too."

Luke had shot her a smile of gratitude, and she had locked eyes with him for a wonderful moment.

She got into a cab and heaved a sigh of relief, glad all that was behind her. She had paid her dues, had her script credit both for *Mom & Meg* and *Pete Winston*, and now she was ready to go on with her plan. She had wormed an idea out of Gwen that was going to change everything.

19

"For God's sake, babe, not out here," Luke said, wriggling away from her. "You want to give the neighbors a free show?"

Diana swallowed her hurt and bit her lip, refraining from telling him that a year ago he had been delighted when they had rolled all over the deck of the house like a couple of dogs in heat. This year was very different. Luke stayed away from her, in bed and out. She tried coaxing, seducing, touching. She even rented a porn tape and played it to tempt him, but nothing happened. He sulked, claimed to have a headache or to be tired. Christ, he would have said he had his period if he could, Diana thought bitterly.

She readjusted her shirt and shorts. She was a little woozy from her drink. She had fixed margaritas, Luke's favorite, and had gone to the trouble of laying in a stock of tequila, Triple Sec, coarse salt, and limes. She had even bought an ice crusher to be able to make the drink properly.

But after asking her to make one for him, Luke hadn't touched his, and she felt doubly rejected. He reminded her of a spoiled child who first demands a double-scoop ice-cream cone and then lets it melt down the sides. Luke was certainly being hateful, and she wished she could hate him.

But that was difficult when he had such wonderful shoulders that tapered to the most perfect male backside she had ever seen. She couldn't stop staring at him as he lay sprawled on his belly surrounded by magazines and thumbing through an issue of *People*.

Diana licked the salt off the rim of her glass, trying to understand how the tables had turned. How had he become the master and she his slave? She hated it, yet felt helpless to do anything about it because she craved his love so badly.

And he was pushing her more and more. Weekends they drove in his open-top Jaguar, regardless of the weather, and she either had to wear a headscarf or arrive windblown and headachy. With his goggles, and one arm extended to the wheel, he was like a racing driver manqué. She felt reduced to baggage but didn't dare say a word. She was treading water, fearing at any moment that he was going to pull away and let her drown in the sorrow of her love for him. It was only the middle of May, and she didn't see how she would survive the summer.

Molly had a pretty good idea of what she was going through, and had called her on it. Dear, honest, tactless, infuriating Molly.

"Each Monday you come back from the island looking thinner and more unhappy. You're wasting away out there with that guy. As far as I'm concerned, the silk purse is still a sow's ear. It's nauseating, the way Luke turns it on and off. You're useful to him, bingo, he loves you. He doesn't need you for his career anymore, oops, he loves you not. Jesus, if this were a script you'd be writing exit lines at this point."

It was true. She even rehearsed a few. "This isn't working out, Luke. Success has gone to your head."

Or, "Luke, I'm sick of your selfishness, your indifference, your goddamn actor's temperament."

Or, "I've had just about enough. I created you and I can reverse the process anytime I like. You need me."

But that wasn't as true as the fact that she needed him. No matter how angry or unhappy she was, the one thing she couldn't imagine was life without him, her bed empty, as it had been before him.

There simply had to be a way to win back his love. The thing she clung to was that there didn't seem to be any other woman in particular. Flirtations, yes, but the more the merrier, it seemed.

Diana sighed and turned another page of a paper she might as well have been holding upside down. She put it aside. "Where would you like to have dinner, darling?"

He shrugged his magnificent shoulders. "Wherever. I'm

just reading about a guy who didn't get half the raves on his show I got on mine and he's been offered a movie role costarring with Meryl Streep. But my Hollywood thing fell through."

Diana hesitated. In her opinion, Luke wasn't ready for a movie just yet. At any rate he would have no time. In July they'd start production on the fall series. "Wait until next year, darling—"

"Oh, Lord, I can't wait until next year. I'm ready for something right now." He rolled over and sat up, his arms hugging his strong tanned legs. God, he was gorgeous.

Diana forced herself to respond to his remark. "You'll do lots of other things. But right now *Pete Winston* is hot. It's top-rated and you're in a good position to negotiate a lot more money when you renew your contract. . . ."

As she talked, she remembered how he had been behaving on the set and that awful last taping when he had antagonized everyone. He needed this time off. They had all been overworking.

Diana stood up and forced a tone of gaiety. "How about a nice walk on the beach?" she asked, holding out her hands to him.

Avoiding them, he stood up. "I'm not in the mood." He turned and walked into the house.

Diana followed him in. "You're not much fun today."

"No, and I won't be much fun tomorrow. Every time I talk about my career, you change the subject. I'm bored with *Pete Winston*. What I need is a movie."

Feeling very anxious, Diana wondered if she could help him get something in the works—anything to make him happy.

Monday afternoon she got on the phone to Hollywood and spoke to everyone she knew. The responses were polite without being enthusiastic, because everyone knew Luke was tied up with the series. However, while talking to an old friend at Coastal Studios, she learned that there was going to be a three-day conference for TV writers, producers, and so forth, and if she would like to be a speaker they would be delighted to pay her expenses.

Diana's mood perked up, and she went right home to tell Luke about it.

He was sitting in the living room, the stereo blasting,

having what was apparently breakfast—coffee and a roll—at two-thirty in the afternoon.

"Wonderful news, darling," she announced, turning down the sound. "I'm invited to Hollywood for a few days—"

"Hey, I was listening to that. Do you mind?" He got up and turned up the volume.

Diana's ears hurt, and with angry deliberateness she snapped off the stereo. "Yes, I do mind. I'm trying to tell you something that concerns you, too."

He glared at her but she went ahead, making an effort to stem her anger. "Come with me to Hollywood. We can make some valuable contacts. Then, when the time comes. . . ."

Diana talked on, trying to convince herself as well as him. The film would have to be tailor-made, of course, but she knew a lot of people. If she could submit an idea for a screenplay, someone might bite. "And as long as we're on the Coast we could spend a week relaxing. Have you ever been to the Monterey Peninsula? There are wonderful places we could explore." She elaborated, with growing enthusiasm. "How does that sound, darling?"

"Not bad." He smiled at her, a real smile for the first time in so long she felt tears rising and quickly turned away her head.

In the kitchen, she looked for the makings of lunch. "Can I fix you something else to eat?" she called out.

"Yeah. I'm hungrier than I thought." He came in behind her and kissed the back of her neck.

Diana felt a delicious shiver. When he moved his hands to cup her breasts and she felt his arousal, she went limp with desire. Within moments they were fumbling with each other's clothing. Buttons, snaps, zippers were undone, and then they were naked, grabbing at each other, getting as far as the living-room couch, where the lovemaking was quick and terribly exciting.

They spent the afternoon in bed. At one point, Diana did cook some eggs, which they ate in bed. She felt as if a burden of worry had been lifted from her, leaving her happier than she had been in weeks. Diana told Luke how much she loved him, and he said he loved her too.

She had the first true, blissful sleep in ages. She had done it. She had won him back.

Then a blow fell from another quarter. Ann Earle was going to England to make a couple of films, and ATN canceled *Mom & Meg*. The series had slipped in the ratings anyway. Five years had been the limit. Molly would, of course, work on *Pete Winston*, but the loss of *Mom & Meg* meant letting several staff members go, and the atmosphere around the office was somewhat depressing.

Diana dragged Molly to lunch, trying to cheer her up, without much success. "I don't know what you're so chipper about," Molly grumbled. "*Mom & Meg* were like family. I just don't feel the same about *Pete Winston*. That show is too iffy, with Luke acting up the way he is."

Diana hated to add to Molly's worry but felt she must be honest about Luke's wanting to make a film.

"That ungrateful wretch! I hope you're not encouraging him. We won't make any money on *Pete Winston* unless it runs for a couple of years. Christ, we gave him his big chance and he'd better sign a run-of-series or I'll personally kick his ass. And, by the way, I'm disgusted with the way you let that creep lead you around by the nose."

In a rage, Diana threw money on the table and walked out.

She was in a spot. If she helped Luke get a film, Abbott and Sinclair would be out a lot of money. But if she didn't help him, he might find someone else who would and then she would lose him.

The day they were to leave for California she came home from the office and found Luke drinking a beer and watching a ballgame.

"Hi, darling," she said, going to him to be kissed. "I'd better pack. I assume you're ready to go. The limo picks us up in an hour . . . Oh, not now," she demurred, pleased at the way he was nuzzling her neck with his lips.

"Babe, sit down. I want to tell you something." He sounded happy, excited, and she decided she could spare a moment.

"I've been having second thoughts about Hollywood. I'm not sure a film is the right direction for me to go in."

Diana stared at him. "But you said that's what you wanted. I've set up appointments for you—"

"I know, and I'm grateful. But I've been thinking it over and I'm not convinced it's such a good idea. I'd have to live out there while the movie was being made, away from you." His smile made her feel weak with love.

"Not necessarily. More and more movies are being made elsewhere, many right here in New York. Nobody's going to force you to make a movie out there."

"That's for sure."

He sounded strangely vehement. There was something he wasn't telling her, and she wasn't sure she wanted to hear it at this time.

"Uh, why don't we talk about it on the plane, darling."

Luke stood up and put his hands into his jeans pockets. "It's too crazy in Hollywood. All those bozos looking me up and down like I was some sort of freak. Judging me. Well, I don't need their okay. I've proved myself on TV and that's where I want to stay."

"Okay, fine," she said, feeling relieved. "But it might be well to keep the appointments. It never hurts to have contacts, to maintain goodwill. Anyway, let me just throw a few things into a bag—"

"Yeah, in a minute. I've got something else to tell you."

She hesitated apprehensively in the doorway. "Can't it wait?"

"No, ma'am. It's been waiting all day." His smile reassured her. He sounded like such an excited kid that she said, "Okay, shoot."

"Well, I started thinking about what was bothering me, and I figured it out. It's not TV I'm tired of, it's playing a role. That was fine for two seasons, but I've had enough. I'm a personality now. The way I figure it, I ought to be able to play myself. Me, Luke Merriman. I want my own show."

Diana stared at him. His own show! Jesus. She loved him, but not so much that she could overlook his professional limitations. Luke not only needed special material, he needed structure. She had to make that clear without offending him.

"It's very unlikely that you could have your own show after a career spanning only two seasons."

"How long doesn't mean as much as how good, and I'm real good. Almost forty million people watch *Pete Winston*."

"Yes, and that's roughly about a third of the TV audience, so two-thirds, or say eighty million, maybe never even heard of Pete Winston, let alone Luke Merriman."

"Bill Cosby has his own show."

"Bill Cosby has been around for years, and even he's not playing himself, but a doctor named Huxtable."

"Yeah, well, he's black so it's harder—"

Diana's patience ran out. "Luke, who put that idea into your head? Tell me. I'm serious. I'd really like to know. Because whoever it was doesn't know beans about this business."

"Lordy, you think you know everything, don't you? Well, there's a few things you don't know."

"Luke, you're new enough at this that if someone tells you something you want to hear, you don't consider ulterior motives that person might have for filling your head with such garbage—"

"You think it's garbage for me to get my own show?" he challenged, his eyes blazing. "You know, you're not thinking of me at all, but yourself. Because *you* write and produce *Pete Winston*, and that's all you've got, with *Mom & Meg* canceled."

"Oh, Luke, for heaven's sake! It's true that Molly and I have an investment in *Pete Winston*, but that's not the only reason—"

"Damn right, it *is* the only reason. You want the show to run for years, and never mind how I feel, being in a rut."

Diana put her hands to her throbbing temples. "I do care how you feel, but what you want is totally unrealistic."

"I want my own show, and I'm gonna get it, whether you like it or not!"

"Okay, go ahead and try it. See how far you get," Diana said angrily, looking at her watch. "I'm getting packed."

In the bedroom she saw that the suitcase she had laid out for him was still on a chair, open and empty. "You haven't packed a thing. We're going to be late."

"I'm not going," he said sullenly from the doorway.

She didn't turn, but continued to pack her own bag. "Please don't sulk. Of course you're going. We'll talk about it on the plane."

"I hate the way you don't take me seriously."

Now she did turn to stare at him.

"That's right," he continued. "I'm tired of falling in with your plans. You have something to do in Hollywood, fine, you go do it. I'm staying right here and working on my career. I'm going to call Harriet. She may not think I'm as crazy as you do."

Diana's annoyance turned to fear. "Please, darling, let's not quarrel. I promise you I'll consider your idea, but right now we've got to catch that plane."

"So catch it. I'm not stopping you. You're going to be busy for a couple of days anyway. Meantime I can be doing myself some good right here. I just want to explore the possibility of getting my own show."

Warning bells went off in Diana's head. That wasn't Luke's way of speaking. He was surely quoting someone. But before she could ask who, the doorman buzzed to announce that the limo was waiting.

Diana looked at Luke framed in the doorway, hands in his pockets. He really had no intention of coming with her.

God, it was ridiculous for him to get worked up over nothing. The idea of getting him a show at this time was ludicrous, unless . . .

"Luke, have you been approached by another network? Because if you have—"

He held up his hand and said sarcastically, "You have no time to talk about it, remember? You just go ahead and catch your plane. Don't worry about me. I'll do okay."

Doubts, fears, and rationalizations began to race with Olympic speed through her brain.

She snapped her suitcase shut and picked up her handbag. Okay, he didn't want to come to Hollywood because he had a new obsession. But after he tried it on somebody else, he would realize it was unworkable. Fortunately, Harriet was a sensible woman and a crackerjack agent. She would soon set him straight.

"All right, if you're sure this is what you want," Diana said tensely.

"Yes, ma'am, it is."

She felt suddenly forlorn. "I'll miss you. I wish you'd reconsider—"

"Why don't *you?* Why don't *you* stay in New York and get me my own show?"

His unreasonable attitude gave her the impetus to start for the door. "My conference will be over on Saturday. I've made a reservation at Carmel for us. This is my phone number. You could take a morning plane on Saturday and meet me—"

"Maybe." He shrugged. "I'll see how I feel."

Her doubts returned. "You'll call me?"

"Yup."

He gave her the merest peck on the cheek.

A moment later she was in the elevator, feeling terrible, panicky, wondering if she ought to go back, then realizing she couldn't keep humoring him as if he were ten years old.

All the way to the airport she pondered, flip-flopping a dozen times.

Before boarding her plane she tried calling but got a busy signal. Maybe she should phone Harriet. No, it wouldn't be ethical to interfere between client and agent.

Even when Diana was fastened into her seat, she had a terrible feeling that she ought to rush off the plane. In half an hour she could be in Luke's arms. Maybe she was risking too much, leaving things the way she had. In the last hour she might have wiped out all the gains she had recently made.

Go back, Sinclair. You love him, you want to keep him.

But his demand for his own show stopped her. There was no way she could deal with that now. He would have to discover reality for himself.

In fact, the more she pondered, the more she saw that she had to let him make a few of his own mistakes at this point. When he erred, he would find out just how human he was and he'd be ready to listen to her advice once again.

20 Luke sat in the little French bistro facing the door. He liked the place, dark and candle-lit. Several couples were striking romantic poses around him. At a few of the tables, women were seated alone, waiting no doubt for their dates, as he was waiting for his. He saw them giving him the eye, and wondered if it was because they recognized him or because they found him so attractive.

As he sipped his kir he had a fantasy about one of them, a stunning woman with long dark hair and full lips. Her date doesn't show, and neither does his. She joins him for dinner, they talk, she invites him home . . .

Lord, it felt wonderful to be free again, not having to account to Diana about where he had been and why and with whom. He didn't have to hold things back or tell lies, nor worry about being found out. He hadn't been with a lot of women since Diana. In truth there had been very few, and each time he had felt a little guilty. He felt guilty now, but Diana obviously didn't appreciate him, so why shouldn't he be with someone that did? She had gone off to do her own thing and he felt free to do his.

He loved women too well, and that was why he had to be especially careful. He knew he'd made a big mistake with Gemma. Early on he'd been flattered by her attentions, but who wouldn't have been? She'd been trying to get him in the hay from the word go, and he'd restrained himself, especially because they were costars.

But seeing her every day, and performing all those teasing romantic scenes had turned him on. And she was smart. She'd worked on him during odd moments, telling him Diana was getting too possessive, acting like she owned him, and they weren't even married. He'd always wondered what it would be like to screw Gemma, and he'd finally found out.

Gemma sure talked a better lay than she gave. Lots of technique, no real passion. Not like Diana, who was like an active volcano on the verge of erupting.

Even so, he didn't mind putting it to Gemma every once in a while, just for variety. Especially when Diana had started to take him for granted or given him the silent treatment, acting like he was poison. She had called them business worries—some bullshit about the fall lineup. She had stopped appreciating him, and he was damned if he'd take second place to her work.

Then again, Gemma was a little too eager to appreciate him. She had come at him with both hands out, wanting him to drop Diana and take up with her. But he wasn't planning an escape from one prison only to be locked into another.

So when Diana began getting pissed about him and Gemma openly flirting, he had decided it was easier to quit seeing the actress. But then she had started sticking pins into him. He hoped he would soon be rid of Gemma and *Pete Winston* both.

"Oh, Luke, I'm so glad you made it. I was afraid you might have gone to California after all." Nikki flounced into her chair and smiled at him with such pleasure that he was glad he had remained in New York.

He ordered a drink for Nikki, pleased that she had decked herself out with special care because of him. She was wearing something frilly and flimsy and damn near transparent. Yeah, Nikki was cute, and sexy too. She also understood him. When it came to Diana, Nikki was in the same boat as he was—Diana's pupil, having to do what teacher wanted.

"Luke, I've been thinking about you all day. And what we talked about yesterday. What did Diana say when you told her?"

He hesitated. "Well, not too much. She was running sort of late."

"Oh, I guess I was wrong. I thought she'd be thrilled. Like, your own show is such a natural at this point. I hope you didn't tell her it was my idea."

"Nope."

"Good. Because I've been thinking, and now I know just the kind of show it should be. You should be doing what Pete does best and millions of viewers have seen him do: give advice to kids and grown-ups about their problems."

While they ate, Nikki explained. During the warm-up period, people in the audience would ask their questions. Luke would pick out the ones he liked and consult with, say, a child psychologist or a marriage counselor (all behind the scenes, of course) and mentally frame the answers. Then, at taping time, he would call only on the people who had asked the pre-chosen questions and he would be ready with the answers. "Like, you're so good at ad-libbing, you don't need every 'the,' 'and,' and 'but' put down on paper."

Luke felt a flush of warmth at the confidence she had in him. She talked on, and the more she said, the more intrigued he became. Instead of having to memorize speeches, he would only have to get a few points clear in his head, such as what to tell a kid who wants to drop out of school, or a girl dating a married man, or a husband thinking of leaving his wife.

"Oh, Luke, I'm so excited. It's the perfect format for you."

But would Diana go for the idea?

"The trouble is that she isn't really a free agent, with Molly shooting down everything. God, I detest that woman," Nikki burst out. "She's been out to get me from day one, and never misses a chance to be bitchy."

Luke sighed. "That goes double for me. She's like a porcupine, that old gal."

"I know," Nikki said, looking at him intently. "I hate to say this, but I think she has a terrible influence over Diana. After all, Molly controls the purse strings. Like, it must be tough to be so much under another person's thumb that you can't make a move on your own."

"Yeah."

There was a pause.

"If Diana isn't interested in *The Luke Merriman Show*, what are you going to do?" Nikki asked softly.

The Luke Merriman Show—it was music to his ears. He looked uncertainly at Nikki. "Uh, I don't know. It depends. Any ideas?"

"Well," Nikki said pleasantly, a confident smile on her lips, "Diana isn't the only writer/producer in town. Maybe it's time for you to do what *you* want, for a change."

Nikki's glance didn't waver, and why should it? She had written and produced a dynamite show, certainly as good as anything Diana had ever dreamed up.

Nikki fingered her empty wineglass, and Luke hastened to fill it.

"One thing you've got going for you is the rivalry between the networks," Nikki confided, leaning forward. "Now that Continental is second, ATN is having a fit. They want to stay number one. And the best way to do that is to acquire the star that's number one in the ratings. Namely, Luke Merriman," she finished, pointing at him.

He felt a growing excitement as Nikki talked on. This gal had a lot more between her ears than a pair of baby blues and a come-hither smile.

She was a budding Diana. And she had been flaunting herself at him for ages. He remembered the last time they had had dinner, in the Italian equivalent of this joint. How she had tempted him with those ripe golden apples of hers. He had longed to take a bite then but hadn't dared because she'd been Diana's right-hand gal. Well, now the troops were moving up, even if they had to promote themselves to do so.

Nikki went on dropping the names of several people in high places at ATN. She seemed to know them quite well—where they hung out, what they were looking for. She pointed out that Luke didn't owe Continental any particular loyalty. On the contrary. Even after *Pete Winston* zoomed to the top, he was still pulling down a pathetic salary.

"If I sign another contract, they're going to pay through the nose." Nikki smiled, and he realized he had said "if" and not "when."

Nikki continued to smile, reminding him that Continental only paid the production company a licensing fee for the right to air the show, and it was actually Abbott and Sinclair who paid his salary. And even if Sinclair was prepared to be generous in a new contract, Abbott, the millionaire partner, was as tight as a noose with money.

Besides, Nikki knew for a fact that Luke was going to

be forced to sign a run-of-series contract, which meant he might be tied up for four or five years. But if he decided to do *The Luke Merriman Show*, he could make an entirely different arrangement with another network.

When she told him how he could bring it about, he sat back in his seat and looked at her with undisguised admiration. She knew something that neither Diana nor Harriet had ever even hinted at.

Harriet, Nikki reminded him sweetly, had been recommended by Diana. Nikki was implying that he was now big enough to negotiate his own contract.

Luke ordered another bottle of wine, mulling over Nikki's revelations. The more she said, the more he was convinced that she was right. Diana had been steering him wrong, holding him back to protect her own interest in the show.

"Of course, Diana has been valuable to both of us, Luke," Nikki said a little later, putting her hand on his wrist and smiling into his eyes. "But let's face it. She's so used to thinking of us as beginners she can't seem to understand that we're both pros now."

Hadn't that been his exact complaint to Diana?

Nikki moved her lovely face so close to his that he couldn't resist kissing her. And when she opened her lips and flicked her tongue invitingly into the corners of his mouth, he felt an immediate response in his groin.

Nikki removed her face, to his regret, but she had whetted his appetite.

"Of course, the whole thing is so complicated," she said. "Like, when Matthew Sayles first bought *Pete Winston*, he only did it to please Diana."

Luke frowned. "Why should he want to please her, particularly?"

Nikki's smile chilled him. "For the most obvious reason in the world. Why else does a head of entertainment in a third-place network take a chance on a sitcom from a female indie prod whose one credit is for an action series? And with a lead actor in this sitcom nobody ever heard of? I mean, surely you know about Matthew and Diana?"

Luke felt such rage gripping him that he couldn't reply.

"Oh, God. I'm sorry." Nikki clapped her hand over her mouth. "I was sure she told you . . . Oh, please, Luke, don't ever say anything. Diana would kill me. I mean, she gave Matthew up once you moved in, I guess. Still, he's the kind of guy that blackmails people to get what he wants. When he's alone with her, who knows? And now they're both in California. . . ."

Luke felt hot with fury at the way Diana had tricked and betrayed him, claiming to have met Matthew at a party when all the time she'd been screwing him, the stinking little bitch.

"Sometimes," Nikki said softly, "when a woman acts very possessive and jealous, it's . . . well, like she's covering up her own actions. I mean, she knows what *she's* been doing so she suspects her guy of doing the same thing."

She touched his arm. "I can see you're upset, Luke. It really hurts to trust someone and then find out . . . Anyway, it's better not to brood about the past. Not when you've got such a terrific future. If you want it." She reached out her hand and gently stroked his cheek and his ear.

Luke shut his eyes for a moment, feeling the very surface of his skin contract with desire.

The Luke Merriman Show. It was her wonderful idea, and she would make it come true.

Nikki got out of bed quietly so as not to awaken Luke. It was a glorious sunny day, and she felt absolutely marvelous. Everything had gone even better than she had planned.

She took a quick shower, washed and blow-dried her hair, then carefully applied makeup and little dabs of perfume behind her ears, on her wrists, her breasts, and just a dot on her thighs, smiling as she admired herself in the mirror. The cat that swallowed the canary. And what a canary. Nikki ran her tongue over her somewhat swollen lips.

Last night had been simply fabulous. She and Luke had been at it like a couple of rabbits, only dozing at brief intervals before climbing on each other again.

Never before had she been with a man who had such energy, whose arousal was so instant and so constant. God, no wonder Diana had been keeping him caged up. Everything had been just as Nikki had always imagined it would be. Good-bye, Gwen.

Slipping into her best negligee, Nikki consulted her watch. Nine-thirty exactly. Humming softly to herself, she tiptoed into her kitchenette and boiled water for coffee. Luke was sprawled out on her convertible bed in the large studio room in deep sleep. The guy deserves to be exhausted, she thought.

She fixed herself some instant coffee and sat sipping it in a chair near the window. Everything had gone like clockwork, telling Luke about his own show just the day before Diana went to the Coast. Whatever that bitch had promised to do for him out there in the way of a film couldn't compare with his own show. His face had lit up just to hear about it.

Of course, she had already laid the groundwork with ATN. She had chosen them after she heard some gossip that Oliver Feranti, their director of East Coast development, was handling his mid-life crisis by developing as much East Coast feminine talent as there were nights in the week.

"He's strictly hit-and-run," one veteran female, a highly placed assistant to a vice-president, had assured Nikki. "However, no woman gets to first base around here unless she's open to a quid pro quiff arrangement."

Nikki's next step was to introduce herself to Oliver Feranti at a network party she managed to get herself invited to. She had watched his ears wiggle with interest when he learned of her connection with Luke. That very night, after she had sweetened the business part with a romp around his pad—complete with loft bed, track lighting, and Prince on the stereo—he had assured her he would be very much interested in developing *The Luke Merriman Show*.

During all of this, Nikki had lied to Gwen that she was taking acting classes a couple of nights a week, which left her exhausted and needing to sleep in her own bed.

Sometimes Nikki had to laugh as she pulled strings and pushed buttons to get the older woman running around in circles just to accommodate her. Whatever Nikki wants, Nikki gets. At times, she found it almost touching. If Gwen had been her mother instead of that cold bitch she had been dealt, her life might have gone in a different direction.

Nikki smiled as she reviewed her last night's performance with Luke at that bistro. His guard had been down. He was annoyed with Diana, and flattered out of his mind at the idea of his own show. The lie about Diana and Matthew had been pure spontaneous inspiration. Luke had certainly eaten it up. Anyway, it might even be true, for all Nikki knew. Diana wasn't the virtuous little flower she appeared to be.

Nikki picked up the phone, carried it into the bathroom, and with the door shut dialed Feranti. "Oliver, it's Nikki," she crooned pleasantly. "I've been chatting with my friend and he's absolutely crazy about doing what we talked about. Of course, I would be the writer/producer."

"Of course, that's understood, sweetie." Feranti's voice came through sounding warm and very pleased.

"The only thing is to do it quickly. Because when my friend's friend gets back from the Coast . . ." Nikki went on cryptically (she knew better than to drop names on the phone), and was assured that a preliminary meeting could be set up that afternoon, and a contract readied by Friday.

Nikki smiled and quietly cradled the receiver. Perfect. Once Luke's name was on the contract, Diana could bang her head against the wall—she'd be out. And Nikki would be in.

She returned to the living room, sat down on the bed, and felt under the covers. God, Luke was unbelievable. He had one made of wood for sure.

"Wake up, hon," she murmured, flicking her tongue against his ear.

"Mm. I already am, hon," he said, grinning, his eyes closed.

"About ATN," she said as she stroked him lightly. "Oliver Feranti has invited you to lunch."

Luke's eyes opened wide. "Hey, that's super."

"It sure is. You're super, too. How about one for the road?"

"You've got it."

In a flash, Nikki was naked and slithering all over him. She wanted him to think that she was constantly horny, although in truth she felt a little sore this morning. But she could take advantage of her talented mouth and her deep throat. Maybe Luke would get his rocks off that way and she'd have a few hours to recuperate.

However she did it, she had to get Luke even more hooked on her than he had been on Diana. Nikki felt supremely confident that anything Diana could do, she could do better.

Luke lay back on his pillow, his eyes closed, a satisfied smile playing around his lips. This was the life. Lord, that girl had some tongue on her.
He could usually make it half a dozen times in a few hours, but last night he had stopped counting. Yet, here he was again, rarin' to go—or at least be gone down on.
As his excitement increased, he raised his head and looked down. The sight of that gorgeous gal swallowing him to the hilt was like being in a porn film. It was a total turn-on, and he gave her everything he had.

Oliver Feranti hung up and immediately buzzed his assistant. "Evvie, get in here."
When she did, he looked at her sleepy face and snapped his fingers. "Hey, look alive, this is going to be a big day. Cancel my lunch with what's-his-face and set me up for twelve-thirty with Luke Merriman." Oliver enjoyed the look of surprise Evvie threw him. "That's right. I thought that would open your eyes. And at eleven sharp, get me Jerry at his home number in Beverly Hills."
Oliver leaned back in his swivel chair and positioned his feet on his desk, admiring the way his Gucci loafers gleamed from their professional shine.
His phone rang but he didn't pick up. He had told Evvie to hold his calls. This moment was so good it had to be savored. Today and tomorrow, if all went well, were going to be the best days he had spent at ATN in a long while.
From the moment *Pete Winston* had hit prime time, the chairman of Alpha Television Network, Jerry Sirota, had been making Oliver's life miserable. The network had *Mom & Meg*, so how come they hadn't been offered a crack at *Pete Winston*? Oliver had been forced to admit they had been, because he knew that Diana, that sneaky little operator, had written proof of the offer as well as the turndown.
Jerry had hit the roof, calling Oliver every name he

PROTÉGÉ 253

could think of, and ordered him to meet with the program committee and get something competitive opposite the successful series.

But that was much easier said than done. For two seasons they had tried everything. A couple of their best sitcoms had performed shamefully against *Pete Winston*. Next they had tried made-for-TV movies designed to have family appeal. ATN had increased their share only marginally and only for the given nights. They hadn't made a dent in *Pete Winston*'s continuing popularity, and the very next week whatever small part of the audience they had lured went right back to Continental.

Oliver had suggested counterprogramming. First, sports events, hoping to give the men of the *Pete Winston*-hooked households an alternative. Sports hadn't done the job. Neither had action drama or a talk show. In fact, at a meeting in L.A., the research boys hd chewed him out for not taking into account that women dominate the viewing choices in a three-to-two ratio, and women watched mostly comedy.

Jerry and the head programmer had both been screaming for Oliver's head because after throwing about fifteen shows opposite *Pete Winston*, the network was stymied.

And what was even more infuriating to them was that the audience stayed with Continental to watch *Turning Tides*, a revolting nighttime soap that under ordinary circumstances would have sunk in its own suds after a couple of weeks. In fact, the audience remained glued to Continental even for the so-so action drama following the soap. Thursday night, in other words, was a total washout for ATN.

In desperation, Oliver had rushed into production what he thought was a canny imitation of *Pete Winston*. It starred an actor with three decades of proven TV popularity as a grandfather raising five kids. But although *At Home with Gramps* earned some decent reviews, it simply couldn't grab the female audience away from *Pete Winston*. Damn all these yuppie women who were gumming up prime-time programming strategies that had worked for years.

Gramps had been moved and was doing well. But the fact remained that Thursday night wouldn't go away. And

Continental had capitalized on Thursday's popularity by arranging a bang-up lineup for Friday, and Jerry was screaming that soon Continental would have dynamite primetime shows for every night in the week and would edge ATN out for the top spot.

Oliver rued the day he hadn't taken Diana Sinclair seriously as a sitcom writer. He had not only been eating his words to her but also choking on them.

To add to his problems, the network had to cancel *Mom & Meg*. Even before Ann Earle had said she was leaving, the series had been dropping in the ratings. Five years was a long time; the program had expired from old age.

And with the fall schedule in front of him, and no way to remedy Thursday nights, Oliver had been plucking his mustache bald in an attempt to pull a rabbit out of a hat. Of course, ATN could try to recruit the whole show. That had been done in the past, but the trouble here was Diana's good memory.

Oliver had tried sounding Molly out, when they were discussing the demise of *Mom & Meg*. Before he could even talk money, Molly squelched the discussion. "You could have had *Pete Winston*, but you passed, and not very nicely, as Diana remembers. Continental gave us a break and there's no reason not to stick with them. Yes, I know you'd pay the earth, but so will they when we negotiate our new contract next month. End of discussion."

There was one final possibility, and that was to try to get Luke Merriman himself over to ATN by making him an incredibly lucrative offer. That, however, would have to be very delicately handled, particularly because of the Diana-Luke connection.

Oliver had been mulling over it for weeks. And then his luck had turned. He smiled now as he thought of it, and took a sip of his coffee. It had gone cold, but he didn't care.

At some industry bash he had been routinely scanning the chicks when a perky little redhead had approached him, leading with her tits and smiling in an unmistakable way. Oliver had wondered what this one wanted and had weighed her possible demands against his probable pleasures.

As soon as Nikki had broached her idea for *The Luke Merriman Show*, over a drink that very evening, Oliver had been sure she was a flake. Then, when she told him Luke was tired of Diana—who happened to be going out of town—Oliver had realized that she wasn't entirely crazy. She was simply too consumed with her own ambition to see that ATN was panting to get Merriman under contract. That bimbo was delivering Merriman tied up in a ribbon, yet she had actually slept with Oliver for the privilege.

It was a delicious irony, and he sat at his desk enjoying it. He enjoyed, too, telling Jerry in a casual tone that he was about to sign up Luke Merriman. How wonderful it felt, for a change, to get a little praise, and to be able to tell his boss to get his ass to New York pronto if he wanted to be present for the ceremony.

21

"Hi, there, I can't come to the phone right now, but if you'll leave your name and number—" Diana hung up before the beep sounded.

All right, if Luke was going to play hard to get, she would tough it out. Already she regretted having left one message for him to call her at the Hilton; she was damned if she'd leave another. She was too annoyed with him. It was already Friday, and he still hadn't said whether he was coming out or not.

Fortunately, she hadn't been thinking of him too much because she had been busy. She had left Coastal Studios a novice and returned a pro, a tremendous success, and a role model for every little scriptgirl and gofer who wanted for herself exactly what Diana had achieved. It had been wonderful to be made a fuss of by executives who would once have scorned to greet her in the commissary.

She wished Luke had been here to see *her* get some kudos for a change. He might remember that he owed his success to her efforts.

His own show. Every time she thought of it, she wanted to scream.

By Saturday afternoon it was clear he wasn't coming. All right, she would go to the Monterey Peninsula herself. For most of her life she had been on her own, and if necessary she could be again. She had let Luke get beneath her defenses, and it was time to assert her independence.

She flew to San Francisco, rented a car, and drove to a small, secluded inn a couple of miles south of Carmel, where she had reserved a suite with a balcony.

She dressed carefully for herself, dined in style by herself, and on Sunday took the Seventeen-Mile Drive, which was as beautiful and awesome as she remembered it. It was delightful to watch sea otters lazing on rocks companionably with gulls and pelicans, and to sniff the mingled aroma of ocean pine and eucalyptus.

Yet by evening, and with no word from Luke, she couldn't help feeling bleak, with time heavy on her hands.

Diana gritted her teeth and forced herself not to phone him. He was probably trying to interest someone in his show and being stubborn about admitting defeat. Maybe Harriet hadn't been firm enough with him; or maybe she had been too firm. Maybe he was embarrassed to have to admit he was wrong. Or he could have been spiting Diana by staying away.

Monday morning those few moments of sleeping-to-waking without Luke's warm, fragrant body beside her were painful. She got up quickly and dressed, even though it was only a little after dawn.

As she drove the short distance to Carmel, she saw the misty outline of the sun rising over the Santa Lucia Mountains. The town was still asleep, the streets quiet and uncrowded. She was the first patron at a coffee shop, and her reward was freshly brewed coffee and a hot blueberry muffin.

Carmel was as picture-perfect as she remembered it—the quaint, twisting streets, the neat little shops, the charming houses tucked amid lush greenery and shade trees on the residential streets.

When she stopped for lunch at a wonderful little seafood place, she felt a sharp pang of loneliness. Eating by herself was becoming more depressing by the meal.

She drove back to the inn wondering if Luke had called after all, or if he might even be there to surprise her.

She had dinner alone in her room, and with a heavy heart, tried calling him. But when she heard his phone ring three times, she hung up. She would leave no more messages.

She awoke on Tuesday feeling awful, panicky, and unable to face another day in Carmel. It would be unbearable during social hours, with tourists strolling in pairs or groups, sharing thoughts and impressions. How she had wanted to show all this to Luke. Damn him!

She preferred to be isolated within the protective mantle of natural surroundings, so she spent the day on the beach and walked for miles. She watched the gulls diving into the blue-green waters for fish; studied the cypresses, twisted into bizarre shapes by the wind; felt the sand cool beneath her bare feet; heard the rhythmic pounding of the surf against the rocky shore.

Every once in a while she thought about her predicament and regretted the day she had allowed Luke Merriman to gain a privileged place in her life. And yet, in the next moment she wished he were there with her.

He was punishing her by not communicating; she saw that clearly. He had probably guessed—rightly—that she would miss him in this place where she had no work to do, while he was undoubtedly living it up every night.

Diana didn't want to give in to him, yet at the same time she found unbidden ideas flickering through her brain for Luke's show. Forget it, she told herself sternly. But possibilities kept cropping up.

Maybe it wasn't as absurd as she had first thought. Maybe Luke was right, and she was sticking to *Pete Winston* because it was a bankable series. Really, had anything been more ridiculous than her idea for *Pete Winston* last year? Everyone had scoffed, but she had carried it off.

She walked along the windswept beach until exhaustion claimed her, then sat watching grains of sand scuttling almost imperceptibly over the dunes. Maybe a series could be made out of Luke roving with his camera, interviewing interesting New York types. He had done something of the sort so naturally, the day she had first had the inspiration for *Pete Winston*. However, on-location shooting would be too expensive. Maybe interviews in a studio setting would work better. She was doubtful; Luke was no Dick Cavett or Johnny Carson. He didn't have the breadth of knowledge needed to run a talk show. But with help . . .

She decided it was time to fly home. As she drove to San Francisco, all sorts of formats for shows began to come to her.

She would catch the red-eye flight and be in New York by six-thirty or seven, and in Luke's arms half an hour later.

Diana got off the elevator and came up to her door feeling weak with anticipation.

Luke was in the bedroom, up and dressed and getting something out of a drawer. Her heart filled when she saw him. "Luke. Oh, Luke, darling."

She ran to him and flung herself in his arms, holding him tightly, pressing her lips against his. "I'm so glad to be home," she murmured between kisses. "I've missed you terribly."

After a moment, she realized that he wasn't responding, but was standing woodenly, his arms at his sides.

She backed off, fear tugging at her backbone, and stared at him. "What's the matter?"

He looked uncomfortable. "I didn't expect you back so soon. I thought you'd stay out there until the weekend."

Thought or hoped? He was certainly not showing any pleasure in seeing her. He wasn't even looking at her, and his face was devoid of expression.

As she looked him up and down, a growing terror within her, she noticed for the first time two suitcases standing by the bed.

"Where are you going? You weren't coming out to the Coast, were you?" she asked, forcing a little laugh.

He made a face, lifted one bag to the bed, and opened it. Turning his back to her, he began to empty a drawer of underwear. "I was going to leave you a note," he mumbled.

"A note about what?" she whispered fearfully.

His answer didn't come for a long time. With great deliberation he stacked a pile of bikini shorts and T-shirts into the bag and then put his socks on top.

No, not that way. She had an absurd impulse to point out that he would save space if he rolled the socks and put them in the corners and empty spaces of the bag. . . . She wiped her forehead and waited for him to speak.

He opened another drawer and loaded a few sweaters on top of his other things. The bag wouldn't shut. Good. He wouldn't be able to go—wherever it was he was going.

"Oh, shit," he muttered, pulling out the sweaters.

Finally he turned and looked at her fleetingly, the look of a stranger. He sighed, took a deep breath, and said, "I can't go on with our affair."

Diana stood motionless, feeling her insides stop functioning momentarily. The room was as silent as a nightmare.

"Our 'affair'? Is that what you call it? Is that what I mean to you?" she quavered.

Luke rolled his eyes toward the ceiling. "Please don't make a scene, Diana. It had to end sometime."

"Why?" she cried. "Why did it have to end?"

"Because," he snapped irritably. "Look, I don't want to talk about it. We had it out before you left—"

"We did no such thing." Diana came closer, as if by closing the physical gap she could banish whatever grievances he had against her. Forcing herself to stay calm and speak reasonably, she continued. "We had a tiff, okay. All couples do. But I've thought it over. In fact, I've got lots of ideas for you. I've reconsidered, so there's nothing more to quarrel about."

Luke backed away and didn't meet her gaze. "You're making this harder than it has to be. Hell, fifteen minutes more and I'd have been out of here and not had to deal with this." He spoke as much to himself as to her, and his attitude was chilling.

"Where are you going?"

"To a hotel. Until I find my own place."

Diana took several deep breaths, warning herself to be careful. What she said in the next few moments could be crucial. "We had a simple disagreement, that was all. You wanted your own show, I thought it was too soon. Well, I've come around to your way of thinking. So if you just stop packing for a minute and listen—"

"Okay," he agreed, his voice hard, "so tell me."

Shakily, leaning on her bureau to keep from trembling,

she started on her first idea, but hadn't said ten words before he broke in.

"And you'd write it, wouldn't you?"

"Well, I'd write some of it. There would be other writers, of course, and we'd need your input—"

"*My* input?" He sneered. "You need *my* input all right, but I don't need *yours*. You want to keep me your protégé forever, a slave to every word you write." As he spoke, his eyes blazed and his mouth curled in anger. "Well, I'm tired of memorizing lines; I can speak for myself."

Shocked by his outburst, Diana played for time. "Okay, okay, if that's the way you feel. Luke, please, please stop packing," she implored softly. "People should never make important decisions hastily. I mean, just because we've had a difference of opinion—after a year together. I thought we had something wonderful. You can't throw it away, just like that."

He was silent as he pulled a suit, some slacks, and a couple of jackets from the closet and looked with dismay at his remaining bag. His wardrobe was too big for his bags, and he was too big for his breeches. She had to make him see reason.

"Luke, don't do something you're going to regret. Please, darling, let's talk it over. I'm sure there isn't anything we can't work out. . . ." She went on, her voice soft, soothing. She had regained control of herself, but her years of persuading people would mean nothing if she couldn't persuade him now.

Luke folded his arms and listened impassively, his eyes as cold as the Atlantic in winter. "I can't work anything out with you," he broke in icily. "You don't appreciate me. You act like I'm some puppet you can dangle on a string."

Marionette, she corrected silently, miserably, shutting her eyes as if she could shut out his hateful words.

"I'm not the shit-kicker I was a year ago, but you just can't take that in. You still bitch away and never take anything I say seriously because you think you know best. Well, I've had enough and I'm getting out."

"But I love you," she cried, suddenly engulfed by fear, by doubt. "I thought you loved me. You did, didn't you?

How could you stop loving me just like that in a week, just because of a little disagreement?" She suddenly couldn't utter another word, as tears welled and spilled over, and she was shaken with sobs. Oh, God, it couldn't be true. This couldn't be happening. Yet, she had been fearing this very thing for a long time.

She moved to the night table for some tissues. She simply had to control herself so she could get him to reconsider. She didn't really expect her tears to soften his resolve, but when he kicked off his shoes, for one glorious moment she thought he was staying. Then she saw he was simply intending to wear another pair.

"I love you, Luke—"

"Oh, Lordy, shut up about love, will you? It makes me sick to hear you say that when you've been screwing Matthew Sayles and making a fool out of me all this time."

"*What?*" Diana went up to Luke and gazed into his face, wide-eyed with astonishment. "*What* did you say?"

Luke brandished his shoe at her. "You heard me. Everyone knows all about it—everyone but me. I've been a real rube, listening to you, believing every lying word you've ever told me—"

"Luke, it isn't true. Who told you I've been with Matthew? It's a ridiculous lie! I've never even been out with him, except on business."

"The two of you have been laughing at me behind my back, in East Hampton, in California. You were glad I stayed here, glad of a chance to be alone with that little creep."

"That's crazy," she yelled, grabbing Luke's arm.

"Don't touch me," he snarled, flinging her angrily from him.

Her mind in a whirl, she saw that someone had been lying to him, and it was surely a woman. But who hated her enough to fill his head with such appalling lies?

Luke refused to tell her who the person was, pretending it was common knowledge, but she knew that couldn't be so. Of course, she could imagine that some unsubtle types, seeing her lunching with Matthew or having a drink with him, might misconstrue their relationship.

Mastering her voice, Diana said quietly, "Matthew and

I have never been more than friends. I'm amazed that you would think I'd lie to you about something so important. Someone has been feeding you poison, and before you swallow it whole you ought to consider what that person has to gain by bad-mouthing me."

Luke finished tying his shoes and stood up. "I'll get the rest of my gear when you're out. I'll leave the key with the doorman—"

"Please don't go like this."

"It's gotta be like this," he said tightly, reaching for his bags.

Diana dug her nails into the palms of her hands until they hurt. She mustn't beg him. It would be better to let him go to a hotel for a couple days. If Luke was jealous of Matthew, it meant he still loved her. She could straighten that out and get him to see the truth. "What hotel, Luke?"

He didn't reply.

"We have to be in touch about the series—"

"Oh, no we don't," Luke snapped, his eyes sparking. "I'm not renewing my contact."

"What?"

"What? What?" he mocked. "You heard me all right."

"But it's all set for next season! They've approved our thirteen shows. They believe in you, and so do all the others members of the cast, and the crew—"

Luke shrugged. "Screw everybody. I don't give a fuck about any one of them. Listen, every berry-picking son-of-a-bitch in this whole wide world is out for number one. Lord, even when I was bone ignorant I knew that much. Learned it at my mama's knee."

Diana was incredulous at his hard cynicism. "You're going to walk away from a successful series just like that?"

"Nope. Not just like that, for something better to do. Like *The Luke Merriman Show*." He smiled triumphantly and picked up his bags.

Diana ran after him. "Wait a minute! For God's sake, tell me what you're talking about." She barred his way.

"Sure I'll tell you. It makes me real proud to let you know you're not the mover and shaker you think you are. Life does go on without you. *The Luke Merriman Show* was bought by ATN. Matter of fact, I just signed an exclusive contract with them for five years."

Diana's hands flew to her face. "You did *what*? I don't believe it! Harriet wouldn't let you do something so stupid."

"You mean Harriet wouldn't let me do something so smart! She's your gal, all right, trying to keep me in line so's I don't get tired of you. Well, I didn't ask Harriet's permission. She'll find out soon enough when she gets a copy of the contract. Don't worry, she's got no kick coming. She still gets her ten percent for doing nothing. Hell, I can be my own agent."

Diana grabbed her head with both hands. "Oh, Luke, you don't know what you've done!"

"I've gotten rid of you, that's what I've done. Of you and Molly and Continental and all the shit I've had to take for a year—"

"You idiot!" Diana shouted. "You've just thrown your career out the window! ATN doesn't have to give you any show! They said they would because that's what you wanted to hear. Jesus, you went up there and signed a contract that your agent didn't see and your lawyer didn't see . . . I'll bet you everything I'm worth that when someone knowledgeable goes over the fine print, you'll learn that the show is something they dangled as bait. And like any greedy fish, you bit and will get stuck with the hook in your throat! Don't you see? ATN has been losing ground to Continental. They'd do *anything*, pay *anything* to get you off the rival network because you've destroyed Thursday night for them! They can keep you from working for five years!"

She saw Luke turn a little pale as she went on, appalled that he could have done something so idiotic. This was the old double-whammy, a ploy used by the networks quite a bit during the seventies. It sounded fine at first, but concealed in all the mumbo jumbo and legalese were a million ifs and buts. Had they given him a *written commitment* to broadcast *The Luke Merriman Show*? Or was the only written commitment on his part—to bind himself to ATN for five years?

Luke's frown vanished, and he smiled. "I've got it in writing that they're going to pay for production of the show without a pilot, and they're going to put it on the air. Says so right in the contract."

"And does it say how many episodes? Or what happens

if the show isn't a hit? Does it specify prime time? No network will commit itself to keeping a failure on the air."

"They're paying me a million and a half! Three hundred thousand a year every year for five years, so you can bet your ass they're going to keep the show going."

"Wrong! They're paying to get you away from Continental and to kill *Pete Winston*. It's worth it to them. And, by the way, it's not enough. You could have gotten four hundred thousand a year, maybe more."

"You're just pissed that Abbott and Sinclair are losing out, because you won't find another hick so fast to be Pete Winston. Well, tough, lady!"

"Without you, there is no *Pete Winston*, but we'll do all right," Diana snapped. "Anyway, if you think I'm going to help you write a show for ATN—"

"Listen to you!" Luke shouted. "Talking about egotism! Hey, I don't need you, lady. *The Luke Merriman Show* is already in the works."

"Oh, really. And who, might I ask, is producing it?"

"Nikki," he snapped.

"My Nikki?"

"Nikki De Paul, that's right, but she's not yours any more than I'm yours! You don't own people!"

For a moment Diana was speechless. It was simply impossible. Her voice returned. "I've helped Nikki, promoted her, she's been with me for almost two years. She would never be so treacherous—"

"You call it treachery, she calls it opportunity."

Now Diana remembered that dinner with Nikki that Molly had warned her about. Luke and Nikki had denied that it was anything but innocent. Innocent! If Nikki had already put together a show for Luke, she must have been conspiring against Diana for some time.

"If you go with Nikki you'll be making a big mistake," Diana said tensely, "because her talents are strictly limited to production details and, apparently, intrigue. For your information, in two years she came up with only two usable ideas, after submitting dozens, and I had to rework her scripts word for word because she's a lousy writer."

"Bullshit. She couldn't be that bad," Luke challenged, "when you kept her, promoted her, defended her against Molly—"

"Well, I was wrong," Diana cried. "I was giving her a break, hoping she'd succeed. I tried to help her. And she was so goddamn sweet, so goddamn loyal, so goddamn hypocritical. She's only using you to produce a show for ATN, and that will do her no good when they see her work."

"Who the hell are *you* to talk about using?" Luke shouted. "You used *me*. You were stuck in a rut with *Mom & Meg* when you met me. Feranti wasn't interested so you went crawling to Sayles, offered yourself on a plate, and that's how you sold him *Pete Winston*! The series happened to work because *I* made it work!"

Diana shook her head, trying not to take his nastiness to heart. It was Nikki who had put such grandiose ideas into his head and lied about Matthew. And Luke had believed her because he wanted his own show. That little bitch had cleverly pushed all his buttons, making him jealous of Matthew and therefore doubly determined not to renew his contract with Continental.

Diana took a deep breath. "Luke, I wish you'd reconsider. Have your lawyer go over your contract. It might not be too late—"

"Don't tell me what to do! I've had enough of that."

"Oh, Luke! Doesn't it occur to you that the very woman who lied so convincingly to me is also lying to you?" Diana cried. "You can't believe her—"

"I'll decide who to believe, and it's not going to be you! Okay, you helped me get my start, but it was *my* talent, first, last, and always. And now Nikki's giving me a chance to show how much more I can do." He was so proud of himself that he told Diana the gist.

As she listened, Diana walked up and down, shaking her head. "You're confusing yourself with Pete Winston. He's just a character I created for you to play, not to be. And now you're planning to . . . God, do you really think you're capable of advising people about their problems?"

"Damn right I am. I'll have experts helping, but I don't need someone to write every single word I say."

He picked up his bags and strode to the door.

Diana felt panicky again. She couldn't let him go. "Please don't, please don't," she kept saying, unable to salvage any pride or dignity.

"Get out of my way," Luke demanded, brandishing his bags. "I don't owe you anything more, lady. I paid you back for what you did. You got out of drama and into sitcom, right? And not only that, I taught you about love. I gave you more pleasure than you'd ever had with any man in your life, right? So we're quits. Now let me go!"

While Diana shrank from the door, Luke resolutely opened it.

Hating herself for asking, Diana quavered, "And are you paying Nikki back in the same way?"

He walked out without another word and let the door slam behind him.

Diana collapsed in tears.

She stayed at home all day trying to deal with her pain and jealousy, feeling as if she had lost control of every aspect of her life.

Molly, who had left endless messages on Diana's machine, insisted on coming over. "I tried to get you in Beverly Hills but you'd already gone. I knew damn well something was going on. Nikki suddenly turned into the viper I always knew she was. We had words and she called me every obscene name in the book. And then she quit. Quite honestly, none of this surprises me. You're well rid of the pair of them. No more protégés, okay?"

Diana nodded miserably. Unfortunately, Luke's defection wasn't only her personal tragedy. "I've made a mess, Molly. We're practically back to square one. No *Mom & Meg*, no *Pete Winston*. Continental is getting kicked in the teeth for having had faith in us. When I think of all the work on that script and those twelve episodes, the fight I had with Phil and the program board . . . Oh, Molly, I can't stand myself. If I were a horse you'd shoot me."

There weren't enough shows for the series to go into syndication, so Abbott and Sinclair would never make back their losses on *Pete Winston*. Affiliates needed close to a hundred shows for syndication because they ran about five per week.

"Buck up, kid," Molly told her. "We made a fortune on *Mom & Meg* and we're still getting residuals. We're in good shape. Besides, we've got ourselves. You haven't run dry, even if you think so at this moment. We'll put plenty of shows together, while that rat, that prick, that world's biggest narcissist will wind up back in the berry patch with his balls in the brambles. . . ."

While Molly went on ranting, Diana wished she could feel so vindictive. Anything would be better than the misery, the aching feeling of loss.

"How about I spend the night?" Molly offered.

"Thanks, but I'd rather be alone." Diana needed to get a grip on herself, and leaning on Molly wasn't the way to do it.

It was two A.M. and she was wide-awake, seeing Luke for what he was: childish, egotistical, cruel, self-seeking. There was almost nothing to put on the plus side, except that she loved him. She just couldn't stop so quickly, after a year. And she kept fluctuating between rage and aching jealousy.

It was three-fifteen; four-thirty. Luke was with Nikki, she was sure of it. And every time she imagined them together, she wanted to die.

22

Gwen Van Ryck sat at her typewriter staring at blank paper. Her secretary would be here in minutes to pick up her plot outlines, and she had hardly made a start. She lit another cigarette, although she hadn't finished her last one.

She got up, pulled her robe tighter around her middle, and shuffled to the bathroom in her slippers. As she rinsed her mouth, she caught a glimpse of herself in the mirror. Her hair was gray an inch from the roots, and the skin on her face was hanging. She had lost eight pounds in three weeks and looked absolutely horrible.

It was three weeks to the day that she had last seen or heard from Nikki. One night they had had a wonderful time together, close and warm and intimate, Nikki asleep in her arms, and the next night there was nothing. No phone call, and even worse, no way of reaching her.

Gwen had called Nikki's office, only to be told that the company had gone out of business. It had seemed crazy. Nikki didn't answer her phone at home at any time of the day or night. Had something happened to her?

Gwen had gone to her apartment and rung the bell downstairs but received no answer. She had even waited for the mailman, who confirmed that De Paul's mail was being removed from the box each day.

So Nikki was here and avoiding her.

Gwen had been a corpse ever since.

She had experienced disappointments in the past, but never like this. Nikki had been her all-time love. Didn't the girl realize Gwen would do anything for her?

She had had to curb her impulse to do something drastic, like wait for Nikki to come out of her house and throw herself in her path, threatening suicide.

It wasn't only pride that stopped Gwen, but the knowledge that it wouldn't work. As soon as a person was needy, that person was shunned. Nobody loves a loser. Gwen couldn't bear to make a greater fool of herself than she had already done. Because if Nikki didn't love her— the thought was killingly painful—there was really nothing she could do.

Nikki was young and unserious. She claimed to want to be an actress, took a few cockamamie lessons, but had never followed up one of Gwen's leads. Yes, the girl had faults aplenty. The trouble was that Gwen loved her and wanted her back. That was it in a nutshell.

If only Gwen had gone ahead with the face lift she had planned—except she would have been unable to be with Nikki for a couple of weeks, and that would have been unbearable.

But it was unbearable now. Nikki had undoubtedly found some new interest. But nobody would love Nikki as Gwen did. Nikki would be back.

Christ, she had to stop this and do her work.

As she stared at the paper in her machine, an idea came to her. Frederick has suddenly been dumped by Toni, without any warning. He's twenty years older, he feels vulnerable. Has she left him for his son? What can Frederick do? He's rich, he's successful, but he stays at home, unshaven, trying to work out a way of getting Toni back. One thing he can do is throw his son out of the business. . . .

Gwen found a measure of solace in her misery by assigning it to someone else.

As her fingers clicked over the typewriter keys, she thought wryly that such deeply felt, monumental unhappiness was the stuff of literature, and here she was squandering it on a soap, just to earn a buck. But she needed the money more than ever. Perry was in his senior year, tuition had skyrocketed, and he had a girlfriend.

Besides, she had to plan for Nikki's return. If not a face lift, certainly a new wardrobe. At least unhappiness had taken off the weight that jogging didn't make a dent in.

When her secretary arrived, Gwen had her work almost ready. Then depression descended. She didn't know what to do with herself, fearing to leave the house in case Nikki phoned.

Gwen had given away her answering machine years before after some sadist who knew about her lesbianism kept leaving revolting anonymous messages. Anyone who really wanted to reach her—her son, for instance, when he needed money—always managed it.

It was a lovely sunny day in June, and she felt wretched. She sat on her terrace and began to turn the pages of several publications she had been neglecting. The *Times*, the *Village Voice*, *Variety* . . .

Although the item was inconspicuous, the name Nikki De Paul hit her between the eyes like a jackhammer. Luke Merriman, of *Pete Winston* fame, was not renewing his contract to star in the popular series in the fall. Instead, he had signed with ATN and was going to be doing *The Luke Merriman Show*, devised by Nikki De Paul, former executive co-producer with Abbott and Sinclair.

Gwen shut her eyes, then opened them and read it again. It was true. She had been had.

She threw down the paper and stumbled inside to get a drink. The Scotch bottle was the first thing she grabbed. With shaking hands, she poured a big glass and gulped it down.

She drank until she passed out.

* * *

The longest two weeks in Diana's life had gone by. She was a hermit, barely leaving her apartment, refusing to see Molly or anyone, monitoring all her phone calls.

When Luke finally called it was only to say he had found an apartment, he was coming to pick up the rest of his things, and did not want her to be there.

As soon as she hung up she had another crying fit. But she honored his request. She did go out, wearing a headscarf and dark glasses, and hid behind a magazine in a store on the corner so she could watch him emerge from the cab—he had the driver wait—and reappear less than ten minutes later with his stuff. She knew better than to accost him looking like a creature from another planet, but she was pained to see her beloved looking so handsome, and to know he no longer wanted her.

Diana forced herself to return to her apartment. Luke's things were gone, but not his aura, his aroma. The closets and drawers still emitted the faint scent of his cologne. She threw herself on the bed and cried until no more tears would come.

Yet, no matter how she tried, she couldn't shake her obsession with Luke. As the days went by, Diana tried to imagine how her lovely little assistant who had never raised her voice had turned into her enemy, but it simply didn't register. Diana had to see for herself.

Nikki's phone was either busy or she wasn't answering. Very well, if Diana couldn't arrange a meeting, she would force one. She knew that Nikki was working for ATN on Luke's show, so she waited outside her office one noontime. It was drizzling lightly but she hardly noticed.

When Nikki emerged, Diana moved forward, planting herself in the younger woman's path. "I want to talk to you."

Nikki looked startled, then a little fearful. "I can't, I have a lunch date, and it's raining—"

"This won't take long," Diana persisted.

Nikki shrugged and fell into step beside her.

Diana barely felt the rain dampening her exposed hair and thin summer suit. "I trusted you," she began softly. "I hired you, befriended you, mentored you, for almost two years. How could you bring yourself to tell Luke such lies about Matthew and me? How could you do it? Ambition I can understand, but why me? I was always in your corner."

Nikki walked alongside without answering.

"I promoted you, against Molly's advice. She always told me to watch out for you, but I believed in you. And you repaid me with the worst sort of treachery. Why?"

As they stopped at a corner to wait for the light, Diana turned to look at her.

Nikki glared back. "Listen to you, Diana the do-gooder. Everything for me, right? Wrong. What you call friendship I call humiliation. What you call mentoring I call tyranny. Only *you* know what's right, only *you* know how to do everything. Treating me like I was a stupid baby, giving me all the shit work to do. Even worse, encouraging me to submit script ideas, then shooting them down. You tried to destroy my confidence. Telling me, 'Here, go over this script, dear,' and when I did, you tore it to ribbons. You gave with one hand but you grabbed back with both hands, you bitch," Nikki cried, growing louder and shriller.

Diana's temper flared. "Goddammit, I tried my best to help you develop, but you didn't because you haven't one ounce of creative talent, and that's the bottom line! Two decent ideas in two years, and not one playable line of dialogue. As for being a producer, well, you're okay on the production details but you don't have a grasp of the overall product and you can't hold a production together. My mistake was in not seeing, as Molly saw right from the start, that you're strictly a production assistant, period. I blame myself for having had too much faith in you. That's what put all those grandiose ideas into your head—"

"*My* grandiose ideas! Listen, the only thing you get off on is finding protégés because you've got to feel superior. Every time you told me to take over a rehearsal or a taping, you sneaked behind my back and got Molly to step in and crack the whip, just to make me crawl. You're a sadist, that's what you are! You and Molly would talk back and forth in a kind of shorthand and ignore me as if I didn't exist. Molly was hardly there, yet she had more say over the production during her few hours on each episode than I did working my ass off on the show full-time. In fact, you're even worse than Molly, because she hated me out front. But you—you acted like my friend while you shafted me every chance you got!''

"If you were so unhappy with our working arrangement, why didn't you ever say so? I would have listened. We could have cleared up some things. But no, you pretended to hang on my every word, you were always hugging me, thanking me. How could you be so hypocritical? Did you expect me to read your mind?"

"No, but I could read yours. You only want grateful pupils around you. Well, I hated it, and so did Luke. That's why he split. He got tired of being told what to do."

Though Diana recognized a grain of truth in Nikki's words, she felt compelled to retort, "I can't help it if some people need to be told what to do or they mess up. Luke isn't Pete Winston. He's talented, yes, but he needs the proper vehicle. Not a show where *he* gives advice. Christ, can't you see that won't work?"

"You're only saying that because it's my idea, not yours. That's right, not Luke's, *mine*."

"Yes, I can well believe it," Diana snapped. "And that's what this is all about. Self-promotion. That's why you've stabbed me in the back and filled Luke's head with lies—"

"I didn't do a thing to you," Nikki shouted. "I was there when he needed me, that's all. I've been watching him seething and getting tired of you and your demands, and wanting me but not daring because you had him so pussy-whipped he was afraid to say 'boo' unless you wrote it down for him."

"Damn you," Diana shouted, as the realization hit her, "you've been after him from the beginning! You've been conspiring for months—a drink here and there and that cozy dinner Molly saw you having, the day I was sick—"

"Listen to the pot calling the kettle black," Nikki yelled over the rain that now poured down. "You kidnapped Luke and held him prisoner, servicing you like a stud so he could break into TV because you knew you couldn't get him any other way! And you're the one who met Matthew at a party and put your ass on the line to sell him that series. Okay, that's the way of the world. Everyone plays it like that, but *you* pretend to be above all of it. You act like you're pure, when you're filthier than anyone else! Well, you've lost, and I've won. And now you're being a bitch in the manger, telling Luke ATN won't air his show, and more bullshit.''

"That's right, they won't, not for long anyway."

"I have a commitment to write and produce thirteen episodes—"

"After which you'll be booted out because they'll be so lousy."

"You can't bully me or Luke anymore. Because now he knows the truth, and since he's been with me he sees what he's been missing. I really know how to love him," Nikki said, suddenly grinning smugly at Diana while pushing her soaking hair out of her eyes. "We do it day and night. He's so hot for me he can't leave me alone, and he tells me he's never seen such a perfect body, young and firm, without any thirtyish sag. He loves my breasts, and my belly, he loves to put his head between my legs. . . ."

Diana felt her stomach constrict. She ran down the street through the pelting rain, hearing Nikki's salacious, vicious laughter ringing in her ears.

Nikki stood there laughing, not caring about the rain that was dripping off her hair and into the collar of her dress, soaking her to the skin. She had been waiting two years for the opportunity to tell Diana off.

For a few moments she savored the memory of the pain on Diana's face when she'd heard the way Luke made love to her. Savored, too, how skinny and ugly Diana had looked, with the curl out of her hair, plastered to her head. The rain pouring down had looked like tears.

But when Nikki began to walk again, the rain let up and her triumph suddenly felt hollow. It had been a shock to hear Diana talk like that about her abilities. Not true, of course. Diana would say anything now. A woman scorned was always prepared to be vicious.

Still, such words as "not one ounce of creative talent" rankled.

Nikki shrugged. People learned from doing. The more shows she wrote and produced, the better she'd get.

23 Matthew watched Diana walk into the Grill Room, and his heart contracted at the sight of her, looking so thin, so pale. He hadn't seen her in a month, and the news of Luke's defection had come only three weeks before.

She seemed a little dazed, for she didn't immediately notice him, apparently having forgotten where his regular table was. She appeared utterly defenseless, as if everything she had ever believed to be true about herself had turned out not to be so. How well he knew that feeling. It had lingered long after Lorrie had left him.

"Hello, Matthew," Diana murmured, greeting him shamefacedly as he stood up and held her chair. "I'm glad you're still speaking to me, after we've put such a hole in the fall schedule."

"Never mind that," he said softly. "It's you I'm concerned about. Not taking care of yourself, obviously."

She forced a smile. "It's called the Luke Merriman diet. Pain, mostly, and it really works."

He put his hand on her arm and squeezed it. "I realize that nothing I can say will really help at this point, but I do want you to know how sorry I am. And I don't want you to worry. We have a great fall lineup, even without *Pete Winston*. Anyway, we deserve some of the blame. If we had insisted on a run-of-series, this couldn't have happened. At the very least, we'd have a winnable suit on our hands." He sighed, remembering that particular battle. He had wanted to pay Abbott and Sinclair more so they could meet Luke's demands for a bigger salary for r.o.s., but Phil had refused.

Diana ordered a gin and tonic, and the alcohol helped her to open up to him.

"I saw it coming, in a way, Matthew. I saw Luke's head inflating with his fame. But the thing that came as such a shock was Nikki." As Diana elaborated, he could hear the hurt in her voice.

"I feel like such a fool," she whispered. "You order for me, please. I don't care what I eat."

Matthew did as she asked, and then he sat back and compressed his lips, empathizing with her pain. Her vulnerability touched him greatly.

"Molly warned me," Diana said. "She knew just what was happening, but I couldn't believe it. You knew too, didn't you?"

He hesitated. "Well, I had my suspicions about Luke from the start, as you know. But I had little knowledge of Nikki. One time she bent my ear at some party, singing her own praises. I was not at all impressed. I never thought of her as producer material."

"That's what makes me feel so angry at myself. I mean, I know better, Matthew. I know what a cutthroat business this is, and how many people want to be producers because of the glamour, the power, the profits, no matter how untalented they are. Of course the only way they can survive is to scheme and undercut their rivals. And I didn't see it when it was right under my nose. Can Molly be that much smarter?"

"She's that much more wary," Matthew replied softly. "She's a New Yorker, and that means a born cynic. Whereas you, from a small town, were probably taught to give people the benefit of the doubt, and to believe they were innocent until proven guilty. And it's a nice way to be, quaint though it may be nowadays. And sometimes, of course, it backfires."

"I've stopped giving people the benefit of the doubt from this moment," Diana assured him, looking uninterested in the shrimp dish the waiter put before her.

"Whatever we believe, Diana, there's no way to keep from making mistakes. I have cause to remember mine every time I see the unhappiness in my daughter's eyes. I should have known better, but I wasn't thinking of consequences. I was simply in love."

He had met Lorrie when he was twenty-five and a hotshot in research, and she was a gorgeous eighteen. That was part of the trouble: she was too young, too inexperienced. She had latched on to him, but it had taken years for him to realize that she wanted someone to take care of her while she bopped all around Hollywood flirting and teasing, even though they were living together.

"When Lorrie got pregnant, she wanted an abortion. I talked her out of it. And once the baby was born"—Matthew paused, feeling the pain all over again—"I assumed that all mothers loved their children. Well, this one didn't even want to try. We had help, but Lorrie hated being tied down in any way. She felt her pregnancy had ruined her figure and interrupted her career. Acting, of course."

Matthew didn't feel as bitter as he may have sounded. And he supposed he was telling Diana all this so that she would feel a little less ashamed of her own poor judgment. He went on relating how many times he had ignored the signs of his wife's dissatisfaction and her neglect of their child. He had hoped she would change until the very day Lorrie had decamped.

A week before Andrea's fifth birthday, Lorrie had run off with a British rock singer who had been in town making a film. Matthew had found a note saying simply that she wasn't cut out for motherhood. There was no forwarding address.

"Unbelievable," Diana murmured. "And since then?"

Matthew sighed. "Since then, nothing much. I had her traced, wrote asking her at least to be in touch with Andy, but she sent back two lines refusing, saying that Andy would be better off forgetting her. The trouble is that she can't face the truth that her mother doesn't love her. In fact, she tends to idealize Lorrie, remembering the pretty clothes her mother dressed her in. Andy tried so hard to please her, but Lorrie simply wasn't interested."

Diana's expression was compassionate. "How awful for Andrea. She's lucky to have a father like you."

"Yes, maybe, but I can't make up for the loss of her mother, no matter how hard I try." He still felt responsible. He had forced Lorrie into something she couldn't handle, and Andrea was the innocent victim. Yet, to wish there had been no Andrea was impossible. He loved her too much.

"When Lorrie left, you must have been miserable," Diana said softly.

"I was, but for my daughter's sake more than my own. I'd realized by then what a mistake I'd made. I think you'll realize yours, too."

"Yes," Diana said, sighing. "I already do, but it just won't sink in. Molly keeps telling me that the best medicine for someone in my condition is to get back to work. That's what she did when her husband died. Let my ideas flow, she says, spend time thinking about what's possible instead of what's beyond my control." Diana smiled sadly. "But my head is devoid of creative thought. I just can't stop going over everything, and thinking if only I had done things differently. I keep thinking about Luke and Nikki, and feeling so . . . so angry and helpless." She paused and swallowed.

Matthew nodded. "You're in mourning, Diana, and you have to go through it. Denying it doesn't help. If it's any comfort, the pain gradually goes away. When you're let down by somebody the way you were, so much is left unsaid. It really is like mourning a dead person. In fact, it's almost worse because you know the person's not only alive but having fun with someone else. The pain recedes, and just when you think you have it beaten, it comes back with a vengeance. I guess there's no shortcut. You have to go through all the stages of mourning until the wounds finally heal."

She looked at him with very bright eyes, and he saw two tears detach themselves and roll slowly down her cheeks. Curbing an impulse to wipe them away with his finger—or even kiss them away—he glanced up at the waiter, now asking about coffee and dessert.

Diana quickly mopped at her face with a tissue.

"How about treating yourself to something gooey and wicked, Diana, like the chocolate velvet cake? The good news is you can eat a slab of the stuff and not worry about calories."

Diana laughed a little hysterically and agreed. "God, I'm sorry to be such a drag, Matthew."

"Don't apologize. And if there's anything I can do, anything at all, call on me. I really mean it." He took out his card and wrote his home number on the back of it. "Anytime. Don't worry about waking me. I'm a charter member of Lost Loves Anonymous. We know how to help others in the same predicament."

Diana smiled wanly at his little joke, while tears again threatened but didn't fall. "Thanks, Matthew, for being so understanding and so thoughtful. For having more faith in me than I have in myself. I can't help feeling so . . . so stupid." She leaned forward, looking at him intently.

"How could I have been such an idiot? I mean, misjudging Nikki so completely? You know, I confronted her, and what I saw was another person. Hard, dangerous, ruthless, a total bitch. All that sweetness and loyalty was an act, and I fell for it. And the vicious lies she told. Not only about me. I . . . I guess I should let you in on it, just in case you should hear rumors. I mean, she told Luke that you and I . . . that it's how you happened to buy the series in the first place. . . ."

Matthew felt himself growing warm, and he had to look away for a few moments. Nikki, and maybe even Luke, might have seen in his face what Diana apparently had no inkling of—that he was in love with her. He almost blurted out his thoughts, but contained himself. It was much too soon. Diana didn't need another problem to deal with at the moment. It was friendship she needed from him, and that he could give with all his heart. "The main thing, Diana, is that you know the truth now. It could have been worse. You could have married the guy."

"Well, I don't hold Luke entirely responsible for what happened," Diana said tensely. "I mean, how can I blame *him* for believing her lies when I was conned by her myself? For two years!"

Matthew grew angry as he listened to Diana's defense of Luke and her insistence upon putting all the blame on Nikki. Luke had been thoughtless—even cruel—but it was his naiveté. He'd never before been in a position to be lied to because he'd never had anything of value to offer anyone. So he had trusted, and Nikki was so deceptive . . . "Luke really is sweet, underneath. . . ."

Matthew sighed and didn't contradict Diana, because she wasn't ready to face it. Luke Merriman was her creation; she had turned a shit-kicker into a golden boy and had to defend that to herself for the time being.

"Mama, I d-don't like this here show," Joey complained loudly.

"Shh." Sara Coles nudged him sharply. "Be glad our neighbor lady's lettin' us watch her TV at all. Besides . . ." Sara didn't finish her thought. Instead, she gazed as if hypnotized at Lucas Merriman prancing around and looking mighty pleased with himself.

It was hard to take it all in. Her Lucas, the boy she had more or less grown up with, now a big star on the TV. How had he done it?

It was a mystery, and as she watched him, she realized that as an actor he must be earning a good salary. It was something to think about, because if he had lots of money, he ought to give her some; it was only right.

Maybe she should write him a letter. Could she find out his address? No, writing was no good; he might not get her letter. She rejected telephoning as well. The thing to do was go there and see him herself. The idea excited her at the same time that it made her fearful. It was a big step to take, and she wasn't sure she could take it.

"Where's my daddy?" Joey asked suddenly, watching Pete Winston hugging his young son.

Lordy, her boy was spooky sometimes. "You hush now, wait till this is over." Sara was riveted to the program, observing that those TV kids lived in a house for rich folks with every gizmo you could imagine and then some. They wore fine clothes, had money to burn and food to waste. She paid so much attention to all the details that she found it hard to follow the talk and was startled every time the audience laughed or clapped. There must be something funny being said, but she failed to see just what it might be.

Her kids weren't laughing, either. They were too busy wanting everything they saw. And Sara could hardly blame them.

"Wh-why can't I have a bike?" Joey asked.

" 'Cause you're too little," Daisy said. "But I'm big enough. I wanna bike, Mama."

"Shush, you kids. That's just make-believe on TV," Sara lied. Lord, it was so unfair. Her kids were as good as anyone's. Sure, this was TV, but plenty of kids really did have bikes and nice clothes and a permanent place to live.

The minute the show was over, Daisy and Joey ran outside with the Garcia kids, and Sara thanked Rosa and

Julio. The Garcias were good people, the salt of the earth. The kids were nice too, though they barely spoke English.

This was partly what was worrying Sara. Each season fewer Americans worked the stream, and Daisy and Joey were more comfortable speaking Spanish than their own language.

"Hey, you kids, bedtime," Sara called into the wind.

She sighed and wiped her forehead. Let them run around for a bit. Maybe they'd finally tire out. The energy they had amazed her. Well, she'd been that way once, before bending and stooping at least ten hours a day had taken it out of her.

This was a good chance to work on the car. At least the kids wouldn't be underfoot, and it was time to get moving again. The lettuce was finished, and blueberries were ripe for picking in Oregon. But would the Dodge make it all the way there?

Sara was suddenly sick of everything—of picking whatever, of trying to coax another few hundred miles out of the car, of having to stay one jump ahead of Walt. That man never quit, and Sara had no idea why. She was nothing to him, had never cared much for him, and the kids weren't kin to him either, but he wouldn't leave them alone. Of course, if she could get off the stream, that would be that. Walt was afraid of towns.

The Dodge had three bald tires, and the spare had no tread, either. If the sheriff caught her, he'd surely haul the Dodge to the junkyard.

Sara suddenly noticed that one of the tires had a leak and was getting flatter by the moment. Then the fan belt snapped with a bang.

"Oh, Lordy, no." Sara turned off the engine and sank to the ground. It was no use. She no sooner scrimped to replace one part than another broke down. Could she afford three new tires, a fan belt, and a brake job? Not only that, but the car had been stalling on her lately.

Sara went into the house and untied an old sock in which she kept her savings. There simply wasn't enough to fix the car; she would finally be forced to sell it for scrap.

Well, if she was going to have to get on a bus, it sure as heck wasn't going to take her to another farm. No, she was going to New York City. Lucas had done mighty well for himself, and he owed her.

"Thanks for meeting me, Diana," Gwen Van Ryck said, nervously hoisting her cup of coffee to her lips. "I know how busy you are, and I won't take up much of your time."

"That's all right." Diana observed her curiously. She had been greatly surprised to receive a call from the woman because she hardly knew her. The most they had ever said to each other, when they came face-to-face at the occasional industry function, was "hello." She did know that Gwen Van Ryck was highly regarded as a daytime head soap writer and had for years been associated with the top of the line, most recently *Night and Day*, FAB's big success.

Gwen had sounded very upset, and although she hadn't been willing to reveal why on the phone, Diana had been unable to think of a good reason not to meet her. Besides, wasn't misery supposed to love company?

The first glimpse of Gwen had confirmed Diana's impression that she was suffering. Diana had remembered her as being attractive and self-possessed. Now she seemed very drawn and on the verge of hysteria. Jesus, Diana thought, she looks the way I feel.

"I understand," Gwen began, "that Nikki De Paul used to be your assistant? For how long, may I ask?"

Diana compressed her lips angrily. "She started as a p.a. almost two years ago. She was pretty good at detail but she had delusions of grandeur, to say the least, of breaking into writing/producing. And like a goddamn fool, I helped her. I . . ." Diana stopped herself. "Before I go on ranting, I guess I should know why you're asking."

Gwen's face, which had turned even paler as Diana spoke, suddenly crumpled, and she put her hands up to hide her tears, but her deep, wrenching sobs were audible.

Diana sat in shocked silence, waiting for Gwen to regain her composure, while feeling the tug of the woman's desperate grief because it very much mirrored her own.

"Forgive me," Gwen snuffled, finally calm. "I'm so sorry to inflict all this on you. I thought I was over it, but it suddenly hit me again."

Amid sighs and pauses, Gwen told the story of her

relationship with Nikki—of how they had met, of the lies Nikki had told her.

"I never dreamed she was associated with Abbott and Sinclair. Or that she knew Luke Merriman. She told me she wanted to be an actress."

"She *is* an actress, and a bloody good one," Diana hissed through clenched teeth.

"Diana, I . . . I've hesitated to approach you. I've always been such a private person—"

"I understand," Diana said, feeling a great deal of compassion for the woman. "You can count on me to keep this confidential. And I know exactly how you're feeling. God, how could Nikki pretend over something so important?"

"That's just it. I don't know if she used me from start to finish, if it all was just to pick my brains for ideas— Luke's own show was one of them, by the way—or if she ever really cared at all. . . ."

As Gwen talked on, Diana realized the lengths to which Nikki had gone in her ambitious zeal to move up to writing/producing. Nikki's two script ideas had been courtesy of Gwen as well.

"There wasn't any need for her to make up stories," Gwen said. "I'd have lain awake nights thinking of ideas for her. I just don't understand why she lied the way she did."

Diana felt she understood only too well. Nikki was rotten through and through, and lying came more easily than telling the truth, especially to Gwen. Diana doubted that Nikki was genuinely bisexual; she had always shown a keen interest in men. Diana said as much to Gwen, who looked skeptical.

"I guess it's common knowledge that Luke and I were living together—"

"I didn't know it," Gwen said. "I'm very far removed from industry gossip."

"Well, we were, and Nikki admitted she's always been after Luke. And now she has him—" Diana stopped, as emotion welled up in her.

Gwen looked doubtful. "I can't believe she's really interested in a man. She must be faking in order to get him to go along with her plans for him at ATN." The tears began to come again. "I couldn't have been so blind. I'm not a kid, I've been around. Nikki was the only one I ever cared for quite so much."

Diana's eyes spilled over. "I'm exactly in the same position with Luke." She attempted a smile. "Look at us. We're sort of in the same boat, aren't we?"

"I guess we are. But I should tell you that I've seen Luke at a couple of charity affairs from time to time and he was flinging himself all over the place, never missing an opportunity for a flirt. I saw him with Gemma Lopez, for instance—"

"And I've seen Nikki playing up to men," Diana broke in, piqued that Gwen was going to blame Luke for what had happened. "I'll grant you that Luke is a flirt, but he's also really quite naive. A country boy at heart—"

"Oh, come on. I've seen the guy in action."

"Well, I lived with him for more than a year, and he's always been honest with me, whereas Nikki has been a hypocrite from day one. When I had it out with her, you wouldn't believe the things she said." Diana told Gwen the gist of their rain-spattered interview.

Gwen listened unmoved. "How Nikki felt about working for you I can't say, since I know nothing about it—"

"But you know she's a liar, Gwen," Diana cried. "She lied about her job, for a mythical company—"

"Yes, she did, but I can't believe she lied about her . . . her feelings for me."

"Then why hasn't she been in touch for a month?" Diana challenged.

"Maybe she's still dazzled at her success. Maybe she feels she has to have Luke's total allegiance while they're working on the series."

Gwen was apparently besotted with that little bitch and would continue to make excuses for her.

"It occurs to me," Gwen said finally, toying with her spoon, "that you and I have something to gain by breaking those two up. That is, if I'm correct in thinking that you want Luke back."

Diana leaned forward tensely. "Yes, I do. And I think if Luke knew about Nikki and you, it would make a difference. Of course, if you don't want him to know—"

"I'll do anything to get her back. Even backing up your

story to Luke, if I have to. I'm just no good without her," she burst out. "I can't eat, I can't sleep, I can't work. My life is a shambles."

Yes, those were Diana's symptoms exactly, and as she agreed to Gwen's plan she felt a ray of hope. Luke's eyes would be opened. He'd be furious to realize how he had been fooled.

"I'll wait to hear from you," Gwen said, standing up. "And don't get discouraged if it doesn't have an instant effect." She smiled grimly. "He's not likely to believe you. What's more likely to happen is that in spite of her charms, Nikki won't hold his attention for long. I don't think anybody could."

Diana, bristling, couldn't let that pass. "And I don't think Nikki's interest is in any particular man or woman, just in what that person can do to advance her career."

As they said good-bye, the two women eyed one another ruefully. Diana was sure that Gwen was wasting her time and emotions on a person unworthy of her. And from the expression on her face, Gwen seemed to be thinking the same thing about Diana.

Diana dressed carefully for her interview with Luke, trying not to pin her hopes on it. For the hot day she chose a cool pale blue cotton dress, sleeveless, buttoned low in front, and almost totally bare in back. The dress was a little big on her but she belted it tightly and festooned her neck with three strands of pearls and put on pearl-stud earrings. The total effect was one of elegance, something Luke had always admired in her. Nikki was pretty and pert, but more trendy than elegant. Since Diana couldn't compete with her rival on her terms, she might as well be herself.

She and Luke were meeting in a little park off Beekman Place overlooking the East River. It had been her choice. She felt she would be unable to eat or drink while she was trying to win back her man.

When she had first phoned him, Luke had sounded surprised, guarded, and he had hesitated before finally agreeing to see her.

Diana had come into the office looking so much better than recently that Molly had immediately noticed. In a burst of optimism, Diana had confided in her, knowing she could count on Molly to keep Gwen's secret.

"Diana, don't do it," Molly had said flatly. "Let Gwen fight her own battles. Never mind Nikki's lies. You're rid of a bad guy, believe me. Bad from the toes up. Did he ever repay the money you lent him?"

"What money?"

"The money you advanced him to take acting lessons, the outlay for his wardrobe, the watch, the camera—"

"Oh, come on, Molly. Everything changed because we were living together. I didn't want the money back."

"That's not the point. The point is that he never even offered it because he took it as his due. Believe me, that guy was used to getting paid for his services long before you ever met him."

Diana stalked out angrily. Yet she was unable to dismiss Molly's words. Even if Nikki had lied, Luke didn't have to believe her. If the situation were reversed, and somebody had come to her with stories about Luke, wouldn't she have let him tell his side of it?

And yet, every doubt in her mind vanished the moment she saw him coming down the stairs and loping toward her in fashionable off-white pleated pants and a vivid Hawaiian print shirt, a jaunty straw hat on his head and dark glasses obscuring his eyes.

She stood waiting for him, feeling her knees begin to buckle and a tingle of arousal throughout her body. God, how she wanted him. She was glad she had not had anything to drink and that they were meeting in a public place. Otherwise, she felt sure she would have jumped his bones.

"Hi," he greeted her coolly, pecking her on the cheek. "Lord, it's hot, even in the shade. Why don't we duck into the Ambassador and have a drink?"

Diana shook her head, visualizing the place he suggested, in which there were mirrors all over so you could see yourself reflected about twentyfold. And Luke would be recognized. No, here in this neighborhood park, with only children and their nannies, she had Luke's complete attention.

"I don't want a drink," Diana said softly. Before she could say more, he began to talk. He had moved out of his sublet and into a condominium which he had just purchased, furniture and all.

Diana restrained herself from asking if he wouldn't rather have furnished the place to his own taste.

"It was real easy this way, not having to go out and buy a thing. Folks who sold it were getting divorced and didn't want to be reminded, but it's terrific stuff, antiques. Anyway, you said you had something to tell me." He removed his sunglasses, and the sight of those wonderful blue-gray eyes made her want to weep.

Take it easy, Sinclair, don't break down now. "I had a meeting with a woman named Gwen Van Ryck. . . ."

Diana had rehearsed what she was going to say, leading into it gradually so that it wouldn't come as such a shock. She had braced herself for Luke's angry denials but not for him to laugh in her face. "I never heard such bullshit in my life. Nikki, a lesbian? You've gotta be joking."

"I didn't say she was a lesbian, only that she pretended to be in order to get the ideas she needed."

"Bullshit."

"Are . . . are you in love with her?" Diana asked in a whisper. "Is she living with you?"

"That's none of your business," he snapped, and then in effect answered the questions. "I'm not planning to get myself tied up with any gal ever again, thank you, ma'am. I don't want anyone owning me. I own myself."

Diana couldn't help feeling a touch of hope, even though she was basing it on very little.

"So," Luke said, glaring at her, "you got me here to tell me some stupid stories. Hell, I thought you'd be above that sort of thing, Diana."

"I've told you the truth, and if you don't believe me, talk to Gwen. I'll give you her phone number—"

"I don't need her phone number," Luke snarled. "I don't need to listen to a lot of filthy lies from some over-the-hill dyke who just hates men—"

"That's not true," Diana interrupted. "Gwen isn't a hater. She's a decent, sensitive woman, and she really cares about Nikki—"

"I won't listen to this shit," Luke yelled. backing away. "Nikki, getting her ideas from a soap writer, for Chrissake. You must be off your nut to think I'd believe that, or that she'd go to bed with a dyke. Listen, Nikki is the most feminine woman I've ever met, and what's more, she's crazy about me. I think you cooked this whole thing up with that dyke just to get back at Nikki and me because we wised up and stopped being your puppets!"

Diana's eyes misted. "That's not true," she whispered. "I love you and I miss you—"

"I don't want to hear it! Leave me alone, and leave Nikki alone. We don't need you spreading lies and interfering in our lives. You've done just about enough of that."

Luke whirled and strode away. As he went up the stairs, two at a time, Diana remembered how strong his thighs were, hard and muscular. At the top of the staircase he was recognized by two young mothers wheeling strollers.

Diana watched Luke's angry scowl dissolve into a smile. He played with the children for a moment and scribbled his signature for the mothers.

Then tears blurred her vision. Molly had been right, as usual. But Diana kept telling herself that Luke wasn't receptive to the truth now because he was still at the beginning. Wait until things begin to go wrong, she thought. It's inevitable.

24

Luke awoke to sunshine pouring in through his window, yet the thermostat was set to make the room just the right temperature. He smiled and stretched to his full length, luxuriating in his king-size bed—the only bed he'd ever slept in where he didn't have to scrunch up to keep his feet from hanging over the edge.

It was wonderful to have such a big bed in a big apartment to himself. Two bedrooms and a dining room, a forty-foot living room, a river view—the price was astronomical, of course, but he could afford it. He had a guaranteed income for five years; it was a miracle. Both Harriet and his lawyer had bawled him out for not consulting them about the contract, but he felt they were simply annoyed that he'd gotten something fantastic without their help. They said he'd done the wrong thing, but it was bullshit.

He had learned something about rich people: they were far too concerned with "what-ifs." He had grown up only a meal away from starvation, and it had taught him to take the good stuff the moment it was offered and worry about tomorrow when it came. A rich bitch like Harriet couldn't get that through her head, though she still accepted her ten percent after he had negotiated his own contract. Agents, lawyers, brokers—everyone came sniffing around as soon as they thought they could get something.

He reached out and turned on his coffee machine, as well as the stereo. Loud, wonderful sound filled the room. "We Are the World" was the song, and it was just the way he was feeling.

Luke had two cups of coffee in bed, then ambled into the kitchen and heated up a croissant.

Today they were taping the fifth of thirteen shows. On tape day, little gofers for ATN gave out free tickets on Fifth Avenue. People heard his name and they gobbled up the tickets and filled every seat in the studio.

It was too easy. The warm-up guy got questions going, and the p.a. made a note of who asked each one. Then Luke started the program by introducing the guest star. They chatted informally, and then he called for questions, pointing only to the folks whose questions had already been chosen during the warm-up. Of course Luke had his answers ready.

No memorizing, no dealing with a bunch of other actors who were always trying to block you out of the camera. No sir, it was his show. He was the big deal, and even the guests knew it.

Just as he finished his breakfast, the phone rang. It was a girl from Continental who said a woman giving the name Sara Coles had been calling and asking for his address and phone number. "I told her we don't give out that information, Mr. Merriman, but she said she knows you, so I thought . . ."

Luke shut his eyes as a tremor went through him. "Yeah, you did good. Where'd she call from? Lord . . . well, give me her number."

Sara in New York. How had she gotten herself all the way here? He hadn't thought about Sara Coles for years. Hadn't she found someone else in all that time? She probably had, but now that Luke was somebody, she would be wanting money, of course. He'd better get this over with, because he didn't want it hanging over his head.

He called the number he had been given and heard a Hispanic accent say the name of a hotel he didn't catch.

Sara's drawl was shockingly familiar, though. She was here, all right, and with the kids. He thought of going to see her but dismissed it. He couldn't face the squalor of where she was staying, somewhere around Times Square, so he told her to come to him.

He quickly dressed in jeans and a shirt, and prowled his apartment nervously. He would cut the interview as short as possible and pay her off.

When the three of them walked in, it was as if his entire previous life suddenly confronted him.

"Hi, Sara," he murmured, awkwardly patting her shoulder.

"Howdy, Lucas. This here's Daisy, growed up a bit, and Joey. Say howdy to your daddy."

The children gawked at him, then tittered. Luke, who could charm any strange child on the street, found himself tongue-tied in front of his own kids.

Daisy had to be six or seven. She looked like a string bean altogether—skinny arms and legs, stringy hair. A couple of front teeth were missing. Her skin was blotchy, her nose runny, and she kept coughing. And Joey was real small and skinny, and he never stayed still for a second.

"Please don't touch," Luke told them, in vain.

They all looked so hungry that he rustled up milk and cookies for the kids and a cup of coffee for Sara. The kids wolfed everything down. Looking at them sitting in his antique chairs and rubbing their grubby fingers over his carefully preserved oak dining table made him very nervous.

He wanted them out, but Sara refused to be rushed. She rambled on about home, the state of farming, how the Dodge had broken down . . .

In the meantime, the kids began to run through the house, opening closets, pulling things out, so he could hardly concentrate.

Finally he took them into the living room and sat them down on the rug in front of the television.

"Well, Lucas, I always wondered where you'd got to. It was really somethin', to see you on the TV a while back."

After his first good look at her, he kept his eyes averted. He had remembered her as the prettiest girl in the Willamette Valley. But she had been only . . . what, fifteen? . . . when they had first gotten together. Now she was thinner but lumpier, in her faded print dress, bobby socks, and plastic sandals. Her hair, which had been shiny and light blond, was dull, stringy, dry. And those deep lines in her face made her look like her own mother, but she couldn't be more than twenty-five.

"I don't mean to bust in on you, Lucas," Sara was saying in a low, flat monotone. She kept her pale blue eyes on him, and she never once smiled.

"I didn't think I'd ever want to get off the land, but I do now. Specially with no car. And Walt—he's been followin' us everywheres. I took up with him in blackberries two years after you left us. Well, it was real hard to manage, with two little tykes. . . ."

While she droned on, he glanced at the kids, seeing not one feature of his in their country faces. Daisy kept coughing, and he wondered fleetingly if it could be T.B.

"You done real good for yourself, Lucas. I guess that's what you wanted, why you upped and left us." She paused, as if waiting for an explanation, but he gave none.

"It's been real hard for us, Lucas. I been at my wits' end, tryin' to cope, but there's somethin' new every day. Joey's a hyper—you know, can't sit still—and Daisy, she's got all sorts of rashes dependin' what she eats. You're rich now, Lucas, livin' in a mighty fine place. Workin' steady. And watchin' you bein' so good to those kids and all on TV, it made me wonder if you wouldn't like to do somethin' for your real-life kids. So I come here on the bus all the way from Salem. . . ."

As she spoke, Luke visualized the valley, the old Dodge (how had she managed to keep it going this long?). He felt his nostrils fill with the smell of kerosene in the cabin, and even worse, the odors of the outhouse.

As Sara looked at him with those expressionless, unblinking eyes, he couldn't tell what she was really thinking, but there was no malice in her voice, only a straight-ahead plea for help—a decent place to live, a school every day for the kids, and enrollment in beauty school for her.

"It would sure be nice if the kids could see their daddy every once in a while."

Luke moistened his lips. "Uh, that would be impossible, Sara." He told her of the crime, the danger, the bad schooling in New York, the icy winters, the impossibly humid summers. He had to speak up in order to make himself heard about the TV, which the kids kept playing with, switching channels and messing with the sound control. When he told them to stop that, they simply got up and ran through the apartment, touching everything in sight.

"You stop that, now," Sara called out, in vain. "You see. They need their daddy to get them to mind."

Every time he heard the word "daddy," Luke cringed.

"But if you don't want us here," Sara added flatly, "I reckon we won't stay. Just so long as we don't need to go back on the stream."

"No, absolutely not," Luke assured her. Excusing himself, he raced through the house until he found the children in the kitchen, trying to take apart the toaster-oven and the coffee machine. He herded them back into the living room without putting a hand on them. In truth, he shrank from their touch. There was no telling what diseases they might be carrying.

Sara was sitting just where he had left her, her hands together in her lap, patient, long-suffering, asking for what she needed, yet not really expecting to get it.

The doorman buzzed, saying that Nikki was on the way up. Shit, was it that late already?

Luke hastily gathered his visitors and hustled them into the spare room that had been made into a game room. He turned on the computer game for the kids, anticipating that they'd destroy it, but he had to take the risk. Nikki couldn't be allowed to see them.

When she got off the elevator, Luke was waiting at the door, a seductive smile on his face. "Hey, babe. How about a little loving before we leave, huh?" He nuzzled her neck with his nose and lips while running his hands sensually over her hips and ass.

"Mm. Let's do it."

"Tell you what. I've just got to finish an important long-distance call and I'll join you in a sec." He led her to his bedroom and shut the door behind her.

Then he raced back to the game room, hearing a crash. Those little brats had broken an expensive lamp.

"I sure am sorry, Lucas. They done it so fast I couldn't stop them."

"Never mind," he hissed, glaring at the kids, who cowered as if waiting to be beaten. "Look, Sara, I've got to run. Listen, do you have a place to stay in Salem?"

"Well"—Sara hesitated—"I reckon we could stay at Mary's boardinghouse."

"Fine. Write down the address." He quickly wrote a check. "This'll get you going. I'll send you something every month. Maybe you'd better find a little house with a backyard for the kids." He didn't want her in a boardinghouse, with people asking questions.

Sara looked at the check, her face expressionless. "Thanks, but nobody'll cash this. I don't have a bank account anywheres, and I need money to pay for the hotel and the bus back."

Lord give him strength. Luke frantically looked through his desk and his coat pockets, trying to round up whatever cash he had on hand. It came to almost five hundred dollars.

"Here, put this out of sight. Don't let anyone see how much you have. And don't stay another night in that hotel, but get back to Salem. Open a bank account with the check."

Luke hustled them out and took them down in the elevator. He handed the doorman his last ten and asked him to get them a cab back to their hotel.

When Luke got back on the elevator, he was sweating.

Nikki, wearing nothing but lacy French silk underpants, wondered why Luke had shut her in the bedroom. After all, he had no business secrets from her. Was it really a long-distance call? Or was it Diana?

Nikki threw Luke's robe on and tiptoed to the door. And then she heard a crash coming from the game room. And a woman's voice, and then what sounded like a little girl.

Scurrying back to the bedroom, Nikki kept the door open just enough so that she could peek. It was a woman and two little kids. They looked like they belonged in a thrift shop.

When she heard the front door shut and realized that Luke had gone with his guests, Nikki went to the window and waited.

The woman and children came out, followed by the doorman, who got them a taxi.

Nikki had a fair idea that these odd-looking people were poor relations and that Luke had wanted to get rid of them in a hurry. She could hardly blame him, but why not tell her about it? Why lie to her?

She didn't ask. She was in bed waiting to greet him. He seemed frantic to have sex, yet she sensed that he was acting.

25

"How do they taste?" Diana's father asked, turning from the stove to watch her eating the *sopaipillas* he had just prepared.

Diana, chewing on the puffy, deep-fried bits of dough drizzled with honey, grinned and swallowed. "Absolutely heavenly. Nobody makes them like you, Dad."

Diana's mother, sitting opposite her daughter, said, "Remember when you were little, Didi, you used to call them sofa pillows?"

"That's right, I did." Diana suddenly felt like crying.

Nobody but her parents had ever called her Didi. Indeed, she had refused to answer to the nickname, especially when used by her brother. It was something special between her parents and her, and she hadn't heard it in quite some time.

Her father, standing at the stove with his back to her, hadn't changed much. He was only a little bulkier than she remembered, and his black hair was thinning. And her mother was a little grayer but still slim and just as languid in her motions.

Diana felt that she looked a little like each of them; she had her mother's dark eyes and soft curling hair, her father's impudent nose and wide mouth. She would age as they were aging, and the thought was not entirely unwelcome, even if it was premature.

"Okay, that's it," her father said, putting another platter of fried bread on the table and sitting down.

"They're wonderful but I can't eat another bite," Diana said. Since she had gotten here a few days ago, her appetite had returned to almost normal. Being home and fussed over made her feel like a child again, protected and loved. She was to have come only for the Fourth of July weekend, but she was staying on. Nothing was happening in New York anyway, and being there was too depressing. She had tried going to East Hampton but the emptiness of the place without Luke had driven her away. Here, in the comfortable, sprawling adobe house on Canyon Road, where she had been born, the pain over Luke was at a more bearable level.

The Sinclair house was typically Santa Fe, with its Indian furnishings. The large kitchen was usually redolent of chili, and a pot of pinto beans was always simmering, to be washed down with bottles of ice-cold Dos Equis beer.

Diana loved the daily sunshine; the clean, sharp, unpolluted air, hot during the day but cool at night. Then the glowing fire in the beehive fireplace gave off a welcome odor of piñon and mountain oak.

As one day extended into another, Diana let herself drift. She helped her parents in the gallery and drove to the market with her dad while her mother painted in her studio at the back of the property. Her father painted much less these days, Diana noticed. But he enjoyed growing flowers and vegetables, and he had become an even more accomplished New Mexican cook.

John Sinclair was a man of contradictions, and Diana felt she didn't know him very well. He had a restless, crackling energy, and a hard edge in his voice, strong opinions, and firm control over the family. Yet he was more domestic than her rather dreamy mother, and his bark never led to a bite. Diana had always felt that knowing he could never be more than a little fish in a little pond, he had used the art gallery as an excuse for keeping Martha Kent Sinclair from the fame she could have enjoyed at the center of the art world.

Diana had wondered why her mother put up with it. To some extent, her own battles with her brother were her way of not being like her mother, of not giving in to the male simply because that was expected of her. Yet in other respects her mother was utterly indifferent to convention. "I hope you'll take a lover, Didi," she had said to Diana just as she was going off to college, "but it would be better not to marry until it feels right."

In truth, her parents lived in a world all their own, with art at its center. Diana knew they were proud of her achievement and watched her shows regularly and with enjoyment. Yet she felt that they were thinking: We don't know how you could possibly prefer that sort of existence, but we're glad you're happy and successful.

Her parents were blessedly silent about Luke. A while ago Diana had told them in passing that she was involved with the actor but not that he was living with her, since they hadn't inquired. When she had phoned them to say she'd like to visit and that she would be coming alone, they had simply accepted it.

One afternoon, as Diana was in the garden helping her father set the table for lunch, her mother wandered out, still wearing her smock, with a paintbrush held absent-mindedly in her hand. "Kent just phoned. He's in Albuquerque and would like to stop off and say hello. Isn't it perfect? Didi is here, and then I can give him the painting I did for Jessica's room. Only I can't think where I put it. I didn't sell it to the Porters, did I?"

John Sinclair straightened up from the table and said authoritatively, "No, Marty, the Porters bought something similar. I know just where Jessica's painting is." He led his wife back across the yard.

As Diana continued to put out plates, she had mixed feelings about seeing her brother. She remembered his total antipathy to Luke from the start and hoped Kent wouldn't give her the usual hard time, because she didn't have the strength for a fight; she was feeling too vulnerable.

After the flurry of excitement following Kent's arrival, he turned to Diana. "That's quite a cute show, *Pete Winston*. But if you ask me, it's Gemma Lopez who makes it so funny, not what's-his-face."

Diana hadn't asked him, and she didn't let herself be provoked. However, she felt she had to tell him that the series wasn't being continued because Luke had gone over to another network. She must have sounded ghastly because Kent looked a little startled. "I see," he said, and changed the subject, to Diana's relief.

Kent described how he had brought in a very big client from Albuquerque, and shortly afterward his architectural firm had offered him a partnership. Diana saw that he was so pleased with himself he had no need to be rough on her, as he had been that last time when he had been feeling unsure of his career. Now the situation was reversed, and *she* was floundering. And when the conversation turned to Patty and her second pregnancy, Diana felt a tinge of envy. A fleeting picture of Pete Winston, surrounded by his children, made her eyes a little misty. Luke would be a terrific father, once he could make the commitment. . . .

"Kent, dear, I do hope one of your children turns out to have some artistic talent," Martha remarked in a wistful voice.

"Well, that remains to be seen," Kent said genially. "How's the painting going?"

"She's been very productive," John answered for her, "and selling like crazy."

"Hey, terrific, Mother. Can we have a look?"

"I do wish you'd call me Marty," she grumbled, "instead of making me feel like an old woman. I'm not *only* your mother, you know. Why can't you be more modern?"

"Sorry, I just can't do it. I certainly won't permit Jess to call me Kent. I think that's disrespectful."

Diana smiled, remembering that while her friends had

envied the unconventional informality of her parents, she and Kent had wanted them to be like everyone else.

Later, while they were in the studio, the bell at the gallery pealed.

"There's a customer for you," Kent said. "Aren't you supposed to be open this evening?"

The elder Sinclairs looked at each other. "Do you feel like it, Marty? I don't, much."

"Nor I. Let them come back some other time."

"What a way to run a business," Kent mused to Diana, and she grinned, finding her parents' zaniness very endearing.

"We'll never get rich, true," John Sinclair said, "but there's something to be said for freedom and leisure. My father was always on the go with his oil explorations, drilling morning, noon, and night. He made out well but was dead at sixty-seven. Not for me."

"I agree entirely," Martha chimed in. "I never could see the appeal in a profession that means working nine to five. Oooh." She shuddered at the thought.

Diana thought that was amusing, but Kent bristled. "You can talk, Dad, because it was your father's money that made it possible for you to have this laid-back lifestyle. I don't have the same privilege."

Diana had to admit that her brother had a point. Children rebel against parents, they become parents themselves, and their own children rebel against them. That was an old story. The present generation, for instance, was close-cropped rather than long-haired, and dressed for success. They had discarded flower power for Wall Street.

Diana reached for her notebook and jotted down: "A pair of zany artists now in their forties live in a SoHo loft. Having decided to 'drop out' in the sixties, they can't understand their college-age kids, one of whom wants to study law and the other banking."

Before Kent left the next day, he hugged Diana. "Hope you get it all together, somehow. I'd like to see you happy, I really would."

She hugged him back, feeling affectionate, for once. "Thanks. I think I'm happier already because I have a new idea and I'm going to get right to work on it."

She spent her last morning with her mother, helping her

to hang a couple of new works in the gallery, and watching her pleased smile when she sold a large painting to a woman from Dallas for two thousand dollars.

"Mom, are you happy?" Diana asked her as they went back to the house for lunch.

"Yes, dear, very happy."

"I mean, don't you ever regret not having, uh, gone to Europe, you know, traveled, opened a gallery in New York? You could have been at the center, acquiring paintings from all over, meeting important people from the art world. You could have been right up there, too, Martha Kent Sinclair," Diana added, unable to resist. "You have more than local talent, you know."

Her mother refused to be baited. "John came here from Oklahoma, we fell in love, and we made our life here. John has always been entirely devoted to me."

Diana thought her mother sounded defensive, making excuses for her husband, unwilling to admit that she had sacrificed her career because she feared she would outshine him.

26

There had been no word from Luke, but Diana was too excited about her new idea to dwell on her disappointment. She and Molly had a brainstorming session. "The parents are named, let's see, Bob and Linda, and the kids are Amy and Adam," Molly supplied.

"Yeah, yeah, and the kids insist on calling their parents Mom and Dad instead of Linda and Bob as they would like," Diana chimed in. "Oh, and the daughter is very independent, planning, when she becomes a lawyer, to have a child and raise it herself—"

"Yes, good. But she needs her birth certificate for

something or other and finds out that her own parents never did get married. Then she's horrified at being a bastard. Her brother, too. They're yuppies in the making, and they insist that their parents go right down to city hall—"

"Molly, that's perfect," Diana cried.

They named the family the Streets, and the projected series *Street Smarts*.

Diana pitched Matthew at his office, struck by how tanned and good he was looking, his green eyes twinkling at her.

She felt like herself again, confident of her ability. "If you like the idea, Matthew, Noreen Sanders is interested in playing the daughter, and Madge Murray the mother. And this time, we get run-of-series commitments from everyone."

Matthew liked it enough to ask for a bible. He suggested veteran comedian Selwyn Smith to play the father, and a talented newcomer, Randy Tippet, for the son.

Diana and Molly both thought those were good choices, and they had a wonderful time working out their bible and story lines.

Somehow, Matthew did it again. In spite of Diana's run-in with Phil, and the way Luke had let everyone down, Matthew went out to the Coast and apparently convinced the program board (over Phil's reluctance) that Abbott and Sinclair had the right stuff for sitcom—they had done it once, they could do it again. Matthew came away with approval of thirteen episodes without a pilot.

Diana's good luck held. The cast and crew they wanted were available. By the beginning of August they were in production and shot the first two scripts. Although the network hadn't committed themselves to air *Street Smarts* in prime time (the fall schedule was complete), Abbott and Sinclair were hustling, trying to get several shows on tape in the hope that *Street Smarts* would be considered as a replacement.

Since returning from Santa Fe, Diana had been spending weekends in East Hampton. The pain of Luke's defection was now only a dull ache she occasionally felt at bedtime. She was too busy to be unhappy.

On the first Saturday in August she received a call from

Matthew. "I know it's late in the day but I thought you might be free for dinner tonight."

Diana hesitated, then said yes. She always enjoyed seeing Matthew and didn't at all mind talking business. Especially now, when she was so immersed in the new series she could hardly think of anything else.

Matthew picked her up and drove to a place that had no sign identifying itself as a restaurant. "It's under new management and hasn't been renamed yet. Couple of preppy women called Muffie and Buffie, something like that. From Southhampton. Families are horrified that their little debbies would do something so infra-dig as open a restaurant. So the young ladies are keen to build up a snappy-looking clientele that won't entirely disgrace the family names. Rockefeller and Mellon, probably."

Diana laughed. "You're in a good mood. Could be one of those young women has put the roses in your cheeks," she teased.

"Could be," he agreed.

New or not, the place had caught on, and the few tables were very quickly filled. Diana caught a glimpse of the owners and had to grant that Matthew had described them very well.

"It's a terrific menu," he said with enthusiasm. "They've rediscovered charcoal, for example. No mesquite, no arcane fungi with disgusting names. Just honest old ribs, chicken, mixed salad, and look, mashed potatoes, hot biscuits, just like their southern servants used to make. I haven't seen mashed potatoes on a menu in these parts in ages."

They sipped gin and tonics and talked about nothing in particular. Diana had never seen Matthew so light, and she thought she knew part of the reason when he mentioned that his daughter had gone to camp for a month. The lifting of responsibility, she supposed.

"How does she like it?"

"I'd say a lot, since she's too busy to write and complain. She's with her two best friends, and they've called to say they're having fun."

"I'm glad she's doing so well, Matthew. That's good news."

He sighed. "Yes, thanks."

Diana was reflective. "Her mother might get in touch sometime, you know."

"Yes, that's a possibility. A probability, even. When and if Lorrie ever grows up. I hope Andy will be old enough and mature enough to deal with it."

Diana felt very warm toward Matthew, and she smiled at him. "Thanks for asking me to dinner tonight. I've hardly been social at all this summer."

He nodded. "I thought as much. Working the way you do is fine, up to a point. But that head is much too lovely to be buried in scripts without a break."

Diana felt a strange jolt, and as she looked curiously at him, she sensed, as she had once before, that he was interested in more than her work. His eyes looked glittery and even admiring in the candlelight. She felt awkward and lowered her gaze, saying, "Writing is what I do best. It's hard but at least it's predictable. No painful shocks. The only way for me to get people to say what they should is to write their speeches myself."

"Oh, I'm not so sure. Mr. Right would come up with perfectly acceptable dialogue."

Diana shrugged. "Even if I met Mr. Right, he'd probably be wrong for me."

While Matthew smiled, one of the owners, a laughing brunette, bounced up to their table and asked if they were enjoying their dinner.

"Very much," Matthew assured her. "Best ribs and mashed potatoes I've had in years."

"Could that be Miss Right?" Diana teased him as the young woman moved away.

"Nope." He put his chin in his hands and gazed at Diana. "Not Muffie, not Buffie, but only the fair Diana. She knows who she is. She's blushing."

"She is not," Diana murmured, feeling warm all over, and a little guilty. Why was she provoking him? The answer came to her: it had been three months since she had been with Luke. And it made her feel good to think that another man was interested, especially someone as impressive as Matthew Sayles. But it wasn't fair to him.

She glanced at him warily. "I . . . I think we'd better talk about *Street Smarts*."

"Fine. I can dispose of it in three words. I love it. I also love you."

Diana sat utterly still, staring at him. Then she murmured, "Don't say that, please."

"I certainly will say it. I love you, Diana. And have for quite a while. I don't know if you've been writing my dialogue in your head—in fact, I doubt it—but I've certainly been writing yours. 'It's too soon,' she says. 'I'm still involved with Luke.' " Matthew smiled, such an attractive smile, and at the same time self-deprecating. " 'There would be too many problems, Matthew,' she continues, 'because we work together. And your daughter jealously guards her turf.' "

"I'd never say 'turf,' " Diana balked. " 'Territory.' "

" 'Turf,' " he insisted. "Never use a long word when a short word will do. Especially when I'm trying to fast-forward to the romantic part. To where she says, 'Yes, I'll spend the night with you, Matthew. But it's not love.' 'Lust will do,' he says, 'because, to coin a cliché, I have enough love for both of us.' "

"Oh, please stop, Matthew." Diana began to laugh but she was on the edge of tears. How ironic. Luke had left her because he had believed she was having an affair with Matthew, and now she was actually thinking of it, and "lust" was exactly the word. She didn't need to be told again that she was blushing. Her face felt like a furnace.

" 'I don't want to hurt you, Matthew,' she says, 'because if Luke comes back . . .' "

Diana put her face in her hands, feeling the alcohol whirling through her brain.

She felt Matthew's hands on hers. "Forgive me. I have no right to probe. I'm making a joke out of something serious. Look, you're probably not ready. Maybe never will be, as far as I'm concerned. But I felt that I had to speak. I left it too long the last time. When we first met, I mean. I was attracted from the first moment, but I was waiting for . . . I don't know what. Just when I had decided to make my move, it was too late." He gently removed her hands from her face.

"One reason I *can* speak, finally, Diana, is that I've grown to love you on so many levels that I'm prepared to accept friendship, if that's all you can offer."

He kept her hands in his, and she didn't snatch them away. She still felt dangerously close to weeping and feared to say anything at all. For a few minutes they sat in silence, their hands entwined. His were firm and loving. She could feel the deep warmth and caring, and it astonished her. She hadn't in any way earned his love.

Slowly he put her hands on the table and withdrew his own. "Is there any hope?"

"I don't know," she whispered.

"I see. You think Luke will be back. In fact, I think he will too. After you, Nikki will seem so shallow, so forgettable that even he will realize what he's lost. Not to mention what happens to him professionally. He's going to strike out for sure. And I know you may take him back, but I'm willing to risk it. Don't ask me why. I don't think it's vanity, exactly, but I think I have traits to counterbalance his good looks and charisma. Like loyalty and deepening affection. I need a history with a woman. The better I know her, the better I'm able to love her."

Diana looked at him with bright eyes. "That's so rare. Women are constantly complaining about just that deficiency in men. You'd better not waste it on me, Matthew," she sighed. "I'm so confused. I don't know what I want. I wish I did." She smiled wanly. "It's all so stupid. I mean, it's like a French farce, everybody wanting the wrong person, scheming, willing to believe lies—"

"I'll take the truth every time," Matthew said, "no matter how painful. So don't add guilt over me to your load, Diana. I'm tougher than I look. I won't pretend that I don't see other women, that I haven't tried to care for someone else. It may even happen someday. Until then, I'm yours, whenever you want me. Tonight, maybe," he finished with a hopeful smile.

Diana felt terrible. "I don't know what to say."

"In that case, let me. 'I'm honored,' she says, 'but it wouldn't be fair. I don't want to hurt you.' 'That's okay,' he says. 'Where is there pleasure without pain? Let's begin right now. Your place or mine?' 'I can't,' she says. 'Take me home, please.' He reluctantly agrees."

Matthew summoned the waiter and paid the check. Then he looked at Diana. "Did I get it right?"

She nodded shamefacedly. "I'm afraid you did."

They were silent as he drove her home.

What a strange evening it had been. Just when she thought she had gotten a grip on herself again, this had thrown her right back into the bubbling pit of her own confusion and doubt. And all the adolescent questions she had once pondered rushed back to assail her. What is love? How do you know? Wasn't being comfortable with someone more important than a physical need? Hadn't it started with Luke just this way? He had told her he loved her, and she had been afraid. She was afraid now. She couldn't go through all that again—loving, and being hurt. Matthew had indicated that he didn't do that, but nobody could guarantee such a thing. Love lasted only as long as it lasted.

Work was pure by comparison. One show died, another was born. There was emotion enough in that, but it wasn't the same. Although she had felt bad over the demise of *Pete Winston*, her tears had been shed for Luke Merriman. That was the difference; that was why love was to be avoided.

"Good night, Diana," Matthew said, kissing her cheek gently. "I'm sorry if I've made things worse, but I'm glad I spoke up all the same."

"Good night, Matthew." She kissed his cheek, as she had sometimes done, only this time her lips tingled.

As she alighted from his car, she wondered if she should invite him in. The house was empty, dark, lonely. And she really did like him. He was attractive, and he wanted her. . . .

She put her key in the lock and turned it, waved to Matthew, and went inside.

As soon as he drove away, she regretted it. Yet to invite him to bed with her, the same bed where she and Luke had been so happy—she just couldn't.

Diana got undressed and took a cold shower. That's what horny little boys were told to do, and indeed, the icy water coming down her back almost did the job too well. As she got into bed she was shivering. Pouring herself a brandy, she lay back against the pillows. It was quiet except for the rhythmic crashing of the waves against the shore.

She finished the brandy and dozed off, but awakened an

hour later, her entire body on fire. And for once she wasn't thinking of Luke but of Matthew. Diana shut her eyes again, but this time she pictured Matthew's wavy brown hair, his oblique and exotic eyes, looking as if they belonged to a god from the sea. She longed for his sensual mouth against her flesh.

She got out of bed and put on pants and a cotton pullover sweater. How strong Matthew was, she reflected. It must have taken courage to confess his love for her, knowing that she was still pining for another man.

She slipped into her sandals and grabbed her car keys. Matthew didn't know her very well. If they had sex it would change everything between them, including the good working relationship they had. Going to his house tonight was not only inadvisable, but absolutely wrong.

And wouldn't Luke—when he found out, as he inevitably would—be even angrier with her?

Well, dammit, she was angry with him! Anger suddenly boiled up in her. He had left her. Yes, he might be back, but when? She simply couldn't wait around for Luke to return.

When Diana left the house, it was cold and drizzling, but her body heat was keeping her warm. She got into her car and turned out of the driveway with her brights on in the mist.

Within a short time she was on the road to Sag Harbor, driving slowly through the darkness, and the line between sleeping and waking blurred. Quite a few other cars came toward her, their windshield wipers moving eerily from side to side through the fog.

The clock in her car registered one-thirty. She must be mad. Matthew would be asleep. He might even be with some other woman. She wasn't even exactly sure where his street was, though she had a vague idea.

What if his housekeeper opened the door? Diana visualized herself standing on the doorstep in the middle of the night. It was absurd.

Turn back, Sinclair. You're being an idiot.

She kept driving, knowing she wouldn't turn back. She needed a man, and one was there waiting for her.

The half-hour drive didn't cool her ardor in any way, and she found his street without making one wrong turn, like a homing pigeon in heat.

Fate had even left a parking place a few feet from his house.

She got out of the car and looked for a light. One dim ray shone from between the curtains of a downstairs window.

She rang the bell and waited. Silence. She rang again, more insistently, then heard faint footsteps.

Matthew opened the door, wearing only a robe, and she stepped into his arms.

As he held her to him, stroking her hair, murmuring her name, she grabbed him tightly around the waist and kicked off her sandals.

He cupped her face in his hands and kissed her gently, but gentleness was not what she wanted, and she let him know it by thrusting her tongue between his lips and digging her fingers into his broad, solid back.

"Diana," he groaned, drawing her into the living room, where a fire was burning and only a dim lamp was lit.

Diana pulled off her sweater and slacks, then her bra and panties. He was still wearing his robe, but the thin blue cotton couldn't conceal that he wanted her.

"You're so beautiful," he murmured, touching her breasts.

She inhaled through her teeth and undid the tie on his robe, pulling it savagely off his shoulders. Then she bent her head to kiss his chest, with its patch of fine dark hair.

He drew her down on the rug in front of the fireplace and bestowed feathery kisses on her face and neck, while he explored her form very lightly with his fingertips.

Diana moaned and writhed, and then pulled him forcefully on top of her. "Now, now, please now," she cried, working her hips and straining toward him. He glided smoothly and quickly into her and for a moment she could scarcely breathe, so glorious was the feeling of Matthew's hardness.

She squeezed his shoulders tightly as she came, panting and moaning, holding him tightly and waiting for his release.

But he didn't come. He moved off her and lay resting on one elbow, breathing shallowly and watching her, his eyes glittering like a cat's.

"What's wrong?" she asked. "Was I too quick?"

He shook his head and smiled. "You're so exciting that I'd like to last a little longer."

Then he leaned forward and kissed her lips, her neck, her breasts.

"I'm all sweaty," she murmured.

"Yes. Salty. I love it." He fondled her breasts while moving his head lower, to kiss her belly and nip it between his teeth.

Diana caught her breath and felt that unmistakable palpitation which caused her entire body to shudder. "Oh, oh," she breathed, feeling his tongue gently lapping at her and going lower, lower still, snaking between her legs, licking a path between her thighs, exploring and teasing until he found the right spot.

"Oh, no, no, stop, I can't stand it. . . ." She arched her back, as his tongue, flicking back and forth with ever-increasing speed, was causing her backbone to dissolve.

Then he positioned himself above her and entered, his eyes narrowed and his mouth quivering.

"Diana," he intoned, thrusting into her in a circular motion. "Diana, Diana, Diana. I love you, Diana."

He continued to rotate his hips. "It's so wonderful to be inside you. You are so glorious inside, outside, every side. I wish there were more ways that I could love you."

He flicked his tongue in and out of her ear as a counterpoint to the rotating motion, and she tightened her arms around his neck, lifting her pelvis in keeping with his rhythm, which quickened and drove her to a frenzy. "Matthew, oh, Matthew."

She felt his harder, more direct thrusts, saw him throw his head back, and felt him surrender to her. They cried out with passion as they felt the spasms of their bodies against one another.

She lay in his arms until the fire had burned to embers.

She felt at peace with herself as she hadn't in a long time. Was that all she had needed? Didn't the man matter at all?

Of course he mattered. It wasn't just anyone. It was Matthew, her friend, and now her lover.

27

"Well, that's more like it, kid," Molly said, looking at Diana, pleased. "Smart woman, smart choice. I think Matthew is terrific."

"Gee, thanks. You know, you're worse than my mother. She never meddled in my personal life—"

"She should have," Molly broke in, turning the pages of the new script that was spread across the conference table. "If she had, maybe you'd have had better taste in men before now."

"Oh, shush, Molly." Diana settled in front of her own copy of the script and reached for her coffee. "Anyway, I'm not sure where it's going to lead. It's only been a week."

"A week during which you look human again. I thought it was more than just the work going well. In fact, this puts a new slant on things. I predict that *Street Smarts* is going to make it into prime time before November."

"Molly, for God's sake." Diana raised her voice. "You don't really think Matthew is so unprofessional as to let *that* make a difference!"

"Of course it will make a difference. Oh, not if the show were lousy, but it's good. It's better than good, it's wonderful. I like it better than *Pete Winston*, because the comedy is more pure, without that tugging on the heartstrings of motherless kids. I find it easier to write, easier to relate to. It can't miss. And the cast is great, too—thorough professionals. But the fact that you're getting it on with a big shot on the network can't hurt, and it's nothing to be ashamed of."

But Diana was ashamed. She didn't want the show to benefit because she was sleeping with Matthew, or even worse, to lose out if she were to stop seeing him. That was the problem with mixing business and pleasure.

When the phone rang, Molly picked up, grinned, and handed the receiver to Diana.

"Lunch," Matthew said. "The usual place, the usual time. Be there."

She laughed and hung up. He was like a boy at times, and it delighted her.

However, as the days went on, their time spent together wasn't entirely without friction. He was a strong personality, and so was she, and they sometimes reached an impasse, such as the Wednesday night he suggested a concert at Lincoln Center. Matthew liked contemporary serious music; Diana loathed it. She liked classical and baroque, but mostly on records. What she wanted to do was hear jazz at a club, but he wasn't in the mood for that.

"Let's compromise," he suggested. "How about Mostly Mozart? In this case, all Mozart." As Matthew read the program to her, anxiety gripped her chest. She didn't want to compromise, she wanted to go to the Blue Note or the Vanguard and drink gin and tonic and groove to funky music.

"There's going to be jazz at Southampton this weekend," Matthew continued. "I'll reserve tickets. We could consider a movie tonight. A walk in the park. Dinner al fresco."

None of those choices appealed to her. "Maybe we should just skip tonight."

There was a pause. "Are you saying that if you can't have it your way you don't want to see me at all?"

She suddenly felt irked, remembering how flexible Luke had been. Matthew was already trying to get her to give in to him.

"Diana? Look, I can't stay on the phone. Make up your mind and call me back."

He hung up, and she felt like wringing his neck. She didn't need this, did she? She missed Luke's easygoing temperament. Matthew could be so damn stubborn. Stubbornness might have gotten him where he was professionally, but she didn't like coming up against it in her free time, dammit. She tried to go over the script on her lap but she was seething. Today was going to be a busy rehearsal, and she didn't need anger to distract her. To hell with Matthew, she thought, I won't phone him. After all, he had practically hung up on her.

The day was so involving that by the time she picked up her head it was almost six, rehearsal was over, and she hadn't had any word from him.

She tried his private line, anxiety tugging at her. No answer. Had he left without resolving the evening?

Anxiety alternated with anger. They had made a date tonight, and he had broken it, damn him. Now she had no plans. It was no fun going to a jazz club by herself; when she had tried that in the past, she had spent the time fending off men.

Diana went home and ate a sandwich. She tried to watch TV but grew bored. Restlessly she prowled the apartment. The thought that he might have invited someone else to dinner and to that concert was very upsetting. And if she felt upset, she was probably falling in love with him.

She had certainly been enjoying the time they spent together. He was an interesting companion and a very authentic person, not impressed with his own status or anyone else's. His house, for instance, was not nearly as grand as she would have imagined for someone of his position and probable income.

His friends, the Blackmans, were equally wonderful—"real folks" rather than the leading lights in the TV industry. Matthew socialized with those people when it was necessary—he often entertained Phil and his wife at Le Cirque, for instance—but he wanted his home to be comfortable and without frills.

Diana grabbed her handbag and left the apartment. She felt too jumpy to stay in. Besides, it was a nice evening, cooler than it had been in days. She started toward Fifth Avenue, getting into a comfortable stride. She had felt so confined in the studio all day.

This was the kind of evening that had every pair of lovers in New York out for a stroll. It was midweek, "date night," and she felt left out.

As she waited to cross a street, she realized she had walked to the West Side and was nearly at Columbus Circle, not far from Lincoln Center. It was almost ten, and Matthew's concert would be letting out.

Don't chase after him, Sinclair, he'll treat you with contempt.

The alternative was her empty bed, on a night that she had anticipated having Matthew in it. They hadn't been together since Sunday night, and . . . And what? Admit it, Sinclair, you want him.

Shit. She felt like a lovaholic. In the past, she had gone for months with nothing and scarcely missed it. But the moment she took a sip of love, of sex, she was hooked. She hated it.

Luke had awakened her sensuality and it was now part of her being, to be expressed with Matthew quite naturally, and probably with any other man who might turn her on. But it was Matthew she needed tonight, and she didn't want to need him, because he had broken their date, damn him.

Sex with Matthew was very satisfying. Less frantic and more sexual than with Luke. It was less an end in itself and more a part of their relationship, and that was the trouble.

Outside Avery Fisher Hall she positioned herself so that she could see everyone coming out. She licked an ice-cream cone like a child while she waited. She felt pouty and resentful and worried, all at the same time. She could almost visualize Matthew emerging with another woman, and all the uncertainties and jealousies she had felt in the latter period with Luke came flooding back. Other images plagued her memory too—of being a small girl and wanting to tag along with her brother, who refused to have her. She would trail behind, watching him having fun with his friends, feeling left out. She had girls to play with, of course, and she did, but it had always rankled that she couldn't be accepted as an equal by her brother and his friends.

Matthew was alone. He saw her immediately and came toward her, smiling with pleasure. "How nice to find my love waiting for me." He put his arm around her shoulder and gave her a welcoming kiss.

Diana felt herself softening but she wouldn't give in. "You broke our date and went off to do your own thing."

"Not at all." He fell into step at her side as she began to walk, she knew not where. "I assumed when you didn't call back that you preferred not to see me tonight."

"And that was all right with you?" she queried.

"Well, what could I do? Twist your arm?"

"You could have come to hear jazz with me," she said sulkily.

"No, that wasn't an option. I told you I wasn't in the mood for jazz tonight. I made several other suggestions—"

"You're so stubborn," she burst out. "You want everything your own way."

"On the contrary. I agreed not to go to the concert. I agreed to have dinner, walk, talk. You were the one who said it had to be jazz or nothing."

A disgruntled Diana didn't reply.

"Now what, sweetie? Shall we have a nightcap? Shall we go home to bed?"

"Just because I live in town doesn't mean you can use my place as a hotel—"

Matthew stopped and grabbed her arm tightly. "For God's sake, will you stop all this?" He put his hands on her shoulders and looked soberly at her. "I don't know what angry scenario is rolling around in your head, but I'm not much good at guessing games, so I'll tell you straight, Diana. I love being with you. But there will be times when we want to do different things. If we can't compromise, then we'll just have to be apart. I can't force you, and you can't force me. And that has to be understood if we're to go on together.

Diana stared at him, puzzled yet somewhat relieved. He wasn't angry, he was just . . . "Stubborn" wasn't the right word. She didn't know what was.

"Diana, I would like to spend the night with you. But if you'd rather not, just say no. I'll stay at a hotel, and I'll still love you in the morning."

When he smiled at her, she moved into his arms. "Yes, please stay with me. And . . . and I'm sorry for being so bad-tempered over nothing."

Things went smoothly between them until she learned he was going to take Andrea home from camp, and she was not invited.

A feeling of apprehension took hold of her. Had she been a stand-in for his daughter, just someone to fill the lonely evenings?

"What now?" Diana asked nervously. "Am I not to see Andy? No more weekends together? No more nights in town at my place?"

Matthew sighed. "We'll have to work it out. Of course you'll see her, but on a casual basis at first."

"Why casual?" Diana snapped. "Is that all I am to you, a casual date?"

"On the contrary. That's the trouble. I'm in love with you. More each day. The question is how you feel about me."

They were sitting on her deck in East Hampton that last Saturday, watching the sun set.

Diana took a sip of her white wine. "I love you, of course."

"Of course," he echoed with a touch of mockery. "But you're not in love with me, are you? And don't start asking me to define my words. You know very well what I mean. You're not in love and you're not ready to make a commitment beyond our day-to-day connection. Isn't that so?"

Diana wanted to deny it, but when she opened her lips a deep sigh escaped, so she stalled by asking, "What kind of commitment?"

He looked her straight in the eye and said, "Marriage. That's the only kind that counts with me. I also have to consider my daughter."

"Yes, that's part of the . . . the problem. I mean, Andrea would have to accept me. I would have to see myself as her stepmother. And we'd have to work out if you would want other children—"

"I can answer that part right now. Yes, I would, very much. I would love to have children with you, Diana."

Unbidden tears rose and lingered. This was her first marriage proposal. She wished she could throw her arms around his neck and say yes. She wanted to be married, she wanted to have children. Matthew was a wonderful man, a wonderful father. And she was certain that, given time, she and Andrea would get along fine.

But wanting, and being able, were not the same. There was still unfinished business.

"Luke stands between us, not Andrea," Matthew said, reading her thoughts. "You haven't altogether given up on him, I know that quite well. I can even understand it. He's younger, he's handsomer, he's a celebrity, and most important, you created him."

"You said, at the beginning," she murmured softly, "that you were tough enough to take care of yourself—"

"Yes, and it's true. I hate it, of course. I hate it that you can't let go of that guy, but I can deal with it. But my daughter—that's another story. I can't present you to her as a possible member of the family when you still don't know what you want. She's been hurt too badly. You and I can't even pretend to know what it's like to be rejected by the very person who gave you life. It's so unnatural that a child can't take it in. Children don't reason, they react. And the obvious reaction is, 'My mother left me because I wasn't good enough, because I disappointed her, because—' You can fill in the rest."

"Yes, Matthew, I do understand how hard it's been for her."

"Okay. Then know I can't risk involving Andrea with you on anything but a casual basis until I'm reasonably sure that you mean to spend your life with both of us."

28

Nikki had expected her life to become wonderful once she was writing and producing Luke's show, but it hadn't happened that way. First, no matter how she plotted and enticed, Luke wouldn't hear of her moving in with him, and Nikki had to accept it. Second, when she came down from her euphoria enough to read her contract carefully, she was appalled to see that although she had a commitment to produce thirteen shows without a pilot, ATN had to air only six of them, and there was no mention of prime time. She couldn't believe it, but there it was in black and white. And third, the six programs they had taped weren't well received by the network. Nikki thought they were dynamite, but Oliver, reporting back from the programming committee, was critical and dubious.

Well, Nikki was sure the public would prove the network wrong. Not only did Luke have an enormous following, but he looked gorgeous up there in front of the mike, eliciting questions from a cheering, enthusiastic audience, then coming up with the answers.

The show premiered the first week in October at seven-thirty to poor reviews but it got a solid thirty percent of the audience. Just when a happy Nikki and Luke were asking that the show be moved to prime time, Continental, which had been rerunning *Pete Winston*, switched nights in order to throw the reruns against *The Luke Merriman Show*! Nikki was beside herself with rage, and so was Luke. Diana and Matthew were ganging up on them, trying to make their show fail. Well, Diana wouldn't succeed.

However, when Nikki demanded that ATN move Luke's show, the network refused. Oliver Feranti stopped answering his phone or returning her calls.

And it got worse. *Pete Winston* received a twenty-two-percent share against *Luke Merriman*'s drop to twenty-five. By the end of October, the reruns were getting thirty-one percent while Luke's show had sunk to twenty. Nikki kept insisting that the show would do better in prime time, but Feranti wouldn't buy that, pointing out that it was so lousy it couldn't even compete with a rerun.

"Figures don't lie," he barked at her over the phone. "Name or no name, Luke isn't bringing in the viewers or the ads, but *Pete Winston* is. After six shows we're pulling the plug."

"You can't do that," Nikki yelled.

"Don't tell me what I can do. Read your contract." Oliver hung up in her ear.

Nikki felt a rising hysteria. She had been so eager to sign on with ATN, so eager for that terrific salary she would draw for the thirteen episodes, that she hadn't realized how she was being shafted. Only the last show remained to be taped, and then she was out on the street.

And now Luke was turning on her, blaming her for the format. "The experts feed me a lot of crap. Okay, I've gone along with it, but it sucks. I don't need the experts. Let the audience ask questions and I'll answer them on the spot. All it takes is plain old horse sense."

Nikki felt backed against the wall. Why should Luke give a damn? He was set for five years. If this show got canceled, they would find him another. Her only hope was to do a terrific thirteenth tape, one she could substitute for show number six so that Oliver and the program committee would change their minds.

Maybe Luke was right and he would be better off not trying to paraphrase the experts. He really was a down-home sort of guy. It might just work.

On tape day of the new format, everything that could go wrong did. There was a major thunderstorm so the studio audience was sparse. The guest star had a virus and they had to use a last-minute substitute, a little-known starlet who looked good and giggled a lot but had nothing to say.

The questions the audience asked were pretty boring, too, but the answers Luke gave were so dumb they were laughable.

A pall fell over the entire cast and crew. They went about their business quietly, almost on tiptoe, like unwilling visitors to the bedside of someone fatally ill.

Someone was ill: Nikki. This was it, the end. There would be no substituting this tape for any of the others because it was the worst of all.

Afterward, she and Luke had a dreadful fight at his place, where they had watched the tape several times. He thought it was just fine, and she couldn't talk him out of it.

In fact, she stopped arguing. There was no point. She had badly overestimated Luke. Diana's angry words about his limited abilities came back to haunt her.

But she saw no reason to be miserable over a lost cause. There was only one way out for Nikki, and she would have to take it.

Matthew flew back from L.A. at the end of the October meeting of the programming board feeling a mixture of emotions.

After one viewing of *The Luke Merriman Show*, he had been the one to suggest throwing *Pete Winston* reruns against it because he thought it would be good business, one of those cases of the before being better than the after. Yet, even though he wanted *Pete Winston* to do as well in the ratings as it was doing, there was a personal catch-22 in it. If Luke's show failed—no, *when* Luke's show failed—he would certainly turn up on Diana's doorstep. Especially since her new *Street Smarts* was doing so well. It had been slotted into Wednesday at nine-thirty as a mid-October replacement and had gone from a twenty-four to a twenty-nine share in just two weeks. Moreover, the reviews had been excellent, and nobody had missed an opportunity to cite the phenomenal success of Abbott and Sinclair, who were doing so well without Luke Merriman, whereas he was doing so poorly without them.

No doubt about it, Luke would be back. The question was, would Diana take him back?

It was a chilling speculation. Matthew had walked into this affair with Diana with open eyes, but as his love for her had deepened, his resolve concerning his daughter had lessened. Little by little, Diana had begun spending more time with him and with Andrea, and things hadn't been easy these last couple of months.

Andy had been confused as well as jealous, and understandably so, for she not surprisingly, had had her father to herself for almost five years. If he could have said, "Diana and I would like to get married. We will all be a family," she might have found the situation easier to accept. Especially as she liked Diana, when she let herself. Sometimes Matthew saw Andy having a wonderful time, but she would suddenly withdraw, as if afraid to love and lose a second time.

In a way, he felt the same. He had hoped Diana would come to see how right he was for her and let Luke fade into memory where he belonged.

But that hadn't yet happened. Yes, Diana was closer to him, and he did feel her love. But—and it was a big but—she was still holding back from any commitment. It indicated to Matthew that she was still uncertain of her feelings.

If that weren't so, just watching five minutes of Luke's new show would have convinced her of what an empty shell the actor was. Without Pete Winston's persona to hide behind, Luke was ridiculous. In fact, remembering that first tape of him, taking photos in the park, Matthew saw clearly that the man had lost the main source of his appeal—the ability to project sweetness, friendliness, and lack of guile.

This was quite another Luke Merriman—smug, pretentious, obnoxious, a parody of his former self. Yet Diana, while finding fault with the format, was unable to find fault with the man himself.

Matthew felt stuck with a terrible dilemma, but he had nobody to blame but himself.

On hearing Nikki's voice on the phone for the first time in months, Gwen sat down hard in her chair. Her hands grew clammy, and droplets of perspiration appeared on her forehead.

"I'll understand if you don't want to see me, Gwennie. I know I've been terrible to you. All I ask is a chance to explain. It's been such torture, wanting to call you but not daring, because of Luke. . . ."

"My daughter is here," Gwen finally croaked into the phone. "Can we meet somewhere?"

Nikki suggested her place.

When Gwen hung up she was trembling, and her body felt drenched. "Liz, I'm going out for the evening. If I'm very late, don't worry. I may just stay over at a friend's."

"Sure," her daughter said, not looking up from her book.

Liz had been staying with Gwen for a couple of weeks before her new sublet apartment was ready. And Gwen had been delighted to have her. She had been so lonely without Nikki, and so depressed that she had scarcely gone out at all. When she took a vacation in Provincetown, where her son was working for the summer, she had shunned gay bars, fearing that in her present state she might be desperate enough to take up with someone else who would break her heart.

Gwen had been totally devastated because her own nature had been unmistakably revealed to her in the course of Nikki's desertion. Yes, it was perfectly possible to find another woman to live with, someone decent, companionable, and her own age. She knew several such couples.

Unfortunately, Gwen wasn't attracted to her counterpart but only to someone like Nikki. The phrase "There's no fool like an old fool" didn't apply only to aging men in their passions for beautiful young girls.

As Gwen stepped into the shower, anxiously examining herself for any dramatic signs of aging during the last few months, she told herself not to be so goddamned stupid. If Nikki wanted to see her, she wanted something specific. In fact, after thinking for a moment, Gwen knew exactly what it was.

She had watched *The Luke Merriman Show*. Yes, the idea had been hers but she had assumed that someone would write every word of the show—questions, answers, the lot. To let the man improvise his answers was complete folly. Nikki undoubtedly knew that by now and wanted Gwen's help. Was she willing to give it? Shouldn't she tell that little slut to go to hell? Maybe she would. It would be nice to inflict pain, for a change.

Gwen slipped into a pale pink jumpsuit that flattered her figure and made her look less sallow, more youthful. She applied makeup carefully, artfully. She had returned to Georgette Klinger's on a weekly basis, so her hair looked good.

Then she thumbed her nose at her reflection. Even if she were hunchbacked and missing a couple of limbs, Nikki would willingly jump into the sack with her at this point. Beauty didn't mind the Beast as long as the Beast was an idea machine.

During the short taxi ride, Gwen refused to psych herself up for a teary reunion. She knew Nikki now for the user she was. And although Gwen initially had put the blame on Luke, as the months had passed with no word, she had realized that Nikki was as rotten as he was.

Finally Gwen was climbing the stairs to Nikki's apartment. How eagerly she would have done so even four months ago. But now it all felt hollow, anticlimactic, because she had suffered so much.

Yet, the moment she saw Nikki exquisitely framed in the doorway, her resolution began to waver. Nikki's face was untouched, regardless of what she was going through (and Gwen could imagine the flak she must be getting from the network and probably Luke, too).

Nikki wore a short white linen dress with a dropped waistline. Expensive and chic. White for purity, Gwen thought wryly. With her creamy skin, auburn hair, and cornflower-blue eyes, Nikki looked like a bouquet of autumn flowers in an alabaster urn.

The apartment was artfully candlelit, and fall leaves were everywhere. The music of Vivaldi, Gwen's favorite, played softly. And the phone, Gwen noticed, was out of its jack in the wall.

She mentally gave the girl an A-plus for setting the scene. If Nikki were as talented a writer/producer as she was a schemer, she would have no need of Gwen at all.

The girl's bright, welcoming smile faded when Gwen walked right past her and seated herself in a chair.

Nikki quickly poured her some wine. "I don't blame you for being angry. I would be too, in your place. But when you hear the whole story—"

"I've heard the goddamn, story," Gwen interrupted tightly. "I had a very frank talk with Diana Sinclair."

She saw Nikki turn visibly paler.

"When was that?" the girl whispered.

"Way back in May, after I read that cute little item in *Variety* about you, Luke Merriman, and Abbott and Sinclair."

Nikki frowned. "I'm sorry you had to hear so much from Diana. I can just imagine how she distorted everything. I was intending to level with you tonight, Gwennie. Okay, I did know who you were, I did arrange our meeting, and I did intend to take advantage of the situation. But, like, I never expected to grow so attached to you. When that happened, everything changed. I saw how wonderful it was, being with a woman, being with you. I wanted to tell you the truth but I thought you wouldn't believe me. Then Luke came on to me more and more, begging me to get him out of Diana's clutches. In spite of what he looks like, he's a big baby. He was afraid to pee without asking Diana's permission."

Nikki went on persuasively, saying that Luke wouldn't have trusted her unless she had agreed to sleep with him. "I figured once we had the show in the works—"

"In five months," Gwen interrupted angrily, "you didn't once phone or write or care whether I was living or dead. Are you telling me he had you chained to a wall?"

"No, no, it was just . . . I didn't think I'd be strong enough to call. And as for writing . . . well, I was too ashamed. I knew you'd get the wrong impression. . . ."

Nikki was a sneak, a liar, a phony, and more. Gwen's rose-colored glasses had been yanked off by Nikki herself. Cruel, heartless, loveless Nikki. A killer.

"Oh, cut out the bullshit," Gwen said. "You called me because you probably want me to help you with Luke's show. Write the goddamn dialogue or something. Well, forget it. Nobody can salvage that show. It stinks from start to finish."

"But you're the one who gave me the idea," Nikki cried.

Gwen laughed mirthlessly. "I *gave* it to you? What a little beast you are to complain that the boat you stole has holes in it. So what will you do, sue me?"

Nikki got up and began to pace. "I don't know what to do."

Gwen listened to the terms of Nikki's contract and nodded. "Take it from an old veteran, dear, the only reason the network gave a nobody like you a crack at that show was that they never in a million years expected it to have legs. You know, longevity. And they didn't give a damn. All they wanted was to eliminate *Pete Winston*. So just take your money and run. You can live for a year on what they paid you for thirteen weeks."

"But what am I going to do?" Nikki wailed. "I can't go back to being a gofer, I just can't. Please help me, Gwennie," she appealed. "I'm so ashamed of myself. If you knew how I missed you, how I hated it when that pig got on top of me—which wasn't all that often anyway," she hastily added. "Believe me, he isn't half the man he thinks he is, in bed or out."

Gwen knew she shouldn't listen to all this, yet she yearned to believe it. A second glass of wine helped. Alcohol tended to blunt her critical judgment, to make her more tolerant, and certainly more amorous. She had to guard against that until she was sure that Nikki meant at least some of what she was saying.

"If I agreed to help you—if, I said—first of all, you'd have to forget making it as an independent producer and resign yourself to working for a production company.

Second, you'd have to forget prime time. After this fiasco, you're going to be poison to the networks. Third, you'd have to forget writing and go the producing route." She peered at Nikki to see her reaction.

The girl didn't flicker an eyelid. She had sat down again and was raptly taking in every word.

"I know a lot of people and I could probably get you taken on somewhere, but you'd have to put in your time and really do the job."

Nikki sighed, and then she said, "Whatever you think, Gwennie. I've missed you so much, honest—"

"Where is Luke tonight?" Gwen interrupted harshly.

Nikki shrugged.

"How come he's not beating down your door? He who was so anxious to get into your pants, to hear you tell it."

"We haven't been making it much lately. Half the time he can't even get it up. We've been fighting about the show. Oh, please don't look at me like that. I can't stand it."

Nikki's eyes grew bright with tears, and she let them moisten her rosy cheeks while she gazed at Gwen with remorse, fear, and love. . . .

Like hell, Gwen thought savagely, yet she was moved in spite of knowing that Nikki's tears were induced by self-pity.

What was love anyway but an illusion? Actions were more important than intentions. Gwen had accepted Nikki's "love" before. She yearned to experience it again.

And when Nikki threw herself at Gwen's feet, laid her beautiful auburn head on her knees, and sobbed that she truly loved her, Gwen couldn't help feeling that some of that must be real.

"I've missed your soft lips, Gwennie, your silky skin, all of you. You're the only one who's ever satisfied me," Nikki murmured between sobs.

Gwen's heart turned over. "Do you mean that? Because if you do, I want you to live with me. I mean give up your apartment. No subletting, no way back. You have to come to me for good. Otherwise I can't start with you again. I won't survive a rerun of all that hell you put me through."

Nikki didn't hesitate. "Yes, I will. Oh, Gwennie, I want to live with you." She hugged Gwen's knees tightly.

Only then did Gwen surrender. The reunion turned out to be everything she could have wished for. It was worth it to help Nikki's career in exchange for the bliss of holding her in her arms every night.

Luke paced his living room feeling murderous. Everything was falling to pieces around him, and why? It must be jealousy, he figured. Everyone was out to get him because women adored him—it was pure and simple. Feranti, for instance, had a rep as a tomcat, but had to break his ass in order to line up pussy, whereas Luke had only to snap his fingers. So that bastard had tricked him into signing a lousy contract. Nikki, too, had turned out to be useless. Telling him his tape wasn't good enough—that slut had a nerve to talk. She had promised him paradise but hadn't been able to put together thirteen decent shows.

Dammit, where *was* the tape? He rummaged all over and then realized Nikki had taken it with her. It was his!

He dialed her number and got a busy signal. Who was she talking to at midnight?

He fixed himself a drink and belted it down on an empty stomach. He hadn't even thought of dinner tonight. The burning in his gut only added to his fury. That bitch was out of a job, so she wanted to drag him down with her by keeping back the most original tape of the series. Well, she wasn't going to get away with it.

He dialed again, and slammed down the phone. Grabbing his coat, he left his apartment.

He'd get that tape away from her if he had to break her arm to do it. She was out of it, but he was in—for five years. Nikki needed him to get a show, but he didn't need her.

He taxied to her apartment and bounded up the stairs, then listened at the door, but there was only silence. After hesitating for a moment, he used his key. Maybe she had a guy with her, but he didn't care. He didn't want her, just that tape.

As he stepped into the foyer, he could see two sleeping heads close together on the futon in the living room.

Drawing closer, he peered at them in the darkness, then switched on a lamp.

"For God's sake," Nikki yelled, jumping up. "What are you doing here?"

Luke stared past her to her companion, who was also awake and looking back at him with a slight smile playing around her lips.

"Luke, I want my keys back," Nikki yelled, holding the covers up to her neck. "You have no right to barge in like this—"

He felt an enormous rage boiling up within him. "You fucking little dyke!"

Throwing down her keys, he slammed out of the apartment, knowing if he remained there a moment longer he would smash her face in.

Only when he was in the street did he realize he hadn't even asked for the tape.

For the first time in his life Luke was kept awake by rage rather than pleasure. That little bitch had certainly conned him. Well, to hell with her. He would take care of himself. He sniffed some cocaine, and it put him in a much better mood.

At nine A.M. he was at the studio, putting on a good act for the production secretary. He grinned and flirted, and got his hands on a copy of the tape, which he then delivered to Feranti's office. Evvie assured Luke she would put it on her boss's desk.

Nikki didn't know shit about anything. Let Feranti make the decision.

Luke didn't have very long to wait. He was called to Feranti's office that afternoon.

One look at the man's face, and Luke knew it was bad news.

Feranti wasted no words. "That tape"—he pointed to it on his desk angrily—"is so incredibly bad—any asshole on the street could give better answers."

"It's the questions that are dumb," Luke shot back. "We could plant folks in the audience to ask interesting questions—"

"Save your breath and read your contract. As of now, you're simply on the payroll. So take a vacation. Make it a long one."

"But you promised me—"

"I've kept all my promises," Feranti shouted. "The show sucks! TV makes stars, stars don't make TV! Yeah, yeah, if we get something right for you, we'll call. Now, get the fuck out of here, and take this piece of shit with you!"

After Merriman had gone, Oliver Feranti popped a couple of Valiums. God, he needed to calm down. He was so furious he was ready to quit the business altogether. What did he need all this hassle for? His jaw was aching again. His dentist had just fitted him with a retainer for his mouth because he ground his teeth at night.

Jerry Sirota was such an unreasonable son-of-a-bitch. Heads, he wins; tails, you lose. Sure, Jerry had loved him when he'd gotten Merriman away from Continental. But that hadn't been the end of *Pete Winston*, oh, no. Continental had made a fool of ATN by getting better ratings for a rerun than they did for a new series. And then, out of the blue, Abbott and Sinclair snapped back from the dead. Who in holy hell could have dreamed that they would come up with *Street Smarts* in a matter of months and that it would be a hit so quickly?

"Wonderful comedic breakthrough," the reviews had called it. "Yupcom at its best." "Strong urban appeal." "The offspring of the flower children can relate to Amy and Adam." "Bob and Linda Street show every sign of becoming the lovable dinosaurs of the eighties that Archie and Edith Bunker were of the seventies."

With reviews like that, the ratings for the show had zoomed up. Not only that, but Continental also had a strong lead-in and a strong follower, so Wednesday nights were quickly disappearing into their corner.

And Jerry's newest obsession was that Oliver was to blame for not having gotten Abbott and Sinclair under exclusive contract way back when *Mom & Meg* was making it big. Then ATN would have had *Pete Winston*, too. Abbott and Sinclair produced winners, Jerry now screamed, yet ATN was committed to paying Luke Merriman a fortune when he wasn't worth shit without them.

Continental was edging up to first place, sweeps month was upon them, and Oliver couldn't think of a fucking thing to throw against *Street Smarts* to woo back Wednesday-night viewers.

29

Early in November, Diana received a phone call from Gwen Van Ryck telling her that Nikki and Luke had split and Nikki had moved in with her. Diana's temples throbbed and she felt warm all over. She thanked Gwen and hung up, leaning back in her chair and taking deep breaths.

She was shocked at the news, but not surprised. After all, she had predicted an end to Luke and Nikki, hadn't she? And Gwen had taken Nikki back, in spite of everything. What would Diana do if Luke wanted to come back to her? She had no idea, any more than she could know how brave she would be if she had to risk her life for any reason. One didn't know for sure until the moment of decision.

What she did know was that every time her phone rang, her heart would stop for a moment. Did she want Luke to call so that she might have the satisfaction of hearing him admit his mistake? Or did she want him not to call because of Matthew?

Over the last months she and Matthew had become very important to one another. He slept at her place a couple of times during the week, when Andrea stayed over with the Blackmans. Summer camp had helped her to mature, and she was less dependent on her father.

Diana hadn't closed her house in East Hampton because spending weekends there made it easier for her to be with Matthew. But her relationship with his daughter was still awkward. What disturbed Diana about Andrea, and set her apart from most other children of her age, was her loss of innocence. It was obvious from the expression in her eyes. Nobody that young ought to have gone through so much pain. How Diana wished she could bring the innocence back, but of course that was impossible.

The child was perceptive and knew very well that her father was attached to Diana. She also must have sensed that Diana was quite fond of her, yet she remained aloof most of the time. Diana could, of course, understand Andrea's reticence, and felt she wasn't being fair to Matthew or his daughter by her inability to take that last step forward into their lives.

She wanted to but she just couldn't. Luke still seemed a part of her. So much so that she felt bad when she saw that his new show was hopeless.

"Don't tell me you're feeling sorry for that guy, after the way he treated you," Matthew said angrily.

"I can't help it, Matthew. I can't lie about my feelings. I *am* sorry for him. I'm defending my judgment, I guess. I hate to admit I could have been so wrong. And now he's let Nikki tear down what I built up. It's just such a waste."

"Your regard for that conceited ass is what's a real waste," Matthew said with growing impatience. "You've dredged up every excuse for him. Youth, naiveté, inability to tell flattery from true appreciation, et cetera, et cetera. I'm tired of hearing about it. His chickens are coming home to roost, that's all. He doesn't deserve anyone's sympathy, least of all yours."

"Don't tell me what to feel," Diana snapped.

"I wouldn't dream of it," he snapped back, his anger matching hers. "I just thought by now you might have gotten to enjoy talking in words of more than one syllable."

"It's easy to kick someone when he's down."

"Dammit, I haven't laid a foot on him, compared with what he's done to himself. The reason he's down is that he tripped over his own bloody ego!"

"You're not exactly a disinterested party! You were prejudiced against him from the beginning."

"With good reason."

"And I think I know what that is," Diana cried. "He's like the rock singer your wife ran off with, isn't he?"

"Yes, goddammit, he is! It's a type I loathe, quite frankly. Luke has been indulged by so many women for so long that he's never been able to penetrate his own superficiality, never developed any depth, any sensitivity. It's the spoiled-prince syndrome, the man who thinks beauty alone is an entitlement. Yes, Lorrie was a spoiled princess, of course, and as far as I'm concerned the Lorries and the Lukes deserve each other!"

Diana lost the argument by default. It was fruitless to keep reiterating that Luke was basically good underneath, that now that he had seen what flattery could do, he would learn his lesson. That would mean he would come back to her, and she couldn't discuss that possibility with Matthew, especially since she didn't know how she would react if it happened.

And there was nothing as unnewsworthy as a fallen celebrity. One day Luke's name was on everyone's lips and in all the gossip columns; the next day he might as well have died. Since Gwen's call, not one word about Luke had reached Diana.

His show was off the air. As November drew on, with no call from Luke, Diana began to relax. It was easier to face the fact that he wouldn't contact her at all, because it lessened her conflicts with Matthew.

It was Molly who brought her up-to-date. She had happened to run into Luke's agent on the street and learned that he was meeting with a division of Paramount in an attempt to get another show in the works.

Diana must have looked as startled as she felt.

Molly said scathingly, "You seem surprised. I'm not. His behavior is typical. Each time he shows himself for the user he is, he wears out his welcome. So he has to stalk new game. What did you think, that he'd come crawling to you?"

Diana didn't reply. She was relieved. At least the ringing of her phone receded into what it had always been—just another noisy interruption.

Diana was planning to spend the Thanksgiving weekend in Long Island. Matthew was cooking a turkey at his house, the Blackmans were bringing homemade pumpkin pies, and Diana, who was frantically busy on her show during the curtailed week, had volunteered to provide the wine.

Thursday morning, just as she was about to leave her

apartment, it occurred to her to bring something for Andrea, who didn't drink wine, of course, but was going to be helping with cranberry sauce and sweet potatoes. But buying gifts for Andy was a problem. Diana had given her an elaborate acrylic paint set for her birthday, and on another occasion, a wonderful art reference book for children. Yet the girl had accepted both gifts with a strange reluctance, almost as if she felt Diana was trying to buy her affections.

At any rate, the stores were closed today and she was running late. Just as she was going out of the bedroom, her eye fell on Raggedy Andy, sitting in his customary place on her bureau. On an impulse, she grabbed the doll and stuffed it into her tote bag.

At Matthew's, she presented the wine to him and then turned to Andrea. "I've brought you a little something. It's not a present exactly. It's not new. In fact, it's very old. This," she went on, pulling her doll from the bag, "is Andy. Andy, meet Andy. Raggedy Andy is his whole name. He's raggedy from age, many washings and repairs, and lots of kisses over the years. I've had him since I was younger than you."

Andrea took the doll, staring with somber-eyed curiosity at it. She poked gently at the worn, rather dirty face with her finger, touched the stiff yellow wool hair, and stroked the faded calico overalls.

"You don't want him anymore?" Andrea asked, her clever green eyes probing Diana's face.

She hesitated. "Well, I do want him. I guess I always will, but it seems to me that he's probably not very happy just sitting in my bedroom all day. He needs more attention, more tender loving care of the kind you could give him."

Andrea clutched the doll to her chest and ran upstairs.

"Andy, at least say thank you," Matthew called out in vain. "It's not bad manners," he assured Diana, handing her a drink. "She's just touched because you gave her something so precious to you. She'd rather have that, I think, than the most expensive toy you could have bought her."

"I'm glad," Diana said.

"Diana, my darling," Matthew murmured. "I keep finding reasons to love you more all the time."

She kissed him back. "I love you too."

And she was growing to love his daughter as well.

That day, Andy behaved much more warmly toward Diana, with less resentment. In fact, it was a wonderful day altogether. The food was marvelous, everyone was in a festive mood, and Diana felt very comfortable being a part of two families celebrating a holiday. It could always be like this, she thought.

That evening, after Andy had kissed her father goodnight, she came up to Diana and kissed her too, for the first time ever.

Diana was moved, but restrained the impulse to hug her too tightly. The girl was still wary, and Diana felt she had no right to her love until she had made up her mind to link her life with hers and her father's.

That miserable creep, Nikki thought, showed that tape to Oliver just to spite her. There was no other reason to have shown it to him; the show was finished. That tape would never have been aired. And Nikki was out, so why did Luke want revenge?

He did it because he had caught her with Gwen; because his male pride was hurt. Luke had nothing to lose; he was set for five years. He just wanted to get Oliver on her case, and he had succeeded.

Nikki had called Oliver innocently to talk about something else and for no reason at all he had lashed out at her, calling her a bimbo asshole and a few other gratuitously obscene names, and screaming particularly about that last tape.

Nikki was prowling Gwen's apartment like a caged animal. Gwen's apartment was the trouble. The only thing of her own, Nikki had been forced to give up.

And now she had been reduced from prime-time writer/executive producer to associate producer on a daytime soap. She hated it, but she was stuck with it for the time being, and stuck with Gwen, too.

In a fury, Nikki dialed Luke and got his answering machine. Curbing her impulse to leave an obscene message on it, she slammed down the receiver. Only sticks and stones would break that bastard's bones. She had even thought of hiring someone to beat him up, but the effects wouldn't be lasting. She would probably get caught anyway.

No, bad publicity was the way to get to him. If only she could call up all the newspapers and tell them Luke was a . . . What? Wife batterer, child abuser . . .

She suddenly remembered that tacky woman who had visited him a few months previously with a couple of kids. Nikki had rummaged around until she had found a piece of paper with the woman's name and address written down and had made a note of it, just in case she ever needed it.

She needed it now.

30

"Congolese mammal? What?" Matthew queried as he pored over the New York *Times*'s Crossword puzzle with Diana. "How is anyone expected to know a thing like that?"

"Oh, some people do." Diana wrote "okapi" in the space with her pen.

Matthew nudged her and smiled. "Smartass, you must stay up nights reading the answer books."

She smiled back at him. "Nope. I'm just a wordsmith. It's what I do best."

He nipped at her ear. "I wouldn't say that."

She edged away. "Don't. People behind us are sniggering—"

"The word is 'snicker,' and let them. I expect more for my first-class fare than champagne and caviar."

"It's 'snigger' in my part of the world. Stop being so competitive."

"Look who's talking." Matthew gave her a smacking kiss on the cheek, which made her laugh as she pushed him away.

They were in a plane en route to Barbados for Christmas, a present to themselves to celebrate that *Street Smarts* had been one of the top-rated shows in the November sweeps, and Continental had just nudged out ATN for first place in the overall network ratings.

Andy was spending the holidays in California with her grandparents, so Matthew was free. Diana was looking forward to being away from work and worry and simply enjoying herself for two weeks.

They had decided to bypass the Hilton because they weren't interested in meeting people they might know. Instead, they chose a quietly elegant hotel on the Caribbean (west) side of the island, which was frequented mostly by wealthy Britons.

When they were shown to their room, Diana walked out on the terrace facing the water, while Matthew tested the king-size bed. "Firm but with just the right amount of bounce. To hell with water sports, I'll take bed sports anytime."

She turned to look at him and laughed as she came back into the room. "You may get lonely."

"Oh, no I won't." He pulled her down on the bed and secured her with an intricate leg lock. "I could tell as soon as I saw you sitting next to me on the plane, Miss Sinclair, that you were going to be a hot number."

Diana struggled to break his hold, and as she succeeded (or maybe he let her), she found that she was aroused and as eager to make love as he was.

"Mm, that was lovely," she said later, nestling in his arms. "Bed sports aren't bad at all."

"Neither are water sports, come to think of it. How about a swim?"

"Ready when you are."

The water was wonderful, light green verging into darker aqua, and so warm they were able to plunge right in.

Matthew drew Diana to him and pulled each of her legs on either side of his hips.

"My beautiful water nymph, I love you," he murmured, kissing her. He looked magnificently at home himself, with his walrus mustache dripping, his sea-colored eyes glittering.

"And I love you," she responded. Yet an unbidden image of Luke momentarily flickered before her.

That happened frequently, often when she was happiest with Matthew. It was probably a form of guilt. Luke had been her first love, and she had sworn herself to him forever. But now she loved Matthew. How fickle the human heart was. She wasn't the same with Matthew, of course; every couple was unique. The trouble was that she kept having the lingering feeling that she and Luke belonged together. It made no sense. Seven months had passed. He was no longer with Nikki but still he hadn't contacted her. So why couldn't she give up on him?

She didn't know the answer to that one.

And although she really enjoyed being with Matthew, at times she found herself battling his domination. As, for example, when they rented a car and learned that traffic flowed to the left, British style.

"Oh, I'll drive," Diana said, getting behind the wheel. "I'm used to it. I drove through the English countryside one summer—"

"Well, I've never driven on the left," Matthew broke in, standing near her door. "I'd like to try it. One only learns by doing."

Diana looked at him, her anxiety rising. "Well, I think I should do the driving, truly, Matthew. I've been driving since I was sixteen. I learned on my parents' truck. I can drive a jeep, just about anything on wheels—"

"And I," Matthew said, leaning on the door and positioning his face close to her, "got my license in New York City at twenty-one after taking the test once. If you can drive in Manhattan you can drive anywhere. I think I can keep it straight because the driver's seat is on the wrong side of the car, reminding me to drive on the wrong side of the road."

Diana felt the blood rushing to her head as she recalled the bitter fights that had erupted between her and her brother over driving the family truck, and how often she lost because she was female and younger.

"Let's take turns," Matthew said amiably, kissing the tip of her nose. "You drive us to the Hilton for lunch, and I'll drive us back."

"I thought we wanted to avoid the Hilton," she said sulkily.

"Staying there, yes, but how much shop talk would

there be if we met someone we knew? At the most, two hours over lunch." He got into the car beside her. "I'll navigate and just enjoy the sights."

Diana felt a little suspicious of him, but his good humor held.

The Hilton was much larger than their hotel, with a California-size beach and a rough surf. They agreed that they preferred where they were staying but that the Hilton was a nice place to visit. It was very pleasant in the Terrace Café, where they had their rum drinks and a buffet lunch.

Diana was disappointed in the local specialty, flying fish. "Not only is the taste ordinary, it just sort of lies there like any other fish. I thought it would at least have wings."

"Uh-huh. One more rum punch and you'll sprout wings yourself," Matthew predicted.

When Diana returned from another trip to the buffet table, she found a plate in front of her containing an oval slice of golden yam topped with strips of pimiento formed into the shape of a heart.

Matthew grinned at her. "An early valentine. Just wanted to get my bid in first."

Diana was touched. "Thank you. That's very sweet, Matthew. I think I'll eat it here."

When they were ready to drive back, Matthew held out his hand for the car keys.

"Grr," Diana said, only half-humorously, getting into the passenger seat. She fully expected him to veer to the right of the road before they were halfway home, but he didn't. He was perfectly competent, so that particular little battle ended in a draw.

However, this was the first time they were together for an extended uninterrupted period, and there were other confrontations.

"Let's go to Bridgetown today," Diana said, two mornings later, pulling out of the driveway and onto the road. "This is a duty-free port, and I understand there are lots of bargains. Perfume, crystal, rum. We can have lunch in a local place to see what the natives eat, then walk around the town. There's actually a Trafalgar Square in Bridgetown, just like London—"

"Excuse me," Matthew interrupted, "but I'm not wild about shopping. Certainly I wouldn't want to spend the whole day doing that. What I'd like to do is drive to the Atlantic side of the island. It's supposed to be quite different altogether, not so tropical. It would be nice to take a picnic lunch. There's a place called Bathsheba. Doesn't that sound intriguing? I could pretend to be David," he finished, winking salaciously at her.

"We can do that some other time," Diana said moodily. "I'd rather go shopping."

"Before you make such a firm plan, don't you think I ought to be consulted?"

"Oh, for God's sake," Diana cried, "It's not a firm plan. I just thought it up. I like to do things spontaneously—"

"Good. I'm a spontaneous type myself. So why don't we spontaneously compromise. Go to Bridgetown first, before it gets too hot, then pick up a lunch and drive to Bathsheba. Maybe have an afternoon nap, under our beach umbrella, and whatever else spontaneously comes to mind." He nudged her playfully with his elbow. "What say, kid?"

Diana said nothing as she drove in the direction of town.

"I think we'd better pull over and discuss this," Matthew said, looking at her stony profile.

Angrily she veered off the road and halted with a screech on the gravel shoulder. "Just because I came up with an idea first, you're pissed."

"I am not pissed, but I also don't recall putting you in charge of this expedition."

"Of course you're pissed. You made me stop the car. As soon as I'm enthusiastic about something, you put a damper on it."

"It's more than just enthusiasm, Diana. I think you like having things exactly your own way—"

"And you don't?" she challenged.

"I'm willing to compromise whenever possible."

"Oh, cut it out. You're not talking to your daughter!"

"Don't I know it! Look, this isn't about who gets whose way. It's about two people who love each other doing something they can both agree on. Now, what's so terrible about that? I'm willing to go to Bridgetown for half the day, and I've told you why. What's wrong with spending the rest of the day on the Atlantic side of the island?"

Diana sighed heavily. "Nothing, I guess. But the shops will be cooler than the beach in the afternoon because they're air-conditioned. I think the beach will be murder, with that equatorial sun beating on us, even through the umbrella, and especially in the water."

"Okay. How about beach, lunch, Bridgetown?"

Diana grudgingly agreed.

The day turned out to be lovely. The Atlantic side of the island was dramatically rugged, with huge boulders jutting out of the water near the shore. The surfers were fun to watch, and the picnic lunch of cold chicken, salad, fruit, and beer was just right.

Matthew was very amiable during the Bridgetown interlude, going from shop to shop without a murmur, showing marvelous patience and restraint when Diana tried on about a dozen batik garments and took a long time making up her mind.

As the days went by, it slowly dawned on her that compromise was a workable alternative to winning or losing. Unlike most of the men she had known, Matthew was usually prepared to be reasonable. And any disputes they did have he forgot once they were over.

He was a rare man indeed, in many respects. She played a much better game of tennis than he, for instance, and although he wasn't thrilled to lose almost every set, he appeared more admiring of her skill than resentful of his lack of it.

Of course, he was an excellent sailor, and she was no sailor at all. They both liked swimming and snorkeling, but after a couple of attempts at windsurfing, she gave it up as hopeless.

"One puff of wind and you're overboard. I'll never get the hang of it," she complained.

"If that's your attitude, then you certainly won't."

"Well, I really don't think it's worth the effort."

"Okay, don't windsurf then," he said, blowing her a kiss. "While I'm doing that you can be playing tennis with a worthy opponent."

Diana respected the way he accepted weaknesses in himself, as he did in her—and in his daughter. It was one of the many reasons he was such a good father.

In the evenings they made the rounds of clubs and other hotels, dancing to local bands playing Caribbean music, as well as rock and traditional favorites.

Matthew, who described himself as a minimalist disco dancer, much preferred the slow numbers so he could hold Diana close. She liked that too. It was rather nice to dance with someone close to her in height. They could look at each other, talk, and laugh without either of them getting a stiff neck. She also liked to feel Matthew's thighs caressing hers, especially as the evening drew to a close, and she knew they would ease into lovemaking as soon as they were back at their hotel.

They savored their last evening. Diana wasn't looking forward to returning to her empty apartment and seeing Matthew only on specified nights.

After having made beautiful love before going to sleep, she awoke in the middle of the night with an acute longing for sex once again.

Matthew never minded being awakened, especially for such a reason. And so she began to kiss him lightly on his cheeks, lips, neck, shoulders, chest, belly.

"Ooh," he moaned, "that's beautiful. Don't stop, darling."

Arousal made him fully awake, and he took a more active part, moving sinuously over her, kissing and caressing her.

"Matthew," she whispered in his ear. "My wonderful man. I want you."

"You've got me, darling."

They joined their bodies and rocked together, their rhythms as attuned as their heartbeats.

Afterward, Matthew switched on the light. "Now, let's just see exactly whom I've been making love to," he murmured, earning a laugh and a playful slap. Then they curled up in each other's arms and went back to sleep.

At their last island breakfast of fresh fruit and homemade muffins, under a thatched shed surrounded by palms and breadfruit trees, Matthew looked deeply into Diana's eyes and said, "I love you ten times more than I did when we arrived. We're so good together, aren't we?"

"Yes, we are," she agreed, smiling fleetingly at him. It was true. She did feel a great deal closer to him.

"I can't bear the thought of not sleeping with you every night, Diana. We've had our honeymoon. How about starting off the new year by getting married? I know that Andy would be relieved to have the matter settled."

Diana's glance wavered, as the old apprehension crept up from the base of her spine. She loved Matthew very much, even more than before. But try as she might, she simply couldn't agree to marry him, because Luke's face still appeared before her at odd moments. She knew it was crazy, but she couldn't help herself.

Matthew was waiting for her answer.

Diana sighed.

Matthew sighed too. "Still Luke, eh? Well, it's just not possible for me to go on like this, Diana. When I first heard that he and Nikki were finished, I was so nervous I could hardly stand it. I tried to hide it from you, of course. I realized that putting pressure on you would only make things worse. But Luke hasn't contacted you. As least I assume not."

Diana shook her head.

"We've been together for more than four months, Diana. And these last two weeks have been so wonderful. If you can't make a commitment to me now, after such a beautiful interlude, maybe you never can."

"I . . . I want to, Matthew, believe me, I do. It *has* been wonderful. You're the best friend I've ever had."

"But not the best lover?"

"Lovers can't be compared. It's always different—"

"Diana," Matthew said, a tight edge to his voice, "either you're through with Luke or you're not. And if you're not, I'm going to have to give you up, for Andy's sake as well as my own. We can't go on in limbo. It's just too painful for us both. It also makes me very angry, because I don't think Luke is worthy of your devotion or my contempt. Jesus, what more do you need to know about that guy to forget him once and for all?"

Diana couldn't answer the question. She crumbled her muffin and sprinkled the crumbs on the ledge of the terrace, then watched the sweetly chirping birds peck at each other in their fight over their breakfast.

She clearly saw that Matthew was right for her in every way, whereas Luke was to her what whiskey is to an alcoholic or candy to a diabetic. She would be better off not getting what she craved, and best of all if she could stop craving. If only she knew how.

31 "Happy New Year and welcome back, Diana," Molly greeted her the first morning she returned to the office. "Don't you look wonderful. Tanned, relaxed. I take it you had a good time."

"Terrific," Diana acknowledged, noting a certain excitement in Molly's demeanor. "What's up? You look as if you're bursting with good news."

"I'd call it that, though you may not. I'm certainly happy that we're on *Street Smarts* and not *Pete Winston*, and that the reruns are finished. Most of all I feel good that there's some justice left in this world. It's all on your desk, kid."

Molly had labeled the folder "Luke Merriman," and the newspaper clipping on the top, from *Variety*, was headlined "TV MODEL DAD PROVED BAD." Diana, her heart pounding, read that Luke Merriman, of *Pete Winston* fame, had a common-law wife, Sara Coles, and two children, who had been discovered living in a rented frame house in Salem, Oregon.

Articles from papers throughout the country detailed the history of Luke and Sara as migrant workers, telling how he had abandoned his family more than four years previously, how Sara had been to see him in New York with the children months ago, and how she had been receiving a monthly check sent by Luke's attorney. But Luke himself never called or wrote or remembered his children's birthdays.

Copies of the children's birth certificates listed Lucas Merriman as father. Apparently he had never denied paternity.

Luke had made the cover of *People*, with the headline "FATHER OF THE YEAR?" There was also an in-depth story in *New York Magazine*, a color spread showed Luke dining in three of New York's most expensive restaurants with a model. Next to those photos was one of Sara Coles and her children eating a modest meal in their kitchen. Luke was pictured behind the wheel of his Jaguar; Sara standing in front of the used car she had bought for two hundred dollars. Luke was shown dressed in a handmade Italian suit with a fur coat flung on his shoulders; Sara was pictured in a cheap cloth coat, and the children in equally inexpensive garments.

The close-ups of Sara, Daisy, and Joey looked like photos Diana had seen taken in Appalachia, showing emaciated, worn-out young women with prematurely lined faces, and their dull-eyed children who looked as if they'd been hungry all their lives.

Diana read the accounts carefully for a second time, finding each fact, each photo searingly painful. She was moved to tears of compassion for the Coles family, and of rage for Luke, who, she finally acknowledged, was rotten to the core.

Sara was so unworldly she hadn't realized the extent of the damage to Luke these interviews would create. She had originally been located in November by a young woman passing herself off as a "friend" who claimed to be gathering material for an article Sara assumed would be favorable to her common-law husband. (Next to "friend" Molly had written, "Nikki?")

Sara had made no complaints. On the contrary, her quoted words carried their own irony. The money Luke sent her—one thousand dollars per month—had taken her away from migrant labor, allowed her to settle in one place, send her children to school on a daily basis, and attend hairdressing school herself. They now had enough to eat and a "new" car that didn't need repairs every week.

Even when that first interview was followed up by magazine reporters and photographers, Sara hadn't realized they were planning to show the discrepancy between Pete Winston, all-American father, as shown on TV, and the real Luke Merriman, who had abandoned his children and even now gave them a modest allowance while he lived the good life.

In fact, after the scandal had come to Sara's attention, she had refused any more interviews and had barred TV reporters from her home. Journalists speculated that she feared to lose the support Luke was voluntarily providing.

Because the story had broken just before Christmas, its poignancy had increased. It was a time of joy, of giving, to children most of all. But Luke's children had no Christmas gifts from their father. The press had seized the opportunity to characterize Luke as a Scrooge, and gifts and money for Sara and the children had poured in from all over the country.

Luke had refused comment and had immediately dropped out of sight. He was thought to have fled to Europe.

Molly had been thorough in her clipping. From the most recent *Variety* Diana learned that ATN had no plans to develop another show for Merriman at present. The implication, of course, was that he would be kept off the air until the scandal blew over.

The last clipping in the file noted that Sara Coles had retained the services of a notorious divorce attorney and was suing for child support commensurate with Luke's income. Diana could imagine how the woman had been besieged by lawyers trying to convince her to demand her rights "for the children's sake," while, of course, seeing a way to cash in themselves.

Diana felt a surge of self-disgust that she could have allowed herself to be so deceived. Sara Coles had been an unsophisticated teenager, but what was Diana's excuse? When she remembered the way she had defended Luke to Matthew, to Molly, for almost two years, she felt terribly ashamed.

She had a strong impulse to be with Matthew right now, to hear his voice and feel his arms around her. She longed to tell him she was ready, that she was definitely finished with Luke. But Matthew was en route to L.A. and would be there for three days. That was too long to keep the big decision to herself, so Diana sent him a telegram saying: "YES TO EVERYTHING. MUCH LOVE, D."

Matthew phoned her, delighted and boyish with excitement. He planned to finish his business as quickly as possible and couldn't wait to be with her.

Diana was elated. She was actually going to get married. Yet it seemed a little strange.

Molly was the first to hear the news. "All right!" she exclaimed. "I'm so glad you've finally come to your senses."

Diana blushed, for no reason at all, and was uncomfortable. And she felt even sillier calling her parents only two days after she had wished them Happy New Year but had made no mention of an engagement.

They were certainly surprised, not having heard too much about Matthew, but pleased nevertheless. Martha took over the conversation, inviting Diana to be married in Santa Fe as her brother had been. Maybe in February, over Washington's Birthday. . . .

When Diana hung up, something was nagging at her but she couldn't immediately determine what it was.

They were on a full production schedule of *Street Smarts*, so the three days passed fairly quickly, punctuated by brief exchanges between Diana and Matthew. He would be catching the red-eye flight arriving Thursday morning, would go home to see his daughter and tell her the good news, and then sleep a couple of hours before coming into town.

Thursday began earlier for Diana like any other workday because she was so busy. It was snowing heavily, and she hoped it wouldn't delay the arrival of Matthew's plane.

When her doorbell rang Diana was startled, since the doorman hadn't announced anyone. She looked through the peephole but saw nothing.

Maybe it was Matthew, surprising her.

She opened the door to find Luke standing there in a fur coat and fur hat, looking like the abominable snowman.

"Hi, there," his familiar voice drawled.

Without being aware of moving, she stepped aside to let him in.

"Quite a blizzard this morning," he said as casually as if he had gone out to fetch the paper. "Is there any coffee?"

"Uh, yes, I think so. It should still be hot." She hung his coat and hat in the bathroom and hurried into the kitchen.

The slacks, sweater, and tweed jacket he was wearing were the clothes she had once bought him. And as he stood in the doorway watching her pour coffee, it was as if he had never left. She felt like a robot that had been programmed to behave to him as always. "Have you eaten breakfast?"

"No, ma'am."

His sad smile made her heart ache. Without being able to stop herself, she bustled around toasting bread, putting out butter and jam.

"Have some coffee with me," he said simply as they moved into the dining area. Obediently she poured herself half a cup, then sat facing him, afraid to lift it to her lips because her hands were trembling.

As he ate his toast, she studied his face—thinner, it seemed to her, since she had seen it about six months before.

"I thought you were in Europe," she whispered.

"I was, but there's nothing for me there. Or anywhere. Not without you, babe." His voice was low, dejected. "You were right about everything. Right about Nikki, ATN, that dumb contract."

She had imagined this scene so many times that now it seemed to her she was watching a rerun. Luke was admitting he was wrong, begging her to forgive him, asking for another chance. In the imagined scenario she firmly sent him away. In reality, however, it wasn't going to be so easy, because his arrogance had vanished. This was the old Luke, the humble, sweet Luke she had loved.

"I know I don't deserve your forgiveness, Diana, but I'm asking for it anyway because I need it so badly."

She forced her gaze from his magnetic eyes and took a sip of coffee. It was late. She had to get to the office. It was insane of her to sit here listening to him, knowing that he had come here only because she was his last resort. Then why was she powerless to budge from her seat?

"What do you want exactly?" she finally got out through her constricted throat.

"What I've always wanted. You, Diana. I've missed you, babe. More than I can say. Of all the mistakes I ever made in my life, the biggest was leaving you."

When she realized that he was prepared to lie about loving her again, she finally was able to summon up her fury.

"You bastard! Do you really think you're going to con me all over again? At this point, when the whole world knows what you are? Do you think I don't know it too? Do you think I don't profit from *my* mistakes?" She slammed down her cup with such force that coffee splashed all over her.

Luke jumped up.

"Stay there! Don't come near me!" she cried, mopping up the spills with her napkin. "You're prepared to go through everything all over again just to get me to write a show for you. That's it, isn't it? Why the fuck can't you admit that's what you want instead of telling lies—"

"They're not lies," he maintained, his gaze unwavering. "I do miss you, and yes, I do want you to write a show for me. Why can't both things be true? In fact, they are true. I've found out the difference between your love and Nikki's flattery. I've realized that talent is one thing, and knowing how to use it is something else. I still have the talent, Diana, only this time I'll work like a son-of-a-bitch. I'll take acting classes for the rest of my life so that I can be the very best. I'll do anything and everything you say. Some of my antics during that last period . . . well, it wasn't really me doing and saying those things. I was with the wrong crowd, into alcohol, pot, coke, you name it, trying to keep up with those folks. Forgetting who I was, where I came from. Cocaine makes you think you've got the world by the balls. Then you come down off your high and you can't face the way things really are, so you get high all over again. I've learned the hard way. Like it says in the old blues song, nobody wants you when you're down and out. Man, is that true."

"Down and out," Diana echoed derisively, "on three hundred thousand a year. Tell me about it. And tell me how you would describe your wife and kids, living on twelve thousand."

"I can explain about that," Luke said quickly. "I wanted to forget my past so bad it got so's I did, pretty much. I swear to the good Lord I almost didn't remember about Sara until the day she turned up in New York. I fooled myself about so many things, Diana. Things like people really caring about me when all they wanted was to be seen with a celebrity—"

"You were telling me about Sara," Diana broke in, her voice and face hard.

"I know that. I wasn't forgetting. It's all connected, in fact. You can't imagine what it's like to be born on the land but not to own anything. To follow the crops, to live from meal to meal, getting no schooling, no encouragement, living without hope. I was my folks' youngest and I never even met the other two, 'cause my folks were drunkards and the house burned down with my sister and brother in it."

Luke went on to describe his parents' marriage when they were teenagers, the way their poverty ground them down and turned them into alcoholics. And when they lost their two children it really finished them. Luke had no childhood, no friends, only backbreaking work, living in shacks, often with no running water, no shower or inside toilet.

"My folks got killed in a car crash when I was seventeen, and that's when I got together with Sara. Then Daisy came along. Couple of years later, Joey. I started boozing myself because everything seemed so hopeless. It was like we were repeating my parents' life, continuing the cycle of poverty. . . ."

Luke spoke movingly, eloquently—perhaps a little too eloquently. He was an actor, after all, and quite effective, provided he learned his lines.

"I never set out to abandon them," Luke continued. "It just happened that way. I had a toothache, went into Salem and got it seen to. On my way back to the bus depot I saw a sign in a diner for a waiter. I just walked in. I was thinking if I could earn money doing something else, we could get off the stream."

"Well, didn't you?" Diana asked. "How is it you never sent for your family? Or called or gave Sara one penny in four years?"

Luke shifted in his seat. "I'm sorry. It was wrong. I guess I got corrupted by the city. I'd never had anything. And my first day on the job, the prettiest woman I'd ever seen close up sat at my table and smiled at me. . . ."

She had given him the room number of her hotel. And he had been so intrigued, he had gone. "I'd never been in a hotel, had never ridden an elevator, nothing like that. A bed, with a real mattress, clean sheets, a beautiful gal wanting me. . . ."

Luke had never been with anyone but Sara, and sex with this bored married woman (her husband was at a convention) was exciting. Seeing what a lovely, cared-for young body could be like had been a revelation to him. Before he left, she had casually slipped him a hundred-dollar bill and told him to buy some decent clothes.

After her, there were more. Women kept coming on to him, and he just couldn't bring himself to go back to living in a shack with Sara and two squalling kids.

"I know it was wrong. I always planned to send her something, in the beginning. But that was the trouble. Send it where? We moved around so much. Nobody had a phone, nobody got mail. I would have had to go back, and that's what I couldn't face. Besides, Sara was real pretty. I figured she'd hook up with someone else pretty quick. Then I got a chance to go to Portland, be a waiter in a better place. . . . I've never been back to Salem since."

Although she was already late, Diana continued to listen

to him because the more he said, the more contempt she felt for him.

"The way you look at me, babe, like you don't believe me—"

"I believe you, all right, and that makes it even worse. Because what I can't believe is that you could have run away and left your wife and children to lead the miserable life you escaped from. Oh, don't tell me you couldn't find them! Money makes everything possible. You could have paid someone, a go-between. You could have arranged to send money from Portland every month to a bank account in Salem in Sara's name. Even a small amount would have helped. You could have shown some responsibility to the people who relied on you instead of being so selfish and cowardly. Two tiny, helpless children—dammit, I've seen their pictures! You let your own children go hungry! Didn't know or care how they were. Your own children—"

"I admit I've made mistakes," Luke agreed, squirming.

"That's a helluva lot more than a 'mistake.' You've been a total bastard to your own family, and how do you atone? By giving them crumbs! Their health and education have been neglected for years, yet you give them a measly thousand a month to pay rent, food, clothing, medical bills, dental bills. Jesus, I've been there when you've spent more than a thousand for a rag to put on your back. That fur you walked in here wearing, for instance—"

"That's all been taken care of," he interrupted. "I'm setting up a trust fund—"

"Only because a smart lawyer wants to take you to court," she cried. "Because it was in the papers and magazines for everyone to read! Luke Merriman, quintessential father, abandons his children. And even after they find him—and he's rich by their standards—he gives them as little as he can get away with. Never sees them, writes, or phones. Can't even send them a present at Christmas—"

"All right!" he shouted, standing up. "Sure, parents are supposed to love their kids, but you know what? That's for middle class and rich. Poor slobs like us get feelings like that knocked out of us early on by our own folks. Mine used to beat the shit out of me, especially my father, every time he got drunk. Which was every day. You want the truth? I'll tell you the truth. When Sara brought the kids to see me, I nearly died of shame. I looked at them and it was like looking in a mirror. Not because they look like me but because they looked dumb and puny and sick and filthy and they reminded me of what I once was. I hated to be reminded, okay? Folks like you think it's noble to be poor. *You* never miss a meal unless you're on some fancy diet. *You* don't know what it's like to be really hungry, cold, afraid, with no home and an old man crazy on corn liquor who'll knock your head off just for being alive! That's what I wanted to spare my kids. I never once hit them, but I was afraid I would. That's why I had to get the fuck out of there!''

Luke jammed his hands into his pockets and walked into the living room.

Diana followed him. "Are you saying that poor people aren't capable of loving their children? That's not only a vicious lie, it's a slur on all the decent poor people who've done everything they could, made enormous sacrifices to hold their families together, who want a better life for their children. Sara, for instance!"

"All right! I want a better life for them too, and now I'm providing it. They're going to get a quarter of my earnings, okay? But I can't see them. That's out. I'm not wild about kids in general. Don't confuse me with Pete Winston."

Diana smiled grimly at the irony that he was finally telling that to her.

"Look, I'm not proud of myself, Diana. It would be great publicity if I said I was going to take the kids for weekends, for the summer, but I can't do it. I just can't lie about feeling love for them when it's not there."

Luke suddenly took her hands in his, and an electric shock ran through her before she succeeded in drawing them away. She clasped them tightly behind her back to stop their trembling.

Luke was looking at her with the old intensity beaming from his eyes. He glanced at his empty hands and then back at her. "My feelings for *you* haven't changed, Diana. I love you. I never stopped loving you, and I never will. I don't want any other woman. There's only one Diana, and I want you forever. I want to marry you as soon as possible."

"Don't tell me that now," she whispered. "It's too late for that. I'm going to marry Matthew."

She didn't bother to elaborate, because she didn't care what Luke thought.

He compressed his lips. "I suppose I can't blame you, after what I've done. I'm sure he loves you, too. Who wouldn't? You're a wonderful woman. And you two come from the same world. He's certainly richer." Luke sighed. "I don't know what'll happen to me without you. After everything fell apart, and I fell back to earth again, cold sober and straight up, I watched the tapes of my show again." Luke shook his head. "They were terrible. In fact, they're embarrassing. I don't blame the network. I had all sorts of dumb ideas about how great I was, but now I know. I've quit drinking. I've quit doing drugs. I think I can act, if I work like hell. I need your help, Diana. You're the only one who really understands me. I trust you because you never lied to me. Not even about Matthew. When I found out what a bitch Nikki was, I checked on her story and saw it was just another of her sneaky lies. I need you, babe."

Diana felt her anger draining away, longing for him taking its place. She shook her head. She couldn't—not after what he had done, after all the things he had just told her about Sara and his children.

She walked to the window and looked out. It had stopped snowing but people were walking with their heads down as the powdery snow blew into their faces.

Please go, Luke. Three simple words. All she had to do was say them. She couldn't allow herself to be taken in again. The man simply had no character, no humanity. Even his honesty was opportunistic. The scandal had made him persona non grata socially as well as professionally. So he had nowhere else to go but here. He'd promise her anything now. Yet, the moment he had made it up there again, he'd be the same as ever he was—a rotten, egotistical user. First there was Sara (for seven years!) then the string of rich women who paid for his favors, then Diana, then Nikki, and no doubt countless others.

Diana recalled some of the brutal things he had told her when she had begged him not to leave her, the way he had taunted her about having repaid her by being her stud.

Digging her nails into her palms, she wondered how she could even consider the pros and cons of the situation. She marveled that she had let him through the front door, that she had listened to his tale of woe. Matthew had seen Luke from the start: a prince who thought that beauty was an entitlement.

There was no comparison between Luke and Matthew. Luke was unprincipled and self-serving, whereas Matthew was as ethical in his personal life as she had found him to be professionally. Luke had no true identity. Without sycophants to prop up his ego, he was rootless and adrift. But Matthew was his own man, original, sensitive, educated, and thoughtful, in every meaning of the word.

Luke was immature; Matthew was a grown-up.

Luke was foolish; Matthew was wise.

Luke only used her; Matthew truly loved her.

With Matthew, life was richer, deeper, more meaningful.

She turned slowly from the window. If she had to choose one of the two men for a long stay on a desert island, wouldn't it be Matthew?

Then why in hell couldn't she tell Luke to go? What was there about him that held her? Why was she still so tremendously drawn to him that she could scarcely catch her breath as she looked at him?

Luke smiled uncertainly and took a step closer.

And suddenly she knew. She went for "dumb blonds" for the same reason some men did. Symbolically, the phrase meant a woman who was "dumb" enough to let a man have power over her.

It was *power* that was the aphrodisiac. Diana had simply taken the cliché and reversed it without being aware of what she was doing. And why was power so important to her? Because as a child she had felt so powerless. Her father controlled her mother, and her brother controlled her. Men control women.

That was why she had always been afraid of love. She had feared losing control. It was also why she had failed to connect with any man for so long. Only Luke had been perfect, a special case, neither wimp nor tyrant, but her own gorgeous creation, her very own "dumb blond."

She had fallen in love with Luke precisely because he had allowed her to be in control of their relationship. And now, after having ventured out on his own and failed, he was handing the reins back to her.

Power aroused her, and absolute power aroused her absolutely.

"I love you, Diana," Luke said, instinctively on cue. "And I know that you love me too."

Did she love him? Or did she love only her ability to make him into Pete Winston—or whoever? Did she really want to spend her life creating a series of roles for him to play? Or did she want to join her life to a man who was a fully developed human being, an equal?

Luke came closer, and Diana felt pulled in two directions. It was as if her heart was the ball in a tennis game.

Luke had reached her. He could see her wavering, and he scooped her up in his arms and kissed her.

She felt a tingle throughout her body but forced herself to remain passive, to keep her eyes open.

He was back to his old trick of using sex to enslave. She could imagine how many times that had worked. Certainly it had with her, once. How uncertain she had been, in spite of taking the lead. Yes, even in bed she had needed to be in control.

With Matthew, too, there had been a power struggle in bed and out, but she had learned that being with an equal means sharing power. Matthew was undeniably the right man for her. And yet . . .

Breaking away from Luke's embrace, Diana hesitated, looking at him intently. What she saw was a very handsome man, six-foot-three, with sun-streaked hair tumbling over his forehead, magnetic blue-gray eyes, and a sensual mouth that slowly curved into a seductive smile. He seemed to be saying. "Take me, I'm yours."

She longed to go to bed with him.

She took a deep breath. "Please go, Luke."

"Diana, no!"

"Yes."

He stared at her for a few moments before he realized that she meant it. Then his stricken face, his trembling mouth, were painful to see.

"Please, babe. I need you."

"I can't help you anymore. Find someone else."

"There is nobody else. Everyone's turned their back on me." Luke's voice broke, and he put his hand over his face and rubbed it.

She waited quietly while he wiped his eyes. Then she went for his coat and hat and handed them to him.

He threw her one last hurt look before walking slowly to the door.

Diana sank into a chair. The muscles of her neck and

shoulders ached from the tension, but it was worth it. She had done what she needed to do.

For a long time she sat motionless, thinking. Her last conversation with her mother popped into her head. Her mother had wanted to know whether Diana was planning to move to Sag Harbor. She had been at a loss for an answer, because in trying to solve the big question of whether or not to marry Matthew, she hadn't really dealt with their living arrangements.

"I guess we'll mostly be in Sag Harbor because of Andy's schooling," Diana had said. "At least until June. By September she may be in private school in Manhattan."

"I see. Well, you be sure to make your wishes known, Didi."

Diana had smiled. "Don't worry, Mom, I always do. Matthew will be the first to say so."

Now she saw what had bothered her about that conversation. And for the first time it became clear to her that her father's gruff manner only covered up his devotion to his wife.

Martha Kent Sinclair had given up a brilliant career to live a simple life with him, and he was grateful to her. It was her *mother* who controlled that relationship by means of her sacrifice. She had told Diana the truth when she had said she was happy. Apparently she had the marriage she wanted.

Did Diana want that kind of marriage?

No, she did not. She no longer needed control over the man in her life, because she had gained control over herself, and a new understanding of everything.

She phoned Matthew. "Hello, darling, did I wake you?"

"No. I was just about to grab a nap. I've been telling Andy our news. She took it pretty well. She doesn't think it's as wonderful as we do, of course, but at least she accepts it. What she actually said was that now you'd both be taking care of Raggedy Andy."

Diana smiled. "I think that's her way of welcoming me to the family. And by the way, where are we going to live? Your place or mine?"

"Neither. Ours. We'll buy something we can all agree on."

"Aha, one of your famous compromises. No doubt we'll wind up midway, in Queens or Roosevelt Island, maybe on a houseboat in the East River."

Diana felt a tremendous weight lifting, and as they continued to banter, Matthew's was the only face she saw before her.

About the Author

Justine Valenti is a native New Yorker and former managing editor of *Gourmet* magazine. After spending several years in Europe, where she began writing novels, she returned to New York and now lives with her husband on Manhattan's West Side. Among her novels are *No One But You*, *Lovemates*, and *Twin Connections*.